For Katie

WHITETHROAT

James Henry

riverrun

First published in Great Britain in 2021 by riverrun
This paperback edition published in 2022 by

riverrun
an imprint of

Quercus Editions Ltd
Carmelite House
50 Victoria Embankment
London EC4Y 0DZ

An Hachette UK company

A CIP catalogue record for this book is available
from the British Library

Paperback 978 1 52940 111 0
Ebook 978 1 52940 110 3

10 9 8 7 6 5 4 3 2 1

Typeset by CC Book Production
Printed and bound in Great Britain by Clays Ltd, Elcograf S.p.A.

MIX
Paper from
responsible sources
FSC® C104740
www.fsc.org

Papers used by Quercus are from well-managed forests and other responsible sources.

'A fast-moving thriller... strong characters, dark humour and a terrific sense of place. I was totally absorbed' Elly Griffiths

'A lovely bit of bleak Essex noir: fast, funny, and clever, with a twisty plot and big cast both deftly handled and local colour in spades' Christobel Kent

'James Henry has done it again with another taut, highly atmospheric police procedural!' Simon Kernick

'Perfectly structured, authentically bred from its bleak and watery setting, Blackwater gives us a new Essex reimagined as a noir landscape' Lawrence Osborne, author of The Forgiven

'It's a cracker . . . Henry is aware of the required marks for plot, pace and characterisation and hits each one with devastating accuracy . . . brilliant' Shots

'Brilliantly engineered police procedural' Daily Mail

Also by James Henry

THE DI NICK LOWRY THRILLERS

Yellowhammer

Blackwater

THE DI JACK FROST PREQUELS

Frost at Midnight

Morning Frost

Fatal Frost

First Frost (with Henry Sutton)

'Unrequited love is not an affront to man but raises him.'

Pushkin

PROLOGUE

3.55 a.m., Colchester High Street

Two men in uniform emerged from the ancient passageway through the old hotel, the Red Lion, and turned left on to the high street. The empty road glistened, illuminated by the dull orange street lamps. They hurried towards the meeting place, disturbing the silence of the pale historic buildings with the urgent clip of highly polished shoes. The town hall loomed ahead. There, they were to meet two more men.

'Are you sure about this?' one hissed to the other, risking a glance at the Baroque clock tower atop the town hall as they crossed the road. The hour was nearly upon them.

'Stop saying that, of course I'm sure.' But of course he wasn't, who would be? Who in their right mind would agree to do this in 1983? He quickened his step. Damn, his tinnitus was particularly bad this morning, to make matters worse.

'I have to ask, Cousins – it's my duty.'

'Right, well, don't – it's happening. We're here.'

Atkinson was nervous and was covering his arse; he'd be

court-martialled along with the rest of them if they were caught. 'It's starting to rain,' he said plaintively. 'There must be other ways out of this mess.'

But there weren't, otherwise they wouldn't be there.

As the two soldiers drew nearer the town hall, the glowing tips of two cigarettes became visible beneath the mayor's balcony. Only minutes left to go – time rushed at them, the seconds evaporated, replaced with a compressing panic. On reaching the steps up to the main entrance the full enormity of the situation hit nineteen-year-old Lance Corporal Cousins – he realised he might not live to see the sun rise. He urgently sought Drake's expression in the murky damp, but his opponent's eyes remained downcast.

'Gentlemen, please take your weapon.' The voice, the Northern accent, belonged to Drake's second, a thin corporal by the name of Burnett. It was he who had procured the service revolvers. Each took a gun from him without a word.

Hands were duly shaken in the darkness, and the process was set in motion, as unstoppable as an intercontinental ballistic missile: for honour was at stake. In less than a minute one or both of them might be dead. As they assumed the starting position in the middle of the quiet provincial high street, Cousins couldn't help but wish the circumstances that had brought them here were as honourable as the tradition they were to enact . . .

PART 1

Soldier's Virtue

CHAPTER 1

5.45 a.m., Monday, November, 1983, Colchester High Street

'Is he dead?'

'Yes. Gunshot wound to the chest. Bled to death, doc reckons.' Not that blood was distinguishable from the surface water in the weak street light. Lowry swung the torch along the body, pausing the beam briefly on the man's face. He'd put him at nineteen or twenty. He switched the torch off and sniffed in the wet air. The rain had eased off, leaving a luminescent drizzle.

'So he was left to die.' Suggesting he was on his own, with no one to help.

Sergeant Barnes grunted affirmation.

The street cleaner who discovered the body stood smoking with a constable on the pavement in front of the baroque façade of the Hippodrome bingo hall.

'What do you reckon?' Barnes's features were obscured in the dark.

'Why is he in dress uniform, I wonder?' Lowry peered down at the body; the lad was dressed in full parade garb.

'Ey up, it's your Himmler mate, sir,' Barnes announced abruptly.

Across the street, the small but unmistakable figure of Royal Military Police Captain James Oldham climbed out of a Land Rover.

Lowry smiled in the dark. Yes, he and Oldham did socialise, but he wasn't sure he'd say they were 'mates'. As the man approached, Lowry noticed that even at this hour he was impeccably dressed.

'Good morning, captain. It appears one of your lads has been shot.'

Oldham stepped closer, the peak of his cap masking his expression as he tilted his head forward in the direction of the body. The captain sighed audibly.

'Indeed,' he said, glancing up and down the street, and then skyward, as if it were the heavens responsible for placing him here, in this street in Essex in the rain at nearly six in the morning. 'Perhaps we might discuss this matter indoors?'

6.00 a.m., Flagstaff House, Napier Road

The British Army's Eastern District HQ was not five minutes from the town centre, and Lowry was more than happy to move in out of the rain. The captain's office was decidedly more than comfortable – luxurious, in fact – and Lowry settled into the Chesterfield settee and lit a cigarette. The dead man had been identified as Lance Corporal William Cousins, nineteen years old.

Lowry was clear where the responsibility lay. 'You need to fathom out who he was with.'

The captain, seated in a large winged chair opposite, took exception. 'With? He may not have been with anyone – military personnel, that is. Why, whenever there's a spot of bother, do the local police assume there's more than one soldier involved? We're not wolves, inspector, roaming the streets in packs in the small hours.'

'We both know this not to be true in the ordinary run of life, Jim: how often is a squaddie on the town solo?'

'This isn't ordinary life though, is it?' Oldham's small hands flexed across the leather chair's arms, and his voice rose. 'A man has been shot, left for dead in the high street – had he been discovered in barracks I might be more open to your suppositions but as it stands there is no evidence to suggest anyone from this camp was involved.' Understandably the captain was irritated at being roused so early in the morning to pull one of his men off the street. Lowry rose and paced around the captain's office, choosing not answer immediately. If the man was going to be disagreeable, he'd rather not sit and face him. It was too early in the day. The captain should be thankful that Lowry had been amenable to resuming the conversation at Flagstaff House, rather than insisting on returning to the creaking police HQ on Queen Street, and his own cramped – and shared – office. The sumptuousness here was near palatial: a mix of military regalia and the captain's own delicate taste, all of it from another era. An orderly broke the silence wheeling in a silver tea trolley. Lowry moved to the French doors. Dawn was peeking through the eucalyptus on the captain's veranda.

Finally, Lowry spoke. 'You say there is no evidence. But then again . . . he was dressed in full regalia, which does hint at a military occasion. Maybe he was rehearsing a birthday surprise for the Beard, perhaps with some pals? What do you reckon? Might be worth poking around the garrison?'

'That is a valid point, Lowry,' the captain conceded, calmer now with tea, 'there is no obvious reason why he should be dressed so formally.' Oldham brought the china cup to his lips, whereupon a shadow crossed his brow.

'What?' Lowry asked.

'Unless . . .' he sighed. 'Unless it was a duel.'

'A duel,' Lowry echoed.

The word lingered in the room. Oldham's attention was diverted as a soldier entered, swiftly laid a buff folder on his tidy antique desk and retreated. The captain rose and moved to the desk. 'Hmm,' he scanned the contents of the file, 'Lance Corporal Cousins was a troubled soul. On patrol in Londonderry his unit was firebombed in a truck. Several were killed. Cousins took it hard and spent a good while recovering, it would seem . . .'

'A duel.' Lowry followed Oldham to the desk, his mind

still on that word from another century. 'Yes, yes, that would figure – dressed for a ceremony.'

Oldham closed the file. 'I dearly hope not, of course.'

'Did that come to mind just now, or did the thought occur to you when we were in the high street?'

'Immediately. But the street is not the place to voice these matters.' He smiled thinly. 'Hence my suggestion to return here.'

'I see,' Lowry said. Much as he liked James Oldham, the man played his cards close to his chest and was always keen to keep military matters confined to military space. 'Hence your annoyance.'

The other did not respond.

'It's as much an inconvenience for you as it is for me,' Lowry offered.

'That I doubt.'

'Where did Cousins bunk down on the garrison?'

'His unit is quartered on Hyderabad. We ought to pay them a call.' The captain consulted his watch with an air of resignation.

'Thanks, Jim.' Lowry finished his tea. 'How long was he in hospital?'

'Hospital? He wasn't in hospital,' he said, picking up his cap.

'You said it took him a good while to recover. A few weeks or months?'

'Several months, though not in hospital. The Military Corrective Training Centre.'

'The glass house?' Lowry said, surprised to hear Cousins

had been in the military prison on Berechurch Hall Road south of Colchester.

'Indeed. He was upset by the experience,' he said sardonically, 'and shared his pain on an officer.'

Hyderabad barracks were not on the Abbey Fields site to the south of Napier Road but on the Mersea Road, half a mile east. Lowry had a good general knowledge of Colchester's long and complex military history; it was hard to avoid, given the wealth of army-owned property, literally on the town's doorstep. Abbey Fields alone was thirty-three acres – army personnel were in fact closer to the centre of town than much of its civilian population. From its earliest days in Roman Britain, Colchester was a garrison town, and as such the soldiery was at its heart. Through the ages, if the town were to grow, it had to do so beyond the military camps. It was only in the last decade or so that things had changed.

Lowry jumped up into the dark interior of the RMP Land Rover waiting for them outside Flagstaff House. A soldier slammed the back door and Lowry braced himself on the cold bench seating. The Napier Road HQ complex itself dated to the 1860s when the land was purchased by the War Office from the St John's Abbey estate on the southwest corner of St Botolph's roundabout. Here the cavalry and artillery barracks were built; the temporary canvas and wooden makeshift accommodation that had seen the army through the Napoleonic campaign would no longer do. The Victorians, wishing to control their ever expanding and more restless empire, required a substantial army with permanent buildings, and that vision took shape in the form of the impressive cavalry and artillery barracks right here on Abbey Fields. They were built to last and last they did; the camp saw them beyond the decline of the empire and through two world wars. Now in the early eighties a number of these glorious red-brick buildings lay empty; with the advancement of machinery, vehicles and helicopters it was necessary to relocate to a more spacious area, thus forcing the military to leapfrog the civilians and situate themselves out on the fringes of town off Berechurch Hall Road, to the expanding Roman Way camp close to the military prison. However, some of the grand old Victorian buildings with their Empire-inspired Indian nomenclature remained occupied to house the infantry, such as Hyderabad, and were but a short distance away. As the Land Rover grunted into life, Oldham, seated up front, issued instructions to the driver then sank into silence, while Lowry clung on in the back of the vehicle as they pulled away.

Atkinson's bed wasn't nearest the door, but he could still hear the fast-approaching footsteps over the sound of his squad mates' snoring. He knew what was coming but the bang on the door was still a shock thundering through the darkness. He pulled the coarse cover tight up to his chin – he wasn't going to be the first to move. The door opened and the dormitory room flooded with light, followed promptly by squeaking bed springs, groans and curses from the six men within.

'*Tenshun!*' The bark of a Red Cap sergeant and a *whish* of cold air announced the arrival of a small party of men. Atkinson stumbled upright and fell into line at the foot of his bed, praying he looked like a man rudely disturbed from slumber rather than one who hadn't had a wink all night.

'What the fuck—' moaned Steele, a bad-tempered Scots.

'Button it, you,' the Red Cap sergeant snapped.

There were two Red Caps, followed by Oldham, the most feared man on the camp, and behind him a tall Brylcreemed man in a donkey jacket: Lowry, the civilian police inspector and ex-boxer. Bringing up the rear was the company RSM quartered downstairs and he too was bleary-eyed, as much in the dark as to what was happening as Atkinson's fellow squaddies. The two Red Caps began a systematic shakedown of the quarters, opening cupboards and tearing off mattresses as if the missing lance corporal were hidden there. Nobody said a word.

'Arrgh, fuck's sake.' A Red Cap trod on Pearson's naked toe.

'Gentlemen, we are sorry for this inconvenience,' Captain Oldham said in a soft, measured way. 'Lance Corporal William Cousins has been shot. You wouldn't happen to know anything about that, would you?'

'Shot? Where?' Pearson said, watching the policeman inspect an ashtray. Oldham stepped up to Pearson, who occupied the bed next to Atkinson. Pearson stiffened, remembering too late that speaking when not spoken to was not a good idea. Oldham, shorter by several inches, was close enough now for Pearson to fear his breath might tickle the Red Cap commander.

'In the chest,' Oldham said calmly, then turning to address the rest of the room, 'and left to bleed to death in the high street.'

The policeman meanwhile had gone into Cousins's room.

'When was the last time you saw him? Any of you,' continued Oldham. Atkinson felt compelled to speak; they were friends, the others would think it odd if he said nothing.

'He was here last night when I went to bed, sir.'

'Was he, was he really?' Oldham's eyes questioned the other men, who promptly agreed with Atkinson. 'And what form of conversation was to be had at the evening's end?'

'Shut 'imself up in 'is room, sir,' Pearson offered. That much was true. Deep in contemplation of the task before him, no doubt. Atkinson was pretty damn sure neither Pearson nor Steele had any idea of what had come to pass. No, it was the other two men directly beneath them, on the floor below, that knew. He wondered whether they slept tight, or heard the visitors' arrival . . .

Lowry kept an ear on the questioning in the main dorm while going through the lance corporal's belongings in his quarters. Not that there was much space for anything in here. Drab furniture, the clothing closet was decorated inside with pin-ups of Koo Stark and crammed neatly with uniforms, boots. A ukulele resting in a corner was the only item to stand out. Beneath a mirror was a heavy chest of drawers containing civvy clothing, equally pristine. He shoved the drawers shut. In the corner of the mirror were a pair of cinema ticket stubs. The Odeon on Crouch Street.

In the main room Oldham was concluding his warning – cooperate or else. The military policeman passed on little by way of detail of the death. The man was shot. End of. Lowry took the stubs and left the room. The six soldiers standing in only shorts were barely men, little more than boys; one of them didn't even need a razor yet. He thought it unlikely that any of these youngsters were with Cousins last night. Lads are in the pub Sundays; perhaps he'd been on a date.

'Was he seeing anyone? A girl in town?' Lowry asked, returning to Oldham's side. The soldiers did not respond.

'Answer the policeman,' Oldham addressed the room – then stepped forward and singled out a thin lad at a corner bunk. 'You, speak.' And even though this was said quietly, Lowry was sure he caught the boy tremble.

CHAPTER 2

Chief Superintendent Sparks was in a contemplative mood and leant only a cursory ear to Lowry's account of the early morning robbery in the high street. On this particular overcast November morning, he was feeling nostalgic. He studied the wooden surface of his desk. Countless semicircles; rings from years of mugs, cups, Scotch glasses, placed carelessly and staining the untreated grain. Then there were more pronounced wounds and scars: cigarette burns, knife scores, unusual marks – traces of events only the man behind the desk could read. The gouge where, when drunk, he'd flung the hefty County Marksman Cup across the room in jubilation; a bullet lodged in a top corner, where he'd caught a rat gorging on his digestives. He ran a gnarly fingertip gently along the surface. For all the history it held, the desk was not a large one. Having insisted on this garret office upon his promotion, he had failed to appreciate just how narrow the staircase was and was forced to settle for furniture that would disappoint a village schoolmaster. Yet he would not surrender this office for all the tea in China. The unique privacy it afforded, up above the world. The tiny high windows that allowed only the gulls to glimpse the goings-on within. Walls adorned with boxing photographs throughout the years. The modest (but stuffed) trophy cabinet behind him. It was his true home. With a sigh he returned his attention to Lowry, who had patiently been waiting for his response.

'A duel? Bloody hell. We'll have the whole of Fleet Street descend on us. I remember the last time, the press loved the drama.' Two soldiers had shot each other in Osborne Street one Saturday afternoon, but that was at least five years ago.

'This is different inasmuch as it was premeditated. More theatrical.'

'Premeditated? Were there seconds then?'

'Perhaps.'

'And left a chap for dead?' Sparks tutted. 'Not very dignified: what did Oldham have to say about that?'

'Lance Corporal Cousins had issues.'

'Issues' was a buzzword that Sparks disliked; a catch-all for unquantifiable complications of the bonce. He disliked it almost as much as he disliked *buzzword* itself; one of Assistant Chief Constable Merrydown's words. This rash of county verbiage was spreading, it seemed, even infiltrating his own interior vocabulary. He would resist – Sparks called a spade a spade. And he would continue to bloody well do so until said spade was mercifully shovelling soil on to his boxed up earthly remains.

'I see,' he said eventually. 'Let's see what Oldham discovers.'

Although it was a genuine military problem, the spotlight on the town was a pain in the neck. CID would take the sideline for the present with the hope the military would swiftly put its best foot forward. Besides, they, the police, had their own worries. 'Issues,' he grumbled, 'we've our own issue to contend with.'

'What?'

'That new hospital they're building up at Turner Village has placed us in the firing line again.' He slid a letter he'd been using as a coaster out from underneath his teacup.

'What, to move? Where?'

'Who cares where? We're not budging.' He flapped the letter around. 'They've been trying to relocate us since '67, and failed every time.'

Lowry reached inside his suit pocket for cigarettes. 'This place is listed – there's only so much that can be done. There's no way the building's circuitry could handle electronics the likes they've got at Chelmsford.'

'Don't I know it. This,' he flapped the letter again, 'is a request for a survey, for systems suitability.'

'What's that mean? The plumbing?'

'Nope, what you said, computers and the like.'

'Time's up then – we're for it. Remember we tried an electric kettle last winter? Fused the lighting; night desk was on candles for a week. You have to bite the bullet one day.'

'They'll have to brick me up in here first.'

Lowry tapped a Navy Cut on the box. 'Merrydown will mix the mortar herself.'

Sparks crumpled the letter and chucked it over his shoulder straight into the bin. Off his desk, out of mind. 'Pah, they can't make me move – nowhere in the centre of town that's suitable. Right, crack on. Poke Oldham for a statement; the sooner the army admit culpability the sooner we're off the hook.'

'I doubt he's willing to do that, until there's evidence.'

'Come now – you two are pals . . .'

'Even so, the MOD will have something to say about it first; no one likes to admit to problems. Oldham will come back to us midday after a preliminary investigation; you know how cautious he is.' Lowry stifled a yawn.

Sparks's number two was cautious himself, bordering on stubborn, but probably right; Oldham wouldn't have the power. He let the matter drop.

'What news of Kenton?' Sparks said, changing the subject.

'Nada.'

'Sulking at home won't make him feel better.'

'Hardly sulking; he watched a thirteen-year-old girl hurl herself in front of a train.'

'Yep, but she was mad as a hatter – couldn't be helped.' Sparks knew one had to be hard-headed about these things. He rocked back on his chair. There was only so much good time alone could do. 'Nick, go fetch him back in; it's been long enough.'

8.35 a.m., Rowhedge, three miles south-east of Colchester

A sailing boat moved gracefully upriver towards Colchester. So gently and invisibly did the Colne run towards the sea that a boat hull, carving its course between the mist-laden sedge grass of the Rowhedge sea wall on one side and the pastures of Wivenhoe on the opposite bank, was necessary to remind you that the river was even there. The sudden proximity of these tall triangular apparitions not more than twenty feet away navigating the grassland never failed to surprise Jane Gabriel, no matter how many times she saw them. She watched the boat glide by, smiling to herself, and joined the road towards the stone quay where the river made itself known and several yachts were berthed. Even a drab morning like this had serenity attached to it, she thought, as the smell of the river rose to greet her while walking to the post office. A small boy on a chopper bike wished her a good morning as he pedalled past. Gabriel had lived in Rowhedge for the best part of two years, since moving across from North London, but she was still occasionally touched by the friendliness of the locals. She had picked the small village for its rural charm, out on the fringe of the Colne. The surrounding countryside, military-owned woodland and firing ranges, kept the port safe from encroaching urban development, conserving the impression of isolation. Together with the river, it was easy to forget how near the centre of town was; she could get to Queen Street in under a quarter of an hour. Popping the card in the postbox, she heard raised voices fracturing the stillness. As she made her way back along the waterfront, Gabriel saw there was an altercation on one of the boats. Aboard a large white yacht, a young man in a green fighting jacket was talking animatedly to an older, shorter, thick-necked man wearing a camel-hair coat, silver hair combed back in a quiff. A third person, a wiry old sailor in a peaked cap, moved about the boat attending to ropes. The younger man continued to talk, but the other appeared to ignore him, drawing on a cigarette and looking in the opposite direction downriver. This action heightened the eagerness of the man in the green jacket, causing his voice to grow louder. The older man flicked the rest of his cigarette across to the dock. Then, face like thunder, he turned round and abruptly punched the young man in the face, sending him over the port side into the water. Jane stopped in her tracks. Noticing her, the older man's expression changed instantly, and with the anger vanished, said, 'Mornin', luv. Sorry 'bout that.' He stood directly above the boat's name, *Nomad*, painted blue in stylised calligraphy. She guessed from his gesture he meant the cigarette, which lay fizzing at her feet. She remained motionless. He recognised dismay, as with a sigh, he called over his shoulder, 'Kevin, fish that pillock out, when you've a mo.'

9.00 a.m., Cavalry Barracks, Parade Ground

Atkinson stood to attention, eyes forward, together with the rest of the battalion. He was three rows from the front. The RSM barked on: a disgrace to the uniform, the regiment, 'the whole bloody army'. The squaddie next to him in line started tittering. To anyone not involved it was a source of much merriment. Atkinson knew he should try to shrug it off, deflect any suspicion . . . the other two would be sweating too; he could see Drake's short, squat form and cauliflower ears one row forward. He wouldn't be laughing; he'd pulled the bloody trigger. The RSM stopped abruptly. The sound of footsteps crossing the parade ground was followed by the soft-spoken voice that belonged to Oldham. Perspiration ran down Atkinson's spine – the early morning visit was just the start. Only now did it occur to him they weren't going to let the matter go until they had a result. Oldham began to address the men. In contrast to the RSM, he spoke rather than shouted. Clear as a bell, his voice reached every single one of the assembly on this overcast November morning, his words all the more fearsome for their calm delivery.

'Gentlemen, I shall be brief. Come forward and the matter shall be drawn to a swift conclusion. If questions of loyalty trouble you, cast them aside; it is not relevant in this situation . . .' Atkinson heard this as if Oldham were addressing himself and Burnett directly. *Would they know there were seconds?*

Of course they would, idiot. He stared intently at the back of Drake's unflinching head. Him, the killer.

'. . . Now is your opportunity to speak up. If not here, then I will grant one further hour.' He paused. 'If no soldier is forthcoming, and a full investigation is required, your lives will be abject misery until this is resolved. Do I make myself clear?'

The assembly replied as one gruff voice: 'Yes, sir!'

Oldham then promptly left the parade ground and the RSM, after reiterating the captain's command at a greatly amplified level, dismissed them. Drake snaked off through the rising hubbub. Atkinson followed at a distance until Drake stopped by the gymnasium lavatories, where Burnett lit them both cigarettes.

'What do you want?' Drake spat as Atkinson approached.

'I thought I'd check in with you guys . . . after, after what he said, whether you thought . . .'

Drake dismissed Burnett with a glance, who scurried off, glad to be out of it.

'Thought what, huh? Don't be bleedin' stupid. We're meeting him at two this afternoon. Just me and you; in the meantime don't go drawing attention to us right here – that's why we're on leave. Jesus, what a Benny.' Drake was an aggressive little sod. He wondered how Cousins would have behaved if Drake were dead. The short stocky man jabbed Atkinson in the chest. 'If you so much as breathe a word in your sleep, I'll cut your knackers off. Got that?'

Atkinson nodded.

'And don't forget you're the one that left him to die.'

'Wha—'

'You were his bloody second.'

Atkinson swallowed hard. The gun had made such a noise in that empty street, he panicked and fled, only just remembering the instruction to ditch the weapon.

'Drake, what about the girl? The police might find her.'

'The Red Cap monkeys are too frickin' stupid.'

'No, the townie coppers. One asked me this morning.'

Drake stepped closer. How a girl could bear to be kissed by a fella with such foul breath – rank cabbages – was beyond Atkinson.

'What did you say?' This possibility had not occurred to the little tyke.

'Nothin' – I never met her. Cousins was so secretive, it's only when . . .' Atkinson stopped himself from saying he only even heard her name when Cousins had found out she was two-timing him.

'Keep it that way,' Drake said.

'At least we're not grounded.'

'We're officially on leave, remember.'

Drake moved off, leaving Atkinson alone outside the gym. He sighed and traipsed off. Rounding the corner of the building, he walked smack into two Red Caps.

'Atkinson, what are you doing lurking round here?'

'Nothing . . .'

'The captain wants you.'

'What for?'

'Cretin. You were in Cousins's unit, you're top of the list.'

'But he's seen me already, first thing this morning.'

The sergeant laughed malevolently. 'You don't really think we swallow you know fuck all, do you?'

CHAPTER 3

Lowry prepared to leave the station. He glanced down through the large sash window at the street below bustling with pedestrians. The police had occupied the building since 1943, the year he was born. They'd moved there from their previous residences at the town hall. It had previously been a soldier's rest home. Sparks had a point, it would be hard to find a better location; turn right, a minute up the road, and there was the castle and the east end of the high street and town centre; turn left, walk down Queen Street, cross St Botolph's roundabout and into the heart of the military. Lowry poked his head out the window. The sky was a troubled grey. There would be more rain – but it was mild. He deliberated over whether to take his donkey jacket. He remembered narrowly dodging a half-full milk bottle the last time he'd visited Kenton, just avoiding ruining his suit. He left the coat on the hook and hurried downstairs. It wouldn't come to that – and God help Kenton if it did.

As he exited the building, wondering whether they might possibly move the police station, he almost collided with Gabriel.

'Hey, good morning,' he said brightly.

'Sorry I'm late.'

'No problem.' He noticed she was ruffled. 'What's up?'

'Oh, it might be nothing, but I think I just witnessed an assault.'

Lowry paused on the steps. 'Here?'

'No, at Rowhedge – as I posted a birthday card.' Lowry listened to Gabriel's encounter on the riverside.

'And was the other man okay?'

She shrugged. 'He didn't complain when pulled out of the water.'

'I wouldn't worry about it then.'

'I think they were up to no good.'

He considered his response, glancing over at a wino emerging unevenly from Short Wyre Street. 'Too late now, though, isn't it?' Then, thinking this inadequate, he added, 'Did you get a good look at both of them?'

She nodded.

'Park it up here then,' he said, and tapped the side of his head. 'Now though, I need help on something else: a dead soldier, William Cousins, found this morning in the high street.' Lowry directed her over to the morgue to collect the lad's uniform and personal effects for his next of kin – not much, according to Robinson, a pendant or necklace – and then said finally, 'And check what was playing at the Odeon Friday night.'

'Right you are,' Gabriel said.

The incident she'd witnessed forty minutes ago was a small thing – in reality it had lasted no more than a few seconds – but it had created an uncertainty in Gabriel's mind nevertheless. Maybe she was making a mountain out of a molehill, but she was a policewoman, and it was on her very doorstep, and what if, say, the boy on the bike had witnessed her do nothing? Before leaving for work, anxiety had gripped her so forcefully she had gone back to the quay, where, of course, the boat had since departed, and the men presumably with it. She'd been late for work as a consequence.

Now standing in Queen Street, her worries faded as Lowry brought her sharply to the here-and-now with the news of the young soldier's death in the high street.

'What about you? Where are you going?' she called out as he made off towards St Botolph's roundabout.

'Kenton,' was the single word response he mouthed back at her.

Lowry was fond of Jane Gabriel, the newest CID recruit, who had made the move from Uniform this summer. CID was, until recently in this part of the county, a solely male reserve. Now, the county – in the guise of Sparks's boss ACC Merrydown – was placing the chief under pressure to modernise his operation in more ways than one. Jane Gabriel, in her mid–twenties, was a tall, willowy blonde – and this was a problem for the chief. As far as he was concerned, women in the workplace should be robust, complicit, dull – certainly not cleverer than him – and furthermore should conceal any hint of 'womanliness'. Unfortunately for Sparks, ACC Merrydown was Gabriel's aunt and had shoehorned the woman in, having lost patience waiting for him to move females into the department of his own accord. Merrydown was the very epitome of progress, with nepotism taking second place to propelling change through the force.

Lowry took the left spur up Magdalen Street towards Barrack Street and home to where Kenton lived in New Town.

There was nothing 'new' about the area; the name was ascribed centuries ago, when Colchester was expanding beyond the city walls, and in terms of the military history, this area was actually the precursor to the buildings Lowry had visited that morning with Oldham. Lowry knew much of the town's past but had learnt more from Kenton himself, who had researched the place when joining Queen Street three years ago. Colchester had long been the mustering point for military excursions to the continent, and by the late 1790s, with a lengthy war looming with France, the town required organisation. It was here on Barrack Street where, as its name suggested, the army's first wooden billets were constructed. Now those early buildings were long gone, and all that remained were the occasional pubs – such as Kenton's local, the Bugle Horn – whose names served as a reminder of those days.

Kenton. His last encounter with Kenton had not been good.

As was the way, horrific events brought a man's character to the fore; his strengths and his weaknesses. Sparks's assessment, though blunt and flippant, was not far from the truth: in the wake of the ordeal earlier this year, Kenton had regressed to wallowing in self-pity.

Daniel Kenton recognised only his pale grey eyes in the mirror. The unkempt straggly hair had none of its summer lustre and had not seen a blow-dryer in weeks. The beard was so alien on him that he had to tug it to check it was real. Like every morning for the last month, he had a bit of a thick head. He sniffed contemptuously at himself and left the bathroom. After picking up his tobacco pouch from a bedroom still shrouded in darkness, he entered the living room in only his boxer shorts. His flat situated above an off-licence was pokey, but it was warm and he was in no hurry to dress. The room where he'd spent most of his time these last weeks (when not in the pub) was growing increasingly untidy. By one wall was a stuffed bookcase. Further piles of books were stacked to one side, tumbling into records lazily slipping down the side of a glass hi-fi cabinet further along. By the only window that overlooked the street stood an enormous cheese plant. The green monster was now of such awesome proportions that he could no longer reach to pull down the blind he'd installed. The walls were in desperate need of a coat of emulsion but instead were adorned with only a film poster for *The French Connection* in a clip frame and a large still of Carrie Fisher pouting with a blaster. His windsurf board, which had not seen any action since mid-August, lay the length of the room on the other wall, having nowhere else to go. The sail and boom lay behind it. In the middle of the floor, on a threadbare rug he picked up in the Far East, were a set of weights. He stretched half-heartedly, cracked his fingers and opened the pouch. There was nothing to do until the yoga programme on BBC2. Ever since lashing out at Lowry with a bottle of milk, he'd tried to ease off on alcohol. With some success. But he had increased his intake of pot accordingly. He'd not tried it since college but had discovered that, if one sat around in pubs in east Colchester all day, there it was, as plentiful as ever, despite police claims of stamping out smuggling up the Colne. He sealed the edge of the reefer and lit up. At the turntable he flipped over side three of *Physical Graffiti*, and took a long drag. Nodding his head to the beat, he approached the iron bar in the centre of the room and took up position in preparation for a dead lift. Weightlifting was again something he'd not done since university, but it was essentially one of the best exercises there was and it complemented the yoga in strengthening his core.

Through the drum beat he thought he heard a rap at the door. He continued the move, hands gripping the bar. Another knock. There was someone at the door; he caught it clearly this time. He took another toke on the joint and placed it in the Truman's ashtray he'd borrowed from the Bugle. Winding the stereo down a notch he padded to the front door, which took a third rap. 'Yeah, yeah, Jesus, I'm not deaf,' he muttered, turning the latch.

Lowry stepped into the room.

'You might like to consider opening a window.'

'Morning, sir.' Kenton stiffened. 'Too warm? Does heat up in here,' he said by way of excuse for his state of undress.

Lowry's presence dominated the space. Kenton felt abashed at his near-naked form next to this cleanly shaved man in a pristine pale grey suit, white shirt and neat narrow black tie. This was Lowry's natural state; that Kenton felt acute discord provoked something deeper than shame.

'I'm not interrupting anything, I hope?' Lowry scanned the room, his eye lingering on the slump of books, where he spotted the bird identification book he'd lent Kenton months ago.

'Err, no . . . just a bit of exercise.'

Reefer smoke hung close to the ceiling. Kenton could think of nothing further to say. He needed the grass – besides, it was better than drinking. His boss stepped over the weight bar towards the window.

'Good, that's something,' Lowry said, elbowing tropical foliage out of the way to reach the window frame.

'What . . . what is something?' Kenton asked hesitantly.

Lowry successfully levered open the window, dusted off his hands and said, 'That you're fit. It's time to return to work.'

'I . . . I'm not ready.'

'Of course you are.' He turned and moved to the centre of the room.

'Really, I'm not.' The prospect of returning to Queen Street was not something he'd thought about in any concrete sense. He was still recovering from an experience that would haunt him forever. 'I thought I made that clear when you came the other day . . . I'm sorry I was out of order then, the bottle and everything, but that's because I really, really—'

'Dan, that wasn't *the other day*,' Lowry reached over and placed a hand on his colleague's bare shoulder, 'that was nearly a month ago. I'm telling you, you are ready, because if you're not back at your desk tomorrow there may not be a desk for you.'

'You can't . . . I really am not in a good way.'

'No, you're not. I agree.' Lowry's hand fell away as Kenton stood back in surprise at this concession. 'You were in better shape three weeks ago; you are going downhill rapidly. And that is why you are coming back to work tomorrow.'

'I've been granted leave.' Perspiration was forming on Kenton's forehead; he knew he was losing. He straightened his back in one last ditch attempt. 'Where's your compassion?'

'Compassion?' Lowry returned to the window. 'I'll nick you for cannabis possession if you press this any further. How's that for compassion? Dan, you are never going to find an answer for that girl's death.'

Kenton hung his head.

'But you will lose your job if you carry on like this,' Lowry continued. Kenton watched as the inspector gazed out at the street.

'How much time have you been spending in the boozer?'

'Not much. Now and then.'

'Every day, no doubt,' Lowry said, ignoring him. Kenton didn't argue. 'They're squaddie pubs around here.'

'Infantry use them, yes.'

Lowry then told him of a soldier from Hyderabad who was shot this morning in town. A duel. The drama of the crime pricked his dulled senses. Duels were the stuff of a romantic age, one long since gone, but one he found fascinating.

'The investigation will take two approaches. One to find the man who pulled the trigger and to locate anyone else involved, from the military side—'

'Seconds,' Kenton said quickly.

'Precisely. Oldham will be leading the charge there. We will concentrate our efforts searching for any non-military influences. Primarily female acquaintances.'

Kenton thought this over, then said disappointedly, 'The townie girls never come out here for a drink.'

'There'll be chatter though.' Lowry picked up the spliff and pulled out his Ronson. Moving closer, he said, 'Get your shit together. Shave. And,' he took an impressively large toke, held his breath and exhaled smoke in Kenton's face, 'use your last hours out of shop wisely.'

As Kenton spluttered away, Lowry left the room.

Outside Lowry stood in the street pulling out his cigarettes. It was tipping it down. The rain was warm though, and he was mellow from the joint. Two lads in tracksuits skulked around the off-licence doorway, their talk abruptly ceasing on seeing Lowry pause for a smoke. One of the lads had discernible needle bruising along his thin arms where he'd pushed his trackie top above the elbow. Kenton's pot habit was not the worst thing in the world, and he would soon shake that. Lowry would see to it that he did. In the meantime, the police were adept at containing their own vices.

So long as nothing untoward happened.

If a dealer was attacked, for instance, and CID's attention drawn to the situation, it could well become awkward. Worse if someone died. Even if one of these wasters was found slumped on the street, questions would be asked – and when questions are asked, people have a tendency to talk . . . it was not the kind of area for anyone in Kenton's position to have a casual drug habit. Still. Get him back on the job first, then work it through. Smoking gear first thing in the morning was bad; addiction. Lowry nodded to the lads and made his way down the street. Nobody was perfect. He himself had a Valium habit and drank more than was good for him, but he didn't touch either in the morning. No, the frequency itself was not really the issue, it was filling the space in-between hits where Kenton was currently at risk – the days had to be filled, otherwise they were lost. It was already happening to the young detective, Lowry could see it: his sense of time was slipping.

Sparks had been right, it was time to bring him back into the fold.

CHAPTER 4

Oldham sat at his desk, now clear, elbows on the table and fingertips touching in steepled fashion. He was enormously fond of Nick Lowry, and he did not wish this incident to cloud their relationship. Public incidents such as this brought the spotlight down on the garrison. The brass had already been on the line seeking assurances this would be dealt with quickly and contained. *Contained.* As if it were a virus.

His men had rounded up Cousins's unit swiftly, but Oldham had kept them waiting until the hour had elapsed. Let them sweat. In addition he'd singled out men who'd seen active service in Northern Ireland as Cousins himself had. He wished to see them first. One in particular; a soldier, Reeves, with a record of passing information to the military police.

As the clock reached ten, the captain stirred his umpteenth coffee and realised how truly annoyed he was that nobody had come forward, how much he'd been banking on a confession.

He sighed. 'All right, Sergeant Fairweather. Bring the first one in.'

'Sir.'

After a moment, the man was shown in.

'At ease, lance corporal.'

It was easier to read a face at rest, rather than one frozen at attention. Oldham himself remained seated. He dismissed Fairweather. The men were more likely to talk if there was no witness.

'Now then. Reeves, is it?'

'Sir.'

'You understand the situation fully, Reeves?'

'Sir.'

'We, and the local police, are under the impression that a duel was responsible for Lance Corporal Cousins's death.' The soldier stared blankly ahead. 'A duel carried out in Colchester High Street. What is the word on camp?'

'Surprise. Sir.'

'By that are you telling me that nothing was known of this duel? Not even a whisper?'

'No, not a dicky bird, sir.'

This was not what Oldham was expecting to hear. Such things are seldom kept quiet; this was not a spontaneous drunken brawl but a precise operation, involving forensic preparation. Gossip and rumour would abound in the run-up. At least, that's what history had taught them. If Reeves was right that nobody knew a thing, catching the other protagonist would not be straightforward.

'I see. You knew Cousins well, I understand?'

Strain showed on the young man's face.

'Sir, yes, sir. Not that well, sir. He was a bit of a live wire. Very aggressive, sir.' At times like this soldiers wished they had never made friends. It quickly transpired that Reeves had not been in touch with Cousins since those volatile days in Londonderry. That sort of experience either bound men together or cast them apart; in this case it was the latter. Cousins's losing it had seen to that.

'Did anyone remain on friendly terms with Cousins after the incident?' Oldham asked pointedly. 'That is, any man here on camp?' Reeves twisted his lip.

'Atkinson, sir. In Londonderry together.'

'Good, good.'

Oldham dismissed the man. Fairweather re-entered.

'Fetch me Atkinson, he's our man. And arrange to have him followed once I'm through.'

Bugle Horn, Barrack Street

Kenton sat nursing a pint of Guinness. He'd been ordered to return to work tomorrow, which, although he should have seen it coming, was still a surprise. He thought this news would be best digested over a final drink. He had been away from work for over two months. After the deaths at Fox Farm he took some holiday, returned to Queen Street at the beginning of September and battled through a week, but was unable to focus. He was haunted by the trauma he'd experienced. The image of the dead girl, her small mutilated body. A living nightmare. His initial enthusiasm at Lowry's tale of a duel had swiftly evaporated when the reality of sorting himself out had sunken in. The pub offered immediate solace and maybe he just might, by chance, hear something useful; something to present to CID and shield his arrival at Queen Street tomorrow morning. Jesus. When exactly was the last time he was in the CID office? He lifted the Guinness sombrely.

Lowry probably hadn't considered how awkward his return would be. In particular, Kenton pricked with discomfort at the thought of Jane Gabriel: she had reached out to him, offering support immediately, but like a truculent schoolboy he had spurned her, only to regret it an instant later. And lacking the maturity to go after her and apologise, his pain had since festered and the idea of losing her completely nagged at him. They had not spoken since . . . he couldn't remember. Early September? He lit a rollie, and noticed how stained his fingers had grown. That wouldn't come off by tomorrow. He'd switched to roll-your-own since smoking pot. No one would notice his nicotined fingers, surely. He glanced at the old boy settling down in the corner; he too had a tin of Old Holborn out, though Kenton doubted grandad carried a sizeable lump of Lebanese black in his. He slurped at the Guinness – more filling than cider or lager and good for you. Apparently. He sighed and checked his tin; actually his sizeable lump was not so sizeable. He'd need more, especially with the stress of Queen Street. Julian would be in shortly; he'd have a word.

What would Jane say if she could see him now? He pictured

her beautiful face distorting with distaste. Kenton grimaced and ran his fingers through his beard. He promised Lowry he'd get a haircut and shave, but that could wait until the afternoon. The pub had opened at eleven and he'd been in at five past. The prospect of work had fractured his fragile resolve of recent weeks. Daytime drinkers were a fascination for Kenton and in the last months he'd often been eager for a pint before noon to still his troubled mind. Until he'd moved to Essex, his experience of drinking establishments was defined by the genteel public houses in his hometown in Surrey, and the lively student watering holes up at university in Edinburgh. Neither had prepared him for the grubby boozers now on his doorstep. Most this side of town were not far from spit and sawdust affairs; but what they lacked in sophisticated décor they made up for in the characters who frequented them. He'd been in most of them in the line of duty – barging in on a Friday night to nick someone, or tracking down some shady character who might be persuaded to talk – but it was different being here as a punter. You saw the place through different eyes; peaceful and inviting and shabbily familiar. Flaking paintwork, worn hardwood surfaces, the yellow, cracked ceiling; a naked ageing structure smoothed by the warmth of alcohol and density of cigarette smoke. That said, at 11.30 and still on his first pint of the black stuff, the essential disrepair of the place was not quite as romantic as it would be later as the alcohol and spliff kicked in.

Kenton slipped two ten-pence pieces into the jukebox. There

was always a handful of off-duty soldiers from the garrison in as soon as the doors opened, celebrating – a birthday, leave, arrival, departure – with a day-long session. There were three here now boisterously playing pool, their excitement at odds with the subdued milieu. To liven it up a bit, Kenton proceeded to scan the records, drumming the glass case with his fingers as they flipped by; he had three picks. The landlord pulled a further pint of Guinness and left it to stand. Apart from the military, there was also a handful of civilians. The first to arrive were the regulars. Men in their sixties. Pensioners. One, Wilf, was already in situ, perched quietly at a corner table, steadfastly drinking IPA. He would sit there until last orders, then leave as silently as he had arrived. Around midday the bohemian set – 'intellectual dossers', Sparks called them – would drift in. Young men clutching tatty paperbacks. Sucking the ends of biros and staring pensively into the middle distance.

'About time you were back at work, eh?' The affable publican, in a neat, bright tie, threadbare 'grandad' cardigan and comb-over, reminded Kenton of his geography prep school teacher.

'Not you too.'

'Seen your guv'nor, 'ave you?'

'Tomorrow.'

'Will miss your custom, laddie. This one's on the house. Ain't surprised though, bet they need you.'

'How's that?'

'Like the Wild West out there. Heard on the radio, soldiers

shooting each other in the high street. Want to send 'em back to the Falklands.'

'Yes . . . so I heard.' Kenton doubted he meant that; duelling or not, soldiers paid for the upkeep of this place. 'Hey, let me know if you hear anything, eh?'

The man winked conspiratorially in return.

'Hear what?'

The door went with a clatter. Julian the plumber, unmistakable with a shock of blond hair like Billy Idol, moleskins and karate slippers, a charmer and character. But most important was what he kept in those deep, long moleskin pockets. When frisked by Uniform he'd boast it was a kind of flux.

CHAPTER 5

By the time Atkinson was pushed through into the RMP captain's office he was a bag of nerves. If Oldham recognised him from this morning, he didn't let on. That he'd been kept waiting was a bad sign. Sergeant Fairweather stood a step removed from the side of the captain's desk, statue-still.

'When was the last time you saw Cousins?'

Atkinson had prepared his words carefully.

'Last night before lights-out.'

'What had you done previously?'

'In the Grenadier, sir.'

'That would be the British Grenadier, on Military Road?'

'Sir.'

'And no mention was made of a stroll into the town centre at four in the morning in full parade dress?'

'No, sir.'

'No, sir,' the captain repeated. 'I feel it only fair at this stage to point out that it is widely known you were close to the deceased.' He raised his slight eyebrows. Atkinson nodded.

42

The captain would have wheedled it out of those who'd been questioned ahead of him anyway.

'And how was William Cousins feeling on his last evening on earth in the Grenadier?'

'Playing table football, sir, there was a tournament on,' he replied quickly. 'Cousins is, or was, a tasty player.'

'Hardly a reflective few final hours then.'

'Sir.'

'And how was he?'

'How was he?'

'Yes, as in, did he have the air of a man prepared to fight another to the death, or was his mind more concerned with this table football extravaganza?' Oldham's cold, colourless eyes terrified Atkinson; not a whisker of emotion.

'Not that I know of . . .'

'You were particularly close in Ireland, where Cousins was prey to bouts of unhappiness, and remained so.' Oldham picked up a silver pen and moved it through the air like a small wand. 'He must have turned to his friends for support, what with his family in Northampton.'

'He was . . . a very private man, sir. Buttoned up.'

At this point Fairweather spoke for the first time. 'Pardon me for interrupting, captain, but – come off it, private. Is that really the sort of man that would assault a commissioned officer?'

'Thank you, sergeant. Atkinson, he makes a good point. You were there, in Londonderry. That sort of behaviour is the definition of one who is *un*buttoned.'

Atkinson couldn't think what to say. Just because he knew Cousins threw a wobbly at some dippy unit commander who got them petrol bombed, earning him a spell in the glass house, didn't mean Cousins didn't hold some cards close. Not to mention, the circumstances were not remotely similar – one was publicly going batshit crazy and the other was closely guarding a secret love affair. Atkinson knew only that Cousins was determined to go through with the duel and that the girl was wrapped up in it somehow. The girl who was never spoken of, her name never mentioned but once or twice. Drake, for his part, never gave anything away either; except that, like Cousins, he had no choice either, according to Burnett. That was it. But there was no point telling Oldham any of this. In the end Atkinson said, 'Now that you mention it, he was a bit out of sorts on Sunday.'

'Maybe the table football,' Oldham said. The captain's tone softened.

'Yeah, maybe.'

'Did he win?'

'No, sir, he was beat in the early rounds.'

'Sergeant, get the names of all the men in Hyderabad that frequent the Grenadier.' Oldham's sudden switch back to the Sunday night foxed Atkinson. He stared dumbly down at the man, who met his eye with something akin to a smirk. 'I don't think it was you that shot William Cousins, Atkinson. Unless we unearth some hitherto unknown animosity between you . . .'

Atkinson exhaled. He'd be out of here in a matter of minutes and could start putting it all behind him.

Then Oldham struck like a cobra. 'However, if it transpires that Cousins was in a duel, it would stand to reason you'd be his second.'

'Second?' Atkinson could hardly say the word.

'Yes, I'm sure you know what that is?' Oldham leant forward on his desk. 'And it's highly likely it was a duel, wouldn't you say, Fairweather?'

'Very likely, sir. Dressed up to the nines, very likely indeed.'

Oldham gave a slight nod of the head at the sergeant's complicity and pursed his lips into a thin, terrifying smile. 'For now though, the matter of identifying a second is, you might say, of secondary importance. Our primary question remains – who pulled the trigger?'

Atkinson nodded involuntarily.

'I'm not an unreasonable fellow, am I, Fairweather?' Oldham motioned sharply behind him to the sergeant.

'Not at all, sir.'

Oldham sat back in his chair and considered Atkinson carefully.

'Duelling was not always illegal. The Duke of Wellington himself fought a duel when he was Prime Minister. But that was then, and we certainly didn't see Mrs Thatcher take up swords against Mr Foot in June, much as she may have fancied it.'

Atkinson had no idea what the man was on about.

'No matter,' the captain continued. 'Whatever drove Lance Corporal Cousins to take such drastic measures, his motivation was unlikely to have been political. No, something far more obvious . . . a lady, undoubtedly.' He held his silver pen poised. 'Her name, please.'

Atkinson's face fell. 'I'm not sure that he had one, sir. I said that to the civvy policeman this morning.' Oldham leant forward.

'I'm not the civilian police, am I?' Oldham said in a dead tone that sent a chill through Atkinson. 'You ate, slept and shat with him: how can you *not be sure*? And if you tell me he was a very private man again, I'll have you court-martialled for insubordination on the spot. The civilian policeman, since you mentioned him, uncovered two cinema ticket stubs for last Friday night.'

Atkinson's brain scrambled with fear.

'Does that jog your memory? Was it you he took, or was it perhaps a date? I'm waiting.'

'There was this hairdresser.'

'Ah, now, that's more likely.' The captain smiled sharply, and picked up his silver pen, expectantly. 'And her name?'

Scheregate Steps, town centre

Oldham had come up with a lead.

Cousins had been dating a hairdresser.

No name, but it was a start.

Lowry remembered passing this particular salon's tropical island window display on his way to the Candyman, a subterranean bar next door, a number of times, but never registered it as a hairdressers'. A neat bit of marketing to make the place inviting in the autumn gloom, he thought, as he pushed the glass door open and entered, dripping rainwater on the floor. As a man who'd used the same barbers since a boy, he was surprised to learn there were more than a dozen hair salons in the town centre alone. They seemed to have popped up all over the place. This one, tucked away down Scheregate Steps off Eld Lane, was the last on his list. Inside, three women in their early twenties were working away on clients to the gentle rhythm of 'Cruel Summer' coming from a portable radio in the corner. All three wore big hair and heavy eye make-up, and dressed à la mode in baggy clothing and leg warmers. Lowry's image appeared before them in the long mirror, a stark contrast, drawing curious glances. A hair dryer blasted into action at the end of the row, drowning out the music along with any chance for Lowry to speak. Eventually, a hairdresser with carefully arranged untidy auburn hair took pity.

'You'll want the manager,' she shouted as she promptly plunged her charge's head into a wash basin and set about her with a rubber hose. 'Behind you.'

An older woman with a blonde Mary Quant bob sat on a stool at a cash register by the entrance.

'A soldier was found shot this morning, in the high street. We have reason to believe he may have been dating a lady working in your profession.' The hair dryer stopped and Lowry's voice was louder than necessary.

'You don't "date" squaddies, honey. Not here,' she said, clicking her tongue. 'Women in this town fast learn to avoid that kind. Girls,' she called over her shoulder, 'any of you seeing lads off the garrison?'

Lowry was met with the same *as if* expression he'd received all morning. 'Are you sure?'

'We're not daft, you know.'

'Maybe a man who held out on his job? Soldiers, like policemen, know it's not always a winning line of work.' He smiled lightly, aware he was reaching here – but he couldn't believe Oldham would give him duff information.

'Sweetie, no hairdresser round here'd be dumb enough to fall for that: you can tell a soldier boy by his barnet alone, that's our area of specialty. We'd notice.' She held her middle and forefinger in a scissor motion and then pointed to a felt-tipped sign sellotaped to the wall above her: *We regret we do not serve military personnel.* 'There's one in the window too.'

'Fair enough,' Lowry conceded.

'We do policemen though, if they're cute.'

The row tittered.

'I'll bear that in mind, thank you,' he said, and stepped back out into the rain.

CHAPTER 6

Gabriel stopped at the cinema on Crouch Street. The film advertised outside was the same one they'd been screening last Friday. 'We change on a Thursday,' was the terse response from the manager. *Twilight Zone: The Movie* then. As she left the building she pulled the collar of her waterproof up against the weather and scanned a poster on the steps; she'd never heard of it, probably a kind of spooky fantasy still doing the rounds from Halloween, except not much of a horror, having only a fifteen certificate.

The hospital and morgue were just beyond Crouch Street where Southway became Lexden Road opposite the Hospital Arms public house. Just ahead of her a figure she recognised was climbing out of a white Audi. The quiff and the camel-hair coat were unmistakable from the boat this morning – she quickened her pace. But he was not in a hurry it seemed, and had moved to the rear of the car.

'Excuse me, sir.'

'What?' His attention was on his car keys, presumably to unlock the boot.

'You're on a double yellow line.' She would place him at around sixty years old. 'You can't park here, sir.' Stepping closer, she briefly recoiled as the odour of stale tobacco hit her. 'What are you doing?'

'Ahh, you. A copper, eh? Well, I never.' He turned and grinned unpleasantly at her.

'Sir, again, what are you doing here?'

'Visiting grandma.' He nodded to the hospital across the road.

'Come far?'

'Peldon.'

'Driving licence?'

Gabriel glanced down and noted the number plate. She didn't believe a word.

'Don't have it on me, love.'

'You're to present your licence to Queen Street police station within the next seven days.' It was small thing, a bureaucratic slap on the wrist, but somehow she felt it exonerated her for her lack of action on the assault. She marched across the road at the pelican crossing to find the pathologist.

The sight of naked corpses laid out was a relatively new thing to Gabriel, and it crossed her mind that Lowry was testing her, as she'd not been to the morgue alone before. Her formal entrance to CID would not be until next year after she had sat the exams. She had been on Lowry's team less than six months.

'Ah, a lady of the force.' Dr Robinson, in his late fifties, was from another era, and thought corpses and healthy women an impolite mix.

'I'm here to pick up Cousins's clothes,' she said, unmoved, 'and personal effects. Lowry said there was a pendant.'

'Aha. This young chap was in full dress uniform, belt and gloves, the whole kit and caboodle, immaculate, fit for a parade,' he said, evidently impressed. He pointed to a metal tray resting on a polished cabinet surface to one side. 'The garments contained nothing, no ID, zilch. Just the pendant, as you say, which is rather dainty.' The doctor held out a Petri dish in which sat a coiled link chain attached to a rather beautiful pendant about an inch long, detailed with a jewel-encrusted seahorse. The loop through which the chain was threaded was formed by the curling tail, and its scales were set in tiny blue stones. She picked it up. The chain was a dull steel colour. Different, she noted, different from the very pale silver of the pendant. She turned it over.

'Oh,' she said, 'this is an earring. See here – a tiny circle where the back was fixed.'

'So it is, jolly well done. You've an eye on you.' The doctor's glasses sat halfway down his nose. She wondered whether he ever wore them properly. 'Now to the deceased himself.'

'Oh, I don't think that's necessary.'

'Fiddlesticks, come and have a gander since you're here, there's something you should see.'

She moved cautiously towards the gurney where the dead

man lay. He was not what she was expecting: a pale boy, not a muscle-bound soldier.

'How old was he again?'

'Nineteen. A baby.' The doctor said flatly, 'Come nearer.'

She felt the chill of the place for the first time. On closer inspection she noticed more hair.

'See here,' he pointed with a silver utensil to a bruise along the top of the shoulder, 'and here,' angry red scratch marks on the right side of the ribs.

'Fingernails?' she suggested.

He nodded. 'Yes, and recent.'

'Was he attacked?'

Robinson peered over his glasses. 'Possibly.'

Something deeply unpleasant crossed her mind. 'Or maybe, whoever it was, was fighting him off? Could he ... could he have been forcing himself on a woman?'

'Hmm, could be.' He sounded unconvinced.

'And the shoulder? A bruise?'

'Teeth. A bite.'

Gabriel moved closer. 'A bite that bruises, rather than one that pierces the skin, might be ...' she said, surprising herself, 'the opposite?'

'Exactly,' Robinson said, a shade too loudly, 'a love bite, which leads me to think the scratches, appearing where they are at the side, rather than the front of the body, are a result of some energetic lovemaking.'

*

Having been on his feet solidly since before dawn, and finding Oldham unavailable, Lowry returned home to rest for an hour. Oldham's adjutant, however, relayed the headlines: the army had notified William Cousins's next of kin, his parents, and the civilian police should visit them tomorrow. Northampton.

The early morning call to the high street felt like another time frame altogether. And finding Kenton in such a state of disarray had wound him up. The longer the day dragged on, the more annoyed he became. Bloody Kenton. He could have done with an extra pair of feet trudging the high street this morning. Those first minutes after a body is discovered are crucial.

Sparks was right to bring Kenton back.

Behaving like some university hippie. Jesus.

After a pork pie washed down with a gulp of sherry and a Valium, he retired to the lounge, unbuttoned his shirt, removed his tie and hit the sofa. He'd try to contact Oldham again after a nap. Thinking of Oldham, he noticed the classical LP the RMP captain had lent him a week back, lying to the side of the TV. Lowry had played it once and been pleasantly surprised. Lowry's musical taste had not evolved since a teenager – his estranged wife having no influence in this area, despite countless gigs in the early days. Jim Oldham had decided Nick might be ready for something more tranquil than the Small Faces and The Who ('*at your time of life*' were his precise words). Well, he could certainly use some tranquillity right now. He thought he'd give it another go – eyes closed this time. He slipped the vinyl out of its sleeve. Lowry had a dinner date this evening, and it would help if he had some life in him. Why bother if not. Since dropping out of the police boxing team, his social life had evaporated, and now he seldom left Great Tey and the local pub a few doors down. A revitalising doze on the sofa would give him enough to power through.

'Right then,' he said, delicately placing the needle on the record and making himself comfortable on the sofa, 'transport me.' Half an hour shut-eye, then back to the station. Soon the cat joined him and together they drifted off to the violin music.

Gabriel surveyed her surroundings as she waited on the doorstep. Lowry's house was a bit odd: the single modern house in an otherwise period hamlet. In one direction was a Norman church next to a seventeenth-century pub; in the other direction fields stretched out like a patchwork quilt into the distance.

Lowry appeared bleary-eyed in the doorway, his hair sprouting out at all angles. He blinked.

'Sorry,' she said, 'did I disturb you?'

Clearly she had. A cat meandered past, brushing her legs, pausing for a peremptory sniff of the outside world before gingerly treading into the wet.

'I've been up since five,' said Lowry, stepping aside to let her inside.

The house smelt musty, or – maybe that was Lowry himself?

'We couldn't get you on the phone,' she explained. When

he didn't answer, she told him Sparks had been called away to an emergency meeting at County and had requested that he, Lowry, hold the fort (and to Gabriel's mind that meant Lowry should actually be *in* the fort). Lowry yawned in response. This was the first time she'd ever seen him without a tie. She tried another tack.

'How's Daniel bearing up?'

'Hairy.' He ran his hands through his hair and entered the kitchen and stuck the kettle on. After a bout of coughing he lit a cigarette and made some coffee. That was all he was going to say on the matter, it seemed.

'Is that it?'

'Pretty much. He'll be back tomorrow. How did you get on at the morgue?'

'There was nothing in his clothes. But ... the body was marked.'

'Marked? How?'

He passed her a mug of coffee she had not asked for. Black; no offer of milk and sugar. She took it anyway. He poured himself a mug, then ignored it and drank a pint of water straight down.

'Scratches, from fingernails, and a possible bite mark.'

Lowry raised his eyebrows, exhaled, filling the kitchen with smoke and said, 'Oh. Come through,' and wandered off into the lounge and sat back on the sofa.

'Passion or resistance, Dr Robinson says,' she said, taking the armchair opposite.

'And what do you say?'

'I wouldn't wish to speculate at this stage,' she said guardedly, 'without knowing where and with whom Cousins spent his last evenings.'

Lowry grunted. She couldn't tell whether he was engaged or not. She scanned the room for evidence of alcohol.

'Vivaldi?' she said, noting the LP sleeve lying on the low table in front of the sofa. Lowry was scratching his jaw lazily.

'Yeah, it's all right,' he said, getting up from the settee. 'You know it?'

'Yes, of course – everyone does.' She picked up the record sleeve and flipped it over to read the blurb. 'It's very popular. I didn't know you liked classical music?'

'Well, there's a lot you don't know, I guess.' His tone was brusque.

She realised she'd bruised him and returned to more professional matters. 'Err. Yes, of course. I'm sorry, I didn't mean to . . . Anyway, just one other thing. The pendant Cousins was wearing round his neck? Turns out it was originally an earring. Here.' She removed a small polythene pouch from her bag. 'A seahorse. Might be handy info if you're questioning the girlfriend.'

He took the elaborate, silvery blue piece for a closer look. 'Worth a few bob. I've not uncovered any girlfriend or possible love interest, though there was mention of a hairdresser.' He picked up his tie from the floor. 'Right, let's roll. Any idea what Sparks's emergency was?'

*

Lowry felt drowsy as he settled in the car. Gabriel had not been privy to County's need of Sparks, it seemed. The Fiat was a small space, uncomfortably narrow with a low roof. Not ideal for someone of Gabriel's height. She sat forward, almost hunched over the wheel. He had surprised her by asking for a lift back into town without giving a reason. Her remark about the music was somehow belittling, and he was reluctant to engage. Gabriel, eyes on the road, was talking animatedly about how she'd taken up the piano again, and how Oldham had once remarked he thought she would be a fine player.

'Oldham?' Lowry said, stirring in the passenger seat.

'Yes, last winter I called and he was playing the piano. I recognised the piece. A Mozart sonata, hard to play . . .'

'Oh, right.'

This uncharacteristic chattiness was a weird power shift. A boldness he'd noticed before when junior officers were behind the wheel. But there was more to it than that; the way she'd picked up the record sleeve in the house and commented. It wasn't that he was offended; just aware that their relationship had altered. Since the Cliff case, an air of familiarity had crept into Gabriel's dealings with him. Working in close proximity in stressful situations shifted boundaries. Bonds were forged, dependencies created. Sparks thought trauma experienced on duty – the loss of life, extremes of violence – fostered emotional dependencies between colleagues, especially between men and women. (This was his best, and most thought-out, repudiation of Merrydown's desire to place more women in

CID, which she had forcefully rejected as 'poppycock'.) Lowry didn't think this was the case with him and Gabriel. He could not pinpoint exactly when this shift occurred – but recognised a change since he had taken her birdwatching, in search of a Yellowhammer, after leaving Kate Everett's cottage at the end of August. Perhaps they were friends? He stared dumbly out of the window as they made their way into Colchester, not wishing to engage. He regretted the Valium; his senses were dulled, he only half heard what Gabriel was saying – she'd somehow come across the man from the boat in Rowhedge outside the Hospital Arms in Colchester and issued him with a summons.

'What do you hope to gain by that?' he said.

'I'm fed up with being treated so . . . like a piece of dirt. Men like him don't take women seriously. Even a police officer.'

'What was his name?'

'I didn't ask.'

Lowry turned his attention from the passing countryside to examine her profile, hands firmly on the wheel, staring steadfastly ahead, blonde fringe just below her brow. He wondered if she could see clearly.

'Why not?'

'It's immaterial – I have no interest, so long as he presents his documents.'

'Fair enough.' Her logic was weird, but it didn't bother him as much as not knowing the identity of this man who was so dismissive of one of his officers.

Captain James Oldham sat stiffly behind his desk with the telephone receiver to his ear and listened patiently as his commanding officer prattled away. On the other side of the desk stood Sergeant Fairweather, twitching and distracting him. The day had been long since the duel in the high street.

'No,' he said, finally managing to get a word in, 'no, I don't think confining the men to barracks serves our purpose. No, not in the slightest. There is no indication of any civilian involvement or reprisal motive. Yes, I'm sure it's an internal affair. Let them breathe; they're more likely to talk if they are not pent up here.' Locking the doors only added to the likelihood of some sort of a fracas occurring when they were eventually released – venting steam on the unsuspecting townies, most likely. Had his CO, known as the Beard, learnt nothing of managing men? Opposite him, Fairweather continued to fidget and his eyebrows were disconcertingly lively. The man was evidently eager to tell him something. 'We will get to the bottom of this.' Oldham said this authoritatively, even though the only lead he had so far elicited proved to be useless, resulting only in a waste of police time and making him, captain of the RMP, look a chump. He bid the brigadier goodbye and placed the receiver in the cradle.

'Right. Bring him back in,' the captain said, wearily. 'Atkinson.'

'Sir, that's what I was trying to say . . . Atkinson is on leave.'

'Leave?'

'Yes, sir. B company are on leave until they are posted to

Ireland. Though a lot of them are milling around camp because time is short and most of them have run out of money.'

'When do B company move out?'

'Friday.'

'We may have to consider postponing. Meanwhile, continue to keep an eye on him and who he's hanging out with.'

The sergeant nodded and made to leave.

'A gentle eye, Fairweather, a gentle eye. We don't want them running home to mummy.'

'Suspend all leave then, sir?'

'No, did you not hear me just now?' he said, exasperated. 'Grounding them will not help – this business is connected to the outside, the last thing we want is for them to be cooped up in camp. And search the dormitory again. Dismissed.'

He needed time. They could reasonably forestall a departure for a couple days, but not much more. The easy way out was to pack them all off and forget about it, but he felt an obligation to Lowry. They had built a bond of trust over the last year and an element of personal pride pursued him. With a sigh he picked up the telephone again and said, 'Brigadier Lane, urgently.'

CHAPTER 7

Howard Osgood's encounter with plain clothes on his way in had not improved his mood. He wheeled his mother down the polished corridor at speed. Hospitals gave him the willies. He was at the wrong end of his fifties, and a year off the age his father keeled over in the Black Buoy in Wivenhoe.

Osgood carelessly manoeuvred the wheelchair, narrowly avoiding the heavy swing door.

'Careful, son, you nearly had me toe off.'

Howard ignored his mother. Exiting the hospital, he paused under the portico. 'People wouldn't have to park on the poxy street if there were enough parking,' he said to himself, frowning at the rain. 'Right.' They trundled down through the rammed front car park on to Lexden Road. The discharge of Osgood's mother had been a lengthy process.

'The new hospital up in Turner Village will be open next year,' his mother said.

'You might not be around next year,' he muttered.

'Charming. You might be pleased I was out.'

They halted at the curb. He looked down at her. 'Course I

am, Mum, course I am.' But it was inconvenient to collect her; he'd not have punched Cooper had he not been pressed for time. Well, he probably would, jumped-up little turd. They'd missed the morning tide as it was, what with picking up his old dear. He wheeled her across the pelican crossing to the car, which was ticket-free, thankfully. That woman copper was plain clothes, that's why – detectives were not in the habit of issuing parking tickets.

The high street being shut this morning did not help the situation. A dead man right outside his new bloody premises. The decorators were due to have started but couldn't get access out front to unload their gear. They could've come the back way, winding through the cobbled nooks and crannies of the Dutch Quarter, but you had to know the place well to know that. After securing Mrs Osgood in the back seat and collapsing the wheelchair, which just fit in the Audi's boot, Howard pulled a U-turn and shot off up Head Street.

'Err, where you going?'

'Just gotta make a quick stop.'

His mother mumbled something disparaging.

The high street was thankfully open and clear apart from press photographers milling around, and he stopped directly outside the Hippodrome. He could make out the lofty figure of Trevor behind the glass doors. Something was up. He was out of the car in seconds.

'What you looking so shifty for?'

'The rozzers, boss, been here.'

'What for?'

'That soldier that was shot outside the town hall.'

'To be expected; it's practically on our doorstep. The whole town is buzzing about it.'

'Yeah, they wanted to know whether there was anyone here last night.'

'That's straightforward enough. No?'

Trevor's uncomplicated features moved in a way to suggest it was not a straightforward question at all. 'Almost. They'd like you to pop into the station when you've a sec, you know, just to dot and cross ... but, there's something else too.' He turned and went into the downstairs office, previously the ticket office. Howard followed.

'Look.'

On the desk lay a pair of shooters. Military handguns.

'Where'd these come from?'

'Underneath the junk mail on the floor.'

Osgood grunted. 'Makes sense they'd thought it best not to leave them lying on the street,' he said, though he didn't really believe that if you'd shot a man in cold blood you'd want the weapon to be discovered on a doormat like that. He picked them up by the barrels and slipped them into a drawer. 'And we don't want them lying out here bold as day, do we, attracting attention.'

'No, boss, that's cool.'

'Then what you giving me that dumb look for?'

'Err ... I think there's squatters on the upper floors ...'

'Squatters? Show me.'

Trevor hesitated. 'What about Mrs O?'

Osgood waved his hand dismissively. 'She'll be fine. C'mon. Show me.'

Up in the roof there was clear evidence of squalid habitation: a sleeping bag, burnt candles, bean tins and cans of Carlsberg Special Brew. The building had stood empty for months, and it was capacious enough to lose a football team up here.

'They might not have been here last night.'

'Oh, they were. I chucked them out an hour ago.'

'How'd they get in?'

Trev shrugged.

'Any sign of drugs?'

He shook his head.

'Well then, there's no need to call the police. On any score.' After Howard's run-in with the female copper, the rozzers were to be avoided. 'Check the doors and windows, I want it airtight. And get rid of this crap.' He didn't have time for this, if they wanted to catch the evening tide.

By the time Lowry entered Queen Street he'd regained his equilibrium and was ready for the sturdy figure of Sergeant Barnes waiting by his desk.

'What we got?' he said, sipping an extra-strong coffee.

Uniform had swept up and down the high street. Colchester High Street displayed every style of architecture the county had favoured in the last four hundred years. Most of the buildings were non-residential these days; anyone within earshot of the shooting was likely to be either a publican or a guest at one of the two large hotels – the Red Lion and the George, further down. Two residents at the Red Lion had claimed they'd been woken by a loud bang, but had not seen anything from the window. The night porter had heard nothing. One gunshot can be missed in the dead of night in the town centre. A single snap, and people were never quite sure what it was; two, even in quick succession, and they were certain it was a gun (even if they'd never heard one before). For Lowry, one shot, one bullet, confirmed it was a military duel.

'The only door we didn't have an answer from was the Lamb,' Barnes said. The pub nearest the shooting.

'The landlord was probably asleep. I'll wander up and take a look. What about the Hippodrome, that still empty?'

'No, there was a chap there, managing the refurbishment.' The old bingo place had changed hands. It was to become a nightclub.

'Presumably he wasn't there overnight.'

'Expect not, but we asked the owner to check in, all the same. Not a lot else for us to do.'

'What do you think?' Barnes was an experienced policeman and knew the streets well.

'Over a bird, I reckon.'

Lowry nodded. 'Do you know there's over a dozen hair-dressers' in town?'

'Ahh, that's what she does.'

'We haven't got a name though.'

'Well, someone will have seen them together, might come forward once the photo is in the papers. Wait until the pubs open. That's if yer man Oldham doesn't shake her out sooner.'

Lowry was not so sure. Military didn't mix with towns-folk in broad daylight, it was the unwritten rule of things round here. Not to say they never interacted, but contact was generally furtive and kept to night-time. That morning, trolling around the town's hairdressers, he was reminded of the stigma attached to dating soldiers. Casual liaisons were frowned upon. Here today, gone tomorrow, that's what young girls were warned. That was the polite deterrent. The less civil line was garrison boys were unclean. Girls known to have been with squaddies were tarnished by association, labelled as dirty, so they kept quiet about boyfriends unless it was serious.

'Has the press release gone out?' the sergeant asked, reading his doubt.

'Tonight's evening paper.'

'We'll see what that flushes out.'

Lowry wasn't hopeful. Reporters were preoccupied with the army's role in all this rather than the crime itself. The times he'd picked up the telephone, the questions were the same: nothing about the victim or his family; more did the police think the army had acted outside the law.

The sergeant left Lowry to his thoughts.

The tiny silver earring lay on his desk. This was something that had missed the press. Would the owner have come forward? He doubted it, whoever she was.

CHAPTER 8

'The last duel fought in this town was on the street outside here, you know that?' Drake said, then drained his pint. He and Atkinson were here, the pair of them, in this busy soldiers' pub, meeting with the man whose threats had placed them all in the high street this morning.

'The last *but one*, to be precise,' Topize corrected. 'Yes, my Saffron saw those white chalk outlines on the road every day from the school bus.'

'You telling me you got the idea from *her*?' Drake said incredulously.

Topize took a breath and regarded Drake as one does a tiresome child, his face minutely rippled with annoyance.

'Relax, sunshine, relax. Same again?'

Relax was the one thing they couldn't do, no matter how many drinks he bought them. Atkinson didn't think he should be here. He didn't think *any* of them should be here, but Drake had insisted – convinced of the need to show they were not intimidated by the slick Mauritian. Bit late for that now Cousins was dead. Two heavy-set black men eyeballed them from their game of pool, moving around the table languidly. White boys loitered in the background wondering what these intruders were doing here – this was a squaddie boozer. Being soldiers, they didn't notice race like the townies. What disturbed them was not the colour of the men's skin, but the fact that they were civilians – that much was obvious from their build.

Topize didn't care. He leant on the bar as if he owned the place, smiling and shooting the breeze, murmuring along to 'Mirror in the Bathroom' purposely to draw attention to his presence. He was lean, unlike his companions at the pool table, wearing a mint green collarless shirt, unbuttoned to reveal several gold chains.

Drake did himself no favours being arsey. Cousins's death was of no consequence to Topize. He should realise that.

'Now then. I want you to do something for me.' Topize smiled a broad smile, revealing a gold incisor.

Atkinson cut in. 'I think it would be better if we had no further contact with you. At least for a while.' Over at the pool table, one of the men was in dispute with an impatient squaddie, a bandsman.

'I'll be the judge of that,' Topize said, sipping a brightly coloured drink. 'Besides, you boys are going on holiday soon, so we make the most of it now, eh?' Topize turned his head to check the situation brewing at the pool table, and as he did so, Atkinson caught sight of a white line running across his throat.

'Oi, d'you say *holiday*?' spat Drake. 'I'll give you fuckin' holiday ...' Atkinson swiftly placed a hand on his forearm to restrain him. He unexpectedly felt for this ugly, angry squaddie – he'd just killed another soldier for the love of this man's daughter. He must be in turmoil.

Topize appeared not to hear. He had to get his men in check. He raised his left hand, clicked his fingers and glared across at his associates. Seeing their boss, they immediately stopped arguing with the soldiers, lay down their cues and left the table. Satisfied, Topize turned back to Drake. 'Hear me out, my hot-tempered soldier boy – I'm about to offer you what I believe you whiteys call "a nice little earner".'

They weren't expecting this.

Drake reached for a fresh pint. 'Oh yeah, what?'

'I've got a little problem I need help to sort out.'

'What sort of problem?' Atkinson asked, finding solidarity with Drake, and determined not to be belittled. With Cousins gone, he had to get on with him.

'Just lean on this dude a bit, nothing heavy – no more than a scare. A few pounds in it for your trouble.'

'Why not send them?' Atkinson gestured with his chin towards the men in the shadows.

'They, uh, shall we say, stand out.'

'Not at night,' Drake muttered.

'Why?' Atkinson added. 'I can't imagine anyone giving you any grief.'

'Hush, boys.' Topize waited. 'Do you know how hard it

is being black in this town? Trying to get on in the world? Prejudice everywhere.' His brow rose in an expression the boys had not witnessed before. They exchanged glances. Was he after sympathy?

'My heart bleeds for you,' Atkinson said, 'but you look to be doing all right to me. All the jewellery and the flash clothes.'

'Appearances are deceiving; image is everything.'

'Stop talking in riddles,' Drake said, lighting a cigarette. 'How much and who?'

'Wait,' Atkinson asserted himself, the beer giving him confidence, 'why us?'

'I like your spirit. You're brave lads. You are men of honour, like myself. I like that. Not everyone would carry through what you did.'

Not everyone is as dumb as us, surely, Atkinson thought to himself. 'And if we don't?'

Topize shrugged. 'No big deal.'

Drake held his hand high, in front of Atkinson's face. 'How much?'

Gordon Topize left the Robin Hood to the soldiers and sent the two minders back to Romford where they worked as bouncers. He had no need of full-time protection, but liked to flash it around where necessary to create an impression. He had been back in Essex a week, having spent three months in Mauritius, and had two problems to contend with. The first, his Saffron dating soldiers. He had put a stop to that immediately and rather brilliantly, he thought. Suggesting a duel. Honour was at stake – were they men or were they men! The second still preoccupied him – the rejection of his bid for the house in Copford. Not an easy one to fix but he had now arrived at an ingenious plan, which he would set in motion using the same men who'd carried out the previous job. Hence his visit to the pub.

As he moved along Osborne Street, Gordon smiled at his portrayal of himself as victim, appealing to the white boys' better nature; soldiers were many things, but not, in his opinion, racist. They disliked whoever they were fighting, of course, and in general that meant foreigners, but they were not casually racist. Possessing a broad worldview, soldiers only had time for real enemies, ones that might shoot them; their discipline didn't allow for trifles such as skin colour. Indeed, he'd seen more prejudice from the squaddies here against Irishmen than anything, since the IRA had recently struck at the garrison and an officer lost his legs. What was a ponce of a landowner like Hughes-Ropers to them, compared to a paddy with a petrol bomb or an Argentine with a rocket launcher? They could do the job this week, before they buggered off out of sight and out of earshot. It was perfect.

Topize turned right, off St John's, and up the Scheregate passageway towards the Candyman in search of Lester Pink, the bar's proprietor and the man who operated as Gordon's trusted eyes and ears while he was abroad.

Lester Pink did not always relish Gordon's custom at the

Candyman – he had a habit of getting hammered on rum and frightening away the well-heeled students – but he did appreciate Gordon splashing the cash in return for Lester keeping an eye on his wife Silvia and her hair and beauty salon, Maravanne, located in the premises next door. In fact, the long, thin underground late-night bar built in the old city wall stretched *beneath* the salon, and in the early days when Gordon himself spent late nights totting up the week's takings, the pulse of the music acts below would send tremors through the floor, occasionally toppling the piles of copper and silver stacked on the counting desk. Now, Silvia did the count and was sure to be gone before nine, when live performances started. Gordon had been especially generous with his money over the last three months, wanting Lester extra-attentive while the salon underwent a makeover. The once-plain old hairdresser had morphed into a snazzy upmarket salon, replete with beauty treatments and sunbeds upstairs. It was now, in Gordon's view, the perfect complement to the travel agency he'd been busy setting up in Mauritius.

'Aha.' Lester's reedy voice travelled from the tiny stage at the far end of the club, where he crouched behind a large Marshall amp. 'Good to see you, buddy.'

'How's it hanging, Lester?'

'Same old, same old.' Lester was a skinny jazz dude with a junk habit to rival Burroughs, and was just as adept at handling it. The place did not open until later that evening, but Lester seldom left the premises. He apparently preferred to lurk in this poorly lit cave below the city wall, a perpetually nocturnal environment. Low-volume blues drifted through the bar. 'Bit of bother with that soldier this morning is all. The police were next door earlier and in here too, as it happens.'

'Uh-huh.' Gordon was not troubled by that. 'You seen my Saffron, Lester? Is she going to be singing in here?'

'Err . . . well, she asked about that. There's five of 'em in the band as it is. It'll be a squeeze but we'll give her a go. She has a top voice, buddy, shame not to hear it.'

Topize knew he couldn't clamp down on his daughter completely. He'd have a full-scale rebellion on his hands if he did. Plus he'd face untold aggro from Silvia, whose own dreams of making it as a singer had never been realised. No, this would take careful management from every angle.

'Right, that's fine – but you have to make sure she gets home safe after the gig.'

'I can't, Gordon, I gotta run this joint – she'll be on early, I promise. I can't drive her—'

'Not you personally, goddammit, outta your mind on whatever crap you shoot up.' Gordon pulled out a fiver. 'Just sort it.'

'Sure, sure, no sweat. And shush – less of the shooting-up schtick, the vibe is the drugs squad are undercover.'

'I don't care. Just get her the hell home once the set's finished. Now, give me Morgan's and ice.'

'Don't be a poof all your life, Atkinson. You might be dead in a month.'

Drake had a point.

'We'll be in Londonderry this time next week,' he continued, draping his arm across Atkinson's shoulder, 'and if, *if*, we're lucky, we might be home in the spring when everything will be forgotten. C'mon, mate.'

By 'everything' he meant Cousins.

Ever since their last tour, Atkinson had been plagued by an existential crisis. He had seen what he had seen and it left him with a clear sense that life was chaos, tenuous, uncertain – there to be lost or taken away. This crisis underpinned the many foolhardy escapades they'd agreed to since they returned. A gruelling period of death and wounding had the side effect of producing a recklessness that knew no check; when Cousins and Drake had agreed to the duel, it was with the same disregard for life as any game of 'chicken' in Northern Ireland. They had barely considered whether Topize himself posed a threat. Drake was flushed with beer, and his appearance had undergone a transformation from surly Lancashire farm lad to rosy cherub. Atkinson was reminded that in times of merrymaking, Drake could be good company; it was only when they were in barracks and out of danger or bored that he became a disagreeable sod, aggressive and picking fights for the hell of it. In Northern Ireland or in the boozer, he was generally fine.

'I dunno,' Atkinson said, 'we do ship out soon, that much is true.'

'Right, and you don't want to rock up to Brize skint. How

you going to win your money back off Castleton if you've nothing to play with?'

They were to be posted to Northern Ireland at the end of the week, flying from RAF Brize Norton to Ebrington Barracks on the River Foyle, and he'd not a pot to piss in.

'Let alone a final blowout in town before we leave . . .' he said, thinking aloud.

'Aye, night on the tiles in Collie, gotta be done. Score us a hangover to last us through.'

'It would be nice, just once more.'

'Go out with a bang, eh? Won't see any skirt for months . . .' Drake egged him on.

True, all grimly true. The crunching reality of Ebrington loomed; the only women they'd clap eyes on would be copped through binoculars from the sangars while on guard duty, ogling as lasses made their way to the RUC disco Friday nights.

'Right, okay,' Atkinson said, decisively, 'birds aside, be daft war zone brassic, eh, mate?'

They both laughed, slightly manically.

The thought of women prompted Atkinson to ask Drake, 'You gonna risk seeing her then?'

Drake's smile fell. His wet bottom lip pouted miserably.

'Forgotten about her already, wherever she is,' Drake said into his beer.

That was blatantly untrue. They'd seen the cuts on his arm. Drake was anguished to the core. He had not remotely recovered from losing the most beautiful girl in the world to a slippery weasel like Cousins. He still wanted her. He wanted her more than ever. And her father's appearance and interventions, crazy fool that he was, had done nothing to quash that lust.

CHAPTER 9

The jeweller raised his head from the glass cabinet, loupe still lodged at his eye socket.

'Beautiful, very delicate.'

'Where's it from?'

'Not from round here,' he said.

'Oh,' Lowry picked the earring up, 'where then?'

'Subcontinent. India's my guess.'

'That far away?' Lowry was expecting Hatton Garden or Southend. 'How can you be so sure?'

'Oh, I'm not *sure*,' the eye-piece popped from his face and into his hand, 'one can never be totally sure. But . . . it's finely crafted, there's no hallmark, it's light – indicating purity,' Lowry tossed the tiny object in his palm as if to validate this, 'and these tiny jewels that make up the creature's scales are sapphires. What we call Ceylon sapphires, because of the pale colour.'

'Expensive?'

'Certainly not Ratners.'

'How much?'

'If you press me, I'd guess a couple of hundred.'

Lowry thanked the man and left. An earring worn as a pendant was a love token of some kind. He exited Red Lion Walk on to the high street to meet Gabriel. Colchester's main thoroughfare bore no trace of what had occurred before sunrise. He stood outside the Red Lion Hotel watching the traffic slowly rumble by down towards the castle. A veteran stood nearby selling poppies. A mother and a toddler son slipped coppers into his collection jar and hurried along. The green beret rubbed his hands against the cold. Lowry rummaged around in his donkey jacket pocket. The old marine raised a smile of anticipation. But retrieving a crumpled pack of Players Navy Cut, Lowry lit one and moved on to the pavement. The police were empty-handed. The press release appealing for witnesses had gone out in time for the evening papers, which were already on the newsstands, but he wasn't going to hold his breath. No, if there were any clues to uncover, they would surface within the soldiery. That was on Oldham. He had done his best to close ranks and cover tracks. Lowry's job was looking impossible.

As the cars moved slowly down the high street, it seemed unimaginable that less than twelve hours ago a man lay dead there in the middle of the road. The way the world closed over tragedy and moved on. Gabriel appeared across the road shaking her head. She had been in the Lamb questioning, the resident landlord, evidently to no avail. A blow, since the pub was right next to the old Hippodrome theatre, close to where the body had been discovered.

'His bedroom is at the back, out like a light,' she said. 'There's activity at the theatre next door but the guv'nor has yet to arrive. What you thinking?'

'Nothing, just watching the world go by,' Lowry said. Two men in white overalls were entering the old Hippodrome with a ladder. The three-storey, red brick Edwardian theatre with its stone stucco and baroque façade had cut quite a blot on the landscape while it had lain empty. An impressive building with a prominent central position in the high street boarded up for months was a depressing sight for the local community. Eventually the town council had reluctantly agreed to a controversial sale to a property developer who was to transform it into a nightclub.

'Waiting for the murderer to return to the scene of the crime?' she suggested. 'That's what we say.'

'Imagine the kind of resolve needed to carry this out. Holding their nerve that long; setting out from the garrison – that's a good fifteen-minute walk.' She looked up to the clock tower. 'Would this road have any significance to soldiers?'

'Not that I'm aware . . . perhaps it conferred some sense of drama? But yeah, to leave Hyderabad and walk all this way together, only to stand twenty paces apart and shoot – easier to just do it on the parade ground. So I agree, this,' he nodded towards the broad high street before them, 'may have some meaning. The man who pulled the trigger will know . . .'

'. . . Or someone who's lost an earring.'

*

The chief entered the small office, bringing with him an aura of discontent and an ill temper. 'You're back,' Lowry said. 'What was the crisis meeting all about?'

Sparks had been summoned to County HQ in Chelmsford at the bequest of ACC Merrydown.

Hot on Sparks's heels lurked a timid uniformed officer, who wished to attract his attention.

'Football hooligans,' the chief said, ignoring his pursuer. 'London clubs coming out to the provinces and bashing the locals.'

'What?'

'Chelsea fans running riot in Sussex last weekend.'

Lowry had seen the reports. 'That was a first division match, against Brighton ... London clubs won't be troubling us at Layer Road for a while, Colchester's at the bottom third of the division.'

'Exactly, the woman knows bum-all,' he said, adding, 'no offence,' as he considered Gabriel, who had taken to using Kenton's desk. He turned to avoid eye contact, only to be greeted with the uniformed officer in the doorway. 'What in the blazes do you want?'

Both his wife and a man from a firm of surveyors had been trying to get hold of him, he was told. Sparks dismissed this angrily. 'Jesus, if I'm out, I'm out; they'll have to try later.' Lowry noted he regarded his wife and the unfortunate firm tasked with assessing their HQ with equal scorn. Gabriel excused herself, allowing Sparks to vent his vexing domestic circumstances. 'I mean, don't get me wrong, I am a hundred per cent up for this nipper, one hundred per cent, breeding is natural and I'll do my bit for mankind . . .'

'Very decent of you,' Lowry said.

'. . . But since hearing the news, Antonia's parents have been all over us like a rash. Coming to *dinner* and inviting themselves to *stay*, just like that. That's all very well, only Antonia can't seem to sort it out herself. She's pestering me twenty-four seven. It's always *shall we do this*, or *shall we do that*, or *can you nip to the shops on the way home and pick up this or that*. Can I *nip to the shops*? With all this nonsense going on . . . ? Jesus, woman. Get it yourself, you could use the bloody exercise.'

He sought support in his inspector.

'She *is* pregnant. And dare I say she's just excited . . . But hell, if you think it's bad now, wait until further down the road. This is just the start.'

Sparks adopted a grimace that suggested both discomfort and mild horror, and promptly changed the subject. 'So. What can I do for you then?'

'You wanted regular updates on the high street shooting?'

'Only if Oldham had something to offer. Has he? Ought to – the public's reaction being what it is. Like a massive dump on the Goose Green liberator's shiny hero image. You should have heard Merrydown on the subject, Jesus.'

'Nothing from Oldham yet . . . But I have been thinking about the location of the duel. Why did they do it there, of all places? It could not be a more public arena.'

'The middle of the fucking high street, you can't miss it.'

'Exactly.'

'Exactly what?'

'Was it significant?'

'Yes. I see your point. If it had happened on camp, the rest of the world would be none the wiser.' Sparks tapped the desk with his cigarette lighter. 'The matter would be brushed under the carpet . . .'

All manner of nastiness happened within the confines of barracks, of which thankfully the civilian police were never informed.

'All the same, I fancy the ball is in Oldham's court, don't you reckon? First catch the bugger who shot him; then ask why, eh?'

Flagstaff House

It was dark outside the captain's French windows by the time his sergeant reappeared. But he returned bearing news. Fairweather had been impressively sly in employing a private from the MCTC, a face unfamiliar to the infantry, to tail Atkinson and another from camp into the town centre.

'And what did he get up to?'

'Spent the afternoon in the pub, sir, the Robin Hood, on Osborne Street.'

Oldham knew it, a traditional squaddie watering hole and scene of many a fracas in the past, including a shooting – a drunken episode which locals at the time had called a duel, though nothing like the current situation, which was escalating by the hour. The national news coverage was horrendous.

'Who was he with?' he said, not wishing to dwell on the past connection.

'A Corporal Drake, sir.'

Oldham consulted a list of names before him on his desk. 'He isn't in the same unit.'

'No, but he is in B company and quartered in Hyderabad.'

'And who did they fraternise with? Any ladies?'

'No, sir. Kept to themselves for the most part, though they did spend some time chatting with a civilian.'

'Who?'

'A coloured gentleman, sir.'

'A black?' He paused. 'Of what kind?'

This caused Fairweather some hesitation. 'A sort of spiv, in fancy clothes.'

'Most irregular.' Oldham was surprised. 'West Indian?'

'I couldn't say, sir.'

'Hmm.' Afro-Caribbean people were a rarity around here. 'I wonder where this fellow hails from,' Oldham muttered.

'Never seen 'im before. Had two pals with 'im. There was a bit of argy-bargy on the pool table.'

He sighed. 'That's all the modern soldiery ever seem to do. Pub games. Did you search Atkinson's quarters?'

'Sir, yessir. Nothing, sir.'

'The man he was with today, also on leave?'

'Yes, sir.'

'Watch Drake too, but equally discreetly. If he leaves camp, alert me, and we shall search his quarters together. Meanwhile, have a detachment from the MCTC search the bins in Hyderabad. That'll be all for now, sergeant.'

This was disappointing; a row over a pool game with some coloureds in a public bar hardly screamed the behaviour of a guilty man and one who'd possibly won his sweetheart's hand fighting a duel . . . Nevertheless, this soldier was a friend of Cousins, and one could never predict the actions of men about to be posted in a hostile environment. 'Bring Atkinson in tomorrow,' he said. 'It's time for the thumb screws.'

CHAPTER 10

Gabriel ventured up to Barrack Street in the dark and drizzle. She was on her way to see Daniel. Her progress was slow and reluctant. He had been scornful of her offer of friendship and they had not spoken in weeks, and on top of that it had been a long day. It would be an awkward evening, but if he was returning to work tomorrow it was worth trying to break the ice.

To her surprise there was no answer when she rang his doorbell. In her mind's eye she saw him brooding, hunched over at the kitchen table or listlessly pacing his flat.

'He'll be in the Bugle,' a neighbour called out, coming up the steps behind her. Gabriel acknowledged the tip and went back outside. The Bugle Horn was just across the road. Its signage glistened in the rain. She hesitated. She really did not want to see him in a public space. The spray of a passing bus was the push she needed, and she made a dash for it, jumping over a puddle in the gutter and nipping under the dully lit sign into the warm fug of the pub.

*

Kenton was in full swing, enjoying himself in his second home.

When Kenton's jukebox picks ran out, he went back to his place for a bong. The grass intake was closely followed by a nap. Kenton had woken some time later with a ravenous hunger. He'd been out to grab a takeaway, but passing the Bugle he had felt a sharpener was in order. There had been a pickled egg and a packet of KP dry-roasted peanuts, but the ratio of solids to alcohol was not, by any measure, in harmony. The alcohol soon punched through. His darts were not flying as smoothly as usual, and Julian the plumber, already back in situ having replaced two ballcocks, was making short work of him. The lanky blond had a loose, lucky way about him. Kenton was on the verge of calling it a day. Work tomorrow; it wouldn't do to start with a hangover. Julian was again scoring high and Kenton was off the mark, starting to go wide; one then five.

The plumber polished him off, finishing on a double three; a tough one, for anyone – but more so for a bloke of his height.

'You're on.' A call from the boy on the pool table.

'I'll be back,' Daniel said to the plumber, though he doubted it. A game of pool then home. Spliff then bed.

The boy racking the balls on the felt was short with cropped hair, obviously a squaddie. He was mid-conversation with his mate, sat at a table to one side, sporting the same hair, casual clothes, neat and clean.

'Fuckin' Red Cap monkeys.'

'At least they didn't ground us.'

'Aye, they'll be a reason for that. Oldham'll be sniffing about, you can be sure on that.'

The alcohol had loosened Kenton's lips. Ordinarily he'd have been more circumspect, but too late heard himself interrupting, 'Was he a pal of yours?'

The soldier shot him a sideways glance as he slipped the triangle beneath the table. This could go either way.

'Yeah, he was.' He pushed up his sweatshirt sleeves and reached for a cue.

'Unusual, a duel in this day and age? I imagine it would be frowned upon by your superiors.'

'Frowned upon?' said the other lad in a Northern accent. 'Aye, and the rest.'

'Put up to it, I reckon.' His pal stepped to the table and sized up the reds.

'Not for love then?' Kenton said, genuinely intrigued.

They both snorted. 'As if! The risk is bleedin' huge!' With that, he made his shot and the pack split with such a blast Kenton sloshed his pint.

'Somethin' iffy. Blackmail or the like,' his companion said sagely. 'Ey up, some lass lookin' for you.'

Kenton swung round unsteadily and gulped.

Gabriel waved smoke away from her face. The two young men continued with their game and Kenton stood mute with a hangdog expression.

'How long have you been in here?' she asked.

'Oh, not long,' he said, finding his voice. 'Just had the one. Here, let me get you a drink.'

She hesitated; she didn't really want to be here. He'd very obviously had more than enough. His eyes were glassy and his face had gone slack, the way drunk men get.

'No, you're busy . . . with friends. I'll leave you to it.' She took a step backwards. His hair and awful beard were quite shocking.

'Stay, just a quick one, as you're here?'

'I just wanted to see how you are. Fine, it seems.'

'Please,' he pleaded, 'I have missed you.'

She sighed. 'Go on, then.'

'Great.' He ushered her to a bar stool. 'Just here.'

She ordered a lime soda, against his protestations to have a proper drink. The pub was not rowdy, apart from the occasional exclamation from the pool table. It had the feel of a giant front room, sociable and amenable, and they were easily able to talk. Kenton spoke perhaps too loudly and repeated himself. Fox Farm this, Lowry that, she had heard it before. Circuitous and rambling. It might have yielded nothing; if anything, it revealed how little she really knew him, but she felt better for doing it.

'Anyway . . . *anyway*, I thought if I hung out here,' Kenton slumped forward and whispered, 'I might find out a thing or two about the duel this morning.' Even he realised the topic of Kelvedon and the farm was exhausted.

'And have you?' Gabriel said, bringing the straw to her lips.

Kenton's face compressed in muddled thought. 'I . . . maybe. Those lads playing pool over there were talking.'

This was pointless. She'd go home, make something to eat, have a bath, then go to bed with a book. Or maybe practise the piano. How odd for Lowry to listen to classical music – a far cry from the racket that was crashing out of the jukebox right now, chosen by Kenton.

He was twenty-six, a year older than her, but here he was reduced to a teenager.

'I – I don't know it . . .'

Her gaze strayed to a tall, nondescript fellow chatting to the barman. He was in his late thirties, perhaps. He had a squint and mostly he struck her as somehow out of place here. For a second he caught her eye, raised a pint and winked. Everyone was suspicious. She'd had enough for one day. In a little under half an hour, she was at home and in a hot bath.

All day she'd been surrounded by men, pathetic men – yes, pathetic. Starting with the bully on the river, then Lowry moping at home and finally Daniel. Pitiful. The only one with any backbone was, loath as she was to say it, the station commander Sparks.

Roman Road, Colchester

Their conversation had been light and gentle. They kept to interests outside of work, veered away from anything harder. The matter of his son and wife was avoided – she had not asked, and he had not offered. Keen to show interest in her, and deflect attention from himself, Lowry seized upon the bookshelf behind her as a conversation piece. Lowry didn't read, hadn't since school. Becky did a lot, obviously. She was an English teacher but her passion was for Russian literature. *War and Peace, Crime and Punishment* were titles he knew but not in any context, and he soon accepted he was out of his depth.

'Boxing and birds are my limit, I'm afraid. And I'm not much good at either.'

'But what about when you're at home? There's nothing nicer than a glass of wine and a good book.'

'Telly,' he said, through a mouthful. 'There's four channels now. Plenty of it. And having a video recorder helps.'

'It's garbage, though. What do you watch? I can't imagine what's worth recording.'

'I don't know, whatever. *The Gentle Touch*, know that?'

'A police show?' Becky laughed. 'Thought you'd want to get away from all that! What else?'

He shrugged. 'Re-runs of *Steptoe* on BBC 2.' That was it. He watched the same thing over and over, interspersed with confiscated videos. A seized copy of *Straw Dogs* was doing the rounds. She was looking at him. Properly looking, in a way that suddenly made him intensely self-conscious. 'Err,' he said, uncomfortably, 'this is absolutely delicious.'

'This is the third time in a row we've eaten at mine.' Becky topped up Lowry's wine glass.

'I wasn't keeping count,' he said, twirling the pasta on his fork. 'I have never cooked anything more sophisticated than a sausage.'

'That's not what I meant.'

They continued to eat in silence. He avoided his own house.

'It's not you. I don't enjoy being there. I'd never choose to stay in,' he said truthfully.

'What about your cat?'

'He's fine, dining out himself tonight.'

'What, you mean you chucked him out to forage?'

'Cats are nocturnal, it's what he's built for . . .'

'Isn't keeping a cat at odds with being a bird fancier?'

'Bird*watcher*, actually. Pigeon fancier is something else.'

'Oh. Sorry.'

'The cat is just fine, he's not really into birds; they're too quick. Voles and rats supplement his diet.'

'We might dine out?'

Lowry'd rather not. Here was just fine: soft folk music flittered in the background under the low light of a standard lamp, partially illuminating the floor-to-ceiling bookshelves. A warm ambience permeated the room. He didn't like eating out. It was hard to relax in public. Colchester was not a big place; the few restaurants were often filled with faces he half recognised from work: villains, suspects, victims, usually someone with a grudge.

'I think you want to keep me secret,' Becky said, looking down at the candle between them. He put it as succinctly as he could: the discomfort in town.

'That doesn't mean I never go out. If you want that, of course we can . . .'

'Did you never go out with your wife?'

'Very rarely. We . . .' *have a child* was what was on his lips, 'she works shifts,' which was also true. 'So, most of the time, we went out separately – she has her friends at the hospital. And I . . . I . . .'

'. . . Have Stephen Sparks?' Becky forced a smile and steered the conversation away from his family, her initial curiosity gone. 'Tell me about your friend the soldier.'

'Oldham?'

'Yes, Captain Oldham. Does he have a girlfriend or wife?'

'No idea.' He almost laughed.

'You went away for the weekend together after the farm murders, right?'

'Hardly a weekend; we went up to Maldon on his boat overnight, got drunk, came back the next day. He's a bachelor, he's married to the army. As far as I know.'

They talked about the army, the impact on the town. As a teacher she was familiar with the history. Soon enough they were back to bantering, and he was off the hook. It had been a long time since he had given any consideration to whether or not a woman he cared about was upset. This relationship with Becky had stirred up some long-dormant feelings and the more he thought about it, the more it confused him. Did he always need to understand why he felt what he felt? Worry about how he was making her feel? At what point would he blow it?

When he had arrived, she had welcomed him in generously and with real affection. She'd been looking forward to seeing him and he had seriously contemplated staying over if the opportunity presented itself. Now, however, he felt he should just leave and spare them both the disappointment. He wanted her to take the initiative, he was too unsure of himself to decide on anything. He picked up the napkin that lay neatly folded, and thus far ignored, to one side of his plate and lightly dabbed the corner of his mouth.

'I ought to be making a move.'

'Wait.' She placed her hand on his. 'We might go away, for a long weekend . . . what do you think?' She leant forward and shook his hand to loosen the tension. 'That way you don't have to worry about being seen out in public, or feeling trapped in your own home. It'll be neutral. What do you say? Nothing complicated. I'm sorry to go on. Come on, it'll be fun.'

Did he want that? Escape from everything, just for a couple of days?

'I guess Pushkin could go over to Sparks's,' he says. 'Antonia hasn't enough to do.'

'Pushkin?' Becky said, unsure.

'The cat.'

'That's great. How funny.'

'What is?'

She got up and turned to the bookcase.

'A great Russian, Pushkin. Killed in a duel.'

Becky pulled down a copy of *The Captain's Daughter* and offered it to him.

'Here. You can read it while we're away to remind you of your cat.'

Now they had a plan, the rest of the evening passed enjoyably, without a hint of pressure. Lowry didn't stay and there was a tacit understanding this relationship, if that's what it was, would be consummated on the south coast.

Creffield Road, Lexden

Antonia was on tiptoes searching the cupboards. 'We're definitely out of paprika. Drat.'

'Your mother isn't down until Friday, for heaven's sake,' said Sparks. It was getting late. She should be in bed. They both should. Sparks sighed and poured another solid measure of scotch. It usually helped his headaches, but it wasn't working. Maybe he was becoming immune to its soothing properties.

'It doesn't hurt to plan, Stephen, a bit of preparation.'

This was the second time today he'd heard those exact words. Merrydown said the same thing this afternoon: he ought to be prepared for a move out of Queen Street should the premises be deemed 'not fit for purpose' following the survey.

His entire world was about to change. Both work and domestic horizons were shifting and he had no control over either.

'You're absolutely right, preparation!'

Antonia beamed at him lovingly; he smiled limply back. What was the matter with him? Lowry was right, she was just excited, and why shouldn't she be? Taking the bottle, he moved to the sitting room and sat in his armchair, preoccupied, swirling Scotch in his cut-glass tumbler. One of his favourite programmes, *Minder*, was on but even the antics of the hapless Arthur Daley could not distract him. *Preparation*. The baby wasn't due until next year but already it was all-consuming. A father for the first time at fifty-five. Fifty-five. Why had he left it so late? Of course he knew the answer; Antonia was his third wife. He winced at the thought of having children with the previous Mrs Sparks and gulped a mouthful of peaty single malt. Thirty years ago his first marriage had ended. 1953. He remembered the year vividly not so much for the divorce, which was messy, but for the night he pulled that young black fella out of the gutter. First time he'd seen blood in the dark. Did something to him. He took another mouthful of Scotch.

The past is a trap. All things considered, he was in a much better place now, and the station move aside, there was a lot to look forward to. This is what he must keep telling himself. The mother-in-law wasn't too bad either. He'd not seen her since the wedding in February. Loaded too. Having wrestled himself to a peaceful juncture, he suddenly felt very, very tired.

'Are you okay, honey?' His wife had followed him into the sitting room. 'You worried about something?' She ran her fingers lightly across the nape of his neck. That was nice. All would be well. He shut his eyes.

'There's tomorrow, the shops will be there tomorrow,' he said, and placing the tumbler between his legs, promptly fell asleep.

CHAPTER 11

Howard Osgood had managed to catch the evening tide. They'd motored over to Brightlingsea in a shroud of rain yesterday evening. Now, early the next morning, his persistence had been rewarded with a break in the weather and he was greeted with a freshening breeze and a chance to unfurl the main one last time before bringing the boat in for the winter.

Osgood was relaxed out here aboard his yacht, hand on the wheel, pointing upwind across the mouth of the Colne. Away from business worries and family trouble alike. The boat carved effortlessly through the water. Brightlingsea to port, East Mersea sitting low to starboard; the Mersea Stone just peeking out. Osgood especially relished the stretch of water before him, Brightlingsea Reach, a smooth sea with the shoreline either side giving definition to the estuary. A horizon was good, and he was comfortable at this distance out – beyond the channel was the open expanse of the North Sea, with a huge undulating swell that made Howard seasick. He liked to see the land, know it was there, awaiting his return.

He smiled down at Gill on the foredeck, in sunglasses

with her brightly coloured headscarf catching the freshening south-westerly wind.

'See, told you we'd get a sail in!' he shouted down at her.

Yesterday had been a washout. The morning's fine drizzle had matured into a persistent grey torrent shortly after Howard had walloped Colin into the Colne. Gill had said the rain was punishment for thumping his nephew, but the skies had cleared overnight. The fine spell held this morning, though heavy cloud loomed on the horizon to the west. All the same, the break from the autumn deluge was a palpable relief and had helped to clear Howard's mind of woes, even if only for now. This would be one of the last such days of the year. He was determined to enjoy it.

Kevin passed Gill a champagne flute. Life was good, but it did have a price and required constant maintenance. His bolshie little prick of a nephew yesterday, for instance, Colin Cooper, bleating away about Osgood being 'out of touch' with things in town. Colin may be family, but that did not give him the right to mouth off – and on Osgood's boat, too, the little twerp. The more Cooper insisted that it was time for Howard to relinquish his empire to younger hands and give him more of a cut, the more firmly Howard would hold his grip. Retirement (for want of a better word) was more unlikely a prospect than ever. Still, he should have contained his anger in the open: Osgood hadn't made the bird on the quay as a copper. He'd heard from Colin there was a policewoman in the village – there always was, they had to live somewhere

– but he wasn't expecting one so pretty. Strange, she hadn't even asked him for his name. But, there was nothing to be gained by slapping the lad in public. Gill beamed up at him from the foredeck.

A fluke gust caught them, forcing the boat to keel. He let the main out a tad, Kevin attended to the jib, and the yacht powered forward, cold spray catching his forehead. White caps appeared across the estuary with the increase in wind, the swell sparkling as the water reared up to meet the low morning sun. Ahh, what a beautiful day; he should do this more often, did him the power of good. Out here, nothing else mattered; just wind, water and the sensation of the present moment.

Queen Street HQ

Lowry stood in the station's narrow kitchen waiting for the kettle to boil on the hob. Cracks ran down the wall like forked lightning in search of the damp it was sure to find behind the cabinets. A strange odour reached out from the sink. Funny that Sparks was so defiant about the building – absolutely nothing by way of maintenance had been undertaken in years. The light on the hob was so feeble he checked twice that it was even there. He heaped two spoons of Nescafé into a chipped Charles and Diana mug.

He had woken at two and not nodded off again until six, and then been disturbed ten minutes later by the cat purring in his ear wanting food. Unusually for him, Lowry could remember the dream he'd interrupted. In it, he stood alone in the high street. It was dark and he was fighting a duel against an opponent he could not see. He remembered hearing a gunshot, waiting to see if he was hit, and then, looking up to the sky, he saw a silhouette of St Helena on top of the town hall. And that was it. He drifted into a reverie, trying to shed light on his subconscious adversary, until the kettle began its shrill whistle.

There was an all-staff briefing at nine. Loath though he was to attend, he thought he should, if only to check Kenton had made it in. He took his coffee through to CID and rang Oldham. A newspaper lay on his desk, the headlines leaping out at him: *PISTOLS AT DAWN.*

'I'm sorry you have been unable to make progress investigating our leads.' The line was bad and Lowry could only take the remark at face value. He wondered how much heat Oldham was getting: scanning the front page, the army came out in a very poor light.

'We tried every hairdresser in town.'

'Perhaps it was further afield.'

'What is your next move?'

'Conduct further interviews on camp.'

'Can we be involved?'

'I don't think it necessary.'

The bitter black coffee burnt Lowry's lip. 'Okay, well, I have something for you. A piece of jewellery we found on the body. I'll drop by later this afternoon.'

They hung up. If Oldham was under pressure he hid it well, and the same time Lowry was not surprised that the military captain was being so guarded. He had encountered this sort of furtive behaviour before. The army didn't like to let anyone interfere with their practices. He didn't like it one bit, but there was nothing he could do about it and meanwhile there was other stuff to deal with. Underneath the newspaper was a report on escalating drug abuse and an advisory note on racial tensions. Both could wait until later. He looked across at the empty desk opposite, disappointed, then made a move to the briefing.

For DC Kenton the early start was a shock to the system.

The sound of his alarm clock was so unfamiliar that it rang for several minutes before he twigged first what it was, then where it was, and furthermore that it was incumbent on him to make it stop.

In under twenty minutes he had arrived – still late – at a briefing meeting that was being held, unusually, in the CID general office on the second floor. Uniform and plain clothes sat casually on desktops as Sparks spoke quietly at the far end of the room. Sunshine burst through the large Queen Street sash windows, the gentle autumn light lending the worn wooden furniture a warm golden glow. Kenton, however, found the brightness a bit much with a hangover that had made its presence known only on his arrival at Queen Street; if he'd had it earlier he hadn't noticed in the rush to get ready. Gabriel flicked him a look he couldn't decipher, and he suddenly felt self-conscious. How did he leave things with her? This coffee was rank, and he was too dehydrated to drink it.

Kenton had been expecting to hear more on the duel, but as far as he could tell the chief was talking about something else entirely; studies undertaken and wiring infrastructure – what had he missed? He was not up to speed. He scanned the room for Lowry but could not see him.

The chief dismissed the assembly abruptly and as the officers filed out, he caught sight of Kenton. Sparks strode over.

'What's all this?' he said, reaching for Kenton's chops.

'Growing a beard, sir. I thought it would help.' This was a lie. It was only while brushing his teeth he'd remembered Lowry's instruction to shave and in haste attacked his face with the kitchen scissors.

'Help? Help what?' Sparks snapped. 'Undercover work with vagrants?' He didn't wait for an answer and moved off. Kenton watched him go, dismayed – he might have said welcome back.

'Welcome back,' Gabriel said. 'How's your head?'

'Err . . . fine, fine. Thanks. What have I missed?'

'Someone in Uniform heard a whisper from town hall that we're to be relocated.'

'And?'

'Pigs might fly. Can you imagine? C'mon, we're going for a drive.'

'Really? Where?'

'Northampton.'

Queen Street HQ

'He doesn't strike me as all right,' Sparks said, addressing Lowry. 'Shut the door.'

'He'll be fine – though not straight away, perhaps. That's why we brought him back now, stop him deteriorating, right?' Lowry sat down opposite.

'Well – for a start,' the telephone rang; he grabbed it, holding one hand over the mouthpiece, eyes still on Lowry, 'he might have made himself more presentable instead of resurfacing like a hippie-cum-vagabond.'

He put the receiver to his ear. 'Sparks,' he snapped at the caller. He was greeted by the familiar nasal rasp of his commanding officer, Merrydown.

'*Must* you be so abrupt, Stephen?' She didn't wait for his answer. 'I take it you've seen the papers. Heavens, they portray you as devoid of all law and order.'

'Me? I must protest. The military are a rule unto themselves.'

'It's the bloody high street – the centre of town! *Your* town. As you are forever telling me.'

'At dawn, ma'am, it was empty – no civilians at risk.'

'That you know of,' she said sharply. 'They are smarting – all that goodwill towards the military after the Falklands up in a puff of smoke. Anyhow, the case is with the Ministry of Defence as we speak, I think it'll blow their way. We'll fax you confirmation later today.'

'Very good, ma'am.' He gave Lowry the thumbs up.

'However, the attention has rekindled the hullabaloo about the new nightclub; that was practically on the doorstep. And that is your concern.'

He rolled his eyes towards Lowry. 'The old Hippodrome? It's not even open yet. Besides, we believe they met at the town hall; cigarette butts on the steps. What's the bloody Hippodrome got to do with it?'

'A late night licence, in the high street? Think of the damage if something like this had happened once the establishment was open. These places should be tucked away. Are we really sure this is the right decision?'

Who had been bending her ear? She has no interest in developments within the town.

'Due respect, ma'am, but I don't follow. What's the damage? It's not a residential area. Centre of town, as you pointed out! It's perfect. We've been over this; it's only Fridays and Saturdays—' He personally had to sign off the licence.

'There's the heritage to think of,' she continued, 'Colchester is one of the oldest towns in the country. You should be thinking of the growth of the Common Market; an influx of Europeans.'

Colchester was *the* oldest in the country; the council had posted signage along the A12; motorists couldn't escape the fact. As far as Sparks was concerned, Merrydown might do better to worry about her own town first: Chelmsford had gone to the dogs; all that ostentatious city-boy wealth had created a town full of well-heeled coke-heads. Even the site workers erecting the new housing estates used cocaine.

Of course he didn't say this. Rather, he waited for Merrydown to finish and said, plainly, 'It's a listed building. They can't touch the outside, and very little of the inside.'

'I don't doubt you know *all* about listed covenants.' She paused for the line to hit home: it was a dig at his fondness for Queen Street. 'Just think on our conversation yesterday, and about the future.'

'Absolutely,' he said, though overnight he'd managed to erase everything she'd told him he was to do in preparation.

'Very well. Goodbye, Superintendent.'

'Christ's hole,' he grumbled after hanging up, 'that woman will be the death of us all.'

'What?'

He rubbed his jaw. 'They are deadly serious about moving us out of here,' he said. '. . . Oh, and the army, in all likelihood, will handle the shooting.'

Flagstaff House

'I'm on leave,' Atkinson grunted with as much bravado as he could muster, doubled over as he was, blood pumping through his head. Oldham's dogsbody, Fairweather, had him pinned to the carpet with his arm twisted up his back.

'Indeed. And I very much hope you're enjoying your last few days before the hell that is Northern Ireland. I don't envy you.'

Oldham's clipped words floated somewhere behind him. Fairweather then pushed Atkinson's arm higher up between his shoulder blades; Atkinson feared he'd dislocate it.

'No, I don't envy you at all; the situation in Londonderry has grown worse and I'm sure your arrival will not be a moment too soon.'

Atkinson tried to swallow, but couldn't gulp. Much more of this and he might choke. He didn't care about Northern Ireland; the sooner he was out of here, the better.

'Now, we have tried to do this gently. But to no avail,' Oldham continued.

'Eh?'

'Unaccountably, not one hairdresser in the entire town knew Lance Corporal Cousins. What do you have to say about that, eh?'

'Maybe they're lying – worried that you'd – *ach*—' Pain halted his speech as Fairweather increased the tension. 'Worried they'd get in trouble,' he managed to gasp.

'Like you?' The captain's voice grew softer, more menacing, as he stepped closer. 'Problem is – why would you not volunteer the girl's name? It's no skin off your nose. Unless, that is . . .'

Atkinson felt his heart thrum fiercely against his ribcage as if it might burst right out and plop on to the lurid oriental rug below. He must say something; defend himself.

'Unless, of course, you, in some way, are *involved* with Cousins's demise? Perhaps it was you that pulled the trigger?'

The captain's voice moved away. 'Yes, maybe that was it. What do you think, Sergeant Fairweather?'

'Very plausible, sir, very plausible.'

'You're not dribbling on my carpet, I hope? Pull him up, sergeant.'

Atkinson's head whipped back.

'You will note at this stage, we – I – have so far been the epitome of reason and calm; but not for much longer. Many, including the civilian police, believe there are witnesses to this shooting. I, however, do not intend to waste my time looking for bystanders. I am only interested in finding the man who pulled the trigger. And I would rather we unearth him by unearthing the *reason* for the death . . . It would certainly make things *easier* if there were a romantic aspect to this sorry business, some drama attached to a civilian quarter? It would cast the whole tawdry affair in a somewhat sympathetic light. I would prefer to find answers by reasonable means – a soldier coming forward, voluntarily – and not, as the police inspector joked, have to resort to employing pliers to extract these answers rather more messily . . .'

'Sir, I can't remember every girl's name; they come and go and I'm not really interested in who he's with . . .' By this point he had convinced himself he really didn't know her name; easy enough as he'd never met her. Cousins had been so secretive, almost embarrassed. It hadn't struck him as peculiar at the time, but now, under all this pressure, he began to wonder why not . . .

JAMES HENRY

'But he went on a *date*. An activity a notch up in sophistication from ten pints and a drunken liaison in a phone box. A trip to the cinema on a Friday evening, he must have been vaguely enthusiastic, eh? Fridays are sacrosanct; payday for all the shop girls – all out on the town looking for romance. To surrender a night's pursuit and the company of the lads for a rendezvous at the Odeon sounds serious to me.'

'I swear, I never met her.'

Atkinson trembled at the possibility that the captain thought he was holding out in order to save himself.

He needed to think quick.

He had it.

'Her name might . . . might have been Sh – Sh – Sharon.'

109

CHAPTER 12

Marcus Hughes-Roper was already at the Hippodrome when Osgood arrived. Trevor had placed him in the old ticket office, where he stood waiting, hands behind his back. Howard entered to meet a man of medium build with straw hair – too long – in a well-cut suit and with a large, prominent mole on cheekbone. As Howard held out his hand, he noticed a cane or walking stick topped with what looked to be a silver-plated pheasant's head.

'Good of you to come by,' Howard said graciously.

Although it was Hughes-Roper who had something to sell, Howard knew the first rule of business was move the mountain to Mohammed: Howard could have met him at the property under discussion – it would have been easier and saved time – but he was smarter than that. He had the posh fellow on his turf. And his turf was impressive, conferred respect on to its new owner. They wasted no time getting down to brass tacks.

'What is it you've in mind?' said Howard.

'I'll come straight to the point,' said Hughes-Roper, though he paused briefly and ran his tongue across a thin top lip in preparation for delivery. A typical public school affliction, as if the world hinged on their every word. 'I was impressed with your move to buy this place and convert it into a discotheque. Inspired entrepreneurial spirit.' He smiled an ingratiating smile. 'I thought, this is a man I ought to know.'

'Thank you; though we've yet to see if we can make a go of it,' Howard said modestly.

'When do you open?'

'Next month, December.'

'Perfect timing,' he arched a solitary pruned eyebrow, 'take advantage of all that festive spirit, party night after party night.'

The Christmas period had nothing whatsoever to do with Howard's plans; he'd open it tomorrow if he could. The flooring contractors were not due to start until mid-month, after the decorators, and the electricians . . .

'Can I show you around?' Howard offered. He couldn't resist a chance to show off. The building was as magnificent inside as out.

Hughes-Roper dismissed the invitation with his cane. 'I am familiar with the grandeur. I myself wish to sell a sizeable property on the outskirts of town, in ample surrounds. I wondered whether I could tempt you to take a gander.'

'Why?'

'I think the premises would make a magnificent nightclub.'

'What makes you think so?'

'Because,' he checked the door slyly, 'a fellow has made me an offer for it already.'

'So why ask me then, if you've a buyer already?'

Hughes-Roper sat in a chair, a scowl passing across his ruddy face. 'It fell through, sadly.'

'I'm sorry, but I'm not interested. This,' he gestured, 'is a pet project.'

'Rather flash for a pet project.'

Osgood did not feel obliged to expand. He didn't know this bloke from Adam. 'How did you get hold of me anyhow?'

'Someone makes a purchase this grand, one makes it one's business to find out who.'

'The building was empty for ages, it's no big deal.'

'Come now, it's a magnificent piece of property smack in the centre of town; in the right hands, it will return to its former glory.'

Howard was usually resistant to people blowing smoke up his jacksy, but this fellow, for all his ponciness, was different. He was genuinely flattered to have his approval. That said, business was business.

'I still think there are more than enough nightclubs in Colchester for now.' There were three: the Colne Lodge, Aristos and the Affair – none of them the scale of the Hippodrome, which would wipe the floor with the rest of them.

'Ah, don't dismiss it immediately,' said Hughes-Roper. 'My property, being out of the way, close to the motorway, would offer something different entirely. I think the previous gentleman had upmarket aspirations. And think of the economies of scale. Negotiating with wholesalers, for beverages and so forth.'

Howard rubbed his jaw thoughtfully. 'You've lost the other man's offer, you say?'

'Oh yeah, definitely.'

Howard should keep an eye out for competition; it would be foolish *not* to look.

'All right, when can I take a dekko?'

Colchester High Street

'*Sharon?* What the fuck did you say that for?' Drake flicked a cigarette out of the car window. The black Fiesta idled throatily. Drake had spent the morning tailing the man Topize wanted and had followed him into the centre of town, where after a couple of hours in his office, he took a stroll down the high street and disappeared inside the old Hippodrome theatre.

While Drake had waited for him to re-emerge, he telephoned Atkinson from a call box to check he'd not been banged up and to tell him where to find them. Atkinson had just arrived.

'I had to say something, for fuck's sake. Do we have to have this exchange now?' Atkinson was not going to be intimidated. After all the pressure he'd had from Oldham, he was not about to be bullied by a little twat like Drake. 'Didn't give him *your* name, did I? Be thankful for that,' he said, pulling across the seat belt. 'Thought it was pretty clever if you ask

me – Sharon, Saffron, could easily be mistaken, misheard . . .'
Atkinson sat back. 'It will lead them in a merry old dance.'

This slowly dawned on Drake. 'Yeah . . . more Sharons in Colchester than you can shake a stick at, there's bound to be one, if not more, in one of those hair places . . . By the time they get to the bottom of it, we'll be long gone.'

'And if they ever rumble Topize's daughter, then I can just say I didn't catch it right. Saffron. You don't come across them every day,' Atkinson said, confidently.

'There's only one,' Drake mumbled to himself.

'So you've spent the whole morning sitting here?' No wonder he was spiky. He was just about to comment on it being a waste of time when it suddenly struck him. 'Hang on. This is a bit weird.'

'What?'

'Look.' Atkinson tapped on the window. 'The town hall. We're smack in the middle of the high street, right where . . .'

'Shh,' said Drake, pointing across the dashboard, 'there he is.'

Two men were leaving the Hippodrome; one older, a stocky bulldog-like guy, and a middle-aged fair-haired man, with a rotund lower body. The latter wore an elegant dark suit and carried a cane. The heavier older one wore a long, camel-hair coat that, while it could never be described as elegant, certainly made a statement.

'He's a size, ain't he,' Atkinson exclaimed.

'It's not him we're after – it's the other one, with the stick.

Don't look much at all.' Drake cracked his knuckles above the steering wheel. 'Why he'd need us to put the frighteners on that fancy fanny, I can't see at all, unless underneath all that tweedy clobber he's frickin' Bruce Lee or sommit.'

They watched Hughes-Roper climb into the passenger seat of a white Audi while the burly chap moved round to the driver's side. Drake eased the Fiesta into gear. 'Keep your distance; not too close,' Atkinson hissed. The driver of the Audi had a shifty bearing about him, an awareness, glancing up and down the street as if *he* was on the lookout. If he'd clocked the men in the Fiesta he didn't make a point of letting them know.

'He ain't on the watch for us. And I been tailing him all morning.'

Nevertheless, Atkinson flicked the sun visor down and pulled on a baseball cap. With the rise of terrorism on the mainland, the army had invested in surveillance techniques and had been briefed on making themselves less conspicuous in general. Not that you'd know it, the way Drake had been lurking around the high street.

'If you've been sat out here all morning, you won't have heard – there's rumours our departure could be delayed.'

'Why?' Drake said.

'No reason given,' Atkinson replied. 'Could be to do with Cousins . . .'

'All right by me, means we get the weekend here with dosh from seeing off this wally.'

To which there was no answer.

The Audi eased into the high street traffic and headed east, swinging down on to Queen Street. All the while, Drake waffled on about the plan to get an idea of Hughes-Roper's movements, as if they had weeks to stake out their target rather than a couple of days to execute the operation.

''Ere, check out the bird outside the cop shop.'

A tall blonde woman in her twenties stood on the steps of the Queen Street nick holding a piece of paper. 'Fit as you like,' Drake said enthusiastically. She was standing stock-still, face agog, and Atkinson thought – but wasn't sure – she was watching Osgood's Audi ahead of them. When she clocked them gawping at her, she turned away in disgust.

'Here, wait a sec—'

'What?' Drake said.

'Nuthin'.'

Drake tapped a cassette into the player. Michael Jackson. In the way music can, the mood in the car suddenly transformed. They both relaxed, as though they were off for a night out, not on a mission to frighten the living daylights out of a stranger.

CHAPTER 13

'Howard John Osgood,' Gabriel muttered to herself. Earlier this morning, Uniform had passed on details of the registered owner of the Audi. And there he was, just now, driving by, as bold as you like – a man clearly not prioritising her request to present his licence. Who was she kidding.

Seconds after the Audi, a pair of leering boys drove by in a Ford Fiesta, which brought her sharply back to her senses.

'What's up, love? You've a face like a guppy fish.' The strident voice of the station chief announced his return from the fruit and veg stall by the roundabout.

'Does the name Osgood ring any bells with you, sir?'

'Owns a couple of boozers and restaurants. Just bought the Hippodrome. Fancies himself a big dick,' he said, tossing an apple in the air, 'if you pardon the expression.'

'Above board?'

Sparks see-sawed his free hand indicating iffy. 'Not been done for anything.'

'Only I saw him knock a man into the river yesterday.'

'Oh yes? Where?'

'The Colne. From a boat at Rowhedge.'

The chief's rugged face fractured in thought.

'Hmm,' Sparks pushed his bottom lip out, 'he's probably a bit on the wide side, but generally well respected ... Those his vehicle details you're holding there?' he said, spotting the paper in her hand. Gabriel shook her head.

'No, though I have requested to see his licence,' she said, fearing he'd think her foolish.

She needn't have worried.

'Right, in that case we'll get Uniform to give him a nudge.'

'He has seven days,' she said, surprised at his support.

'Nah, that's not relevant here. It's a matter of respect. To you: he needs to doff his cap, show you some courtesy. And it seems he may need a bit of encouragement.'

And with that he marched up the steps. Wonders never cease – she often thought the chief begrudged her presence in CID, but here he is helping her.

'Thank you,' she said, too late for him to hear. Then she spied Kenton.

'There you are, I've been waiting out back in the car park.' Kenton was ghastly pale. 'What was that about?'

'Nothing. Are you okay?' His complexion was clammy and feverish, and with the memory of his inebriation last night still vivid, she was immediately suspicious.

'I haven't ...'

'No?'

'I'm fine, honest.'

'You better be,' she said sternly. 'Just don't hurl in my car. It's a long drive. My goodness,' she shook her head, 'what a start.'

'There are four ladies answering to the name of Sharon.' Barnes proceeded to reel off the various hair salons as Lowry stood at his window and watched Gabriel and Kenton on the street below. Flinging Kenton together with Gabriel for a long car journey was his best idea to buck up Kenton's ideas. Unpleasant for her, he conceded – Gabriel visibly baulked at the idea of having to travel with Kenton, hungover and reeking like he was – but Lowry was banking on it making Kenton think twice about how he presented himself going forward.

Barnes got to the point. '. . . All deny knowing a William Cousins.'

It was starting to spit. Lowry tried to close the sash window, but the wet weather had caused the wood to swell. It had been a mistake to open it in the first place. 'More rain on the way, sergeant, I reckon. Why would they deny knowing him?'

'Embarrassed? Frightened?'

'Is the stigma of admitting to a relationship with a soldier really that bad? This is a potential murder investigation. If anything, they should be afraid of withholding evidence.'

Oldham had sent a fax with a single sentence. *The lady in question may answer to the name of Sharon.* No phone call, nothing.

'Want me to get alibis?'

'No, no. That's tantamount to an accusation.'

Lowry disliked his position, operating on second-hand information, floundering around in the dark. What was Oldham playing at? At a remove, it didn't make any sense – did the military police know who Cousins's girlfriend was or not? This being in the middle was totally unsatisfactory. And what of the other duellist? Did they have no clue who this man was? He needed to talk to the soldier informant himself or wash his hands of it entirely.

Northampton

Gabriel and Kenton had made decent time to the Midlands. The local police had informed the family in advance.

'Our Billy always wanted to be in the army.' The father's eyes were heavy and all the while gazed at the framed photograph on the coffee table. There he stood, Lance Corporal William Cousins, their boy in full regalia. Pride of place.

'Did you serve, yourself, sir?' Kenton asked politely, even though the answer was obvious from the black-and-white photos on the mantelpiece behind them.

'Arnhem.'

'Had William a girlfriend, do you know?' Gabriel directed the question at the mother, who sat silently beside her husband with her hands neatly in her lap. Mrs Cousins was about to speak but was cut short by her husband.

'He'd been sowing his wild oats, I'll be bound. Young fella like that in his prime.'

'Were it over a lass, then, you reckon?' the mother said, ignoring him.

'We are looking for anyone he might have formed a close relationship with,' Kenton said diplomatically.

'I think there were someone special . . .' She frowned, searching for an answer to her own suggestion. They waited expectantly for more, but nothing followed.

'What makes you say that, Mrs Cousins?' Gabriel asked.

'Aye, what yer talking about, woman?'

'A mother knows her son,' she said firmly.

'Had he had girlfriends in the past?'

'There were girls he was soft on, yes . . .' she broke into a smile, 'always told me.'

'Mrs Cousins, if you don't mind me asking – why do you think he kept this girl – if, as you suspect, there was a girl – from you this time?'

Mrs Cousins's paused and smiled, remembering her boy. 'He's prone to brag, our lad. When he's got something to brag about. *She's so pretty, Mam*, he'd say, *you wait till you clap eyes on 'er* . . . I have a feeling he wanted to say something last time' – her words caught in her throat – 'last time we saw him in September,' she said, softly. 'But he got tongue-tied when I asked . . .'

'Maybe the love interest was out of bounds?' Kenton said.

All eyes – Gabriel's included – turned on him indignantly.

*

'Why did you have to say that?' Gabriel said as soon as the front door shut behind them. 'Those poor people; as if they haven't enough to worry about without you besmirching their son's memory. You all but said their son was a marriage wrecker. Did you see the look on her face?'

'I did not say the girl was married, merely suggested there may have been a need for secrecy. Could be for any number of reasons,' he said gaily, getting into the car. 'One shouldn't shirk from possibilities, however unpalatable.'

'I very much doubt it – he was playing the field, clear as day.'

'But the mother thought that it was someone special?'

'Mothers want to think the best of their sons, that's natural. I'm sure it's not entered her head that he might be whoring.'

'That's an old-fashioned expression.' Kenton turned and watched a Triumph Stag shoot past them on a junction. 'There certainly used to be a lot of it about; so few soldiers were able to marry in the last century that many took to "flattening the corn" in Abbey Fields, with a lady of the night. I read that somewhere.'

'Is that what you've been doing all this time, reading history books?'

'No. I read up on Colchester before I moved here,' he said proudly.

For the first time in many weeks, he felt human. More than that; being here with Jane in the car, he felt a policeman again. They had at least two more hours together.

He ground his knuckle in the palm of the other hand thoughtfully. Sparks had not ignored him altogether either. As they were about to leave, he had collared him about a boxing match next month. That he could do without.

'Have you missed me?' he said eventually.

'You asked me that last night.'

'Oh. I don't remember,' he said, truthfully. 'So, what did you say?'

'You've not been away forever, Daniel.'

'That's not an answer. I thought about you a lot.'

'Not now,' she said firmly.

'Why not?'

'We're working.'

'We're on the M1.'

'Your mind should be on William Cousins.'

'But I haven't seen you in ages.'

'You may not remember, but you saw me last night, and besides, now you're back at Queen Street, you will see me every day.' Not once had her eyes strayed from the road ahead. This weird, contradictory compartmentalisation was one of the most frustrating aspects of her character. Kenton still did not know whether they were dating. He wanted to know, but couldn't bring himself to ask whether she was seeing anyone else. He wondered if she wondered the same thing. The question hung silently, awkwardly, between them.

'So,' he said, 'how about the pictures?'

He stole a glance at her, brow stern in concentration.

To his surprise she said yes. *The Twilight Zone*, she suggested. This evening.

CHAPTER 14

The Audi had stopped outside a large house in Stanway where the two men had been in conversation for a good fifteen minutes. The sky had grown dark. Across the road, under a row of storm-weary horse chestnuts, sat the Fiesta, collecting large brown leaves on its windscreen.

'We can't follow this dude around Colchester all day, can we? A right pair of muppets,' Drake complained.

'What are they doing?' Atkinson said impatiently. The suited man was gesturing with his hands as if sowing seeds on the sizeable lawn that surrounded the property. Even though Atkinson questioned their intent, it was obvious, having noticed the estate agent's *For Sale* sign protruding from the perimeter of the property, that the man they were after was flogging the land. He looked to be quite the flamboyant salesman. Large raindrops started falling. 'If it starts pissing down again, he might get a spurt on.'

Sure enough, the sky opened and soon the two men were retreating to the Audi, still in heated discussion. They knew Hughes-Ropers' home address, a huge place with stables south of here near Copford Green. Topize had nixed any idea they might have had of paying him a visit there. Not in front of his wife and kids. 'Family is sacred,' he'd said. His office in Church Street was difficult – it being a fully pedestrianised area and all. Only viable if he stayed late.

'It's unlikely we're going to get him on his own,' Atkinson muttered, coming round to the idea of a few extra quid to blow on a farewell night of debauchery. 'Why not here and now?' Thunder clapped as the heavens opened.

'What, in front of that old geezer?' Drake said.

'Why not, he'll be too piss scared to say anything . . . when else? There's no one about. It'll take a matter of seconds and if anyone drives by, they're not going to make anything out in this shit with the wipers going ten to the dozen . . .'

'Yeah, probably think we're helping fix a puncture or summit.'

Rain drummed on the roof of the car. Inside, the two of them arrived at the same conclusion; the storm would cloak their move and also their appearance. Yes, in many ways this heavy rain was a godsend for them, a win-win if you will: no man need see the whites of a man's eyes as he's about to give him a black one. If they were quick, he wouldn't know what, or who, hit him.

Readying themselves to get out, the Audi pulled away.

'Damn. Hold on . . . follow them and see where they go,' Atkinson said. The car did not head back to town, but continued along London Road, where buildings soon fell away and they found themselves in the countryside. The Audi slowed and took a left, out across the smooth rise of dark fields on to the Copford plains towards Birch.

This could be their chance.

The empty road was slick with surface water. The spray beat up the wings of the Audi as Hughes-Roper chatted away energetically next to Osgood. His topic was himself. He was keen to impress. A man with some low-level aristocratic standing, apparently. He wished to sell the family manorial home, which had been unoccupied since his father died in the summer. In spite of himself, Osgood was entranced by the man, and had not hesitated to accept the invite back to his 'pad' for mid-morning tea.

'The rates are significantly lower out here than in the centre of town, I can tell you.'

Osgood didn't let on that he'd got a deal on the Hippodrome; town hall were desperate that something happen with the structure, lest it fall derelict. His plans were not without controversy, of course. The elite, who came to Colchester from their luxury homes in Suffolk, were nothing if not vocal in protesting his proposal. But it seemed the more they complained, the more the mayor pushed sweeteners Osgood's way. He didn't have to pay a penny in rates for two years. He shifted down a gear and accelerated over the hump in the narrow road and down straight and clear towards the village green. In his rear-view mirror, a black Fiesta took off down the left fork of the green only to then cut round in front of them. 'Cheeky little fuckers.' He grinned. Kids pratting around in motors. The rain increased and he notched the wipers up to full speed. As they exited the village, the Fiesta slowed down instead of roaring off into the distance. Hughes-Roper continued to prattle on next to him, but Howard was bored of property banter and switched the subject to boats, more of a level playing field. Howard told him of his dash from Brightlingsea on the *Nomad* this morning and was unsurprised to hear Hughes-Roper himself owned a boat, a racing yacht he was in the process of selling. He was trying to entice Howard into viewing that too, thinking it a way of cementing the deal.

'I won't be on the water again this year.'

'Nonsense; you'd be surprised the number of good days that will still be on offer,' Hughes-Roper chirruped. Howard began to wonder if the chap took him for a chump; the season for sailing small craft such as the one he had on offer was well and truly over.

'Weather like this? You must be – hang on, what's that silly blighter doing?' The car in front had braked to a stop in the middle of nowhere. A door opened and a man emerged in a green fighting jacket and baseball cap. 'Bloody hell.' This was not good. Hughes-Roper, still talking, remained blissfully unaware of any danger.

The man went for the passenger side of the car. It wasn't him they were after. Osgood slipped the car in reverse, but as he glanced over his shoulder, he realised Hughes-Roper had opened the car door. 'Idiot,' he screeched, 'shut the fuckin' door.'

It was too late; a pair of strong, young hands gripped him and yanked him out. Howard turned off the ignition. The Audi rocked as his companion was slammed forcefully against the side of the car. Osgood sighed; though he couldn't imagine how this fellow had caused offence other than being a posh twat, he couldn't sit by and let him take a pummelling. The damage to the paintwork alone would be a mint. With a grunt, he got out of the car into the downpour. The not-unpleasant touch of warm rain was accompanied by the smell of wet greenery. He addressed a barrage of threatening expletives at the attacker across the car roof.

'Oi, mate. Leave it.' Another man appeared, approaching the Audi.

The man opposite then nutted Hughes-Roper, prompting Howard to advance and take on the second man, also in a baseball cap. But he was much quicker than Howard and dodged his blow; in return, Howard received a solid clout, square on the ear, causing him to lose his balance. The leather soles of his loafers gave on the wet tarmac and he went down, cracking the back of his head on the road.

Osgood blinked rapidly. Water in his eyes.

He must have passed out. He saw two sets of feet before him, one a plain, scuffed black – unmistakably that of a policeman. The other pair moved briskly away and a second later Osgood felt himself levitating. Nausea raced at him, making it impossible to move his stare away from the shoes on the road.

He thought he had concussion and knew he was hurt.

How and why he could not understand. He tried to apply reason to the situation. Young man. Strong. Black boots. Temper. Green jacket. There could only be one answer. His hothead nephew Colin. Not that he could make him out through the torrential rain. He said the name out loud: 'Colin.'

But wait, it was the other bloke he was with they went for – pinned up against the side of the Audi . . . where was he, anyway?

Queen Street HQ

Lowry held the MOD's faxed statement in his hand. This was what Sparks was waiting for; they were officially off the hook. They concluded they had 'a strong inclination that another soldier was involved' although 'army and civilian police were united in their efforts to catch the man'. Brigadier Lane went on to explain the men were under enormous mental pressure. The gist was it might even have been a suicide pact gone wrong.

Unsurprisingly, Lowry had been unable to contact Oldham and was past twiddling his thumbs in frustration and not being able to act. He just hoped that as part of the military investigation, the girlfriend was flushed out. He was curious as to what sort of woman could drive a man to such an extreme act of recklessness. To kill for love, to die for love, was as old as love itself, but to do so in premeditated circumstances took balls. To get up in the middle of the night and march across town to stare death in the face. With a sigh, Lowry folded the fax, lay it on his in-tray and lit a cigarette.

Still, at sixteen hundred hours – an hour from now – the matter was officially out of his hands. He breathed out and surveyed his desk. At quiet moments like this he was prone to feel lost and without purpose. The cluttered immediacy of his desk gave him reassurance on such days. A typewriter stood surrounded by police paperwork, fringed with an eclectic mix of knick-knacks – lighters, ashtrays, penknives, string, mail order items he'd forget to take home, books and 45s, even a compass. He pulled out one of the records, a Small Faces single. He flipped it over in his hand and muttered, '*Grow Your Own*.' Playing old records and collecting rarities were okay for filling the odd half hour, on occasions when Jacqui was asleep upstairs or he had the house to himself, but now with all the space he'd ever need, the solitary nature of it struck him. A bachelor's life, was that to be it? Hours and hours wasted cataloguing and indexing records and videos. He tossed it on the desk. Seven-inch records were for kids. Not that he could talk – he had twice recently had reason to feel like a child on the matter of music and books. He winced remembering Gabriel's 'It's very popular'. And then his lack of cultural knowledge when discussing books with Becky.

Giving up the boxing might mean fewer aches and pains

these days, but it was a huge chunk of his life gone. The training, the socialising in the Britannia. It might be mindless but he wasn't half good at it. Jacqui never cared what he read or minded the sixties music ... unsurprising now, of course, her mind on other things. He bleakly saw his future before him: running to seed, slumped half-comatose on the sofa watching the exploits of DI Maggie Forbes on the box and working through the confiscated police film library. Getting fat and old. He had stopped running and the birdwatching had petered out too, both activities inexorably tied to the boxing – the running as a complement to it, the birdwatching as a kind of balance for it. Maybe a trip to Rye might reignite his interest in ornithology?

There was a lot riding on this weekend away. He picked up the phone, dialled Becky's number and cleared his throat to leave a message to confirm it was happening – but replaced it remembering she hadn't an answerphone and would be at school.

'Afternoon, guv.' Gabriel and her light blue eyes materialised in front of him unexpectedly.

'Aha,' he said, embarrassed, though why he didn't know. 'What did Cousins's family have to say?' Though really it was of little consequence now that the investigation into his death rested with the military. Kenton appeared at her side, very pale.

They both spoke at once, contradicting one another: Kenton thought the boy may have had a girlfriend, one kept secret from his family, while Gabriel thought the reverse – that Cousins was footloose and fancy free. The parents had been similarly divided, the father suspecting his boy of a somewhat promiscuous sex life, his mother believing her son was sweet on a local girl.

He waited for them to finish talking, and said, 'But there was definitely someone – you're both agreed on that?'

Both reluctantly nodded their heads.

He considered the pair, one alert and aloof, the other with the complexion of a consumptive about to expire. 'Well, it's out of our hands now: the Ministry of Defence have deemed it a military matter.'

A gust of chill wind slipped in under the window, causing the fax from the MOD to flutter in his in-tray. 'Gabriel, write it up and send it over to Oldham. Kenton, get your arse out of here,' Lowry raised a hand to forestall any protest, 'and straight to the barbers. Be sure to arrive with the milk tomorrow. That's the end of it.'

Gabriel watched Kenton leave, her fondness for him creeping up on her again in spite of herself, rekindling as he slunk towards the stairs. She turned to face Lowry, who was doing battle with the window. Slow, uneven spots of rain hit the glass, followed by faster, angled spray, reaching in under the sash window.

'That's as far as it'll go,' he said, giving up. 'Cardboard will have to do.' The inspector looked sad.

'Does it trouble the birdwatcher?' she asked.

'What?'

'Rain.'

'Makes them harder to see and hear,' he replied. 'How was Kenton?'

'Okay,' she said, 'okay.' The swift change of subject was odd, like he didn't want to talk, and she wondered what she'd done wrong. He had grown defensive since the day before. He was embarrassed that she'd caught him napping. She'd overcompensated by talking too much. He didn't care that she was Grade 8 piano. She sighed and raised what was chiefly on her mind. 'That man, you know the one that shoved a guy in the river yesterday? The chief knows him. His name is Howard Osgood. Recently acquired the old Hippodrome.'

'Osgood . . .' he mused, reaching for a pack of Players.

'Sparks ordered Uniform to go fetch him in.'

'Exacting his revenge,' Lowry said quietly.

'Sorry?'

'Merrydown was needling Sparks this morning about allowing a nightclub in the high street, and you presented him with the perfect excuse to vent his annoyance on the new owner.'

'Oh,' she said flatly.

'I wonder if he actually sent officers up there,' Lowry mused.

Gabriel felt deflated. She had believed the chief had wanted to support her – what was the phrase, make Osgood 'doff his cap'? As it turned out, it was all to do with some spat with her aunt. He probably didn't even do anything about it. 'Just words,' she said aloud.

Lowry gave her a quizzical glance and said, 'He probably forgot, he's a lot on his mind. Don't take it personally.'

'I don't.' But she did and couldn't hide it.

'Things are quiet round here. Why don't you and I mooch over there ourselves and see what's happening.'

'Why?'

He glanced at his watch. 'The duel death is still ours for another hour. Let's go and make Howard's life uncomfortable in what time we have left.'

CHAPTER 15

Antonia Sparks frowned up at the heavy sky from the large, front bay window. The heavens would open before long and rain would undoubtedly settle in for the day. She was expecting friends for tea later in the afternoon. If she was going to go today, it had to be now.

Her mother was coming at the weekend and Antonia wished to cook a special meal – that was what she'd told Stephen, anyway. But it was also his birthday on Sunday, a fact he'd forgotten. Since hitting fifty, almost five years ago now, he never seemed to remember. His new wife however, did. This would be the first time she'd cooked for him. It just so happened her parents could make this weekend too. Mummy was bringing up some vintage Veuve Clicquot. It would be a double celebration! But not without hard work first ... Antonia's culinary skills displayed enthusiasm rather than accomplishment; prior to marrying Stephen, she'd been more one for going out than slaving over the stove. With motherhood looming, she accepted those days were over, that she'd be spending a good deal more time at home. She revelled at the prospect of a child and was all for embracing the happy housewife role. Her netballing was – for a time, at least – on hold, so she decided she may as well try something new.

One of her maxims for everything in life was be prepared: plan ahead and all will be well. She hunted out her yellow sailing mackintosh from the cupboard under the stairs. She would nip to the shop on Crouch Street.

Heavy rain meant Gabriel and Lowry took the car for what was a five-minute walk to the high street. Osgood was out but was expected back imminently, and Lowry was reluctant to give up his parking spot – or do anything else, for that matter.

Time, Gabriel had quickly learnt, could often move slowly in CID. Hours were spent on surveillance, or simply waiting, hanging around, whatever you wanted to call it. Sitting in cars was much of what being a detective was all about. She had also quickly learnt how the minutes moved even slower during inclement weather – especially now when they could barely see beyond the windscreen. Lowry wouldn't have them on while stationary. 'The wiper blades need changing.'

He claimed to be people-watching, though how was a mystery – and even if the road were visible, the high street was surely empty. The town hall was to their left across the road, and the Hippodrome a couple of buildings further down.

'Would you mind opening your window?' she asked.

'It's raining,' he said.

'Really, I hadn't noticed . . . No, it's your cigarette. It is rather overwhelming.' Lowry wound down his window an inch. He took a long drag, cigarette hissing as the rain blew through the car, and as he did so a powder blue Scimitar GTE pulled up directly outside the Hippodrome. The car door opened. Lowry flicked on the wipers to get a better look. He thought he saw the top of a head emerge briefly, as if someone was going to get out, but then ducked back.

'Weird, what's going . . .' He craned his neck but couldn't make anything out through the rain. The car promptly sped off.

Gabriel then nudged him and said, 'At the window.'

A figure loomed darkly at the driver's side door. As Lowry wound the window down all the way, a PC poked his helmeted head inside.

'Yes?'

Rain streamed from the peak of the constable's custodian.

'The chief asked me to tell you – Mrs Sparks, sir. She's had a fall.'

Colchester General Hospital, Lexden Road

That Sparks should call on Lowry in a real emergency was not a surprise. The two were close, in an unspoken way. But in all the years Lowry had known the chief, he'd never seen him upset much beyond the frustration of losing a boxing match or placing poorly in a rowing competition. As a man, Sparks was not given to tender emotions. Not so much as a flicker when either of the previous wives had left him. However, the man he saw now was a man crushed. His friend watched helplessly on as two nurses urgently rolled his wife into the theatre. Antonia was critical. She'd lost a lot of blood. Sparks was muttering about the child – Lowry was sure he had yet to acknowledge that Antonia was in danger too.

'Shall we take a seat?' Lowry suggested gently. 'Let them do their job, we're just in the way here.' Sparks acquiesced in silence, as Lowry steered him away from the corridor, a hand placed lightly on his back. Seated on the hard plastic waiting room chairs, Lowry pulled out his hip flask from his inside jacket pocket and handed it to his friend, who took it.

'I might not have been jumping up and down in joy at the prospect, but it was part of me.' He tipped the flask back.

'Try not to think that way, eh? No news yet. It may be okay.' Lowry offered him a cigarette.

'Nope. I think not.' He stared blankly in front of him.

A man in a flat cap tutted disapprovingly as Sparks passed the flask back. 'You head off.'

'Sure?'

He nodded. 'I'll call you when I know anything. Thanks for coming.' He patted Lowry's thigh.

'Hang on to this then.' Lowry passed the whisky down as he stood.

'This is a hospital, not a public house,' the man seated across announced.

Sparks's nostrils flared but he contained himself, took a

deliberate swig and then started to talk. Lowry sat back down again.

She had been shopping for his birthday dinner when it happened. He was going to be fifty-five. Not that he'd told Lowry until now. Lowry absorbed this information, along with the rest of the occupants of the waiting room. The chief spoke openly and plainly of his young wife, the whirlwind romance at Cowes, and of the wedding in February, which Lowry had attended as best man.

'Paprika,' Sparks said. 'Something with paprika of all things.'

Lowry moved to place his arm across Sparks's shoulders, but instead clasped the nearest arm, squeezed the firm bicep and bowed his head. He was winded by a surge of sympathy, revealing an attachment to the older man that seldom surfaced. Even now – more and more, in fact, the older he became – life caught Lowry out, introducing unsolicited emotions and concerns, age bringing with it a new sort of awareness.

'Stay by her side.' Lowry rose a second time to leave. 'We'll manage.'

'Wait, Nick . . .' Sparks's eyes found his beseechingly. 'Wait for me in Ward 9, just for a quick one . . .'

'Sure.' He smiled.

The world outside the hospital was stained grey. Keen to distance himself from Jacqui's domain, Lowry marched straight out into the rain, not noticing Gabriel under the portico.

'How is she?' She stepped forward wearing a tan mac.

'No news.'

'And the boss?'

'He's not too bright.' Lowry remained away from the shelter of the portico, letting the rain wash over him.

'I'm sorry.'

'These things happen,' he said unconvincingly.

'Someone else has had an accident in the rain.'

'Who?'

'Howard Osgood. Just been brought in here.'

Gabriel was fast becoming drenched. She moved back under the portico but her boss did not take the cue. The elements appeared to have no impact on him. She had witnessed this about him. She watched the rain run down his forehead along dislodged locks of Brylcreemed hair and into his unblinking eyes.

'Now's your moment then,' he said.

'Meaning?'

'Go have a word – see what's happened to your new friend Mr Osgood. If he's had a shock, he'll be vulnerable. I got some calls to make.' He ran a hand back over his head, sliding the stray strands back into place, and set off across the car park.

Lowry sat at the bar of the Hospital Arms, pinched the bridge of his nose to shake off the rainwater, picked up the telephone receiver in front of him and dialled Queen Street. Sergeant Barnes needed to be told. Barnes had known the chief even longer than Lowry – they had enrolled together back in 1950. The news clearly affected him but he said nothing out loud, putting the running of the station before personal concern. Merrydown would need to be advised but he'd wait on word from Sparks first.

Lowry ordered a drink. The pub was busy, as it usually was between shifts and before regular visiting hours. The Hospital Arms was directly across the road from the hospital itself, slap bang in its eyeline. Hospital staff referred to it as 'Ward 9' when arranging a crafty drink. Lowry wondered not for the first time this week what impact the 'new' general hospital up in Turner Village, which was close to completion, would have on the town. Colchester had accumulated so many different specialist units down the years, tropical disease and isolation hospitals and asylums (and military, of course) that the County Hospital had always been referred to as the general. But soon there would be a new purpose-built 'general'. This made the future of County uncertain – along with that of the nurses working there.

His estranged wife Jacqui included.

Whenever he had cause to be in or around the hospital, he was on the alert. He was sure the moment he entered the building it went round the bush telegraph. She'd always find him. Like earlier when, as he was heading to see Sparks, she appeared out of nowhere and intercepted him, demanding they speak. Tonight. *Gotcha*.

He glanced at his watch. He asked the landlord to use the phone again.

'Hullo.'

'It's Nick.'

'Oh.' Surprise in her voice.

'Calling as I said I would.'

'You needn't have; I believed you.' A peel of laughter rang across the bar. 'Where are you?'

'Err, the pub . . .'

'Oh yeah? Who with?'

'I'll explain later.' He felt a friendly hand on his shoulder. 'I've got to go. See you soon.'

'Who was that?' Sparks asked, nodding to the phone.

'Becky.'

'Did you tell her?' It was Antonia who had introduced him to Becky over the summer.

'No . . .'

'All for the sake of some bloody paprika,' Sparks said, ignoring Lowry's answer. 'It would have taken two minutes for me to get it. Jesus. Why didn't I go? She asked me half a dozen times.' He shook his head woefully.

'Stephen, you weren't to know this would happen. Don't be hard on yourself. Antonia's able-bodied, can race boats across the Solent, whip a spinnaker up in a trice, has balance and agility – you could hardly expect her to slip on the pavement in the rain.'

'Tripped. She tripped on the curb running across Crouch Street.'

'How is she?'

'She's resting,' he placed his knuckles on the bar, 'for half an hour or so. I'll go back after a quick one.' He pulled back his coat sleeve to reveal a wristwatch rimmed in condensation. He squinted at the timepiece. 'Bloody thing.'

Lowry knew the story of the Omega Seamaster only too well. Sparks had bought it in 1969 from a shop on the Strand in London, while drunk after receiving a bravery award, only to discover the watch was not, as its name suggested, waterproof – or indeed, water-resistant – but for decoration only. After wearing it on a particularly challenging sailing weekend, he took it back, only to receive short shrift from the store manager, who remembered the belligerent police inspector only too well.

'Time enough, it's only over the road,' Lowry said.

'She'll be right as rain soon.' Sparks's face did not carry the conviction of his words. 'The doctor . . . the doctor, he said she . . .'

A burst of laughter from a young medic across the bar made the chief falter.

'Don't worry about the nick, I'll call Merrydown, you stay here,' Lowry said.

Sparks seemed not to hear. Lowry wished to see Oldham anyway, one final time. He doubted it would make any difference were he to stay with the chief. The poor man was so lost in trauma. 'Careful,' Lowry said to his friend, 'just you be careful, eh?' He drank up and left the solitary figure of his chief hunched on a bar stool amidst a lively ensemble of young medical staff.

*

Osgood was in A&E, curtained off in a bed. A nurse wrapped his arm to take his blood pressure. The PC who attended the call stood at the foot of the bed. Gabriel sat to one side. The wounded man was dazed; if he recognised her he made no effort to acknowledge it.

'What about the other fella?' Osgood asked her. He'd refused to say a word until she arrived.

'What other fella?'

'The bloke I was with.'

'You were lying on the roadside alone,' the PC said.

'Are you saying there was someone in the car with you?' Gabriel asked quickly.

'Never mind.' Osgood rubbed his eyes wearily and stared into space, then flung off the sheet. 'Right.'

'You've a concussion. They'll want to keep you in overnight.'

'Like bollocks they will.'

Gabriel looked to the young PC for assistance. 'Up to 'im, miss.'

'Where's my motor?'

'It's been taken to Stanway garage. Would you like to make a statement?'

'No, I wouldn't.' Shrouded in the white hospital garment, Osgood's stature was much reduced. He could be anyone's father, or grandfather even, as he rooted around to find his socks.

'In your shoes, under the bed.' She bent to fetch them.

'Thanks,' he said begrudgingly.

'Do you know why anyone would wish to attack you?'

'No, I do not.'

'We are here to help,' she said, averting her eyes as he hoisted his trousers up underneath the bed garment. 'What about that young man you punched yesterday morning?'

He stood there now in trousers, bare-chested, defiant, proud. 'No chance.'

'Are you sure?'

'Absolutely. Now if you don't mind, I'd like to get my car.'

'I'm not sure that you should be driving.'

'It's none of your damn business.' Osgood flicked a quick glance to the PC, who stood unmoved by the exchange before him.

'Mr Osgood, I find your manner rather hard to fathom. Our chief superintendent assured me you were a respectable businessman, kept your nose clean . . .'

'He's right.' He finished buttoning his shirt and waited for her to finish.

'If so, why won't you cooperate? If someone has attacked you, why don't you want them brought to heel – if not for your sake, for others?'

He sighed and scratched his jaw.

'If you make a statement, we can run you over to collect your vehicle.' Stanway garage was the base for the traffic police.

He smiled. 'You know, I think I'll just get a mini-cab, if that's all right.' He made to go. 'And don't you worry, I will be at your nick by the end of the week.'

Gabriel left him behind the curtain to finish getting dressed. If there was any sign of vulnerability, she'd not witnessed it.

CHAPTER 16

Lowry settled himself in his own front room before picking up the phone to call the ACC at home.

'Shall I come down?' Merrydown asked.

He watched the TV screen as a videotape rewound in the player. The cat lay beside him on the settee and he gently mussed its ear. 'I don't think that's necessary, ma'am.'

'Very well, but I want him to know they are both in my thoughts. Will you tell him, inspector?'

Lowry raised his eyebrows. He'd misinterpreted her question, assuming she meant come down to assist running the station, not to offer some bedside comfort.

'Yes, of course.'

'He's not the easiest man to work with, but he's a damn good policeman. And that poor woman. If there's anything I can do, be sure to let me know.'

'Ma'am.'

'Good night, inspector.'

'Wow. Did you hear that, Pushkin? Mrs Merrydown is worried about Chief Sparks.' Lowry place the phone back in the cradle next to the cat, who stretched out, front legs prostrate off the sofa and back pushed into his thigh. 'I wonder what he'd make of that?'

Was Merrydown's concern genuine or was she exhibiting her 'people management skills'? Since her appointment to the role, the senior members of Queen Street had been inundated with training opportunities, especially for managing staff, all of which had been dutifully ignored. Lowry's own concern was heartfelt, but confined to Sparks alone, not the wife or the unborn child. He reached for the fino. Was that wrong? He couldn't help it. The explanation was probably down to his own estranged family, he thought.

'We are what we think we are, Nick.' A phrase of Sparks's came to mind. In times of doubt over a case, or generally when things were going badly, he would trot it out. It never made any sense in any given context, but was used frequently enough for one to assume it came from somewhere. Socrates, apparently – as Kenton had pointed out to them fresh from university. This had caused much mirth and derision.

'Sparks quoting Socrates, do me a favour!' Barnes had erupted with laughter. Lowry smiled at the memory, and taking his lead from the cat, he shut his eyes and stretched his head back over the sofa. Yes, Antonia's accident had brought Lowry's own situation sharply into relief. Quite literally too; his wife had caught him at the hospital wanting to talk tonight, hence he was home, waiting for her to call.

The tape clicked on the VCR and the digital clock reappeared on the display: 19:57. Jacqui would soon call. And then when that was over and done with, Jim Oldham was waiting for him at the officers' club for a debrief. This accident had thrown the day off-kilter.

He stroked the cat who responded with a purr.

'Just me and you from now on, buddy.'

Lowry knew his own mind and what he must do.

The fact of the matter was that although he loved Jacqui, he could not forgive her, and if he allowed her back, her indiscretion would plague him forever. It was better for Matthew to have his parents apart, apart but amicable, than be stuck in a household embittered with resentment. He knew she saw it the other way. *'For Matty, it's in his best interest that we patch things up, remain together.'* For Lowry the exact opposite was true. These pat remarks drove him crazy; their relationship wasn't a pair of jeans in need of repair, or a spot of rust on a wheel arch.

In fact, everything about her wound him up. Nine months apart was enough time to see her afresh. What he used to consider endearing was now just annoying, and whether it was true or not, he now believed them incompatible.

As he reached forward for the sherry bottle, the phone went.

'Hello.'

'Nick, it's me.' She waited and when he said nothing, continued, 'I need you to make a decision.'

'You're in luck. I have. It's over, Jacqui.'

The news went down like a bombshell. Silence, followed

by a torrent of abuse. *You don't care – you never did. No wonder what happened happened.* So insistent was she that he began to think her right. While her affair may be over for her, for him it shone in his memory brighter than their wedding day. Now he would have to compose himself for his meeting with Jim Oldham.

Kenton fidgeted in his seat. His initial joy that Jane had said yes to a date at the cinema had been replaced by bewilderment at her wanting to see this film. An American teen horror fantasy flick whose selling point could only be that the man behind *E.T.* and *Poltergeist* was involved. Based on a cult TV programme, the film was episodic nonsense, featuring creatures that could well be rejects from *The Muppet Show*, offering neither thrills nor frights. Kenton failed to see the point of it. He glanced at Gabriel in the darkness, who was slowly and methodically placing popcorn in her mouth.

They arrived separately, Gabriel having gone back to Queen Street while he'd gone off in search of a haircut. She arrived and took her seat as the house lights began to dim. If she'd noticed how well-groomed he was – freshly shorn with a smart new haircut – she either didn't say or wasn't bothered.

The hairdresser, now there was a girl with a sense of humour. He'd given his regular barber a miss and tried a trendy new place, and got chatting to this woman, who was entertaining and refreshingly flirty. Kenton quite fancied her but was unable to do anything about it. He'd wound up with a cut far shorter than he'd have liked. If things didn't become clear with Jane soon, he'd go back to Maravanne and ask her out. He'd have a skinhead if it came to it.

'Well, that was different,' he said as they stepped out on to the damp pavement afterwards. Expecting something more cerebral, or at least mature, he was at a loss for comment.

'I'm not sure what I'd think if you'd chosen it,' she announced.

He lit a cigarette. 'Well, I wasn't going to say anything. It wouldn't have been my first choice, I must admit. Fancy a drink?'

'Certainly not.'

'Oh, I just thought – that's what folk usually do after seeing a film.'

'Don't you think you've spent enough time in pubs drinking? I would start to worry, if I were you. Goodnight, Daniel.'

And she left him there in the street. He stepped forward, half attempting to reach for her sleeve, but withdrew, fearing a humiliating scene as couples passed him by either side, arm in arm, a few of the men slipping sympathetic glances. It took several seconds before he registered his wet feet and moved out of the puddle. Maybe she was right, he was damn tired.

The day had started badly, in a sick hungover fashion, and it seemed it was ending back where it started. Worse, in fact, because in the middle of it all, in the car with Jane and right up until the curtains opened, he'd briefly felt like himself again. The movie had proved to be a juvenile piece of tosh and now here he was, standing in a puddle, left on his own like a prize Charlie. He really had sunk to the bottom. He didn't understand her at all. The sensible thing would be to put it all behind him and go to bed, but the enticing glow from the Bull pulled him in. It was still early – no harm in a quick one. Then home for a spliff, just to help him sleep . . .

Wagon and Horses, Colchester Head Street

The Scimitar was a pale cream under the street lights. Raindrops glittered on the bonnet as the car slowed to a stop. The window wound down. The engine remained running. Drake nudged Atkinson forward from the shadows. They'd been sat in the pub the best part of three hours waiting for Gordon to roll up.

Atkinson stepped up to the car.

'Sorted,' he said. It was pitch-black inside the car, and for all he knew it could be empty.

'I know,' came the familiar voice from within, 'estate agent, he phoned me having had a change of mind.'

'Oh right, great,' he bent down to the window, 'good, good.'

'Get your dirty white fingers off my pristine sports vehicle, you hear!'

Atkinson jumped back. A bolt of laughter ensued, before an envelope peeked out the window, resting on the sill. He hesitated. The envelope flapped, indicating impatience. Atkinson grabbed it as if it might bite.

'So long, soldier boy.' And with that, the car sped off down North Hill.

Drake stepped out of the doorway.

'Come on, let's get back inside, those couple of sorts will have gone otherwise.'

They returned to the darker recesses of the cavernous Head Street pub and settled down to another round.

'Well, that was straightforward.' Atkinson counted out the money under the table. He repeated the words again to satisfy himself, not that Drake was listening. Drake's full attention was rooted on two women standing at a centre table towards the bar. Big perms, dressed in all white – blouses, mini-skirts, matching white stilettos, as if it was the height of summer.

'I think we should make a move on these two now we've some readies . . . what do you reckon?'

Atkinson was no coward, he knew that – he'd not have signed up if he was. He was not afraid of death, but he found the more aggressive hardcore soldiers like Drake difficult to deal with. They made the day-to-day unpleasant and intimidating. Until now. The grilling he had taken from the RMP had hardened him and with each fresh pint he felt bolder. He felt the balance of power had been redressed: Atkinson was the dominant male, a shift tacitly understood by both.

With one of their number dead, and money in their pocket for threatening a businessman, Atkinson was bold enough to mention the unmentionable.

'Was she worth it?'

Drake grunted heavily, his face oddly contorted. In his mind's eye, he was flashing a winning smile across the bar to attract the attention of the two ladies in white. In truth he looked like a bulldog with an abscess.

'Does it matter?' he said.

Atkinson picked up his pint.

'No, I guess not. But describe her ... what is she like?'

Atkinson had never met or even glimpsed Saffron Topize; he was not holding out with the police beyond the name. And now, when all was said and done, he was curious. She must be fit. Super fit, to be the cause of all this bother. Neither Drake nor Cousins had any problem pulling the girls – this one must be special.

'Like no other girl I've ever met. A goddess – better than that, a face that could launch a thousand ships – more ... Venus, skin as smooth as a siren, you know, hypnotic, like.' The man waffled on in this vein, mixing metaphors and ancient allegories, while successfully making eye contact with the two women. Atkinson stared too. Even in this dim light, he could tell the women were older than they were. Maybe it was the adrenaline rush of Copford Green and the fifties in his back pocket, or maybe it was Drake's talk of smooth skin and feminine allure, but he felt a sudden lustful desire.

'Come on,' he slurred boldly. 'Let's make a move ...' By now he was sure that his and Drake's combined age would fall short of the younger of these Colchester deities. 'Don't like yours much.'

CHAPTER 17

Oldham greeted Lowry in the foyer of the officers' club and signed him in. The detective's face was drawn, and he wondered if the man sickened for something.

'Two amontillados,' the captain said to the white-jacketed waiter, who seated them at a low, polished table next to a large window overlooking tennis courts. The courts were floodlit despite the weather, large puddles in the uneven surface reflecting the glare, nets sagging forlornly.

'Do you play?' the captain asked.

'Uh-uh . . .' Lowry shook his head.

'Good for the core.' Oldham himself was a fine player.

With the pressure off – or redirected – they bantered convivially. Lowry had only been here a handful of times and would not have detected the slight draft of unease that stirred through the room when the captain entered.

'And with the boxing over, what will you do? Birdwatching is not – I presume – so physically demanding?'

'No . . . it's not. I hadn't given it any thought until I had to let the belt out a notch the other day. It seems like only yesterday I was flat out on the canvas.'

'Hmm. You might try yoga. It works for me – picked it up in India in the seventies – stay trim without leaving one's quarters.' There was an uneasy pause, as each man struggled with a mental image of the other at his physical pursuits. Oldham continued. 'Right, to business. Your mob are officially off the case. I'm sorry you've been given the runaround over this girl, but no need to worry about it now.'

'I heard. But that doesn't mean we just forget about it.'

'Sorry, I didn't mean to imply you would. Only, the burden has shifted . . .'

'It seems strange to me that you have an inkling about the love interest – not an accurate inkling, but a name, nevertheless – yet no idea who pulled the trigger?'

'It is a process, inspector, a slow but sure way. That's your inquisitive mind, can't help itself. We run our investigations . . . differently.'

'It's stupid that we are not able to work more closely on it.'

Oldham sympathised with Lowry, to a point. 'We will be in touch once we have the man,' he said firmly, 'or indeed, if we have any more on the girl. It is early days, remember. The fact we *know* there is a girl is progress, even if we can't find her yet?'

'Sure, sure. Yes.'

Early days it may be, but the unit was shipping out imminently.

'Okay, well, I'll not keep you.' Lowry pulled out a large handkerchief and blew heartily, drawing attention to himself. He downed the schooner. 'Oh, we found this.' He pulled out a sapphire seahorse earring and placed it on the table. 'Cousins wore it round his neck as a pendant, but in fact it's an earring, possibly from Asia, according to a local jeweller.'

Oldham knew exactly what it was: he and Fairweather had come across its match in a dormitory just this morning.

'May I?' he said after a while, picking the piece up. Yes, it was the same. 'Interesting.'

Bingo. They had their man. The girl – whoever she was – had clearly given one earring to each lover. A keepsake. Oldham took the decision not to share this information with Lowry for now. The army had so far bungled finding the girl, so best to wait until they had the man locked. He stood, holding the item out. 'Here, you hold on to it.' He smiled serenely. 'It looks valuable.'

The captain escorted the inspector to the door and watched him disappear off in the night. For a man in the throes of a cold or chill, as Lowry surely was, he might have moved a bit quicker. Oldham stepped back into the warmth and took possession of a room marked private. He had heard the police were under scrutiny again, their powers under review; the public were dissatisfied. This was where the army were markedly different, he thought, as he picked up the phone and issued the arrest order at dawn: he was the law.

*

Brigadier Lane appeared at Oldham's office promptly the next morning. Oldham had already been here an hour to check all had been carried out efficiently. It had. But something was not quite right. Something in Lane's posture – the way he sat in the leather chair, relaxed as if it were the end of a gruelling day, not the start of a fresh one – combined with the fact that he felt the need to show up in person, rather than call on the phone, served to warn Oldham to be on his guard.

Thus far, however, all had gone well. Corporal Drake had been hauled in at dawn. He had resisted at first, startled to be shaken roughly from his bunk, but eventually he calmed down and was transported to the MCTC by armed guard in a bulletproof Land Rover. He would be held there for the foreseeable future.

Oldham did not hesitate to issue the warrant for Drake's arrest after Lowry presented the earring matching the one he and Fairweather had discovered tucked away in Hyderabad barracks, in a small pewter cup on a bedside table. Oldham was convinced that Atkinson, by dint of his behaviour, had served as a second or go-between and should also be locked up. He had been seen with Drake in the Robin Hood public house during the afternoon of the duel, and that was good enough for him. Given enough time, Oldham would wheedle out anyone else involved. Brigadier Lane, however, held a difference of opinion.

'The Army Act is quite clear on this point,' Oldham challenged his superior.

'I am well acquainted with military law, Jim,' the heavily

bearded garrison commander said. 'However, after careful thought, I think we let them go with a ticking off.'

'A ticking off? Good heavens!' Oldham was aghast. 'Why?'

'Less chance of even more newspaper attention; we can't have the nation thinking we allow this sort of antiquated practice to go on. Two men wishing to shoot at each other is one thing, but the involvement of further men gives the affair a ceremonial status.'

'Ceremony? Exactly! Atkinson should have reported this, as soon as it was mentioned. Their loyalty is to the Crown, not to each other. Let him off and it will only serve to encourage this kind of behaviour. I'm sure there's one more too, that is the code. With enough time . . .'

'I've said my piece, James. Let it go.' The Beard tugged his earlobe, a tick that revealed his discomfort. 'This has come from up on high. A slap on the wrist and the matter is done with.'

Oldham sat back. *A ticking off*. He'd have him for this; the streets of Londonderry would seem a walk in the park compared to what he'd line up.

As if reading his mind, Lane said, 'Nothing too debilitating, mind you, Oldham. They've a tough tour coming up. Just make sure they know what side their bread is buttered. The situation is not getting any easier over there and that has no-doubt influenced the higher-ups in their decision.'

'They will serve as witnesses, Whitehall will grant us that?'

'Let's cross that bridge when we come to it – may not be

necessary, eh? Our man confesses and what have you.' Lane started to squirm in the leather armchair; he wanted to be done with it. He leant forward. 'I trust you as always, Jim. You run this camp impeccably when it comes to discipline, I know that, but it would be bad for morale, for the men to see two of their own put away. Their brothers are innocent in their eyes. If this weren't during the Troubles, well, yes, I'd question the decision.'

'Very well.' Oldham took a measured breath. He knew there was nothing to be gained in pushing the garrison commander. They had a fine relationship. The Beard was not lacking mettle, but he was politically attuned in a way Oldham was not. The RMP captain may hold absolute power on pursuit and capture of a suspect, but the top army brass had to want them first. And sometimes they did not.

'Did we locate the root of all this nonsense?'

'That was in the hands of the civilian police. And no, they've drawn a blank.'

'For the best. If she's not been found then she doesn't want to be, which suits us – we don't want some bit of skirt in the red tops, rabbiting on about randy soldiers losing their heads over a fumble in the hay. Advise Queen Street to desist in the search.'

'Very good.'

'I'll leave you to update the civvies, given your man Lowry is on the Queen Street throne. The superintendent has had a bit of a blow.'

'Oh?'

'Yes, his good lady took a bit of a tumble.'

'A tumble?'

'Slipped on the pavement.' The ear was called upon again. The dense brow furrowed. 'Gravid. And the baby, of course. Touch and go. Sparks called me late last night, poor old sausage, had had a few.'

'When was this?' Oldham asked.

'Yesterday afternoon in that downpour.'

'How terrible.' He'd never met the woman. Lowry must have been aware but chose not to mention it.

'So,' Lane continued, 'since Lowry's running the cop shop until Sparks gets back, be a good chap and let him know this business is closed.'

When the brigadier left, Oldham stepped away from his desk and opened the French doors on to the veranda. Even though it was beastly damp out he had to get some fresh air – aside from everything else, the brigadier's cologne was overpowering. Quite unbecoming of a man of his position.

Oldham smiled, thinking about Lowry. He had not mentioned anything about stepping in for Sparks at Queen Street. Did they mistrust each other, even now? Or were they just too similar? They were the same age and between them there was no ugly corner of human nature they had not encountered over the years. Oldham was a ruthless man and he ran to his own code, leading a solitary existence, but he tried to tend to his finer senses. Companionship for him was in music and in his garden, and he was fond of a gin or two. Lowry, on the other hand, was a different animal. There was a hole in the policeman's life. A void. The harder he tried to hide it – from himself and the world – the more visible it became. Every time Oldham saw him these days, he was somehow diminished, less the man he'd once known. He had not looked well at all last night at the officers' club; that in itself was not encouraging. Thinking about it, Lowry had not mentioned his wife or son once these last months and Oldham did not feel it his place to ask.

Something fundamental was lost in Lowry's life.

An orderly arrived with his tea.

Age, he thought, as he surveyed his veranda plants ravaged by the change in seasons. Underneath the eucalyptus, which drooped woefully in the gloom, he noted the roses were in desperate need of cutting back before the first frost.

PART 2

A Dream Fulfilled

CHAPTER 18

A cocktail of fine drizzle and mist flavoured the air. Moisture clung to the fabric of Gabriel's mac and hung densely over the river, cloaking Rowhedge, her own village, on the opposite bank.

A body had been found in the mud in Wivenhoe.

Gabriel was one of the first on the scene. A jogger on the esplanade, where she now stood, had been attracted by the number of gulls fussing over a mound that had been revealed on shore by the outgoing tide. Sutton, the scenes of crime doctor, lived nearby and was there already. Uniform were in the process of cordoning off the whole of the seafront. Gabriel greeted them across the wooden rails.

'I would say he drowned,' the doctor said, breathless from the plod across the mud.

Gabriel ducked between the rails and followed him, her steps sticking to the shingle. The shoreline beyond was an innocent canvas – a smooth, lacquered brown belying the viscous matter beneath. A single misjudged footstep and her shoe would easily be lost to the mud. Sutton's legs were sludge grey up to the knees.

The corpse lay in a star shape, as though the man had been for a swim and lay there exhausted, catching his breath. Though of course he'd not been for a swim. He was fully clothed, his green combat jacket shiny in the weak November light.

'He has a mark on the back of his head, at the base of the cranium, and a nick above his eye.'

'A cut?' At the mention of a facial injury, Gabriel lost all concern for the mud and hurried closer. Was it the man she saw punched on Tuesday? She looked towards Rowhedge. The mist had started to lift and she could see the faint outline of boats against the quay. She was aware of her heart thumping away.

'Oh, look lively. Here's himself.' Sutton squinted up towards the sea wall and the silhouette of Lowry. The inspector's arrival made Gabriel nervous in a way she couldn't pinpoint. 'Great,' she said, and slowly made her way back.

The Hippodrome Theatre, Colchester High Street

'A black Fiesta XR2, you say.'

Howard Osgood took a deep, patient breath and repeated the description of the vehicle into the telephone. Was it him or was there a funny smell in here? The spacious attic room was poorly lit, God knows what lurked in the darker recesses. He wished to convert the attic into something more businesslike, but he'd need more light than the solitary bulb dangling in the middle. At present all that was up here was a cheap desk, a plastic chair and a phone that had only been connected yesterday. His head throbbed. That *smell*. Maybe his olfactory senses had been affected by the concussion? You read about such things . . .

'Young lads – teenagers, early twenties,' he continued. 'I only clocked one of them – ginger with sticky-out ears. Not sure whether he was the driver, but he's the one that nutted Hughes-Roper.'

'Hmm . . . it ain't going to be easy.'

'C'mon, Tony; I'll make it worth your while.'

'I'm not being funny, Howard, but do you know how many of those things roll off the line at Dagenham? This is Essex. Did you clock the plate?'

'I think it's W or X.'

'XR2 models don't come earlier than X.'

'Are you splitting hairs?'

'No, I'm trying to help you find your car,' Pond said simply. 'I'll ask around.'

'Cheers, mate.'

Howard pressed the cradle for the dial tone and tried Hughes-Roper's number from the business card lying on his Filofax. He wasn't answering. Although Howard was certain in his mind the hitmen were after Hughes-Roper, he still wanted to know who the hell they were. Osgood would have to pay him a visit. When Trev appeared . . . where was he?

Howard left the roof space and stepped out towards the upper balcony, where he paused, gazing at the auditorium below. Placing heavy hands on the gilded ledge, he leant forward and took in the enormity of the space; his space. Opened in 1905 as a theatre, the interior itself was something to behold, a sumptuous Edwardian variety hall, seating capacity of fourteen hundred, with ornate gilt boxes either side of the proscenium. The ceiling stood at an impressive height, crafted (according to the auctioneer) in ornate rococo-style to resemble the inside of a shell. Two curved balconies swept elegantly beneath it. The stage itself was thirty-six feet deep, sizeable for its day, and above it, like an enormous crest, was a striking cartouche, also a convex the shape of a shell, reaching the ceiling, where two reclining muses presided over it all.

From the twenties, the Grand Theatre, as it was then known, had operated as a cinema. It was in that incarnation when Howard made his first visit, in March of 1935 for his tenth birthday, to see *Mutiny on the Bounty* with Charles Laughton and Clark Gable. He had been enraptured by the magic of the place even then. The splendour of the theatre felt like a palace to young Howard and from then on in, he went whenever he could, seeing everything from Laurel and Hardy films to *Snow White and the Seven Dwarfs* with his kid sister, a few years later. He continued going well into adulthood, through to his early thirties when he fancied himself as a bit of a spiv, courting girls under the auspices of screen idols like Elvis and James Dean.

The ownership of the building changed hands numerous times over the years, and along the way it was renamed the

Hippodrome. Eventually it was acquired by Rank, who converted the venue to a Top Rank bingo parlour in the sixties. And then too, Osgood was still a devout regular, seated under the muses' gaze as he always had been, but this time with his mother. The bingo offered entertainment of a different kind, with the likes of Jocky Wilson and Barbara Windsor treading the boards. Now bingo's number was up and so the building was again to reinvent itself. Who better to do it than him: Howard Osgood. Howard, the building's lifelong patron and devotee. Howard, whose one sincere ambition was to own a building of great prominence in the centre of the only place he had ever called home.

Howard had bided his time. He was canny like that. First a retail operation tried, failed and chucked it in, leaving the building empty for months. Nobody knew what to do with it . . . But Howard did. Its next stage in life was about to begin. The fresh smell of emulsion rose to greet him. There was no mistaking the odour of paint, even with the pong from the attic still lingering in his nostrils.

A creak on the floor behind him indicated he was not alone. He turned expecting to see Trev, but instead one of the decorators with a question about positioning scaffolding in front of the stage.

'Have you noticed a funny smell anywhere?' said Howard.

The young man shook his head.

'There's a funny smell upstairs. At first I thought it was me hooter playing tricks on me, but now I think there's definitely an 'orrible pong. Tell Trevor to check it out when he shows up.' He'd had Rentokil in immediately after the purchase. 'Decomposing rodents,' he muttered.

Trevor, he learnt, was out to fetch some cleaning materials so maybe he'd noticed it too. What with it all, Howard now had a powerful headache. He left to go home, thought he might take an afternoon nap. Yesterday's drama had drained him, and he wasn't able to bounce back as quickly as he once could. The doctor had said there was nothing wrong with stealing forty winks at his age, so hell, that's what he'd do.

CHAPTER 19

'Is it him, the man you saw knocked into the river at Rowhedge?' Lowry's attention on Gabriel was intense. She didn't like it. They were in the morgue with Robinson.

'Don't pressure me like this.'

She looked the corpse up and down again where it lay on the gurney, fully clothed as found. The mud had been wiped from his face. At first she had been so sure. It was the green fighting or bomber jacket that did it and he looked – didn't he? – like the same build and rough age. But when she had said this to Lowry, he dismissed it out of hand. The jackets were ten a penny round here. Every Mod, skinhead or scooter boy wore one exactly the same. He had given her reason to doubt herself – and so, she did.

If it *was* the same man, then they would immediately turn to Howard Osgood for answers. If it wasn't, the road ahead was far from clear-cut.

'I don't know,' Jane said, 'his back was towards me – I didn't get a look at his face.'

'But when he resurfaced in the river, you saw him then?'

'Not really, sir. My attention was more on Osgood.'

Lowry shrugged, annoyed, and looked to the corpse expectantly, as if it might open its mouth and introduce itself. Not that the name was a mystery. They identified him from a soggy dole book in his jeans' back pocket. Colin Cooper.

Robinson stood to one side and maintained a stoic silence, arms folded patiently across his white tunic. The man, Colin Cooper, had drowned. There was a mark the size of a ten–pence piece at the nape of his neck – an unusual location to be sure, but the feature that *really* held their attention was a graze, and that's all it was, above the left eye. That was enough to go on, at least for preliminary questioning.

'Okay. Don't worry, we've got enough for now,' Lowry said, putting her mind at rest. He placed his hand on the dead man's Doc Marten boot. 'This mud here is surface mud, not absorbed into the fabric, suggesting to me that in the moments before his death he wasn't on the waterfront plodding about.' He moved round the table to where the man's drainpipe jeans overhung his DMs. He carefully rolled back one leg, revealing red laces and a good inch or two of clean black leather.

Lowry sighed. 'Nobody is accusing Howard Osgood of murder. If he knows this man, it's a start, that's all.'

'I think – I thought – I was sure it was him, until you started grilling me,' said Gabriel.

'Oh, so it's my fault,' he said, so plainly and without accusation that it inflamed her.

'It *is* him,' she said decisively, trying to suppress her rising colour, 'I'm positive.'

Lowry looked up from the dead man's feet to face her eye to eye. 'Dr Robinson,' he said, still looking at Jane, 'may we please use your telephone.'

Osgood's headache had eased with the windows wound down on his drive home, and after a fifteen-minute doze and a cup of tea he was refreshed. Apart from his boat, his main loves were his garden and plants. Now he stood in his greenhouse with a mister in one hand, thinking it time to take the geraniums out and wrap them in paper over winter. The week was developing into a real stinker and as such he'd not been able to rest, but he did feel better by virtue of being back home. When situations demanded calm, rational thought, the only place available was often here. The boat was all very good to clear the head, but when it came to complexities, Osgood believed a man should seek the sanctity of the hearth, its particular quiet and privacy, to remind him what was at stake before making any rash decisions.

What was at stake, in Howard Osgood's case, was a seven-bedroom pile with an ostentious standalone double garage on a rise overlooking the village of Peldon, on the edge of the marshes south of Colchester. And the heart of his home was, for Howard, found within the twelve-by-ten wooden-framed greenhouse, which afforded an extra degree of privacy, without fear of eavesdropping from the cleaner, wife or wife's friends. This was important: delicate matters were being discussed.

Trevor had turned up shortly after Osgood woke from his nap. Lean, in frayed jeans and grubby white tennis shoes, and now standing amid Howard's leafy greens. Ol' Trev could, at a push, be mistaken for a surly gardener. Their present business, however, was far from horticultural in substance or essence. Trevor was midway through a delicate disclosure he'd been unable to make earlier in the day: the smell in the attic did not belong to a decomposing rat. It was far worse. Trev had unearthed a tramp up there, dead, covered in vomit and God knows what. Not wishing to cause a fuss, he'd disposed of the body. 'Don't want the police sniffing round,' Trev said plainly.

'Police sniffing around? That's an understatement.' Howard rubbed a geranium leaf between thumb and forefinger and breathed in the scent. A strange peppery smell that soothed him and reminded him of his grandmother. 'I've had more interaction with the bleedin' police this week than I've had in the last ten years.'

'What's up?'

'Doesn't matter . . .' Howard didn't want to go into it. Trev knew he'd punched Colin but he'd not shared anything about the run-in with the female copper. It would only complicate matters. 'You know, the shooting in the high street,' Howard offered, 'and the plod banging on doors, is all. What did you do with the body?'

'Bins by the Stockwell Arms.'

West Stockwell Street, the road through the Dutch Quarter behind the theatre, running north down the hill.

'All right, good move. You sure there's no more, you know, nothing else in the building that needs clearing?'

Trev shook his head energetically.

'All right, these things happen.' Indeed they did, vagrants did expire in unwanted places. Usually in the winter though. This one had choked on his own vomit, a wino drinking meths. 'Good man.'

Trevor grinned and made to light a fag.

'Oi,' said Osgood, 'not in here. It'll mess with the photosynthesis.' Osgood put the mister down on a seed ledge next to a wicker box that contained string, spare secateurs and a snub-nosed Smith & Wesson. The telephone began to ring distantly. He had had an outside bell installed, that he switched on and off as his mood dictated. He could tolerate pretty much anyone, apart from his sister that is, who he could only take in small doses. Whingeing on about how he'd been mean to her baby boy. Jesus. Anyone would think Colin was still in nappies. He couldn't risk it, not now. Gill could field the call.

Right on cue, the upright figure of Mrs Osgood appeared through the huge variegated fuchsia, hands loosely clasped before an ample bosom. 'Darling, a business associate for you.'

She smiled sweetly at them both.

'Top Trev's tea up, there's a love.'

*

175

The unmistakable accent of Tony Pond reached Howard's ear.

'That Fiesta you were after.'

'Yeah?'

'I've found it. An '81 Supersport.'

'That was quick, where?'

'Rolled up on the forecourt.'

'Really?'

'Yeah, unbelievable, really, fella wanted to sell it. Sell it quick. Like seconds after you rang off, and there it is now.'

'Top. Did you get the geezer's address?'

'Sort of . . . he's going away.'

'C'mon, do you know where he's from or what? The day I've had, I am low on patience.'

'It's not that straightforward. Meet me at the Maypole. Howard, it's easier that way, if I explain in person.'

The white roof of a car pulling up on the ample driveway caught Howard's eye. Beneath it the unmistakable orange horizontal band of a police jam sandwich Cortina.

'Oh, fuck off.'

'That's a bit stiff, H, I'm only trying to do you a favour, explain the circumstances – I'll tell ya now, if you want—'

'Not you. Jesus. I'll call you back,' said Howard and slammed the phone down. 'Gill,' he hollered, 'dig out the blasted insurance papers for the motor.'

CHAPTER 20

Howard sat staring at the jaundiced walls, wondering when they'd last seen a lick of paint. The police interview room was cold; the groan of the pipes that came through the ceiling to the floor below indicated radiators existed elsewhere in the building. There was nothing to divert his attention. The frosted glass window was a dirty beige, crusted yellow in the corners, offering no glimpse of life beyond. Even the clock offered no relief, having stopped at precisely six. He wondered whether it was six in the morning or evening, or whether there was an ulterior purpose to the thing, some sinister policing tactic, dividing the face cleanly in two.

The door was flung open. The policeman with the Brylcreemed hair, Lowry, entered the room with the woman, Gabriel.

'Colin Cooper,' said Lowry. 'Name mean anything to you, Mr Osgood?'

Osgood leant forward a little, over the desk. He had been anticipating Gabriel, but not this geezer. 'Sure,' he replied. 'He's my nephew.'

Gabriel shifted on her feet, waited for more. Osgood remained calm, unperturbed and silent.

'Why d'you knock him into the Colne?' Lowry prompted.

'Bit of larking about, that's all.' From somewhere on his person Osgood pulled out a toothpick and started to probe a rear molar.

Gabriel stepped forward, pulled out a chair at the table and parked her long body down, sitting very upright.

'The thing is, Mr Osgood, Mr Cooper was looking very animated the other morning – talking loudly, gesticulating wildly – that's what drew my attention to you in the first place. Sounded like quite an argument to me.'

'Families have disagreements, darlin', even ones as perfect as yours, I bet.' He winked at her. 'Anyway, here it is, like you asked.' He flopped a wodge of papers on to the table, with the familiar green of a driving licence right on the top. He nudged it in her direction. 'So now we can all go about our own business, can't we.'

Gabriel couldn't understand how Osgood could be so calm. It was time to lay it on the line. Lowry, sensing her impatience, paused her with a hand on the shoulder.

'That business yesterday, which landed you in hospital,' Lowry asked, 'what was all that about?'

'Mistaken identity,' he replied matter-of-factly, removing the toothpick and pointing it towards the ceiling. 'It happens.'

'Oh, I see. And you're happy to let that go?'

'Yeah, yeah. Now then,' he shucked his jacket on, making ready to move, 'if you don't mind, I got shit to do.'

Lowry moved away and with an open palm left Gabriel the floor, satisfied with Osgood's answer on the assault.

'You think you're here to present your driving licence, don't you?' said Gabriel.

'Not here for my health, am I.'

'No, Mr Osgood, you most certainly are not.' Something in her tone caught Osgood's attention. Sensing something was amiss, he looked from her to Lowry. She gave it a second to see if Lowry was going to speak, and when it became clear he wasn't, said, 'Colin Cooper was discovered dead this morning on the banks of the Colne.'

Outside the interview room Lowry spoke in hushed tones, not that Osgood would hear, barking down the phone on the other side of the door, as he was. Uniform were dealing with Osgood's sister – Cooper's mother – at the morgue. She had been asked to identify the body and was now evidently on the phone with her brother, each sibling throwing accusations at the other by the sounds of it.

'He's either very clever and ultra-cool, or—'

'Innocent?' said Gabriel.

'Exactly,' said Lowry. 'To come in without making a fuss.'

'What do you make of him?'

Lowry was unsure. The fact that Osgood had taken a beating,

the day before a man that he had recently assaulted wound up dead, was a big coincidence.

'Something seems not quite right but then again, it's all out in the open. Osgood'd have to be dumb to brazenly kill a man – let alone his own nephew – after a police officer witnessed him knock that very man into the drink just days before.'

'And?' Gabriel said defensively; she was convinced Osgood was a lard head.

'Unless it's a double bluff?' Lowry looked at her. 'And you are his cover – the fracas on the waterfront staged for you specifically to see?' This idea visibly appalled her. 'Okay, forget that for now. Examine the death in isolation, until we have a clearer idea of the relationship between uncle and nephew. Osgood said that Cooper did the odd job for him; find out what exactly that entailed. We need background, and we need a full picture of Cooper's movements yesterday.'

Gabriel nodded. 'Right, let's get back in there,' and opened the door.

Osgood had calmed down. He put his anger on the phone to his sister, Sally Cooper, down to shock.

'He was a useless twat. My sister wanted me to keep him off the streets. All that just now on the blower was her blaming me for not looking out for him.'

'So how *did* you keep him off the streets?'

For the first time Osgood seemed vaguely uncomfortable,

as if the weight of his situation – in the police station, being questioned about a dead man – was slowly dawning on him.

'Deliveries, mainly.'

'You're into property; what was he likely to be delivering?' Gabriel asked.

'Bits and bobs.'

'Come on, what? Be precise,' Lowry said.

'I have a number of establishments that need supplies.'

'Yes?'

'Couple of wine bars, and three pubs. Dovercourt out near Harwich.'

'And they need supplies.'

'What I said.'

'And what was Colin's last errand for you?'

'He'd done nothing since last Friday. I'd fired him.'

'So the incident on the boat was more than a family dispute.'

'I'd fired him before that, just to bring him into line, you know? He gets too big for his boots – he was angling to run a bar.'

'And you said no?'

'You kidding? He couldn't run a bath. I told you, he was completely useless. The proof of which is he could never get a job—'

'What did he get up to when he wasn't working for you? In his free time – who'd he hang out with?'

'Socially? How the hell do I know, I'm not his keeper.'

'Okay, let's take a step back. The incident at Rowhedge, you say it was a disagreement. Who else was there that morning?'

'Kevin who pilots the boat, and the missus below deck.'

'The four of you were off for a little jaunt?'

'Not Colin. He lives in Rowhedge, see, and I leave the motor at his as the boat is berthed there. He was supposed to run over to Long Melford and fetch me a rug . . .'

'Mr Osgood,' Lowry interrupted, 'I don't need to tell you that your close relationship with Cooper, and the timing of the incidents on the boat and Copford Green, place you under the spotlight.'

Osgood started to protest.

'Stop,' Lowry said flatly. 'Colin Cooper was pulled out of the very river you were seen to knock him into – I'd be foolish to overlook that, you'd have to agree?'

'Did I do a runner when your boys in blue turned up? No, I didn't.'

'All right, let's start from the beginning.' Lowry offered him a cigarette, which he declined. 'And for convenience sake, let's start with the fracas on the boat, happy with that?'

After three hours of questioning, Howard Osgood was released without charge.

Lowry had Howard Osgood's week mapped out and a broad understanding of the man's business interests, which were extensive and impressive. Osgood simply could not have got where he had today without keeping his nose clean. If there was any dirty work to be done – and there was always dirty work to be done in property at this level – it was carried out at an untraceable remove. This would not, he thought, stretch to the murder of a family member, without extraordinarily good reason. And even then, he would make the evidence disappear – properly disappear. Not wash up on the banks off the Colne.

Gabriel had sat in throughout the questioning, barely uttering a word.

'Osgood may be primeval on women's rights, but given his empire, he is not stupid: I think if he was going to personally take charge of doing Colin in, he'd dump him in the North Sea with weights on or have him wind up in concrete supporting the M25.'

From what little Lowry could make of Cooper, he did not strike him as possessing the guile to wind up a man like Osgood to such an extent that he'd end up dead. No, Osgood had been cooperative, and apart from the altercation by the river, there was nothing to suggest he was involved in the death of his nephew.

'Very well,' Gabriel said, unimpressed, 'Sally Cooper is currently at the morgue. We should talk to her while she's there.'

'Good.' Lowry tried to elicit a smile, but none was forthcoming.

CHAPTER 21

Sally Cooper was a fraction of her brother's size but had a hard edge to her features that identified her with Howard. She was ageless, in that way people over thirty appeared to a twenty-three-year-old such as Gabriel. She could be forty-five, she could be fifty.

'Do you know where your son was yesterday?' Gabriel asked in a low voice.

'No, no, I don't – he'd had a spat with Howard, God knows what he does when he's not running errands for him. All he's good for.'

'Deliveries and so forth?'

'Yes, he'd not much going for him. Learning difficulties; scraped a CSE Grade 2 in metalwork, or was it woodwork . . .'

'So you don't know how he spent the day?'

'I told you, I've no idea, really, no idea . . .'

Gabriel let the words hang there. It was best to give the woman space and time; her son was just beyond the curtain. Lowry told her these moments, when kin were in shock and not fully aware of what they were saying, were crucial for police inquiries. But she was not Lowry and thought it heartless to press a bereaved mother in a morgue. Fortunately, Lowry was elsewhere in the building browbeating Dr Robinson over something or other.

'Has he ever been in any kind of trouble before, Mrs Cooper?'

'He's done plenty of silly things, but nobody ever got hurt. He's daft but he's law-abiding, I'll have you know.'

'If Colin *was* mixed up with bad company, it might help us to know who.'

'Two years back, summer of 1981, he was running about with a bad lot, nothing nasty ... There was this time him and his mate frightened a family in a restaurant in town.' She stopped to take a deep intake of breath. 'A black family. He was scared of being in trouble with the police, when he'd not done nuthin' ... not really. Howard had to hide him away in Harwich, stop him freaking out.'

'Frightening a family?'

'They reported it as an assault; it was all kicking off in Brixton at the time and people were on edge. But I say it was just pranks and what have you. Pullin' faces in the window at the mother, as best I can make out,' she said evenly. 'Seems excessive, I know, moving him and what have you. Anyhow, Howard never wanted the boy to come to any harm, even if he did think him a bit simple.'

'Talking of your brother. Colin was seen arguing on Mr Osgood's boat, Tuesday morning at Rowhedge ... and you mentioned the – spat, did you call it?' Gabriel couldn't bring herself to say Howard knocked Colin in the water; it wasn't appropriate, given where he'd been found.

'Howard has a berth there.' Then, inclining her head towards the curtain, she muttered abstractedly, 'I don't know what my Colin'd be doing by the water. He can't swim.'

'Can't swim?' Gabriel echoed. Sally Cooper nodded.

Did Osgood know this, she wondered. It was not Osgood's intelligence she questioned – it was his temperament. If he knocked Colin Cooper into the river once, what's to say he might not lash out on open water, where maybe it's not possible to haul a man in? Where a drowning man could be swept away in the undertow?

Rowhedge

Kenton used the keys found in Cooper's jeans pocket with the mother's approval to unlock the flat. The place was strikingly similar to his own: a two-bed lad's pad, though Kenton's lacked the view of the Colne, of course. In fact, this place was definitely a cut above his fleapit in New Town. There was even a Star Wars poster (Cooper favouring Harrison Ford over Carrie Fisher). A twinge of jealousy made him itch.

He picked up the envelopes lying on the floor, mainly bills – in Osgood's name, which made him feel better – and walked through to the open-plan kitchen. There were plates stacked in the sink and a cassette radio on the worktop. He pressed play and thought he heard Madness as he inspected the fridge to find two-litre bottles of cider, a single can of Special Brew (already open and half consumed), some mouldy mild cheddar and half a pint of milk. On a cheap Formica table lay local papers open at the property pages and an ashtray.

'Thinking of moving,' Kenton muttered to himself, but a closer look suggested it was industrial land the boy was perusing, not residential. The master bedroom had a Sam Fox poster on one wall, various mulleted footballers on another, and – most unexpectedly – a huge swastika flag draped above a mirror. In one corner rested a baseball bat.

The overall impression of the inhabitant was of a young man with little interest in anything other than alcohol, ultra-violence, football and Page 3.

Outside through the fine drizzle, a goldish Ford Cortina sat alone by the quay, a large gull standing proud on the vinyl roof. He weighed Cooper's keys in his hands then strolled over and opened the car. The inside was rank with stale cigarette smoke. He nosed around briefly, finding nothing, and locked the car with a sense the vehicle had not been used in a while, though there was nothing to substantiate this more than the unpleasant odour. He strolled on to the quay. It had started to rain, dimpling the brown water slipping out into the estuary. Had Colin Cooper departed from here to meet his watery grave?

It was gone six as rain lashed the large black windowpanes of CID with such violence that heads turned, thinking perhaps the glass would give in. If they ever did move, Lowry would not miss the old sash windows. However elegant they may appear by day, in practice they were cold to the touch six months of the year, and so draughty that the scant heat generated from the ancient radiator beneath the sill slipped effortlessly out into the Colchester air.

The squall passed, the noise subsided and the windows let out a rattle, as though seized by a shudder of relief.

'Let's put Osgood's temperament to one side for a moment. The deckhand was there in that instance,' Lowry said, placing a hand on the radiator to see if it was in fact on. 'The assault the mother referred to, from 1981 – that needs digging into. His boots were done up with red laces, after all.' Hand warming, Lowry watched Gabriel for a reaction. There was definitely an edge to her; something was going on somewhere.

'A skinhead thing?'

'Red laces in DM boots are an affiliation or affection for the National Front or British Movement . . .' He waited for it to sink in.

'Fascists?'

'Racists: his mother told you about an assault on a family on North Hill a year after the Brixton riots. We need to wade through all the assault files since July 1981 and pull out anything race-related.'

In the meantime Lowry would deal with the local press on Cooper. At this stage he would be deliberately vague; a local man had washed up on the banks of the Colne and the police were investigating, no indication as to cause of death.

One benefit of Sparks being out of the picture was that Lowry had time to think. The chief would have insisted on keeping Osgood in, possibly indefinitely. Merrydown was at a remove; she had her own show to run and so didn't bother intervening. There was time.

'Hello!' Kenton bounded in.

'Unearth anything at Cooper's flat?'

Kenton described the swastika flag in the bedroom. Evidently Cooper did not keep his sentiments in the closet. This wasn't unusual in itself; many angry young men round here had a thirst for Third Reich paraphernalia, without having the first clue as to the ideology it represented. It did confirm his suspicions, though.

'Anything else?'

'Unpaid bills in Osgood's name,' Kenton said.

'That's to be expected. Osgood has a portfolio from flats in Wivenhoe, wine bars in Suffolk, and listed buildings in Colchester, and now he owns the Hippodrome, which he's turning into a nightclub.'

'The chief signed that off himself?' Gabriel said.

'Eventually it landed on his desk, after passing through various committees and meeting council approval. The building had been empty for ages. Initially, town hall couldn't quite get their heads round the idea of a nightclub in the middle of the high street, not when councilmen's wives had been up there for bingo and a singalong with the cast of *Hi-de-Hi!* only the Christmas before. But after that department store failed and went bust, they realised it was either the nightclub or the prospect of tripping over winos in the doorway of a derelict building after one of their gala fundraisers.' Lowry smiled. 'Osgood has a good business instinct, and over the last twenty years has amassed a sizeable property portfolio. Even so, this latest application was scrutinised to the nth degree. All above board – he would have to be respectable.'

'Meanwhile Colin Cooper is a nobody, and a family nobody at that,' Gabriel said. 'Even his mother thinks him a lost cause and has him on a tight leash, prone to taking a thump every now and then from his uncle. Maybe he was even becoming a liability, his association to extremists?'

This had occurred to Lowry. 'It's possible. An embarrassment and threat to his uncle's position. But again, I think he'd have been more creative, more tidy, in disposing of the body.'

Barnes arrived carrying a cardboard box. He dumped it on the desk. 'This should be the whole of 1981, though not necessarily chronologically, I'm afraid.'

'We're going back two years? I wasn't even here then,' Kenton said, regarding the box distastefully. Queen Street's paperwork was kept in the basement for storage, in the further-most corner beyond the cells. The police keenly denied any suggestion that there was severe damp down there, but every time records were retrieved, the telltale signs were evident. Ignoring the mildew on the uppermost sheets, Lowry turned them face down and lit a cigarette to blanket the smell. If they ever moved out, the disgrace of their records would be laid bare.

'All the more reason you'll find it interesting then, what with your history degree,' Lowry said, dividing the pile into three and bringing Kenton up to speed on the assault on North Hill.

'There's been no trouble of that kind since I've been here,' Kenton continued, 'and stop me if I'm being naive, but race doesn't strike me as such an issue here in Colchester? There's fewer black faces here than in Surrey, which is saying something.'

'It's a lead is all I am saying,' Lowry conceded. 'We know basically nothing about Cooper. We need to find out who he associated with aside from his uncle Osgood – and what he got up to with them.'

Gabriel remained silent throughout this exchange. Osgood's story about being in Brightlingsea overnight the day before the death checked out: he was spotted in the pub and the harbourmaster confirmed him docking that evening. But as far as Gabriel was concerned, the time of death would still allow for Osgood to have killed Colin – intentionally or otherwise. The whole case was straightforward to her. She had witnessed Howard Osgood lash out in violence once and she *knew* an angry man when she saw one. There was no question in her mind that Osgood, if provoked, could easily be capable of the crime. Not that she would raise it again without solid proof.

She gave Lowry a sideways glance, as he expertly thumbed through arrest sheets; each time she'd mentioned her suspicion, he had countered with pointless questions. *How did he hit him?* What difference did that make? Lowry was so attuned to violence, his boxer's mindset so analytical, he couldn't see it for what it was.

Nevertheless, she had a plan.

'Daniel,' she said curtly, 'how about a drink after work?'

Kenton stopped mid-track in his appraisal of the racism in East Anglia.

'Err, yes, sure . . .' He cleared his throat. 'Let's crack on with these first.'

Gabriel and Kenton each took a pile of paper and sat down to the task at hand. As they went about their reading, it gradually dawned on them that they were not alone. Sergeant Barnes had remained in the background after dropping off the musty reports. Queen Street's dependable Uniform who ran the beat bobbies had something on his mind.

'How goes it, sergeant?' said Lowry.

'Inspector, I'm asking after how the super is faring.'

Barnes and Sparks had started their police careers together but their paths had divided when Sparks made the jump to CID.

'He'll weather the storm. He's made of solid stuff – you know that.'

'Mrs Sparks and the little 'un?'

'I'm sorry to report the child was lost; Mrs Sparks suffered a miscarriage brought on by her fall,' said Lowry, swallowing some rising emotion, 'but she herself will mend.'

'Aye.' The sergeant shook his head solemnly. 'But yes, Mrs Sparks. She's young enough.'

They took a second, silently acknowledging the sizeable gap in years between the chief and his wife.

'Exactly, and the chief has his mettle about him still.'

'I'll say.' The sergeant let this sink in. He didn't give much away.

Lowry didn't want them to dwell on the matter and said, 'What's the word on the street?'

'Nobody will miss Colin Cooper, that's for sure.'

Since nobody could challenge this last statement, the remark hung there. Lowry offered to buy Barnes a drink in the Social after work to ease the awkwardness that arose between men when personal feelings and professional relationships began to blur. Barnes gratefully accepted. Nevertheless, the mention of the chief's ordeal had cast a shadow over them all. With the exception of the faint rustle of dampish papers, the room lapsed into silence.

CHAPTER 22

Osgood sat in the recliner, the telephone cord trailing across his ample lap.

It would seem that Trevor had been watching the same local news report as he had – and that Colin's moronic face was just as recognisable on Trev's old black-and-white set as it had been on Osgood's spanking new eighteen-inch Ferguson.

'There's no trouble, boss?'

'Nah. Put the flat at Rowhedge up with the estate agents for letting, would you?'

'Righto. He won't be needing it now.' Trevor's voice relaxed. This straightforward instruction had the desired effect of restoring business as usual, on firm footing. Better to deal with it now than to let it lie empty. They discussed the rent – Cooper had it scot-free – and arranged to get the cleaners in.

'Do we need to let the Old Bill know?'

'They've had a dekko already and haven't said anything. But let his old dear have a butcher's first, eh.' He didn't want his sister bemoaning his emptying the place before she'd had a chance to claim some keepsake, some sentimental essence of Colin.

'If you say so, boss, though all that Nazi shit might upset her.'

'Not for us to hide what sort of son she had.'

There was nothing to debate there. Trev moved on to other matters, listing the materials they still needed for the Hippodrome. It occurred to Howard that Trevor was as untroubled by Colin's passing as he was. The lad was a useless lackey and had created more work for him than he'd saved. Maybe now at least Osgood'd get some dependable support so he could stop running around like a blue-arsed fly cleaning up the mess. Howard agreed to bung Trevor a few extra quid to help him run the odd errand – he didn't want new people – and knowing Trev, he'd pocket it all and graft the extra hours anyway.

He could smell his grub from the kitchen and was about to end their conversation when a report on drug abuse on the TV screen caught his eye.

''Ere, Trev, that vagrant you dumped. Nobody saw you, you're sure of that?'

'Yeah, I'm sure . . . why?'

'No reason,' Howard said. 'All right, catch you on the morrow.'

He hung up and continued to watch the news. The vagrant, probably a druggie, would be discovered any minute. Howard just had to hope there was no way the police could trace it back to the Hippodrome. Prior to Colin's death there would be no reason to suspect they would, but if the police took it upon themselves to snoop around, who knows what they might find. So far they believed him. They'd not asked to search his boat, yet; if they did, he'd be hard pushed to deny them access, given Colin had been pulled out of the river . . . and what if the police wanted to poke about the theatre? He better have a proper inspection himself tomorrow; if they got a sniff that there'd been junkies in the building and traced the dead one back there, he really would be in the shit. In truth, Howard had suffered a degree of surprise at the turn of events for Colin, and he'd completely forgotten about the tramp until he saw the drugs report on the news. Whatever else he was involved in, the news about Colin had come out of nowhere. He might not have given a fig about the boy, but he was nonetheless gobsmacked rolling up at Queen Street in good faith with his documentation to discover the lad was dead.

Why would anyone bump off Colin?

Did the police still see him, Howard, as a potential suspect? Nah, they'd let him go. The death, as reported on the evening news, was presented with the same lack of official concern as the druggie they will inevitably find by the bins in West Stockwell Street. Those who contribute nothing to society while alive can expect nothing back when they pass on.

The lounge door opened, as his wife brought his tea in on a tray.

The only mistake he might have consciously made was not divulging Hughes-Roper's name. The reason for this, maybe ill-advisedly, was that he wanted to keep the toff out of it as far as possible: in spite of himself, Howard was curious about the property out at Copford and, well, in a sneaky way he thought the assault may allow him some leverage over the posh boy. Once all this other stuff blew over, he'd see how far Hughes-Roper could be pushed. If he had the energy, that was . . .

He smiled wearily up at his wife as she handed him the tray. 'Cheers, love.'

As he tucked into his bangers and mash, he remembered his earlier conversation with the car dealer and cursed himself that he'd forgotten to call back, what with all that had happened . . . Why *was* Tony making a big deal of that motor, insisting they talk in person? What was going on there?

Lowry was scanning a charge sheet – an assault on an Asian corner shop in Greenstead from August '81 – when he was interrupted by a call from Oldham.

The captain had news: they had their man.

Lowry was not surprised. Once the military were convinced one of their own was responsible for a matter this serious, they had closed ranks and found answers. He replaced the receiver and relayed what he had heard while continuing to read the report on the arrest of one Nigel Foster.

'So, case closed, then? We don't even get to see him?' Kenton asked, disappointed.

'That's about the sum of it. Only a matter of time before they rooted him out, once the responsibility rested solely with them.'

'So what next?'

'Move on.'

Kenton got up and paced the room. He had taken Lowry's instructions to heart: as well as a tidy beard, he sported a boyish, short – very short – back and sides. 'Be fascinated to know, though, what was behind it.' Standing there, hands on hips, spectacles perched on his nose, he was every inch a school prefect.

'We may never know,' Gabriel said, eyes down as she continued to leaf through her pile. Jane Gabriel was not interested. Hardworking and diligent though she was, she did not seem to get emotionally attached to her cases: which was good and bad. Her detachment meant she could move on from one case to the next in a straightforward way. Equally her zeal for answers could make her unwilling to let things go. Somewhat contradictory, working with her took some getting used to.

Lowry watched Kenton challenge Gabriel's lack of curiosity. She would not rise to it. Lowry himself was curious but had not questioned Oldham about the possible owner of the seahorse earrings. The military police captain had been curt and officious. A matching earring was discovered among the effects of a Corporal Lawrence Drake, which was enough to make an arrest.

'What sort of woman would do that?' Kenton persisted.

'One with a surplus of jewellery, I'd imagine,' Gabriel said.

'No, I mean give two chaps the *same* keepsake.'

Lowry caught Kenton's furtive glances at Gabriel. Gabriel,

for her part, did not acknowledge the interest she'd aroused in Kenton but diligently continued working through her arrest sheets without raising her head.

'Let's take a break,' Lowry said, suddenly unable to concentrate himself.

'Wait,' Kenton said, abruptly. 'Did you say Cooper's mother mentioned an assault at a restaurant?'

'Yes,' Gabriel leant over, 'on North Hill.'

'Aha! The handwriting leaves a lot to be desired but still, we have some names and addresses here. Name of the lady that was assaulted. It seems the restaurant owner reported the incident.'

Gabriel moved her pile away. 'That's enough for now?' she said, seeking Lowry's approval.

'Sure. Call round in the morning.' Lowry rose to his feet. 'Until tomorrow then.'

Lowry had nothing to rush home to but had had enough himself for one day, so went off in search of the sergeant for that drink, as the other two fetched their coats.

CHAPTER 23

Oldham had intended to wait until much later, or even the small hours in the morning, before interrogating Drake. But frankly the whole business had put him in an ill temper and he was rather tired as a result. He hadn't the energy to wait.

'Right, what have you got to say for yourself?'

The soldiery were prone to clam up once incarcerated so the captain would rely on the persuasive power of his own intimidating personality to break the silence.

Drake grunted. He was an obstinate little tick, this one.

'Don't you grunt at me. You shot Lance Corporal Cousins in a duel in Colchester High Street.'

'Prove it.'

'I have no need to.'

'Eh?'

The earring alone was not proof, not in a fair world. Fortunately, there would be no cross-examination at this stage. Military justice was not civilian justice.

'No, you'll just stay here forever. No trial, no chance of getting out.'

'You can't do that.'

'Imagine, never to do the things you enjoy again.'

'He can't do that?' he beseeched Fairweather, who stood to one side as ever.

Fairweather's malevolent grin in response indicated that he most certainly could.

Police Social Club

Lowry's drink with Barnes had proved more sombre than he'd envisaged. The sergeant had got wind of the hunt for new premises and took that as a bad omen; any disturbance of the status quo worried long-serving staff. Talk of *the good old days* did not lift their spirits – Sparks was so much a part of the place, it only served to highlight his absence. The mood in the office had been down, nowhere more so than here in the social club down in the basement. The place was the heart of Queen Street and it was deserted. Sparks was the life force of the place and without him, the heart had ceased to beat. After a couple of pints, Lowry and Barnes slunk off into the wet night, the sergeant to his home in Abberton, and Lowry to the supermarket across the road from the station.

Thursday late night openings were a new occurrence, and now and then Lowry was struck by a whim to stock up before driving home out of town. He tugged a trolley loose and through the window caught the attention of the girl at the cigarette kiosk, who gave him a familiar smile as he trundled past towards the entrance. He would pick up a carton of Players on the way out. The supermarket itself was not so welcoming and somewhat tatty at the end of the day. The off-white lino floor was scored with trolley wheels spreading dirt from the wet street beyond the entrance. Brown sprayback on the untidy heap of crates in the fruit and veg section did little to encourage shoppers.

At this hour it was practically empty, bar a few teenage boys in dust coats wheeling great metal cages down the aisles, blissfully unaware the shop was still open for business as they set about shedding packing materials randomly across the floor. Lowry meandered through the shop, layering his trolley with tins of beans and cup-a-soups, three pork pies from the chilled deli counter. November had spun on its heels. A northerly wind was blowing in and the rain had switched from weirdly tropical to almost sleet in a matter of days. Not that his diet was affected; what he ate did not alter with the seasons – a pork pie was solid and dependable all year round, as was cheese on toast and beans. Alcohol routinely made up the bulk of his shopping bill. His trolley contained four bottles of sherry and a four-pack of Holsten. Half a dozen tins of Whiskas and he was done for another week.

In some ways living on his own was proving more agreeable than he thought. He and Jacqui had never really shared meals, and she had always been quick to criticise his eating habits. Now he had the freedom to eat what the hell he liked. He could leave a pork pie in the fridge without fear of being moaned at. Hell, he could have two. A small thing, but it was the little things that counted.

He wheeled the trolley across the road and round the back of the building to the car park, where he loaded the boot then lit up a cigarette. Only then did he notice the rain had stopped completely and the dark air of the car park was deathly still. He wondered how Gabriel and Kenton were getting on, and where they'd gone for a drink. As he climbed into the car, he remembered his commitment to Becky. A weekend away. It had totally slipped his mind. Why the hell had he just stocked up? He shrugged to himself. No matter – they'd eat out and it's not like any of this would go off.

7.15 p.m., Rowhedge

There it sat, Osgood's yacht, quietly innocuous under a fine mist, the varnished deck catching dully in the inky night. The tide was out and the boat sunk in the mud, the smell of which rose to greet them as they peered over the edge of the quay. It had quickly grown obvious to Kenton that Gabriel's asking him for a drink was a pretext to get him to accompany her to Rowhedge, where her intention was to search the boat and not go to the pub as he'd hoped.

'Shouldn't we wait until daylight?' Kenton remarked, noting the PRIVATE MOORING sign.

'Nonsense,' said Gabriel. 'But you can scoot off if you like.'

'No, no, I'm game.' But his attention was half on the warm

glow of the pub windows further along the riverfront. For all his bravado, he was still jittery at work and needed the reassurance of her company. Just to be with her was enough, although he'd rather the circumstances were different.

'Coming?' Gabriel coaxed, as she clambered down the ladder on to the boat.

He was surprised at her actions; Gabriel was often on the moral high ground herself. Kenton was of the opinion that they should not be trespassing on Osgood's property, when they'd only two hours previously let him go. Especially with moves afoot in Parliament to curb police powers, in the wake of Brixton. This bee in her bonnet about Osgood was leading her to stretch her boundaries in a way he'd not seen before.

'Right behind you,' he said, in almost a whisper, and cautiously stepped on the ladder that squeaked in acknowledgement of his weight.

Neither Kenton nor Gabriel knew their way round a boat. Both Sparks and Lowry were sailors. Lowry's father had forced him into it at an early age, but the experience had been unpleasant and had put him off. Chief Sparks had met Mrs Sparks at Cowes . . . Kenton was a rower back in his uni days, but that was then and counted for nothing. Kenton felt only mounting unease about what they were doing.

'Right down here, I think.' He heard Gabriel click open the latch to below deck, dashing his hope that it was locked.

He immediately banged his head on the galley.

'Careful,' she said, flashing the torch beam across an interior of honeyed wood.

He moved forward and knocked his knee on a low table. 'What exactly is it we're expecting to find?' he grumbled. A second later he was blinded by the torch beam.

'If you have a problem with being here, you can always go home,' she said, annoyed. 'Behind you, to the side of the steps – look in there.'

He turned around, flicked his own torch to life and started ferreting around the concealed spaces at the back of the boat. This area was used for storage, ropes, life jackets, gloves and . . . 'Hello, what's this?'

'What?'

'A hammer.'

'Give me that.'

He hesitated.

'It's all right,' she reached past him, 'I've gloves on.'

Holding the small, almost toy-sized hammer under her narrow beam, she felt a thrill of electricity pass through her. She started to speak, then stopped herself. The word *blood* was on her lips. 'Interesting,' she said, leaning past Kenton to place the item back, 'now let's go.'

She had willed herself to exercise caution. Firstly, she was not sure of her legal grounds; and secondly, inexplicitly, she wanted to keep her discovery to herself.

CHAPTER 24

Kenton flipped down the sun visor. The morning was fresh, the sky a sharp contrast of clear blue against towering grey cumulus nimbus moving in from the west. With a piece of hash under his tongue, he was in a mellow mood as he followed the narrow winding road through green and surprisingly hilly countryside in the direction of Bures, north-west of Colchester.

The previous evening had ended with frank and abrupt disappointment. Having initially seemed thrilled by his discovery of what he had concluded was a fairly insignificant hammer, Jane had announced that she was heading straight home to practise the piano. He had no idea she could play, let alone owned an instrument in her Rowhedge house.

Plunged into despair, he had retreated solo to the Bugle, and without pause, sunk into the solace of four pints followed by a saveloy and chips from the takeaway on his way home. Leaving half the food, and troubled by the realisation that he did not know Jane Gabriel whatsoever, he lit a joint and watched some impenetrable art-house film on Channel Four.

A second joint did nothing to help him make sense of things – not the film nor the woman – and he soon fell asleep on the lounge floor. Waking at four from the cold, he made for his bed and lay there replaying the evening's events. Crashing around Howard Osgood's boat with Jane, vainly searching for signs that she benefitted from – or frankly cared for – his presence. He finally nodded off again at dawn. Awaking an hour later in a cold sweat, with anxiety coursing through his system, he broke off a piece of black Leb to calm down enough to get up, get showered, get dressed and get on the road.

Bures presented itself as he rounded the prow of a hill, down below on to the Stour. He was unfamiliar with this part of rural north Essex but he seemed to have navigated well enough. The town was unusual in that it was bisected by the river, so that one half was in Essex and the other in Suffolk.

Barnes had advised him the tiny hamlet he wanted was past Bures: tucked away beyond the steeper banks of Colne valley along the Stour River. The sergeant had said one could be forgiven for thinking it a forgotten part of Suffolk, with its handful of inhabitants gravitating to the nearby town of Sudbury, rather than Colchester, for anything much beyond buying a loaf of bread – such as banking a cheque or filing for divorce. In that way, it was a place one could literally describe as being 'neither here nor there'. Bordering both Essex and Suffolk, belonging to neither.

He glanced at the notebook on the passenger seat.

Alphamstone. Tossing the notebook in the Capri's footwell, he opened the OS map.

He bore left up a steep incline lined with dense trees, leaves heavy with rainfall. The muddy road twisted and turned until eventually he emerged on to the flat green of the Stour valley. On one side he passed a round-towered church, then a phone box, indicating life though he had not seen a soul. Then nothing. Travelling straight now, he knew he was lost. To his right were lush pastures and presumably, out of sight somewhere, the river; to his left the downs rose up impressively beyond the hedgerow. Checking his rear view mirror, he saw dense woodlands. Where was this damn village? He then spotted a pub coming up on the left, set back from the road. Had he missed a sign hidden in the hawthorn? Maybe he should stop and ask at the pub. Refocusing his attention, he saw something in the middle of the road dead ahead. He braked, suddenly skidding off the road into the grass to the right. Head down, he cursed. He shouldn't have taken the dope. Catching his breath, he turned to see what, if anything, he'd missed, and couldn't help but laugh: there in the road, stretching majestically erect, stood a swan. He laughed again louder, in relief. Not only had he not been hallucinating, he had also managed not to hit the bird. Turning the key in the ignition, he noticed his bonnet was pointing towards a glade with a boating platform. In his rear-view mirror was a woman crossing the road from the pub. He wound down the window and put the car into reverse to meet her.

'Hello. You all right?' she called out. 'Damned nuisance, them swans. Reckon they own the place.'

'Yeah, I'm fine. Thanks, though. Actually I'm looking for Alphamstone?'

She shook her head and pointed down the road. 'Back there.'

Apparently he had overshot the turning some miles back. If he retraced his steps, he'd find Alphamstone up beyond the trees, hidden from sight in a leafy dell. He thanked the lady and got on his way.

Apart from a church and red brick village hall, most of the houses were screened from view by foliage of one kind or another. It took him a further fifteen minutes of trial and error to find the house he wanted behind holly trees and thick laurel bushes. He got out of the car just as it started to rain again, heavily, stinging the bonnet of the Capri with such force as to create a mist. He quickly made his way up the path in the deluge as it tore through vegetation, bringing it wildly alive. As Kenton reached the front porch, he paused before reaching for the large door-knocker and thought: *if I didn't want to be disturbed by a living soul, this is exactly the spot I'd choose.*

'Dad, it's for you!'

It would not be for Gordon. No one called on him at home. He stayed in his study, thoughtfully tapping the airline schedule on the desk with the heavy shaft of his Montblanc. The estate agent had telephoned again, chasing for an answer. The client would gladly entertain Mr Topize's offer for Copford

Grange; could they talk? This persistence annoyed Gordon. So much so that he was beginning to go cold on the idea. His daughter stood in his doorway, both hands raised and touching the wooden beam above her, sullenly chewing gum, midriff exposed between her cropped top and skintight jeans; even he found her appearance confusing.

'Why you dress like that when it freezin' col' out there, girl,' Topize said irritably. 'And rainin' like a goddamn monsoon.' With make-up on, she looked more and more like the *Vogue* girl in the Roxy video. Even her name sounded similar. She had darker skin, of course. Should he be thinking things like that? He felt uncomfortable.

'Wet man at the door, Daddy,' she said.

'What he want?'

'I didna ask, just opened the door.'

'I ain't expecting anyone, sugar,' he muttered, to himself it seemed, as she poked her tongue out, turned on a heel, performed a sassy back kick then walked off singing 'The First Cut is the Deepest', one of Silvia's old favourites.

Sighing, he left the airline schedules and checked himself in the mirror on his way to the front door. He never had visitors. Whoever it was would likely be in for a surprise when they saw a black face all the way out here.

They had been holed away up here for years. It was just dandy when it was the three of them and Saffron was still little, but now with her off up to all sorts about the county, it would not do. He needed to put provisions in place. Instead of taunting his enemies he should be forging relationships. Maybe it was time to let the proverbial drawbridge down and entertain a few . . .

'Dad*dy*!'

'I'm a comin'.'

But for now the fact remained: nobody visited him out here and Silvia was out at the salon.

Opening the front door, it seemed Topize was the more surprised of the two. There on his doorstep stood a fresh-faced white man with short back and sides, drenched through in a collar and a tie underneath a raincoat. Surprise was swiftly followed by irritation and he had trouble containing his anger; in fact, he could not do it.

'I've told you guys not to come round here no more, now beat it! I praise the Lord in my own sweet way – I ain't interested in your goddamn magazine and goddamn Bible classes.' He paused and took a breath in and out. 'Apologies for the blasphemy; just your crowd wind me up bad, man. I told the two women on Sunday to go on back to church; I can't for the life of me wonder how you got the time to come all the way out here to hassle the few . . .'

'Excuse me, Mr Topize? My name is Detective Daniel Kenton. I think you may have me confused with someone else?'

'Ha ha!' Gordon placed a hand high on the doorframe and let out an exaggerated laugh. 'I thought you were a Bible thumper! You know, a Joho – Jehovah's Witness. Once those guys find you, they never let go! Like missionaries in the

Amazon. My mistake.' He exhaled and took a moment to examine the young copper, unsure if he was any less invasive than the God squad. 'Christ, you police boys are looking goddamn clean-cut these days . . .'

'Mr Topize, I wonder if I can ask you about an incident that occurred in July 1981. There were disturbances, racially motivated disturbances, over in Colchester, and we have just discovered the body of one of the men involved – one of the offenders – dead on the banks of the Colne. Now, there's no need to be alarmed here, we are just looking to see if any witnesses can . . .'

'Racially motivated disturbances?'

'We have a record pertaining to you and your wife,' Kenton checked his notepad, 'Mrs Silvia Topize? You were assaulted by two skinheads while dining at the Castle Restaurant, correct? We have strong reason to believe that the dead man is one of the assailants from that night.'

Topize was bemused by this sudden jolt back to the summer of '81, remembered the incident. 'Through the window,' he said. 'That restaurant, up on North Hill, had these big, plate glass windows. Shut now.'

'That's the one,' Kenton nodded, 'large Edwardian bays, modernised like goldfish bowls.'

'Exactly. Me and my family are eating there that evening – the manager, he knows my wife and gives her a nice table right out front in the bay – when these bovver boys march up the hill, spy us sitting there and start giving us verbal – abusing Silvia worst of all.'

'Your wife?'

'She like you.' The young man didn't comprehend. '*White*.' Gordon said it with his teeth. 'Why she with a golliwog, all that; I don't need to spell it out.'

'No, no. I get it. Sorry,' Kenton consulted his notebook, 'it's not clear from this, to be honest. The complaint was actually made by the restaurant – the manager remembered your name, and said you might have got a look at them. We know the dead man was one of the two involved, as his mother told us he confessed the incident to her. Now, if you can see him here and his companion . . .'

'I saw them good, real close. But I turned the other cheek,' he said bravely, 'it's all there is to do.'

That was true at the time anyway – a fortnight later he had seen to it that the real aggressor of the two had received a little visit. Had his index finger removed. He'd not be making the V-sign ever again. It put the proper frighteners on the other kid too. He'd soon disappeared without trace.

'I have some mugshots. The police were not able to identify the two men at the time, but hopefully . . .'

'How many fingers did your dead man have?'

'Fff . . . ?'

Topize held up his hand and wriggled his fingers.

'The normal amount. I have these photos . . .'

'You best come in.' Topize bowed obsequiously, though he only moved back two paces. 'Please wipe your feet.'

He didn't particularly want a policeman inside the house, but the rain was blowing in on to the carpet.

Kenton kicked off his shoes and walked over to a glass telephone table in the hallway. 'May I?' he said.

Topize nodded and the detective went to lay out half a dozen black-and-white photos. The table was low, and the detective forced to stoop.

'All these dudes look the same, know what I mean? Baldie potato-head yobbos . . . hmm.' Topize bent closer, hands on hips, made a pretence of mulling over the six King Edwards before him. He had instantly recognised the two men responsible and was still debating whether to say anything. The policeman explained how they were tracing the last steps of the deceased, one Colin Cooper. Gordon quickly deduced he was the kid with all his digits intact. They were searching for any friends or acquaintances, the policeman continued, and given the records, Gordon'd understand why they were eager to locate Cooper's accomplice from that night.

Did Gordon want the man who killed this utter cretin caught? Not really. But on the other hand, it didn't harm to be seen to be helpful . . .

The detective sensed Topize's hesitation. 'The man in question will not know you identified him, if that has any bearing.'

'Well, I'd like to be of assistance . . . hmm . . . maybe, maybe. I think your man's this charmer here,' he said, and pointed to the man whose finger he'd had removed.

*

Kenton shuffled back to the car in a daze. At this point there was little he could do but accept he was mildly stoned. Between a near-miss with a rogue swan, the extraordinary incongruity of Topize in this quaint cottage and the fleeting young woman who answered the door, his senses were reeling.

'Far out, man,' he mumbled to himself as he opened the car door. Glancing back over his shoulder, he thought he saw a shadow at the first floor window. It occurred to him only then that he had not spoken to Mrs Topize. Although he had barely glimpsed the woman who opened the door, he was sure it wasn't the wife. Leaving the door to ease open on its hinges he was implanted with only the vision of her slender form disappearing inside the house. Not that it mattered, now he had all the necessary information from the husband. He climbed into the Capri. Smashing house, thatched cottage, hidden out here in these north Essex hills. He wondered what the fellow did for a living. 'Never find this place in the dark,' he concluded, sniffing.

His damp Burberry was emitting an unpleasant odour.

God knows what Jane would have made of all this. For some reason she was intoxicated with the hunt for Howard Osgood, and like a dog, she was insistent on piquing Lowry's interest with that blasted hammer. Kenton blinked, shook himself and tried to focus. He imagined their meeting back in Queen Street, the dull, irritated conversation that must have ensued. Far as he was concerned, they'd both missed out on the morning's adventure out here.

He did an enormous sneeze. Too much time in the rain. His head buzzed numb momentarily. He was so glad he'd taken the blow; the world was too dreary without it – added to which, the week, his first back, felt lengthy and was taking its toll. But for now he felt good: he had a buzz on, he had an ID on Nigel Foster, and now it was just a matter of finding him. Which he would, after a few quiet minutes watching the rain trickle, in a myriad of prisms, down the windscreen . . .

The police radio jolted him from his daydream, noisily beckoning him to Queen Street; something about a body in the Dutch Quarter.

CHAPTER 25

Lowry was surprised at Gabriel's action on many levels.

'So, you thought you'd just pop down to Osgood's boat on the way home?'

She stood before him, while he remained seated at his desk. Her elegant stature and height from this perspective seemed incompatible with the ramshackle surroundings.

'Daniel was with me.' Kenton was currently in West Stockwell Street attending to a dead vagrant.

'It was your idea?'

She nodded.

'Okay. And you're sure it was a hammer?' The article in question remained on the boat. At least she had the good sense not to remove it.

'I know what a hammer looks like, Nick – sir. Not a big one ... the diameter around the size of a ten-pence piece. There was something on it ... a substance ...'

'Get forensics in – get them to confirm it's a possible weapon. What material was the boat made of?'

She poked her bottom lip out in ignorance.

'Is it old or new – the galley made of wood or fibreglass?'
'Wood.'

Lowry reckoned they'd come across a caulking hammer, used for repairing wooden boats, sealing leaks between planking. As a lad, his father had him forever plugging that old winkle brig he kept at Geedon Creek on the Fingringhoe marshes.

'Okay, let's look into it, get forensics on it without making a fuss. And well done, but next time run it by me first,' he said. She'd used initiative but he didn't wish to say that; whenever he commended anyone it came across as patronising. 'Meanwhile, check the diameter of the bruise at the back of Cooper's head with Robinson. This isn't strictly proper, but given the proximity, we can get away with it.'

She waited expectantly. Realising there was to be no more said, she nodded and left the room. He didn't want to flatter her at this stage; he just didn't have Osgood down as the culprit. If the hammer size *did* match the wound, he would give it further thought. Open-minded without the presence of evidence as always.

He reached to pull at the desk drawer. The wood was old, like the windows, and reluctant to give. His coffee mug jolted on the desk. He cursed quietly, not that there was anyone to hear. He was after a comb. If he had an affectation, or habit, it was his Brylcreemed hair. Always liked it slick and smooth like his narrow black ties, of which he owned five identical.

Sometimes, crimes were plain as day and solving them required little in the form of detective work. The old maxims always contained an inkling of truth: the killer is likely known to the victim. Statistics showed, etc. Still, he couldn't quite see Osgood in the role. He needed to be able to envision that first incident; the manner in which the punch was thrown would speak for itself. He didn't have Howard as an explosive sort of man. Gabriel's account was neither convincing nor, frustratingly, definitive. She just couldn't tell him precisely how the assault proceeded. Had Osgood a dark side Lowry had not seen? When pushed on the subject, Gabriel grew agitated.

'We're not all boxers, sir.'

She was missing the point, but never mind. Violence was violence to her, and fair enough. They might have enough for a case.

Time and crime move on; another dead body in the town centre. DC Kenton had been dispatched. Lowry was still manning the fort in lieu of the chief. The week grew ever more complicated, and the death of the soldier just days earlier seemed but a distant memory.

Lowry was not given to self-examination but he had a creeping sensation that he was not as involved as he ought to be in the death of Colin Cooper. Likewise, he'd ceded the duel to the hands of the military without raising any real objection. Over the last weeks, any sense of the importance of what he was doing here at CID had, it seemed, dwindled. Did it – did *he* – really matter, in the grand scheme of things? The decision to separate from Jacqui permanently had been on his mind for some time. He'd not seen his son since the school holidays had ended. Without them in the background, his sense of purpose had vanished. He had always told himself they gave his life some meaning, but didn't expect it to be so fundamentally *true*. Valium at lunchtime, for instance. He'd never have done it before, even if he'd been up the entire night. Why? A muted existence, where too much thought was and could be avoided. He was in danger of becoming a cliché. He lit up another Players and chose not to dwell on it.

His thoughts turned to Sparks. There was a man who could never be labelled a cliché in his day. The CS had gotten wind of the two deaths and had requested they meet. Not, surprisingly, at his Lexden townhouse, but at the West Mersea yacht club. Lowry reached for his coat and, as if on cue, the rain started to patter against the windowpane.

A dead vagrant slumped against a steel bin in the rear courtyard of a Tudor pub. Kenton was well and truly back in the thick of it. He winced and turned away while Dr Sutton busied himself with the body. Kenton's clothes were thoroughly sodden now. On the plus side, the more the rain came down, the less overwhelming the smell of death and garbage. He could pick out the mineral scent of wet stone from the cobbled surface underfoot. The alley ran between the pub and a residential building. It emerged on to West Stockwell Street, where two Uniform officers stood hunched in easy conversation. They were untroubled by the situation. It was just another day on the job to them. Kenton scowled.

The buzz from this morning was gone. Cold and shivery, he didn't feel calm in the least.

'Well, it's not exposure. I am inclined to think a drug overdose the cause of death. And yet . . .' Sutton spoke loudly to be heard over the rain, but Kenton's attention was on the men at the end of the alleyway.

'I say, detective, anyone home or am I talking to myself?'

Kenton was sure one of the Uniforms had asked Jane on a date. Maybe she had been seeing him, maybe they'd discussed him and his absence over a glass of wine, maybe—

'Detective!' The doctor's glasses had steamed up in the rain.

'My apologies, doctor. Not an overdose, you say?' Sutton's furrowed brow told him this was not what he had said. Sutton rose and straightened himself up, removing his spectacles and commencing the futile process of wiping them dry. He was known to be brilliant but short-tempered.

'To repeat: I am inclined to think cause of death *is* an overdose, from these puncture wounds. There's traces of vomit around the lips and on the T-shirt, though none to be seen here on the ground.' He took a step away, deeper inside the alley, and studied the litter-strewn cobbled ground surrounding Kenton. 'Indeed, there are no used needles either.'

'So you would suggest the man did not die here, where he was discovered. That the body was moved after death?' Kenton mumbled.

'Quite.'

Kenton moved closer. There was no external indication

of injury. A passer-by might assume the man was passed out. Long hair obscured most of the features, but there was familiarity in the pale face; the prominent nose was distinctive. He thought Gabriel would be more likely to recognise him, to know the street regulars from her time on the beat. He stood back. The landlady had discovered the unfortunate soul when she woke up. Sutton was right: despite the body showing signs of death by overdose, there was none of the usual external evidence to support it. This would, of course, make the death suspicious.

They exited the alley on to the street. Sutton nodded his okay for the body to be removed. Kenton went over to advise Uniform of the situation. The officers greeted him cordially and respectfully. So much for his paranoia. Jesus, he felt cold.

CHAPTER 26

As was sometimes the case during the more volatile seasons, the weather on Mersea Island was localised and markedly different from the wet-grey of the town centre. The sun was out and offered a pleasant, tangible warmth to the air. The south-westerly wind funnelling up the Blackwater came sheering up the bank of cloud, holding it inland.

Sparks strolled down from the yacht club to greet Lowry. He was wearing a spring-like tan leather blouson and, surprisingly, jeans. Lowry took his casual attire as a good sign, more relaxed than he had expected. On closer inspection, he noted sunken eyes beneath the wiry brows, and patches where he'd missed himself shaving, leaving Lowry in no doubt the last days had taken their toll.

'Two dead bodies in as many days? The town is taking advantage of me being out of the picture, eh?' A weak smile ghosted his lips. 'One every morning I've been absent.'

'How's Antonia doing?' Lowry said, ignoring his jibe.

Sparks pulled a face.

'Quiet,' he said, 'very quiet.'

The two men stood close together on the lawn, the sun reflecting off the broad flat white of the clubhouse behind them. The chief was not an emotional man, but Lowry understood the pain it would cause him to see Antonia, who was known fondly by all to be an infernal chatterbox, become silent.

'Why are we here?'

'To look at a boat.'

Lowry turned to face the estuary. 'Which one?'

'Quarter tonner, racing boat; Antonia was wanting me to shell out on one, but we canned the idea when she got pregnant. Thought that now, after what's happened, you know, might be a nice gesture.'

'I can see that. Good idea.'

Two men, both in cream trousers and navy blazers, were leaving the club. They broke into exaggerated laughter as they passed by, making their sunburnt faces glow even more fiercely. County snobbery was never more evident than here among the yachting elite. Lowry knew Sparks was welcomed into the set chiefly because of Antonia's Cowes pedigree. His rank might help a little bit, but Lowry doubted it counted for much down here on the waterfront. Connections and plenty of cash were the basic prerequisite. The commodore drove a Bugatti.

'Come on, we need to find this chap down on the hard.'

As they made their way to the jetty, the air smelt less of cologne and more of fish and wet rope. Lowry had sailed dinghies up and down the creeks as a boy. Until his father told him to focus on the boxing. The sea would always be there, his youth and strength would not. In general, the water was not a competitive arena for the police round here – the fishing tournament off Walton Pier was as close as most officers got to the sea. Sparks asked Lowry when he had last been on a boat.

'Not in a while. And when were you last at Cowes?' Lowry asked as the water came into view, knowing that's where he and Antonia had met.

At the muster point near the lifeboat station, there were a handful of people waiting for launches out to the creek and the boats anchored there. The season was over and most would be making their craft ready for winter. Sparks stood at a remove, scanning the assortment of sailing folk and fishermen milling around. The chief had not met the vendor before. 'Chap called Marcus, a friend of a friend of Antonia's – landed gentry, country set,' he muttered, lighting a cigarette.

'Here, fellow with a plaster across his face, marching over,' Lowry said, tapping his shoulder.

'Mr Sparks, I presume. Hullo, I'm Marcus.' A fair-haired, pear-shaped man, with a distinctive mole on his cheek and a white gauze bandage across the bridge of his nose, held out his hand to greet Sparks. 'Come this way, I've a tender on the pontoon.'

As they chugged through the sailing boats pointing seawards, straining at buoy lines on the incoming tides, Marcus filled them in. This would be his last season on the water and since he had not found the time to haul the boat out for the winter, he thought of selling it now while there was still a good month left to see some action. Sparks stared solemnly ahead at the black hulk of the oyster shed, standing in isolation out on the shingle spit slowly sinking in the channel.

The vessel, a quarter ton keelboat, cut a sleek figure in the water; long and thin with an overhanging stern and scooped-out deck.

'That looks nasty,' said Lowry. 'Took a clunk from the boom, did you?'

'What, oh my nose?' The man self-consciously put his free hand to the gauze. 'Yes, yes, gust caught me . . .'

Sparks made a play of examining the deck. Lowry himself knew the basics, but this was a different class of vessel entirely.

'I've done a bit of patching up, here and here. But in general, you'll find it all shipshape.'

Lowry had inherited a dislike of this sort of casual posh sailor from his father and couldn't help trying to embarrass the man. 'How on earth did the boom catch you there? Were you drunk?'

'What are you, a copper?' He half laughed.

'Yes, he is,' Sparks said. 'We both are.'

Marcus glanced from one to the other. He didn't visibly flinch but was unnerved for a moment before hooting loudly. 'Didn't steal this boat, honest, guv!' he said, both hands raised.

'I'm sure you didn't,' Sparks clapped the man on the back, 'and I'm sure you're giving me a decent price. You mentioned the traveller block needs replacing . . .'

Lowry moved out of the way as they talked about specifics. He watched dunlin shoot by, skimming the surface of the water low and fast.

After a tour of the boat, and satisfied of Sparks's enthusiasm, Marcus navigated them back to shore. Standing once again on the pontoon, he regained his haughty equanimity.

'What did you say you did again?' Lowry asked.

'I didn't.'

Lowry left it. Above all, he was relieved to see Sparks re-engaging with the world, even if purchasing a racing yacht was a little extravagant.

'I own some land, to the west of Colchester,' the man offered, unexpectedly. 'And much of my time is spent managing my concerns. Indeed, I must leave you gentlemen, if you don't mind. Mr Sparks, I have a number of other inquiries for *Shearwater*; I don't wish to be pushy, but . . .'

Sparks looked poised to make an offer, but restrained himself.

'Thank you, thank you. I'll be in touch.'

'Jolly good,' said Marcus. 'I'll look forward to it.'

They watched him go. After a while, Sparks said, 'What was all that about? Hassling the bloke like that?'

'He was nervous.'

'Who isn't around policemen, eh? Come on, I'll get you a beer.'

'He never did say what happened to his face.'

'Hit by the boom, he said. Who cares? C'mon.'

Sparks did not consider beer, lager or otherwise, as serious alcohol – merely refreshment.

'I thought you were going to make that chap an offer.'

'I got cold feet . . . in case it was the wrong colour or something. You know how it is with women. Mine especially. Come on, you need to fill me in on what I've been missing.'

Lowry smiled. This was the Sparks he knew.

Rowhedge

Gabriel watched on miserably from under an umbrella on the quay as a white-suited forensics officer disappeared below deck.

Robinson had already told her the skin on Cooper's neck was not broken. It was slightly bruised, nothing more – a fact that she must have wilfully ignored, or at best forgotten, in her enthusiasm. The only saving grace was that she'd held back from telling Lowry she'd seen blood on the hammer.

At least the foul weather prevented an audience assembling. This was, after all, her village and she could do without the neighbours talking.

The forensic popped his head above deck and promptly leapt across to shore. He joined her under the umbrella, hammer in an airlock bag.

'Here, take a look, detective. I think this here is rust.' He was right. It was clearly not blood. 'But the measurement matches.'

She thanked the man and said goodbye. She shook and collapsed the umbrella and got into the Fiat, rain trickling down her neck. She gave an involuntary shudder. So, what did it all mean? Was she on to something or not?

CHAPTER 27

Stephen Sparks asked for the yacht club members' phone, dialled the hospital and held the receiver to his ear.

'Stephen, please. Just go in. Please. They need you.'

'No, no, honestly, love. I couldn't. I honestly don't know what I was thinking; you are my priority.'

'Stephen, you are no good pacing up and down the ward like a caged lion, frightening the nurses. For God's sake, go, I'll be fine.'

'Okay. But I'll be there for visiting hours this evening.'

Sparks's decision to return to Queen Street had almost seemed impulsive. It happened at the yacht club. An unaccountable surge of energy, a drive to get back into the fray. While he had been at home or at the hospital, he'd not given the station much thought. And then Lowry turned up at Mersea, irritable and short-tempered, sniping at the fellow with the boat, and after sinking a couple at the bar while hearing of the goings-on at CID, Sparks's mind was made up.

He had only half taken in what Lowry had said, but it was enough to deliver a strong presentiment that things were happening without him in a disorganised fashion. Sparks was not, to his mind, being rash. He had spoken to Antonia and she agreed: she was out of danger and would be home next week. Best for all of them if he kept busy.

The division had welcomed him back warmly that afternoon. Condolences and good-wishes were solemnly extended, concern from every corner. Uncomfortable with any expression of emotion, Sparks had been civil, politely dismissive, but secretly very pleased.

Settled back in his garret office, he listened as his team filled him in on the death of Colin Cooper and the questions surrounding the uncle, Howard Osgood. Lowry had let Osgood go, a point he noted then put to one side. Eventually the room fell quiet. Gabriel, Kenton, Lowry and Barnes were awaiting a pronouncement.

'Tell me again about this hammer,' he said, addressing Gabriel specifically.

'What did you call it?'

Lowry stood hunched in the corner of the room by the high window. Outside, gulls paraded on the roof parapet. He listened with interest as Gabriel explained the situation to Sparks.

Lowry couldn't figure it out. The diameter of the caulking hammer, the size of a ten-pence piece, was a match for the bruising on Cooper's neck, but it was circumstantial.

He levied a hard stare in her direction. It was one thing giving her some rope to go ahead and investigate her hunch, and for her to have quietly reached a dead end (which to his mind was clearly the case); it was another thing entirely to have the chief enter the fray midway through and apparently entertain her suspicions. He couldn't allow Sparks to railroad the investigation at this point.

'That the diameter matches the bruise means nothing,' Lowry said.

'No?' Gabriel said, her mouth puckering into a self-conscious grin.

'No. There are thousands of ordinary domestic woodwork hammers that would fit the bill.' To illustrate his point he picked up the hammer Sparks used to rearrange his boxing photos on the walls. 'See? It appears smaller, by virtue of its double head,' he held it up and twirled it around, 'and its shorter stem. And compared to this,' he produced the one he kept in the boot of his car, 'it feels and weighs less, the claw being on the heavy side. But they are identical.' He placed the two heads together.

'Hmm,' Sparks scratched his jaw thoughtfully, 'he's right, but you weren't to know.'

'What does that mean?' Gabriel turned to face him.

'Well, you're a woman; couldn't tell a claw hammer from a barbarian's mace.'

'Excuse me, sir, that is an outrageous, sexist remark.' She was furious.

The chief stood and pushed out his chest. 'So I'm wrong? No, thought not. Nick, carry on.'

'The bruising may not even have been sustained by a hammer

blow.' Lowry picked up the pole used to open the skylight. 'The butt of this would produce the same mark used, say, to push the body down into the water. The caulking hammer is pure circumstance, is all I'm saying. If Gabriel had not witnessed Cooper go overboard, we wouldn't be going down this road. There is no motive.'

'Okay, fair point.' Sparks read the tension in the office correctly. Lowry wouldn't admit it, but he had been terribly soft on Gabriel, sanctioning a wild goose chase like that. It was undoubtedly for the best that he'd returned. 'What about you, Kenton? What do you suggest?'

The young detective had been subdued. Sparks was pleased to see he'd at least had a haircut.

'Well, sir. We have been able to identify Nigel Foster, a local skinhead, involved in some trouble. He seems to have been a pal of Colin Cooper's. A word with him may throw some light on the situation?'

'Okay, you lot carry on. Now, if you'll excuse me.' Sparks felt he had things back on track and was now more concerned about his bladder than anything. Time was he could easily manage four pints after a meeting with Merrydown *and* get back from Chelmsford without needing the loo. They'd only had two at the yacht club.

Lowry exhaled a final jet of smoke and leant across the chief's unnaturally tidy desk to squash his cigarette in his pristine ashtray.

'The vagrant found dumped in the Dutch Quarter,' he said to Gabriel. 'Kenton pointed out you might recognise the guy's face from your time on the beat. Go take a look.'

'Of course.'

'Dan, Foster is yours – check him out.' Kenton frowned and looked like he was about to complain. 'Hey,' Lowry said, 'you agree, right? Jane knows the streets and the Foster lead is yours, what's the problem?'

Lowry was pushing him hard. Sending him here, there, everywhere. Consciously trying to wear him down, get him back into shape, discourage the dope and alcohol habit he'd lapsed into these last months.

'*Fine*, whatever,' Kenton said and marched out.

Gabriel shot Lowry a look – *nice one* – grabbed her bag and hurried after him.

Lowry shook his head. How the hell had he landed himself in this situation with her? He couldn't understand how it could be so exhausting.

Foster was an easy man to find.

Currently unemployed, he lived on the Greenstead Estate. Arrested twice in the summer of 1981, and with a custodial sentence staring him in the face if caught again, these days Nigel Foster thought better of getting involved in the more active conflicts he used to thrive on. Finding Kenton on the doorstep to his council flat, dredging up the past, was the last thing he needed.

'I weren't done for that, on North Hill,' he squinted, trying for a drag on a match-thin roll-up, his pale knuckles displaying a blue swastika beneath fine hair. His index finger stopped short at the knuckle. 'Only words, ain't it?'

'Oh, we aren't interested in you. I'm here about Colin Cooper.'

'Colin, ha, the old tosspot. Yeah, I saw the news. What about him?'

'You two were friends?'

'Knew him from school, yeah.'

'About North Hill. Can I ask what your purpose was that night, taunting that man and his family?'

'Purpose? Dunno – was something to do.'

'And the swastika on your hand?'

'It's a free country.'

Kenton took a note of the school in Old Heath and, after some coercion, the names of the lads they hung out with.

'Anyway, I got my due; geezer in the restaurant was not to be messed with.' He considered his hand.

'And Colin?'

'Scurried off to his uncle, didn't 'e. Disappeared until that autumn, when old Osgood'd had enough of him.'

'And?'

'Wanted some work; I was doing some beating up at Marks Hall.'

'You work on a farm?'

'Nah, had some casual work down the port, with the

livestock. One of the owners was looking for hands – down the Hythe, if you know it round there? Full of dossers hanging about in the hope of cash-in-hand work.' He took a drag of his cigarette. 'Reckon if you want his pals that's where they'd be.'

The port was not a place Kenton knew well; he did not think of Colchester as in any way maritime. The Colne channel was little more than a stream until it met the Blackwater down at Brightlingsea. The surrounding area was vast, and as far as he knew, much of it was deserted. It would be the last place he'd try for a job. However, if this was where the trail led them, so be it.

'What happened to your finger then?'

'Jumped at Balkerne Gate by two geezers with a pair of bolt cutters. Passing on a message, you know, teaching me a lesson. Bloody well hurt.'

'Mr Topize?' Kenton chanced.

'That his name? Couldn't say it was him to be precise, being dark, and I'd never spoken to him . . . but,' Foster rubbed the stump, 'only fella I'd given the V to recently.'

'When?'

'Couple of weeks after we saw 'im in the restaurant.'

'Might he have sought revenge on Colin too?' Kenton said, thinking aloud.

'Kill Colin – what, now, after all this time? Bit harsh compared to this?' He waggled the stump. 'Colin was a skinhead back then – had long hair last I saw. Uncle Howard not so hot on a shaved 'ed. Doubt the black geezer would recognise 'im now. If his uncle dunno what he's been about, have a sniff down the Hythe. It's on the water at least; ain't that where you found 'im?'

CHAPTER 28

Kenton requested a Uniform detachment to canvas the port and surrounding area. Sparks refused outright.

'Dead as a doornail. The town spent the best part of the seventies dredging the river, until the government pulled the plug. That's why it's derelict.'

'That and the recession,' Lowry said coolly.

'Bah,' said Sparks. 'That's nothing to do with it – import/ export is all good for cosying up with Europe, just not here – or London, for that matter. Ships are getting bigger, not smaller; you seen the size of those new container ships? They didn't shut the Isle of Dogs and put all those dockers out of work for the hell of it. The boats don't fit. Big plans for Felixstowe: that'll be the entrance to the East of England for the Common Market. Mark my words. Flooded with whatever . . .'

'Like?' Kenton asked.

'A considerable amount of French and Italian plonk, I imagine. Not since your man Claudius rocked up right here with his amphoras of Pinot Grigio to take the edge off the

Roman occupation has so much wine appeared in this country. We can't get enough of the stuff.'

'And what goes out?'

'Search me. Motors and wheat is what we have but you're not going to get more than a Fiesta and a box of Weetabix through that tiny trickle at the Hythe. There's fuck-all going on down there. That swinging dock was abandoned during the war ... Anything with a draught bigger than a canoe is fucked. Town hall know it too. Point is, you're free to waste your own time, but not anyone else's.'

With his assessment of the situation complete, he went back to the sports pages of the *Telegraph*. The trauma of the last few days appeared to be a distant memory.

'Colin Cooper and Nigel Foster would not have the benefit of your encyclopedic knowledge of the economics of the region,' Lowry said, 'and so if tradition took them in search of work there, old habits die hard. Let's take a look ourselves.'

Harbour House, The Hythe

The little port of Hythe lay in the south-east corner of town, not far from where Kenton lived himself. Kenton and Lowry passed through Barrack Street, descending Hythe Hill eastwards into an area of light industry that had met with mixed fortunes. Paxman's diesels, on the south side, was the largest and most successful employer in Colchester though lately they had been forced to make lay-offs. Eventually Lowry and

Kenton came into an area of disused warehouses and boarded-up vacant business lots, an area at one point on the cusp of regeneration – before the recession struck and shut it down before it could stand. This no-man's land merged into the coal depot then the port itself and King Edward's Quay, the silted-up wharf stretching out beyond, with the road turning east following the river that lay hidden behind high-walled Victorian buildings.

Not far past the bend on the inland side of the road was the old customs house, where Lowry and Kenton now stood chatting with the chief officer at the reception desk.

'No shipping livestock here any more,' the man said. 'A panel beater, broker's yard and an insulation company have since set up shop. Bugger all coming in and going out; rumour has it they'll mothball the port eventually. One of the lads saw surveyors out by the turning circle. Putting another bridge in, I reckon.'

'What are you lot all doing here then?' Kenton asked, noticing a card game in progress beyond the counter. It was well known there were more men in customs than CID.

The chief officer was unperturbed. 'Ain't just the Hythe, you know. Bit of business trundles on below the Hythe at Rowhedge and Wivenhoe, but out beyond here there's one hell of a coastline; more illicit traffic than legal. Drugs squad were here only the other day. Smuggling's been done on this water for centuries.'

'Any trouble?' Lowry asked. 'Demonstrations two years ago as I remember, anything since?'

'There've been rabble-rousers down 'ere since ol' Enoch's "Rivers of Blood" speech back in '68. The dockers are heroes to that lot; been right-wing rumblings round here ever since.'

'This is hardly the Mersey or Toxteth.'

'Makes no difference, there's still unemployment and unrest. Where better to recruit for a bit of Paki-bashing? Two summers ago there was some fair trouble, as you lot would know, but it's gone quiet since. Nobody to take no notice, as there ain't much to disrupt.'

They shared the photos of Cooper and Foster. The man grunted.

'Try the Swan, just back a way – big old boozer at the bottom of the hill on the river, can't miss it. Or the Rising Sun, over the bridge. That's where the National Front were canvassing, dishing out leaflets and the like, but as I say, that was all in '81.'

It was dark and cold when they left the customs men. Crossing the road, they walked close to the damp Victorian dock buildings back towards the bridge. Up above in the gloom, catching on the weak, tall street lights, the century-old paintwork clung to the wall. Old signage indicated a lost trade for livestock, grain. One faded blue sign on a lower floor, perhaps more recent, advertised the *Colchester Vehicle Steam Cleaning Co.* Kenton wondered what decade that would have been added.

'All a bit bleak,' he said, his voice triggering an echo, 'what do you think?'

'About what?'

'The outlook for this place where we live and work: the future, all this decay.'

'I don't let it bother me,' Lowry said, his breath alive in the gloaming as they walked.

'It fuels the hatred.'

'We've not witnessed any.'

'That customs officer seemed to condone intimidation.'

'Half the schoolboys in England scribble NF on their exercise books. Do they know what it means? I doubt it.'

'I didn't.'

'That I believe.'

The warm orange glow of a public house window shone in the distance.

'Ah, behold, some life.'

The Swan was a distinctive, high, two-storey public house standing alone on a bend in the road. It was an impressive construction of eighteenth-century red brick, curved round at one end, with a hipped roof behind a parapet and large windows beneath white lintels. It was an establishment determined to outlast its surroundings. Lowry had been here with Sparks at the time of the demonstrations. It was a grand old place; few of the like remained.

Disappointingly, however, the pub was deserted, apart from a very young barmaid. Lowry bought two pints in silence and took them to a far corner passing a Wurlitzer playing a Two Tone record low.

'Barmaid's not going to know a thing; she would have been at school two and a half years ago – probably still is. We'll have this and poke our heads in the Rising Sun over the bridge, but don't hold out much hope. Sparks is right, the area is dead as a doornail.' He proclaimed, 'Good luck to any smugglers, they'd stand out a mile passing through here. Cheers.' He raised his glass. 'Nice to have you back.'

'Cheers. This is the second Swan pub I've come across today,' Kenton said, but couldn't hold a smile.

Lowry, sensing his unease, sat back in the chair and said, 'What's on your mind?'

Eyes to the floor, shortened fringe flopping forward, he said, 'Everyone's talking about me. In Queen Street.'

'What? What about?'

'You know ... what happened, me cracking up.' He lifted his gaze.

'No, they are not,' Lowry said.

'They are, I know they are.'

Lowry studied his younger colleague. 'Like who?'

'Them. Uniform.'

'What's been said, then?' Lowry understood there might be whispers, but at the same time didn't want to encourage the man's paranoia.

'Uh, I don't know ... things.'

'Stop smoking that shit, and you'll stop hearing things, I guarantee it.'

Kenton leant over, his voice barely above a whisper. 'But I need it.'

'No. You don't. You just think you do. It's a vicious circle.' Lowry considered spooking him with the drugs squad. The possibility was real: the body in the Dutch Quarter this morning would undoubtedly prompt questions over usage and supply in the area. Gabriel had failed to identify the lad, making an intervention from County even more likely. Hash was not the same as the crap they shot up on the streets, but that wouldn't matter during an investigation. If County issued a clean-up, any officer thought to be using would fall foul.

'I just don't understand why I feel the way I do,' Kenton said. 'It was never a problem at college.'

'This is real life. You've a responsible job and you've been absent for a good while, lost in a world of your own. It may have served a purpose then, but trust me – it won't do you any good now. Kick it.' Lowry drained his pint. 'You know better.'

Drawing a blank was often the way in investigations like this, but the bleakness down here was stark and Lowry could feel depression begin to penetrate his bones, like the damp seeping through the pub walls. They left the Hythe empty-handed and down at heart.

Learning the police were clambering all over his boat, Osgood faced the fact that things could quickly spiral out of control. A local had seen them poking around twice now and he'd come to the conclusion he had to confront them. He approached the front desk of Queen Street at five-thirty and asked for Lowry. When informed he was out, he asked to wait and moved to take a seat.

He sat patiently. He figured the police had nothing to go on, and if push came to shove, he reckoned they were after trying to nail him for Colin. The fact they had released him *then* visited his boat meant they weren't on the level. It was too risky, now, holding back mentioning Hughes-Roper. Greed had got the better of him – the prospect of a deal on a property and the possibility of a step up the social ladder distracting him. But really, what need did he have for that? He couldn't afford to get deeper into the mire, not when the Hippodrome was so close to completion.

Lowry entered the building with a younger colleague. Osgood had only been waiting fifteen minutes. The desk sergeant signalled for his attention and he rose to his feet. The inspector saw him but held back, waiting for the desk to confirm that Osgood was indeed there to see him. Howard always fancied himself a quick – and shrewd – judge of character. Usually had a man nailed after ten minutes. But three hours of questioning yesterday and he hadn't the vaguest notion of Lowry. He looked at the copper: tall, broad, hair slicked back, around forty. White shirt, slim black tie, donkey jacket: impossible to make out.

'Mr Osgood?' Lowry approached, unhurried.

'Yeah, inspector. Can I have a word? There's something I want to get off my chest.'

Lowry led him through to a small room and shut the door. 'What can I do for you, Mr Osgood?'

'The geezer I was with when I got attacked in the car, out in Copford the other day? Thought you should know his name. Hughes-Roper. Has an office in Church Street, he was showing me a property he had on the market. He'd an offer but it had fallen through.'

'I see.'

'They might just have been messing around, like young lads do, Billy-big-bollocks behind the wheel. They'd been tailing us pretty close. But . . .'

'But?'

'I think there was more to it. They pinned Hughes-Roper against the car – I reckon they knew him.'

'I see. Well. Thank you, Mr Osgood.' He nodded appreciatively, showed him to reception and made off back inside, leaving Howard all alone and more confused than ever.

Did they suspect him or not?

Lowry took the stairs two at a time. He filed the name Hughes-Roper away for later. Osgood was clearly spooked; Lowry knew a frightened man when he saw one and Osgood's sudden need to give him a name confirmed as much. He'd have heard they'd been poking around his boat. Yes, Osgood was afraid, uncertain and weary. He looked exhausted, his face saggy and drained. Funny, that. To all intents and purposes, the man was on the up.

But all this could wait. Captain Oldham had called, requesting he visit at his earliest convenience.

CHAPTER 29

To whom it may concern:

I took my life willingly and with clear and sound mind. I confess to shooting William Cousins by duel. I have no regrets and if asked to perform the task again, I would not hesitate. There were no witnesses, no seconds.

Now, my thoughts can only turn to her.

The love that took hold of me, dies with me.

Lawrence Drake

Oldham read the letter over, and the words did not change. Fairweather stood over his shoulder. Oldham tossed the paper aside.

'How?' he asked.

'Razor blade,' said Fairweather, stepping to the side of the desk. 'Concealed in a strip of leather and carried in his mouth. Think the struggle we had with him yesterday was cover.'

'Don't they search people, for heaven's sake?'

'Couldn't say, sir.'

'Bloody fool.' Drake was clearly mentally ill. Serving in a

war zone loosened men's minds. The physical wounds could be treated; it was the psychological scars that always went unnoticed until it was too late. He picked up the note again; something jarred. The phraseology, the composition, was unusual. He refocused on Fairweather but decided not to share his thoughts. 'Very well, notify the next of kin.'

'Sir. The CO will wish to see the letter.'

'I shall pass it to him.'

'Very good, sir. Inspector Lowry is here.'

'Show him in.'

With the brigadier wishing to draw the investigation to a close, and the man who pulled the trigger on Cousins dead, there was little he could do from his side. But that didn't mean he could not, in a subtle way, help Lowry get to the bottom of things if he wished.

'Captain Oldham,' said Lowry.

'Thank you for seeing me. Well, not to waste time, I'm afraid I've some rather disappointing news. I thought you should see this.'

Lowry scanned the letter. It was neatly written in pencil, unhurried, on foolscap paper. 'Thank you. Have you seen many of these before?'

'Suicide notes? A few, yes.'

'Any in these circumstances?'

'None quite like this, no. Broken hearts, yes, depression, yes, but aftermath of a duel, no. What do you make of it?'

'*If asked to perform the task again.*'

'A duellist does not ask, he challenges. This letter suggests to me that his involvement came at the request of—'

'– someone other than William Cousins?'

'Yes, my thoughts exactly. That's how I read it.'

'Then we are in accord.'

'Maybe I'm a policeman, after all.'

'Come off it. There was never any doubt from my side.' Lowry was amused that Oldham felt slighted in some way. 'Maybe this woman – this breaker of hearts – demanded they fight for her?'

'Maybe.'

Lowry had been surprised to get the call after shutters had so unceremoniously come down on this case. That the young man had died by suicide was terrible: the torment that he must have suffered to bring him to this decision. Lowry knew Oldham must in some way feel the weight, despite the granite exterior. The army did not release statistics of those who took their own lives; Oldham was under no obligation to share the letter. He needed Lowry's input. He still wanted answers.

'What a waste of life,' said Lowry, wondering if it could have been avoided. 'Obviously he saw no hope of being with the woman in question.'

'That isn't the point. The sad fact is that a soldier's mind could have been so reduced. All his powers of reasoning turned to mush by conflict. While the Troubles continue, casualties will continue to accrue both on and off the battlefield.' Oldham spoke in a monotone, no trace of emotion. It was not for Lowry to contradict him.

'Did you ever connect anyone else to the duel? Seconds?' Lowry asked, ignoring Drake's claim to the contrary.

'Well, Lowry, that brings me to the point. The brigadier is keen to draw a line under the whole affair – end of the road, from our perspective. I'm simply sharing this recent information with you as,' he hesitated, 'well, as a matter of interest, let's say.'

'That is thoughtful of you.' Lowry knew what Oldham was saying.

'Here.' Oldham passed him a small envelope. Lowry had no need to open it, feeling the seahorse inside. 'I wish you the very best in reuniting it with its owner.'

'*Sharon.*' He almost laughed.

'Ah, yes. I'm sorry. That wasn't exactly helpful. Anyway, there we are. It's out of my hands now.'

Lowry returned to Queen Street. Sitting alone at his desk with nothing but the desk lamp on, he immersed himself in thoughts of Drake's suicide note. Two men fighting to the death over a woman in a premeditated fashion was crazy.

Mentally, Lowry had tried to switch off from this case once the military had assumed responsibility. But now he could not but help wonder about the woman behind this. What, if anything could he do? With Drake's death, all avenues of inquiry via the military were firmly shut.

He had taken a day's leave tomorrow – the trip to Rye, and

not before time. Some distance may offer clarity. Adjusting his posture and releasing a crick in his neck, he saw he'd scribbled Osgood's name and 'another large property purchase?' on his blotter. He poured himself a large measure of J&B Rare Scotch into a Wombles mug and picked up a biro. He should write down what he could recall of Drake's letter. But his mind kept veering back to Osgood.

Why was the man eyeing another building? What for? Another nightclub? Not in Copford, surely. Besides, the one in the high street was not yet up and running. What sort of money was he pulling in? Lowry was impressed. To go from running a couple of free houses in Suffolk to this level of dealing was no mean feat. Still, interesting as it was, did it really matter? After all, if he didn't make Howard Osgood as his nephew's killer, what reason could they have to pursue him?

'The man found in West Stockwell Street did not die there.' Gabriel's voice pierced his thoughts and the silence of the office.

'Oh, I see,' he said, absorbing the implications of the discovery. He stopped doodling round the 'o' in Osgood on the desk pad and turned his attention to Gabriel. 'I was with Daniel earlier, he didn't mention anything.'

'Well, he should have. There were traces of vomit on the corpse's beard but none in the street where they discovered him.' She flicked on the wall light. 'According to Sutton, Daniel took off sharpish. Sutton was rather put out, actually. Anyway, clearly he got distracted.'

'Good that you picked it up then,' he said, diplomatically, eyes adjusting to the increased light. Maybe he was pushing Kenton too hard.

She pulled off her gloves and sat down opposite. 'This hot?' she said, reaching for his mug. 'May I?'

'You bet ... be my guest.' He waved absently with his pen, surprised by this familiarity. Not for the first time, it puzzled him to think that there might be a connection of any kind between them. It was, to his mind, the least likely thing imaginable. She possessed a fragility that warned him off, an element of purity that was beyond his reach. But that might just be youth and health that he couldn't recognise.

'Ugh,' she protested, expecting coffee perhaps, but she took a sip anyway. 'What is it with you men and alcohol? Daniel the other night, and him upstairs.'

'It's easy, comes in a variety of flavours and there's plenty of it,' he said, as she plonked the mug back on the desk.

'Yes, but you don't need to try and drink it all at once.'

'Anyway, the photo of the dead man in West Stockwell Street has done the rounds then?'

'Yes, I shared it with Uniform. There's all sorts going on in the shadows round town at night, as you know, but all the pushing and dealing is concentrated around New Town. The beat bobbies have been questioning the homeless population this evening. If we can't ID him and no one's reported him missing, he may be from out of town.'

This was a real consideration and already on his mind. 'Sutton positive that it was an overdose, is he?'

'Yes, heroin.'

'Okay. Run through the missing persons list, here and in Chelmsford and Southend.'

'What about the fact he was moved?'

'Someone probably didn't want him lying in their doorway.'

'There was dust and traces of spiderwebs on his clothes.'

'Maybe he snuck inside somewhere. All the rain we've had would make shooting up in the street difficult ...'

'What next?'

'Wait until Uniform finish poking around the town centre. Check in with them tomorrow?' He feigned a smile. 'Nothing we can do till then, is there?' This appeared to placate her. He rose to his feet, heavily. 'I've the day off tomorrow, by the way. Have a word with the chief now he's back. He should know about the OD – though he'll want to downplay it for fear of County thinking we're going to the dogs.'

'Doing anything nice?'

'Not really ... just time out.'

'Looking at birds?'

He shook into his donkey jacket. 'Maybe.'

'Do you fancy a drink?'

He declined abruptly and departed, leaving her still sitting opposite his desk with her hat and gloves. Stopping on the stairs to light a cigarette, he nearly turned back. The urge to accept the offer had been strong and instinctive, and if he was honest with himself, that was why he'd been so quick to say no. Just occasionally he realised how lonely he was, and it shocked and scared him in equal measure. But he knew it could have seemed rude. He walked down the stairs and, with a tinge of regret, hoped she would let it go.

CHAPTER 30

Lowry had woken early. Unused to free time, he didn't really know how to spend it.

After leaving the remains of the bread out for the birds, he ran the hoover round, but by eight he was pacing around waiting for the washing to finish. Taking a coffee and cigarette into the lounge, he decided to put on a The Who record. He'd heard a track on the radio and realised he'd not listened to them in ages. He quickly grew frustrated at not being able to locate the album he wanted, one thing led to another, and soon he was dividing the LP collection into his 'n' hers. Performing this separation was cathartic and revealing at the same time. He tossed *Rio* by Duran Duran (hers) one way, *White Light* by The Velvet Underground (his) another. How could two people with such vastly different tastes coexist? Depeche Mode (hers). Eventually he found *Sell Out*, slipped it from its sleeve and flipped it on the turntable. Jacqui was right about one thing – he'd not progressed his music taste beyond 1969.

Pushkin lay on Oldham's Vivaldi, quietly observing this

ceremonious splicing of a joint life, occasionally tapping a seven-inch picture cover tossed his way.

Becky phoned at nine wanting to know why he hadn't told her about Antonia. He didn't really have an answer, only that he didn't think it his place. By the time he'd got off the phone, it was nearly time to go, as he intended to walk the three miles into the village to meet Becky. Lowry deposited the cat on the patio, with an extra serving of food. He'd not tapped Sparks up to look after the animal, as Lowry had downgraded the weekend away in his head to just one night.

Since jacking in the boxing, he'd stopped running, and had this past month released a notch on his belt. Not that it would offset the inevitable middle-aged spread – to that he was resigned – but a walk would do him good. It was a beautiful day, with a light breeze gently nudging copper leaves from the grand oak on the bend in the road. Shotguns sounded off in the far distance. Closer by, the click of a robin in a yellow hawthorn framed the morning.

After fifteen minutes he heard a toot from behind. It was Mrs Richardson, the librarian, who gave a friendly wave from behind the windscreen of her 2CV. She insisted she give him a lift, would not hear his protestations about walking, and so he jumped in. Ever polite, the librarian did not inquire as to the purpose of the policeman's trek to the village with a gym bag; the pair simply chatted gaily about the glory of the morning.

As a consequence of the librarian's kindness, Lowry arrived at the Woolpack ahead of the appointed time by a good half hour. The pub was empty until, halfway down a second Guinness, Lowry found himself surrounded by beaters from a nearby shoot, rich in the mulch smell of the cornfields where they'd spent the morning chasing birds to the sky for what was very likely their last flight. The shooting season was in full flow, and the Woolpack was a popular venue for shooters and beaters alike.

Lowry budged up to allow several green-jerkined men room at the bar as he sipped his Guinness. The shoot was one of those rare occasions that extremes of the social scale would meet. Farmhands, labourers and the seasonally unemployed like Nigel Foster, rubbing shoulders with the upper-class set. Or something close to it. Lowry observed how outside the pub, beaten up Hillman Imps touched bumpers with gleaming Range Rovers. But inside, the class divide was upheld – puce, jowly men wearing waxed Barbers on one side of the saloon bar, beaters in mud-spattered snorkel jackets on the other, public side.

Lowry checked his watch. Becky was only ten minutes late but his early arrival made it seem longer. The pub was crowded now and he didn't fancy another pint, so he drained it and decided he would wait outside. It was his fault, insisting she collect him from the pub, a Coggeshall one at that – some sense of unease at being seen, of questions being asked, had made him want to avoid his own village and the Chequers.

As he placed the empty glass on the beer mat, a face he recognised appeared in the mêlée across the other side. Lowry couldn't place him at first – but the second he heard the man's ungodly guffaw, it soon came to him: it was the bloke from Sparks's yacht club, the one with the boat for sale, only the plaster across the nose had gone.

The man saw him and raised his glass in acknowledgement, froth on his moustache.

Lowry tapped the elbow of the beater next to him. 'What do you know about that fella over there?'

'You're the copper from up the road . . .'

Lowry turned to face him, a farmhand he knew by sight. 'I am. Allow me.' He caught the barmaid's eye with a crisp pound note between index and middle finger.

'Don't mind if I do,' the beater said and nodded across the way. 'That's Mr Hughes-Roper, landowner out over Copford way.'

That name again. Interesting.

'Tell me, do you know a Nigel Foster or Colin Cooper, by any chance? Both been known to work periodically on shoots?'

'Yeah, know 'em both. Ain't here this time, though; just know 'em from before, like.'

Cooper. Osgood. Hughes-Roper. What was he missing here? Hughes-Roper was a man to have a word or two with. But not right now, in a crowded pub. Turning his back to the bar, Lowry slipped out to the lavatories and used the public phone to call Queen Street.

Having told Gabriel to find out Hughes-Roper's address and

that he was on his way back to collect her, he exited the pub. Standing on the step of the sixteenth-century wooden doorway, Lowry saw Becky in a bobble hat close her car door and skip across the road. Her smile fell as she drew closer, meeting his neutral expression. He held up his sports bag in his defence.

'All's good,' he offered, 'just something has come up with work.'

She scrutinised him, looking for some explanation. 'What, literally this minute – in there? What could—'

At which moment he put his hands to her cold cheeks, leant down and kissed her.

'Can you drop me home, I'll be as quick as I can.'

Berechurch Hall Road, South Colchester

The Jag XJS slunk into the Maypole car park. Osgood shook his large head wearily, and then pulled out a comb to realign his quiff. If you needed any further proof that Colchester was a decade behind the rest of civilised twentieth-century society, Tony Pond was it. The geezer *genuinely* thought he was a TV celebrity-stroke-local-hero, poncing about in a pipelined suit and handlebar moustache like the bastard child of *The Prisoner* and Jason King. Osgood was feeling lighter, having decided he was off the hook. The police hadn't bothered him overnight, Lowry had all but brushed him aside at the station, and the overall effect was to encourage him to find out for himself just what kind of trouble Hughes-Roper was really in.

Tony Pond glanced warily around the empty car park, shiftily smoothing his lapels. As if they'd be spotted. As if anyone either of them knew would be loitering around the big old pub on the fringe of Friday Woods under the heavy horse chestnut tree canopy.

Pond climbed into the Audi.

'What happened the other day?'

'Nothing. Detained.' Pond was rumoured to be a gossip; if he hadn't heard of Howard's brush with the law, Howard wasn't going to be the one to enlighten him. 'So what is it that warrants this furtive behaviour, skulking about in the woods?'

Pond seemed more interested in a line of soldiers jogging past along the main road than answering questions.

'You know what's on that side of the road, eh, Howard?'

'The new garrison camp, married quarters.'

'And this side, in the woods?'

Howard rubbed his jaw; where was this going? 'Army land, firing ranges.'

'No, the MCTC, Glasshouse or, as we know it, the nick. Squaddies up and down the country call it "Collie". The car you were after was owned by a soldier.'

'A squaddie? Are you sure?'

'Positive.'

'What the hell would a soldier want with Marcus Hughes-Roper?' Osgood muttered without thinking.

'Hughes-what?'

'Nothing. Well done. You're a pal ... Sorry, just a bit distracted.'

'Mate, I heard, sorry.'

'Colin's dead,' Howard said, bringing it into the open.

'How?'

'Dunno, found washed up on the mud in Wivenhoe. Drowned.'

'He was a pain in the neck, but I'd not wish him dead. What do the plod say?' Tony asked.

'Clueless. They gave me a grilling.'

'You'd not ...'

'For Christ's sake, no. Trouble is, Colin didn't have much going for him, and so the police have precious little to go on.'

'What do you reckon?'

'Fallen off a speedboat drunk, for all I know; the harbour-master says it happens. Anyway, what the hell we doing here outside the army lockup? You're not telling me the man who owns the motor is in there?'

'I reckon I am, H.'

'Fuck's sake.' He'd have to brace Hughes-Roper himself and screw any possible advantage he'd thought to gain on the sly. Unless the driver was out anytime soon. 'What's he in for, any idea?'

'Shooting another soldier in a duel. You know, in the high street.'

Howard did. 'Course I know – it was on my bloody doorstep.'

What on earth was going on in this town?

262

CHAPTER 31

'Ah, inspector, I wondered when you might make an appearance – please, do come in. I saw you slide out of the Woolpack.' Hughes-Roper beamed at him from behind the solid-oak farmhouse door wearing an open-collar check shirt and beige cashmere sweater in a relaxed fashion, with the air of one assured that the world's problems were, by and large, beneath his consideration. 'You're lucky to catch me, I have offices in town.'

'I might have been here a lot sooner, if you'd been forthcoming in the first place.' Lowry wiped his feet as he and Gabriel crossed the threshold. It was near dusk. Lowry had waited until late afternoon before making his move. Hughes-Roper did not know they had checked with his office to be certain he was at home.

'Now, now,' he wagged a playful finger, 'there's a time and a place for these things. Aren't you going to introduce your colleague?'

Gabriel introduced herself with a slight nod, as they entered the polished wooden reception area.

'Marcus,' he said. 'Charmed, I'm sure.'

They followed Hughes-Roper along a passageway to an elegant room at the back of the house.

'I spoke with your chief again only this morning; he's terribly keen on *Shearwater,* you know.'

Lowry had since put Sparks right on Hughes-Roper, reckoned he was trying to pull a fast one and the chief might be able to get the boat cheaper. He had a sixth sense about Marcus – a dodgy bastard if ever he'd sniffed one. *What is it with people with money, always introduce themselves by their Christian name, as if they're the only one in the entire country.*

'Make yourselves comfortable.'

The room was large, lined with sculpted oak panelling and softly lit by standard lamps in the corners, which, by design or accident, accentuated an impressive view of the Copford plains beyond – verdigris, swathed in a low mist, framed through large latticed windows. Lowry imagined the landscape unchanged since the dawn of time. Only the privileged few could enjoy such a preserved view; the rest endured the changing world. Some, like Osgood, welcomed it, wanted to be a part of building it; others, like Sparks, resisted, clung to the status quo by their fingernails.

Hughes-Roper sat down behind a large desk, ornate with figures carved in the inlay. Lowry noticed a solitary ivory crucifix on the wall behind.

'I am sorry, inspector,' Hughes-Roper continued, 'I thought about reporting the incident, of course, but one mustn't allow these little trifles to get in the way of business, or indeed pleasure, such as boats.'

'It may have been trifling for you, sir – Howard Osgood, on the other hand, ended up in hospital. Weren't you curious to see how the man was?'

'We weren't that close.'

Hughes-Roper sat back, arms folded. Here was a man who knew what was, and was not, worthy of his attention: the police, yes, they required courtesy and due respect. But that was it.

'All the same, it's admirable that you are able to wave it off like that.' Lowry took a seat in the Chesterfield. It was much like Oldham's, only the leather was more worn and forgiving – now he thought about it, Oldham probably rarely entertained visitors – and here he was seated lower than his host, who was effectively looking down at him, gently rocking his chair on its back legs. Lowry found something contradictory in the man's manner given what had happened. 'I'm afraid the police can't be so dismissive, you understand. Youths hijacking cars in broad daylight down country lanes, like highwaymen, roughing people up? Come on. It is intimidation, and this is not the eighteenth century.'

'I agree. Did you know Dick Turpin was an Essex man? Born in a public house and started out as a butcher disposing of deer poached in the royal parks. The graduation to highwayman came later.' He paused and smiled lightly.

'Is that so? Fascinating.' Lowry knew all this, every schoolboy in the county knew the Turpin myth, but he kept schtum, indulging the raconteur. 'Well, all the more reason to nip it in the bud now then, while they're still young,' he joked.

'I'm sorry to digress, inspector. But I can assure you that we – I, at any rate – we were not robbed.'

'Robbed or not, I'm sure you understand our interest,' Gabriel said.

'Yes, yes, quite.'

Lowry indulged the man so because he wanted as broad a picture as possible before bringing up Osgood's nephew. 'For a man like Osgood to wave it away is one thing, but for a gentleman like yourself is something else . . .'

'I'm surprised you chaps can't see beyond the class barrier – I thought it essential in your line of work, eh?'

Lowry gave an involuntary snort. 'So are you telling me *you've* something to hide?'

Hughes-Roper looked appalled. 'Does Osgood? No, I'm suggesting that both of us are man enough to shrug off a bit of tough play by a couple of kids.'

A small laugh escaped Lowry's lips as this chinless wonder drew comparisons between himself and Howard Osgood.

'You are right, my apologies.' Lowry leant forward. 'But forget Osgood for the moment – think, think hard; why might anyone want to put the frighteners on you?'

'Might it not be, as I have assumed, a random act of aggression?'

Lowry thought not. Osgood's instinct was right: it was Hughes-Roper they were after.

'Well, if so, I reckon we've all the more reason to catch them.'

'Look. I'm sorry, I didn't *fess up*. I was spooked, okay? And I will admit I didn't want to lose the sale of the boat to your guv'nor. Seriously. I see now it was foolish of me.'

Lowry remained unperturbed. 'Who were they?'

'I have absolutely no idea, and like I said – even if it weren't so random, why would it be me they wanted and not Osgood?'

'It was you they pinned to the car.'

'I was first out of the vehicle!' he retorted boldly.

'And what was said?'

'Abuse. Foul language and nonsense: kids larking about. They were driving incredibly recklessly and had been trying to overtake us for some time. I put the whole thing down to meaningless violence, to which the youth of today seem prone.'

Lowry pulled out a Navy Cut and sparked up without asking. 'For all your manliness, you still scampered off like a frightened rabbit. Didn't hang about, leaving Howard knocked out cold on the tarmac.'

'I went to fetch help. You know where the incident took place, so you'll realise it was not far from here.'

'The emergency services were alerted by a passing motorist, who called from the box on Copford Green. What happened to the help you went for?'

'All right.' He snapped shut a gold cigarette case and inhaled deeply. 'Pleasant though he is, I didn't want to connect myself to Mr Osgood over anything like this. Looks bad, you know. Happy to strike a deal with the man on the manor house, but I'm not after any public association; especially should the police be involved. If he says later I was in the car with him, so be it. Just because I chose to say nothing does not mean I know who the thugs were.'

Lowry's dislike for this man grew every time he opened his mouth. He spoke with the assured authority of one with an inflated sense of entitlement. But that aside, his logic was persuasive.

'Three things, if I may, inspector.' He ran a finger across his top lip then proceeded. 'First, either you've rather taken your time in coming to see me or – I suspect – Osgood was not immediately forthcoming. If so, why is that? Because, my second point, it was Osgood who ended up in hospital; I was able to "scamper off", as you put it. And finally, you seem to be overlooking what, to me, seems the glaringly obvious fact that it was *Osgood*'s Audi I was in.'

A slight flush was creeping above the man's neckline. Lowry could not fault the reasoning, and he was more determined than ever to find out who was behind the attack and why. 'Fair enough – let's just say we can't have this sort of carry-on in country lanes. You'd agree there? So for now I don't care who they were after – when I find them, I'll ask – but as a member of the public, are you willing to help? What do you remember?' He pulled out his pocketbook. 'Starting with the car?'

'Not my forte. A black one? Small, common, boxy; a Dagenham offering no doubt.'

'Number of assailants?'

'Two. Wearing baseball caps. The one on me had terrible halitosis.'

'Age?'

'Early twenties.'

'Clothing?'

'Nothing you'd ever find me wearing, that's for sure.'

'Okay, and the purpose of your jaunt with Howard?'

'I invited him to the house for a cup of tea, after viewing a property, Copford Grange, I have on the market.'

'Tea,' Lowry repeated. Why would such a snob ask a man like Howard – a man he confessedly didn't want to associate with outside of a bit of business – home for a cuppa?

'Yes, I offered him tea, why not?'

Lowry nodded to Gabriel.

'There's just one other thing, Mr Hughes-Roper,' Gabriel said. 'Did you know a man by the name of Colin Cooper? He occasionally worked on the shoot.'

Hughes-Roper's face was expressionless. 'I don't think so, I know most men by sight, but some names escape me and casual labour comes and goes, you know . . .'

'He was found dead Wednesday.'

'I saw on the news. . . a man on the banks of the Colne. Well, if there's anything I can do; I mean, if he was in my employ, I'd like to help if possible . . .'

'No, no, it was seasonal only – he usually worked for his uncle, Howard Osgood.'

'Ah. Small world,' he said succinctly. 'All the same, I am here.'

Gabriel asked for the gamekeeper's name to check out any of Cooper's associates – which Hughes-Roper politely gave. As she folded away her pocketbook, Lowry sprung a question.

'Could one of the hands have taken exception to you?'

'*Me*? Whatever for?'

'Jealousy. Haves and have-nots. It's a constant burden, being skint; men get frustrated, want to take it out on easy targets like you.'

Hughes-Roper's face twisted; he'd never imagined his presence might provoke hostility among his staff.

'I . . . I really can't think of anyone. By all means ask Beswick, the gamekeeper, if there's any animosity percolating among the lads. As far as I'm aware, they're frightfully fond of me.'

Lowry had hoped to ruffle him and was disappointed – Hughes-Roper quickly regained his composure, settling down to smoke his cigarette in peace. Evidently there was no more to be said.

'One final question: had you much interest in the manor house before taking Mr Osgood for a viewing?'

'Hmm, some, why do you ask?'

'Osgood said a sale had fallen through.'

Hughes-Roper rose and ground out his cigarette demonstrably; their time was up.

'No, no, I was being, shall we say, *creative*. You see, Mr Osgood had concerns about its suitability as a potential nightclub. I was just trying to get him to see its potential.'

'And is it? Suitable, I mean.'

'If an Edwardian theatre can cut it, I don't see why not.'

'You don't like his sort, do you?' Gabriel paused by the Saab's passenger door, breath misting in the sharp air.

Lowry at the driver's side watched Hughes-Roper, who had followed them out of the house and was approaching a gardener raking leaves. Eventually he said, 'You always say that. I don't have an opinion.'

Lowry's call had been unexpected. It was his day off, and after giving her the cold shoulder yesterday evening, his was the last voice she'd expected to hear. But it was a welcome surprise – his curtness last night had left her feeling upset and she'd not slept a wink. Her initial surprise and relief at hearing from him had soon been replaced by concern: why, on his first day off in ages, would he be sitting in a pub mid-morning? Was he okay?

Unable to voice any of this, she said what presently troubled her more.

'You shouldn't wind people like him up,' Gabriel said. 'People with money invariably have power. And clever people hide it well.'

'Ah, I was goading him to see what sort of man he is.'

'I would say it's pretty obvious what sort of man he is.'

'Perhaps,' he said, opening the car door.

'He's the same type as my aunt, you think.'

Lowry turned to face her as she pulled on the seat belt. 'The thought hadn't crossed my mind.'

'Would you want my aunt's job – stop doing all this foot-work?'

She watched his broody eyes flicker in the failing light. Afterward she would think she asked the wrong question. *Could you do it?* would have been more appropriate.

'No. In fact, I'd rather not be doing any of it,' he said, 'however, I am, and it never stops and right now I want to rule out Hughes-Roper's involvement in Colin Cooper's death. And no, he's nothing like your aunt; we may not always agree with Merrydown's methods, but she is a grafter, unlike this low-level aristocratic parasite.'

They watched Hughes-Roper finish admonishing the gar-dener before making off towards the stables, ignoring them entirely. Lowry turned the ignition on.

'You're right,' he conceded. 'I probably don't like him.'

As they pulled away down the long beech-lined drive, Gabriel said, 'They're both Tories undoubtedly.'

'What makes you say that?'

'They're right wing, obviously, both in grand houses.'

'That's a generalisation – Wedgwood Benn owns a large stretch of land, right here in Essex, and is a socialist. Or purports to be.'

'Tony Benn, the politician?' Politics was never discussed in the police, they were ipso facto the government's enforcer. 'Where?'

'Stansgate. Owns a beautiful pile south of the Blackwater; refuses public access to a sea wall on his land – the only part of the Essex coastline closed off. So much for *land belongs to the people*.'

'You know a lot about this place, don't you?'

'My father told me that. He did a lot of walking along the coastal path once upon a time.'

Lowry never mentioned his family.

'Well, my aunt is a Tory, that I can say with certainty.'

'Most of the country is, given who's in Number Ten, and you're right, odds are this bloke Hughes-Roper is no exception. Everyone has prejudice in them; for me it's moneyed classes like him, and for you, men like Osgood.'

'You mean hatred is a defining human quality? How sad.'

'Stands to reason.'

'Yes, of course,' she said distractedly. Her pursuit of Osgood had come to nothing. They had let him go, and in the end she wondered if her tenacity had anything to do with the man himself. She'd not thought about him all day.

'We are all different,' he said, 'and as such we must each play to our strengths: you're best suited to having a word with that upmarket estate agent on Head Street; I'll go and nobble Beswick, the gamekeeper.'

'Sure.' She sighed. 'Most of this country's problems generate from envy.'

'There'll always be a pecking order. That's inescapable.'

'I noticed you called him "sir".'

'False humility, let them believe they're in charge – works on some.'

'Like my aunt?'

'Your aunt is in charge,' he said, grimly. 'And Merrydown is not remotely interested in what we think of her, I can tell you that for free.'

CHAPTER 32

Head Street crossed the west end of Colchester High Street. Lowry double-parked to let Gabriel out, engine idling, and watched her glide across the wet pavement towards Moss, the estate agents. Curious conversation they'd just had, sending him back to his drunk father raving about Tony Benn. He shouldn't be surprised; his father always crept into his consciousness this time of year. Lowry's old man had returned from the war and taken to rambling. He was often gone days at a time. Thomas Lowry, known locally as the Blackwalker, was thwarted on his journey along the coastal path at Stansgate Abbey farm, where he ran up against signage warning him away. The land was private property. Lowry was familiar with hearing about 'silver-spooned hypocrites' long before he understood what it meant.

He smiled as Gabriel reached the estate agents' and looked back at him once before going in. He raised his hand lightly from the wheel in acknowledgement. Lowry had no politics in him, and in truth he accepted that Hughes-Roper was guilty of nothing other than unwarranted but perfectly legal inheritance.

'*People with money invariably have power. And clever people hide it well.*' Before joining the police Gabriel had worked as a model, a world as alien to him as the rings of Saturn, but he wondered if that experience had taught her to be wary of powerful men. She was right. Hughes-Roper would surround himself with legal barbed wire at the drop of a hat should he even get a whiff that he was suspected of so much as litter dropping; Osgood, on the other hand, though far from perfect, had suffered a borderline harassment-level of intrusion.

Hughes-Roper's gamekeeper was a hard man to track down given the nature of the job and the extent of Hughes-Roper's estate, but Lowry eventually met him in a pub at Eight Ash Green in heated debate with a Chanticleer breeder over grain feeders. Beswick was a rosy, solid man, more at ease with partridges and posh chickens than men and women. He was not an eloquent man and he stumbled over phrases and words. It took Lowry less than a minute to decide he wouldn't want to be on the wrong side of him.

Asked about Hughes-Roper, it was clear Beswick was unquestioningly loyal and proud of his position. He had no qualms stating the men that worked alongside him in the fields were just as fond of the guv'nor; 'a top man,' apparently.

On Colin Cooper, he dithered over whether his boss would know him or not – and though Hughes-Roper had told them he would recognise an employee by sight if not name, Beswick wasn't sure. 'Flat caps and parkas all look the same to the shooters at a distance, you know. Gaffer, 'e might of heard 'im though – bleedin' foghorn of a gob on him, Colin – birds woulda done 'n all, long before 'e 'ad any use for a stick.'

Outside the pub, leaves swirled round Lowry's feet as he tried lighting a cigarette. Turning to go back inside, he spied a telephone box underneath a large oak tree beyond the pub signpost. The weather, like his mood, had altered for the worse and heavy splats of rain hit the glass of the telephone box as he splayed his diary against it in search of Becky's phone number to rearrange meeting up before returning to Queen Street.

Back at the station, Gabriel had not fared any better. The estate agents, Moss & Co., were reluctant to give any client information away. All she found out was when Hughes-Roper placed the property on the market – three weeks ago – and that the owner was personally involved in all matters regarding the sale, '*to see that the property passed on to the right hands.*'

Lowry clearly thought she had been fobbed off. As did Sparks. Why he was even in CID this close to the weekend, not attending to his wife, she didn't know. Rain was coming in through the window. It seemed they'd given up trying to close it properly.

'*The right hands* . . . What does that mean?' Sparks snapped, as if she herself were responsible.

'It means Hughes-Roper is particular about the property and does not want it falling into the hands of riff-raff, I imagine,' she offered flatly, refusing to be bullied.

'If he's getting rid of the place, why should he give a toss where it goes, so long as he gets the price he wants?' He turned to Lowry. 'Do you read anything into that?'

'Had there been any other interest?' Lowry asked Gabriel, not answering the question.

'The estate agent wasn't disposed to say.'

'All this snooty reserve is getting on my tits,' Sparks barked. 'Nick, go down there and give him a slapping.'

Gabriel rolled her eyes, forbidding herself to be annoyed by this unnecessary testosterone. Lowry moved from the desk, adjusting his tie. He was not at all perturbed by the chief's behaviour; if anything, he was buoyed by it.

In the dark drizzle of Head Street, lights were going out as shops and businesses slammed their shutters, and people dodged puddles as they hurried home. The working week was drawing to a close. Lowry waited patiently, leaning against a wet Range Rover parked neatly against the curb. Gabriel stood across the way under a barber's shop awning and nodded at Lowry as the man she had spoken with earlier hurried along the pavement in his direction.

Upon reaching his car, he was startled to see the imposing figure of Lowry, seemingly oblivious to the foul weather, waiting for him. Gabriel watched at a distance as the man's earlier bravado almost visibly drained away with the rainwater down the gutter beneath his rear tyre. She pulled up her collar and stepped out to try and hear the exchange.

'I'm an estate agent,' the estate agent said, blinking rapidly in the wet.

'And I'm a policeman.'

The man bravely tried to reach round Lowry for the door handle. Lowry remained steadfast.

'Please move away . . . wait; how did you even know this was my car?'

'Private number plate parked on the street outside an office bearing the proprietor's name in two-foot-high letters above the windowpane; not exactly subtle and it sure had the desired effect – you are Moss?'

Moss nodded, squared his chin and tried to stand a little taller.

'Excellent. I am curious to learn Mr Hughes-Roper's instructions as to the sale of Copford Grange.'

'Instructions?' The word triggered alarm bells. 'As I said to your colleague earlier, inspector, these are private business matters. Any inquiries really do need to be directed at Mr Hughes-Roper himself, and if you leave a message, we'll certainly see that he gets it.'

'Did you know Mr Hughes-Roper was assaulted after showing a prospective buyer around the manor house?'

'No?' Moss stepped back on to the pavement, his wet face transformed into a ghostly mask in the pale orange as he backed up to a street light.

'Yes, and it could happen again . . . to anyone.' Lowry spoke deliberately. 'The man he was with was taken to hospital, which is how come we know. A passer-by called the police.'

'Wait, when?'

'Tuesday.'

The man's mind was churning. 'But we didn't have any clients out there this week.'

'A lot you don't know, it seems.'

'You're trying to frighten me,' he said, frightened.

'Suit yourself.'

'There was one.'

'I'm waiting.'

'A Mr Topize made inquiries on the telephone, offered the asking price, I never met him . . .'

Lowry inclined his head, leant in close to the man. 'Say that again?'

'Topize. He spelt it for me: T-o-p-i-z-e.'

'Unusual.'

'Yes, with an accent I couldn't place. I don't think him a local gentleman.'

CHAPTER 33

Only a story with real excitement would grab the attention of CID and Uniform alike at the end of the day on a Friday at Queen Street, and the name Topize was certainly an unexpected new twist in the tail end of the week. It was rare news that could halt the general inexorable drift down to the social club in the basement.

Gordon Topize. A revenant from the underworld of the nineteen-fifties – a legend in his day: the older Uniforms grumbled knowingly, the younger ones fizzed with curiosity.

Gordon Topize's activities may have predated Lowry, but he'd been around long enough to hear of the man and his myth. As far as Lowry knew, Topize spent long periods abroad, and when here in the UK, did nothing more dangerous than live quietly on the Suffolk border. But give a dog a bad name, and it would stick – even thirty years back. Barnes, and even Sparks himself, fanned the flames, and gossip crackled around the station like wildfire. The commander even saw fit to hold an impromptu meeting for anyone interested in hearing the story before heading off for the weekend.

Lowry stood at the back, intrigued, as Sparks took centre stage.

'What does the word "Whitethroat" conjure to you all?'

'Migrant songbird, sir, arrives in May.' All eyes turned to Kenton. 'A small warbler from Africa.'

'You what?' Sparks said, deeply unimpressed, unlike Lowry who felt a surge of pride (he had lent Kenton his *Hamlyn Guide to Birds* in August but hadn't expected him to read it). 'You, sonny, are keeping the wrong company,' Sparks pronounced. Lowry took the criticism with a shrug. 'Gordon "Whitethroat" Topize is a six-foot Mauritian, and evidently he returned to his old stomping ground in November.'

Mutterings circulated the room.

'Wait,' Kenton said, surprised. 'I know that name! He was the man that Colin Cooper and Nigel Foster assaulted two summers ago.'

Heads turned, alert, serious.

'Yes, I paid him a visit. Funny sort of fellow, lives out of the way near ... Bures? Foster claims it was him who snapped his finger off, you know, for insulting his family.'

'He done Colin Cooper, plain as day,' someone shouted.

Other voices pitched in, increasingly incendiary. In the past Lowry had put racist remarks down to fear of the unknown, not out-and-out hatred. The word Whitethroat, as Topize was known, was instantly seized upon. He was an immigrant troublemaker, even if his last known criminal activity was recorded over two decades ago – his skin colour triggered all manner of unpleasant insults. Kenton was surprised and embarrassed by the reaction.

'Steady on. It's only a finger,' he said defensively, 'and that was over two years ago.'

'Still, it's a bit of a game-changer, Kenton. You might have mentioned it,' Lowry said.

Kenton turned pink above the collar. 'I didn't realise he was such a big deal.' He cast around the room for support. Finding none, he said, 'You all knew we were looking into Cooper's history of racial assault, hoping to find associates, mates who'd help fill in the blanks – of which there are many – and this death has yet to be pronounced murder, let alone racially motivated. Jesus, talk about condemn a man before proven guilty.'

'Fair enough,' Lowry said loudly to quell the dissent, 'and Whitethroat's crimes, whatever they were, are in the past – the incident with Cooper on North Hill that summer would have passed anyone here by. Especially if the only complaint came from the restaurant owner. Topize went back to Mauritius in the sixties. Sergeant Barnes, am I correct?'

'Yep, couldn't make any headway here. Anything he turned his hand to met with prejudice.'

'Why Whitethroat?' Gabriel asked.

'A knife wound,' said Sparks, so quiet it was chilling, 'here.' He drew a long line across his throat. 'Left scar tissue, pale against his skin. Can't miss it. Guess it's not alert enough, eh?' he said, looking at Kenton. 'Anyway.'

'Actually, he was wearing a turtleneck sweater, high.' And tapped his chin with a deflective forefinger. 'What happened?'

'Attacked by some teddy boys outside the Hippodrome, cinema as it was then,' Barnes said, eyes carefully on Sparks. The sergeant rarely spoke out but when he did, he was blunt and to the point. 'Promises were made and not kept by those that brought his kind here. He was told he would become a teacher, but ended up little more than an orderly teaching handicapped kids how to speak.'

'He ran a gang of thieves, I heard,' a Uniform said loudly.

'Bad times back then; led to frustration from all corners. He's no different from anyone else, except maybe more reason for it. Educated too, that one.'

'From over there, though, ain't the same.'

Lowry read disgust in Kenton's face but said nothing.

'Maybe Topize had been misled, or maybe he was naive, a victim of circumstance, but he'd had enough; one day he was here, the next gone, back to Mauritius before anyone could say how's your father,' Barnes said levelly. 'He resurfaced many years later, a respectable businessman. A phone number was listed in Alphamstone, and he owns a couple of shops – beauty salons, I think they are – one in Sudbury and another right here in the town centre.'

'You knew all this?' Sparks addressed Barnes.

'Aye, I seen him once or twice, but his missus runs the shops. He don't have much call to come in 'imself.'

'Beauty salons? As in what?' Lowry said.

'I dunno, I've not been in one,' Barnes replied uncertainly. 'Hair and nails?'

'I have been in plenty,' Lowry said, annoyed. 'You might have said, given I tramped up and down the town salons at the beginning of the week . . .'

'What's that business got to do with any of this?' Barnes said.

'Nothing in itself, just saying, as a man with a criminal record . . . never mind,' Lowry said, dropping the subject.

'I resent the implication,' Barnes said, getting wound up, 'did you cross-examine the background of every shop in town? Or just the girls that worked there?'

'All this is very well, sir, but why did Hughes-Roper reject Topize's offer?' Kenton asked finally.

'Have you not been listening?' Sparks said. 'Because he's black.'

PART 3

To Mourn a Mischief

CHAPTER 34

Police Social Club

'Point taken, but I'm sorry, just because there's a surge of racial hatred in parts of the country, we cannot assume Hughes-Roper's involved,' Kenton said stiffly, 'he's the last person under threat from immigrants. And—'

'And why not? Because he lives in a nice big house and has a double-barrelled name and doesn't have swastikas inked on his knuckles? Bollocks.' Sparks blew a jet of smoke up at the bar's sunken ceiling lights, where it swirled and lingered like a spell. He picked up his pool cue and marched up to the table to take his shot.

Friday evening was the start of the weekend, for CID at least; Uniform were on rota seven days a week. That was the one 'us and them' grudge Gabriel was well-versed on. She watched the chief hunker down over the pool table and wiggle his hind, like a cat about to pounce. Terylene trousers, tight, with a seat so shiny it reflected. She shook her head and spun round on the bar stool to face Lowry, counting out coins for a round of drinks.

'He can't talk like that,' Gabriel said, staring at him as he examined the change in his hand, smoke curling round fingers. Pushing the coppers to the fore of the bar, he raised the cigarette to his lips.

'He just has.'

'Why isn't he with his wife, instead of giving us a hard time?'

'Her mother's arrived – he's giving her time alone with her at the hospital.'

'You're pleased, aren't you – seeing him charging about like this.'

He met her stare, thinking he really ought to be making a move to meet Becky. In truth Lowry was concerned about Sparks's almost maniacal behaviour. This disassociation from trauma was excessive. 'Yes, I'm relieved they're both okay – I think it's his way of coping. Losing a child like that.'

'Yes, sorry, even for him,' she demurred.

Especially for him. Lowry sighed; he was painfully aware of all the internal wranglings the chief had struggled with over approaching parenthood – only to have it snatched from him.

'So what does that mean, exactly?' Kenton blurted. He was sitting on Lowry's other side, perspiring, eyes already glassy. 'This chap, Topize, might have killed Cooper over a grudge? Is that honestly his assessment? Cos if you ask me, it stinks.'

'No – *that* he did not say.'

'That is the implication,' Kenton said.

That was indeed Sparks's conjecture. Topize had meted out his revenge on young Colin, not only for the part he played in the racist attack on his family that summer, but also as an employee of a man who had refused to sell him a property purely out of prejudice. A triumphant roar and a raised pool cue were followed swiftly by jeering from the shadowy fringes of the basement.

'Can't we at least *ask* Hughes-Roper why the offer fell through?' Gabriel said. 'And while we're at it, maybe think about whether Gordon Topize would really think it worth his while to kill a man who gave his family the V over two years ago? You can't leap to conclusions based on his past . . . all that gang stuff was thirty years ago, people can change.'

'Not if the occupants of this bar are anything to go by,' Kenton muttered.

'The chief is, perhaps, joining the dots prematurely,' Lowry conceded, 'but if Hughes-Roper *is* a racist, then that is a con-nection to Cooper – links his past crime with this business with Topize.'

'There may be more to it,' Gabriel said.

'I'm sorry, but I don't think that just because Colin Cooper was possibly a member of the NF and Hughes-Roper refused to do business with a black man, we can conclude Topize is guilty of murder,' Kenton said.

'Calm down, you two. You're missing the obvious;

Hughes-Roper denied there was ever an offer,' Lowry said. 'Jane, remember when we were there, and I asked him about Osgood saying a sale had fallen through? Hughes-Roper dismissed it as being creative – to get Osgood's interest – but, as we know from the estate agent, Topize offered the asking price. We need to find out why Hughes-Roper is holding out on us.'

'How do we do that?'

'Spend a bit more time with him,' Lowry said, 'see whether he actually knew Whitethroat.'

'Do you have to call him that?'

'It reminds us that we are not dealing with someone that straightforward.'

'Out of interest, whatever happened to whoever it was that sliced his throat in the first place?'

'Topize and some of his friends were jumped by a bunch of teddy boys down East Stockwell Street. They'd been selling weed to some girls queuing up to see a film. That right, guv . . . ?' Lowry levied the question at Sparks, who had returned to the bar victorious.

'Sweets: they were selling sweets, pear drops.'

'That so?'

'Yeah. Sweets, not spliffs. Time embellishes the facts; easier to explain the attack.'

'That's outrageous!' Kenton burst out. 'How do you know?'

'I was the one that found him. His throat was slit open by a flick-knife. He was bleeding out on the cobbles. Twenty-seven years old I was, 1955. Funny how these stories change. The punishment did not fit the crime.' He drained his Guinness.

'Well, you kept that quiet . . . wonder if he'd recognise you, after all this time,' Kenton said, thinking aloud.

'We will find out tomorrow.' The chief had a look about him that unsettled Kenton.

'Tomorrow? But tomorrow's Saturday.'

'So what?' said Sparks. 'One more, please, Phyllis love.' He raised an eyebrow at Kenton. 'Yes. Thought we'd take a drive, you and me.'

The thought of weaving through those country lanes with his tanked-up chief made Kenton shudder. 'All the same,' he said bravely. 'It's the weekend.'

'Exactly, Kenton. All this back-biting about CID not pulling their weight. Uniform grumbling about shift work. Be good for morale to see me chip in. Besides,' he grinned, 'I'll have *you* with me.'

With that, Sparks picked up his cue, puffed his chest out and strode towards the rectangle of light that was the pool table, to the sound of cheers from all corners.

Lowry returned upstairs and Gabriel followed. For once he had something besides work to do with his weekend – Becky was waiting.

'I'm out of here,' he said, unhooking his donkey jacket. 'We'll pick up on Monday.'

'That's it then?' Gabriel remained standing opposite.

'There's nothing more to do tonight. We've made an appeal for witnesses in the Cooper case; until someone steps forward, there's little more we can do. Same with the druggie in the pub alley.'

Lowry sensed there was something she wished to say, but rather than ask, he busied himself searching his desk for a book he'd found in the second-hand shop, Greyfriars.

'Let's get a drink next week? Away from here,' she said, 'and you can tell me more about your father.'

Lowry would not say no a second time, and surprised himself by feeling strangely pleased at the prospect. 'Sure. You'll be disappointed though; he disappeared while I was still at school . . .'

The telephone rang as his fingers touched the book under a pile of race-related arrest sheets. It was a little after six.

Gabriel went to reach for the receiver. 'You're leaving, remember.' Her pale blue eyes, veiled with icy reserve. 'DI Lowry's phone . . . oh, hullo. Yes, this is her. Funny, we were just wondering where you might be. Uh-huh. Where exactly is that? We'll be there shortly.' She replaced the phone. 'It's Osgood – he's found the car.'

Osgood had started to lose his nerve. Lowry's silence was not helping. He couldn't figure out why the coppers were all over him one minute, then the next nothing. Since his talk with Tony, he'd convinced himself again he was the main suspect in Cooper's death and had spent the entire afternoon going round in circles, trying to figure out how best to handle it. In the end, he decided to call Lowry to say he'd found his assailant's car. He was confident it was the wise move, given it was such a big deal to the police.

Now, however, he wasn't so sure.

They turned up in force; lights flashing, illuminating the gleaming vehicles on Tony's forecourt. A panda car, a comma van, what he took to be forensics and Lowry himself in a Saab 900. Tony and Howard waited outside Pond's port-a-cabin office, watching the arrival.

Tony Pond, himself not unused to the police, was all the same surprised at the alacrity with which they pulled up and the numbers in which they came.

'Impressive,' he said, 'they must want this motor something rotten. What you got yourself mixed up in, mate?'

Howard stood stoically and shrugged in his camel–hair coat.

Lowry and the WPC made their way over towards them.

'Logbook, please, Mr Pond,' Gabriel asked, holding out her hand.

Pond passed her the folded green paper. The name on the document meant nothing to Howard, a fella from Lancashire. It did, however, trigger a reaction from Gabriel, who showed it to Lowry.

'Not local,' she turned and spoke quietly to Lowry.

'Know who owns it?' Osgood grunted, but the police

said nothing. Desperate to know more, Howard pushed. 'Lancashire's a distance to come to sell a motor?'

The police gave him a cursory glance. 'Thanks, Tony,' Lowry said.

'No worries.' Pond smiled ingratiatingly. 'You goin' to be long? 'Aving your mob all over the place is not good for business . . .'

'We won't be long. We might ask for a statement – just to confirm it was the owner that sold the vehicle,' Gabriel said.

'How about the lad who sold it?' Lowry asked. 'Was he looking to replace it?'

'Nah, nah, just after the readies – reckon he was movin' out. Squaddie. I've had a fair few soldiers in over the last weeks, flogging their wheels. Happens all the time; charge around in a motor while they're in camp, then flog it when they're shipping out.'

Pond's explanation sent a crease of concern across the woman's forehead. Lowry did no more than nod towards the dealer and start walking sharply back towards his car.

'I've a right to know!' Howard called out. 'It was me they punched out cold!' But the detectives climbed in their car.

'You know it was a squaddie, H, I told you already, mate,' Pond said as they watched them pull away.

'I know that, Tone, but why the hell would CID know a soldier's home address, eh?' For the first time Howard felt he was losing his touch, clutching at straws. 'And beside all that, it was me who tipped them off! And not so much as a by-your-leave for the trouble.'

He felt Pond's hand on his shoulder. 'It's just business with them, Howard. When they want you, they'll let you know about it, I'm sure.'

CHAPTER 35

The heavy, dark shapes of military vehicles moved almost invisibly about the empty streets. Normally Lowry would pay them no notice, but this evening the quiet rumblings signalling an imminent departure prompted him to put his foot down. A car horn went as Lowry cut up a motorist, turning sharply off the St Botolph's roundabout.

'The difficulty with the military, as you know by now, is that once a soldier disappears into a war zone, that's pretty much it,' Lowry said, by way of an excuse for his erratic driving.

'You really think this Ford Fiesta holds the answer?'

'Don't ask me how ... but yes, all the puzzle pieces do not make up a whole picture without it; or to be precise, the driver.'

'And arriving five minutes earlier will make a difference?' Gabriel dug her nails into the leather of the seat. 'Or better to get there than not at all.'

Lowry gave no sign that he'd heard her as he bumpered aggressively up on to the curb outside the army building, just as a man in olive drab was leaving.

The Saab's lights clearly picked out the serpentine grimace of RMP Captain Oldham.

'In the nick of time,' said Lowry.

'Inspector, do I detect some urgency in the manner of your arrival?' Oldham asked courteously and, sighing, led them back inside.

'Drake's car has been found,' Lowry announced as the military police captain settled behind his desk.

'His car?' Oldham said, as if a car was the least likely thing in the world for a soldier to possess. The captain's manicured fingers adopted the steeple position, his elbows neatly at the corners of the leather inlay of his desk. 'Where?'

As Gabriel gave him the particulars, Lowry studied his sometime friend's features. The dark recess around his eyes Lowry had previously attributed to his Mediterranean complexion, but now he thought it tiredness. Long vertical creases he'd not noticed before carved through smooth cheeks. Lowry wondered when Oldham was due to retire. The army wouldn't be that dissimilar to the police force. There must be a limit to how rewarding castigating naughty soldiers could be.

'Well, let us have the garage owner's details, and we shall notify the family.'

Lowry shook his head. 'We need it in a civilian investigation.'

'Of course. Of course. I see – why trouble to make a visit otherwise?'

'Two local businessmen were attacked by two assailants on

a country lane outside Copford,' Lowry explained. 'In addition, one of the victims of this attack recently lost a close relative in suspicious circumstances. So, I'd like to rule out any question of whether the two incidents are related.'

'And how may we help?'

'We would appreciate your assistance in identifying Drake's close friends.'

'Very well.'

'There may be a degree of urgency – the car dealer said the soldiers were decamping?'

'I was just on my way for the falling-out. It is beyond my power to stop the wheels turning, but I think I may be able to root out the individuals you wish to speak to before they leave. Give me five minutes.'

The captain rose. Lowry moved up slowly.

'We'd like to inspect the deceased's – Corporal Drake's – accommodation and personal effects for his movements over the last week.'

'The room has been cleared: his belongings itemised.'

'Find anything unusual?'

'He had rather a lot of cash on his person.'

'How much?'

'Nearly three hundred pounds.' Oldham stood behind his chair, manicured nails resting on its back. 'Gambling, maybe? For the single men, their salary's often fully disposable. Not many are inclined to save, especially when on leave. There's endless tournaments in the NAAFI, table football, darts, you name it . . .'

'And off camp?'

'Now that you mention it, a few lads – Drake and another – were spotted in an altercation with some coloureds over a pool table in a pub.'

'Coloureds?' Gabriel uttered her first word since arriving.

'Black gentlemen.'

'He was there with a friend? Where and when?'

'The Robin Hood in Osborne Street, that afternoon – after Cousins was found.'

'Why, when we were jointly investigating the death in the high street – the duel – didn't you mention this? We were hunting high and low for any link to civilians.'

Oldham's expression changed.

'Come now, we were looking for a girlfriend, not a West Indian pool player.'

'West Indian? Know that for fact?' Lowry said curtly.

'I – I didn't see for myself.'

'So, Drake's companion that afternoon – you know who the man was?'

'That I *can* tell you.' The Beard may not want them looking into this business of seconds, but this was different: he could hand Atkinson over to Lowry. 'Undoubtedly the same man you seek to question.'

'Are you sure?'

'Yes, I am certain. You must hurry though; the men

disembark at twenty hundred hours. Fairweather will take you in the Jeep.'

Lowry was at the doorway already.

'One more thing, inspector. The men do not yet know Corporal Drake is no longer with us.'

Hyderabad Barracks

For the third time, Atkinson checked under the bed, the chest of drawers and the wardrobe. All empty. He had everything, no doubt – his kitbag sat slumped stoutly in the corner – yet he couldn't remember packing a thing. Since Drake's arrest his mind was in turmoil. Unable to focus and full of nerves, he was so transfixed with getting out of Colchester he was basically on autopilot.

He just wanted out. He could take the streets of Londonderry; anything would be better than this, this uncertainty.

Drake's ugly mug haunted his every moment. Rumour was rife that he had topped himself in the clink. Atkinson didn't believe it: they would have to have told them. His company were out at eight p.m. He was plagued by visions of being pulled from the unit at the last minute. The sooner he was on the truck and out of Essex the better.

The surfaces were largely bare but a tin of boot polish and a cloth sat ready on the chest of drawers. He lit a cigarette and set to work. As he rubbed away at his boot leather, he played over the scenarios for the millionth time: Drake was not his friend, so there was no reason on earth for him to keep quiet. But then again, that was what he had done. There was a code and he'd followed it: Burnett and he had done what was expected. They had accepted the role of seconds, and they had not grassed. Even Oldham, that bastard, even he, somewhere deep down, must understand *that*.

The door was flung open and his heart jumped. The sound of laughter put him a little more at ease; top brass never laughed. It was Pearson and Steele.

'You'll never guess what,' Pearson bounded over, an excited jumble of embarkation nerves and camp gossip, 'there's a civvy copper on his way over to see you.'

'Me?'

'Heard the sergeant take the call from Flagstaff – 'ere, look, down there.' The pair were craning their necks at the window. 'It's the boxer and some bird.'

Atkinson froze. Lowry – he was here the morning Drake shot Cousins. He leapt over to the window. Sure enough, there below was a figure in a donkey jacket and pale grey suit crossing the quad under the spotlights.

'What the f—'

It was one thing dealing with the sadistic Oldham, but this guy was different – his reputation extended beyond the canvas of the boxing ring; those that had crossed his path in town said he was impossible to get a measure on. No clue what he was after until it was too late.

CHAPTER 36

'Mind if I smoke?' Lowry gestured to the tin ashtray on the soldier's cabinet.

The soldier shrugged. 'Sure.'

Atkinson celebrated his twenty-first birthday in July. Pale skin not yet razor-tough, this lad had four years' service under his belt, including a tour of Northern Ireland, and he was now off for a second.

'All set?'

'Reckon.' He seemed calm, but his eyes betrayed jitters.

'I won't keep you long. A friend of yours, a Lance Corporal Drake, recently sold his car to a dealer on Clacton Road. A Fiesta. And a car fitting the same description was also recently involved in an incident on the lane to Birch, outside Copford.'

'I don't know the area.'

'West of here, not on the way to anywhere really; a few Blackwater hamlets, that's all.'

'Oh, right.'

'Do you know anyone living that side of Colchester?'

'I don't know the area.' Atkinson repeated himself, more

than likely unaware he'd done so. Lowry was spooking him. He didn't know how to take authority if it didn't come with stripes on the arm or stars on epaulets.

'Two men were hijacked and roughed up. One of the men targeted in the attack, a Mr Hughes-Roper, was just heading home for a cup of tea.'

'Oh, right.'

'I'll cut to the chase here. There were two men in this Fiesta, two men involved in the attack – and I think you, Atkinson, were one of them. Now, listen closely. The car has been dusted for fingerprints, and Captain Oldham has granted permission for us to take yours. But matching them up will take time and you've pressing business in front of you, right? So I thought, to save both of us some bother, you can just tell me in confidence if you were involved.'

Lowry let the words sink in. The sound of moving furniture scraped and thumped through the ceiling and shouts echoed along the corridors. An exodus was in full flow.

'Are you nervous?'

'About what?'

'Northern Ireland; what else have you to worry about?'

Atkinson's lips parted slightly, about to speak, then changed his mind.

Lowry ground the cigarette out. 'I'm sure it's not something a man takes lightly. Ireland, that is.'

They sat without saying a word. In the main dormitory space, soldiers shifted kitbags about and spoke in hushed tones. Lowry pushed up his sleeve to reveal his watch. 'Nearly eight.'

'I need to go. If I ain't on the truck, there'll be hell to pay.' This was the most Atkinson had said, but the words had no teeth and he started to fidget.

Lowry offered his olive branch. 'There will be no charges brought. Against the men in the Fiesta.'

Atkinson met his eye, but was cautious, wary of a trick. The policeman's voice was soft and low, no trace of Oldham's menace. He wanted to trust him. Or her, the beautiful WPC woman who was all the while quietly watching. Beyond the door, heavy boots approached, and a cropped head poked round the corner. ''Scuse me, sir, all right to say cheerio to our lad here?' a Northern voice asked politely. Lowry held open his palm. Another head appeared and salutary well wishes were exchanged, then the soldiers left and the building emptied.

'You not gonna let me go then?' Atkinson said eventually, breaking the silence.

'Not until I find out who was in the Fiesta that morning. Now, no doubt you'll be thinking, why does he need to know who was in the car if no charges are being brought?'

The soldier inclined his head a fraction.

'Understandable – the men assaulted were inclined to over-look it,' Lowry continued. 'The incident was no real bother to them. Not compared to other aspects of their lives. Let's put it this way: these men, they can do without the attention.'

'So why not let it go?' Atkinson said, almost angrily.

'Because this – frankly irritating – incident has become pivotal to a whole bunch of other stuff. Stuff that I need to get to the bottom of.'

'I've done nothing wrong.' Springs creaked as he shifted on the bed. 'Please let me go,' he said beseechingly to Gabriel.

'Were you in the car?' she asked.

He nodded at her.

'Now, why would a pair of battle-toughened soldiers be roughing up two middle-aged businessmen?' Lowry held up a finger to prevent Atkinson speaking. 'Yes, I know the other was a soldier. But it's you I'm talking to. Now, I'm guessing someone paid you to take a swing at one of them?'

'This'll not get back to the captain? Not that it matters, I could be dead this time next week. If,' he paused, 'I get on that truck.'

'You have my word. And you'll be on the truck in no time.'

'Some fella me mate met down the pub wanted frighteners up a bloke with a posh name. Dunno who it was. You'll have to ask me mate, Drake. His car, innit. Only trouble is, he's locked up right now. And Drake's not really a mate – just sort of know him, same platoon, like. We didn't mean to hurt anyone, just warn the posh one he was making a mistake crossing this fella that give us a couple of quid – we were skint, cards 'ad burnt a hole in our pockets ... dunno how. No one was hurt until the fat one fell over.'

This was the confirmation they needed. It *was* Hughes-Roper they were after.

'What did you say to frighten him?'

'Told him to rethink this fella's offer and not to worry, he'll "not paint it black". Those exact words.'

'And what was the man's response?'

'He just nodded.'

'This man in the pub, was he black, by any chance?'

'Yeah, wears fancy clothes, bright like a peacock. Can't miss him.'

'This in the Robin Hood pub?'

'Yeah, not really 'is sort of place, stood out like a – a—'

'A fancy-dressed black dandy in a pub full of squaddies?' Lowry finished the sentence for him. It was unlikely it could be anyone else. Topize. Had to be. As soon as Oldham had mentioned black guys, Lowry had made the jump. But he hadn't had time to figure out anything beyond that.

'You know the geezer, then. Please, can you let me go?'

'Okay.' Lowry said. Atkinson rose. 'But the Robin Hood, was that where you met him in the first place? His name is Topize. It's an unlikely place for him to be.'

'Honest, I don't know where Drake first met him. I went along for the ride. It's his car; ask him.'

Atkinson already had his pack on.

'Is there anyone else who might know? Just curious.'

'Cousins. But he's gone.' And with these words, the young soldier clattered off to join his comrades in one of the most perilous places on earth. Lowry wished him luck but his words only echoed in the empty dormitory room.

He stood. Everything was starting to fall into place.

'I've not met Gordon Topize,' said Gabriel, 'but if that's who you think might be behind this, what would he be doing posturing in a pub like that – it's not the picture Kenton painted of the man living quietly in the Stour valley?'

'Good question. Bizarre, contradictory behaviour, drawing attention to himself like that. He's either stupid or crazy.'

'Or very clever.' Outside, the bark of a sergeant major could be heard shouting 'fall out'. Gabriel moved to the high, small window.

'Why do you say that?' Lowry asked.

'Every witness in town is halfway to Northern Ireland. Tomorrow all those boys in the Robin Hood will be gone.'

Lowry joined her at the window. 'So he's either stupid, or crazy, or lucky, or – or he's very familiar with troop movements, which is no less bizarre.'

Atkinson ran with all his might and tossed his kitbag into the rear of the truck. Arms reached down to haul him aboard. Once inside, multiple hands patted him on the back, while inside his ribcage, his heart pounded ten to a dozen.

What had just happened made no sense whatsoever. How did the police locate Drake's car when the men involved hadn't pressed charges? He'd had no bother about describing Topize – of course they were seen in the pub; it was obvious to Atkinson now that Oldham must have had them watched.

In hindsight, it was crazy to meet that weirdo in there. The whole problem was Drake, thinking with his dick.

The only thing that eluded him was why he – or Burnett, for that matter – had not been done for their role as seconds. Either Drake must have held his tongue, or the army valued their soldiering more than it cared about the letter of the law.

Lowry watched Becky's lips, moist with wine. He was listening to what she was saying, but his mind was on Gordon Topize. It was almost certainly him who had commissioned the squaddies to frighten Hughes-Roper. An extraordinary, daring move, brazenly entering a favourite army watering hole, flamboyantly dressed. He must have known the soldiers were about to ship out, but how?

Still uncertain about what tack to take, Lowry had not yet briefed Sparks on developments. The night desk had said the chief had left and was at home with his wife. He and Kenton would leave for Alphamstone first thing, so unless Lowry caught them before they left, it'd have to wait until they returned. His stomach rumbled. He had not eaten all day; now the prospect of food stirred his hunger.

'Hello, hello, are you with me?'

'Couldn't say,' he said absentmindedly, tapping the menu. 'Come on, what do you fancy?'

'We're in no hurry, surely. We *should* be in Rye after all.'

'I am famished, that's all,' he said and tore off a chunk of bread to demonstrate. And whether he heard her every word, he was aware that a need to talk to someone, or a need for contact, was driving him. As he placed the wine glass down, their fingertips almost touched.

'Do you miss it?'

'Miss what?'

'The boxing! Jesus, you aren't listening at all . . .'

He reached forward and clasped her hands. 'I am, promise. No, I've not given it a second thought. I don't really do anything now, not like you.'

'Not done much twitching by the sounds of it either. Why don't you take up something else?'

'Like what?'

'There are a ton of things.' She herself was very active. Netball, painting, yoga, theatre; the list was endless. Lowry had long suspected teachers had too much time on their hands, and Becky was living proof. 'Golf? Isn't that good for contacts?'

'We have the masons for that. You'd not find a copper on a golf course. No, I could do with more exercise; golf is the least energetic sport . . . if it is even a sport, you should hear Sparks on it. I used to run all the time, but stopped when I quit punching people. Tell me, have you heard of a village near the Suffolk border by the name of Alphamstone? No reason why you should.'

'No, why's that?'

Lowry briefly outlined Topize and his history, then proceeded to describe the remote part of Essex where the man lived. He was curious that a village in Essex could be so hidden.

'And strangely, it's not more than ten miles from here, near Great Henny on the Stour—'

'Sounds enchanting; we should go there some time.'

Lowry had unimaginatively taken Becky to the Woolpack. She had once mentioned she thought it was quaint, and he had seized upon this, sparing himself the effort of thinking further about places to go or things to do together.

Quaint and cosy it was, and as such perfect for a date. Dating, if this was what it was, gave him a phenomenal thirst. Nerves or whatever – a wine bottle would be empty as soon as he looked at it. Pronouncing the bottle of French red done, Lowry made to the bar for another, where stood the man he'd spoken to that morning.

He gave a faint nod in the man's direction. He evidently had not left the spot since then.

'Boasting about his uncle all the time,' the man muttered to no one in particular, slumping forward with eyes swerving this way and that. 'Unless he were deaf, couldn't miss 'im,' the man continued.

'Who?' Lowry moved closer, realising the man was attempting to communicate with him directly.

'Colin Cooper. You never said 'e was brown bread; 'eard it on the radio.' The man's voice rose in drunken aggression.

Lowry regretted getting into it. He signalled the landlord, ordered his wine and suggested ejecting the drunk. Lowry took his bottle back to their table. How would he ever escape the job if he kept himself to this area? It had been so long since he had been anywhere outside of Essex. Becky looked up at him in the candlelight. Never mind the Suffolk border, would it really have taken that much effort to drive down to the south coast tonight?

He sat down heavily, emphatically, planting more than his body. Since his separation from his wife, an uncertainty had crept into his existence. The steady trundle of the week, bodies, crimes to be solved, punctuated by booze and tranquilisers. The latter – for all his castigation of Kenton – had become a dependency. Quitting boxing had slowed him down in all manner of ways. Physical and mental alertness were inseparable. Here he was with an attractive, intelligent woman – who for some reason seemed to *like* him – and the only things on his mind were police work and plonk.

What the hell was wrong with him?

He topped up her glass.

'So, what's going to happen to the legendary Whitethroat?' Becky had clearly listened to him better than he had to her. She saw this was the only way to communicate with him; through the job.

'Oh, we're going to pay him a visit in the morning,' Lowry said.

'What, arrest him?'

'Ask him some questions.'

'Shame, the world needs colourful characters like that to

break the monotony of the drunken bores that litter this place.'

'Don't worry, it's only for a chat; we're not arresting him, as such.'

'Hmm, I wonder whether he'd see it that way.'

'Enough about that,' he said. 'Let's talk about . . . travelling.' The word sounded foreign on his lips.

'I'll drink to that!'

A wave of relief rushed through him and, unsteadily, he lifted his glass and said, 'Here's to you.'

'Not us?'

He smiled weakly and clinked her glass. 'Us.'

CHAPTER 37

The chief's Brut aftershave filled the Capri and Kenton wondered whether he could risk winding the window down.

'There's no guarantee he'll be there, but early Saturday morning, there's as good a chance as any. Remember the way?' Sparks asked.

'Of course. Thanks for asking me to accompany you.' Kenton, without wishing to appear obsequious, thought it best to appear keen. He had not taken any dope this morning and his hands were sweating on the steering wheel.

The chief and he did not historically get on, and Sparks could commandeer any Uniform driver, so he had to make an effort. The chief's disparaging look this morning as Kenton appeared on Creffield Road, and the exaggerated groan as he lowered himself into the passenger seat of the Capri, did nothing to dissuade him from believing there must be an ulterior motive. The only time Sparks had shown any regard for Kenton whatsoever was over his ability as an athlete, so Kenton could only assume there was some sporting challenge he wished him to undertake, representing the force – swim

the Blackwater or some such notion. Or perhaps some excru-
ciating post-mortem on the whole Fox Farm incident was on
the cards . . . but no.

'You, sunshine, need to be educated if you're going to understand this place. You want that, right? To be serious about
police work out here?'

'Sir, yes, sir. Of course . . .'

'Good man, now put your foot down, it's about twenty-five
miles away; we don't want to take all day over it.' Sparks lit
up an Embassy. Kenton caved and rolled down the window.

On the winding route cross country, Sparks gave an account
of the region's dealings with, as he put it, 'ethnic groups'.

'Essex. East-Saxon. That's where we start. After the Romans
skedaddled, the Saxons cruised up the Thames, took a liking
to the north shore and promptly injected ancient Kraut-Nordic
genes into our make-up. They settled, and for the next four
hundred years lived more or less peacefully – the odd skirmish
with the neighbours aside – until a violent period of slugging
it out with the Vikings.'

Kenton frowned into the mid-distance; the chief's rhetoric,
even when tinged with truth, was difficult to follow.

'What about the Normans?'

'That's the south coast, your Sussex mob. The Norseman is
essentially the same deal, albeit with a touch of the Frenchman
about him. Here on the east coast, our gene pool was settled
at the Battle of Maldon in 991. The point is, we are a hell

of lot closer to Thor than to Chicken George, as defined by geography.'

'I can't argue with that.'

'Exactly: any colour blending with our pasty complexion will have been imported, with the exception of the Second World War. A lot of Americans over here in East Anglia during the war. Everyone knows about the airfields, stretching up through Suffolk and on into Norfolk, but what they forget is the infantry. The entire black infantry division for D-Day, five thousand of them, were stationed here.

'If ever a nation held back the progress of civilisation, it's the Americans. It should lead by example. But does it? Does it, hell! Their Civil War was fought over slavery – but segregation was enforced right up until the sixties. When the US Army wound up here in 1942, whites in one camp, blacks in another, it set a tone. You know? Our impressionable community, many of whom had never seen a black face anywhere but on a jam jar, saw segregation and thought, *black people are different*.'

'Buffalo soldiers,' Kenton said. 'I didn't know they were in Colchester, but that makes sense given the town's place in the war.'

'Don't get me wrong. Personally, I never had a problem with them.'

'*Them*, sir?'

'Yes, them – as in, not us. Don't interrupt. My old mum worked at the Red Cross social club, a place for coloured troops in St Botolph's, and it never did her any harm. Loved the music they played. Anyhow, guess that had an impact on me; I didn't think twice before helping Topize when I found him that night. There's those that would have left him to die.'

Kenton drove on, faintly moved.

'Anyhow, the Americans weren't here long, they shipped out. Three years later in 1948, the Windrush crowd came to Tilbury. You wouldn't know Tilbury, nothing there but a fort . . .'

'. . . Where Elizabeth I reviewed the fleet before taking on the Spanish Armada. On the Thames, where your Saxons disembarked,' Kenton said.

Sparks laughed loudly and slapped Kenton hard on the thigh, causing him to momentarily depress the clutch. 'So, yeah, the UK imported those people to help rebuild Blighty – but they had no impact out here in Essex: over half of them found refuge in an underground shelter at Clapham Common, and sought work through the nearest labour exchange at . . . ?'

'Brixton?'

'Correct. It was not until the fifties, when the NHS cast the net a bit wider, that a number of Mauritians were recruited as nursing staff for Turner Village.'

'And that's when our man appears?'

'Exactly.'

'When did you last see him?'

'Not for many years. Whitethroat had a theatrical element about him. He would pop up now and again but then disappear, often for months. Until finally he went away for good, it seemed . . . to set up a travel business in Mauritius. I guess he comes and goes.'

'Why is he back now?' Kenton was more curious than ever to see the man again.

'We shall ask him, but my guess is he's making sure the travel company is selling Mauritius properly. Tropical paradise. Coral reefs. Very exotic.'

Topize was fascinated. The man standing before him bore little resemblance to the slender young man with the thin moustache who had pulled him out of the gutter back in 1953. *This is the man who saved my life*, he thought.

'So, you are top of the pile now!' Gordon greeted Sparks warmly.

'You're not doing so bad yourself, sunshine – sitting on a pile yourself. Classy gaff. You've landed on your feet.'

'Hard work and enterprise: pennies earned here on earth.'

'No doubt, no doubt. May we?' The old policeman gestured to enter the house.

'Of course, please do. But I suspect you are not here for a reunion, eh?'

Ever since Sparks's young companion had called a few days earlier, Topize anticipated they'd return and had made provisions accordingly: one being moving Saffron out of sight. They bantered on, touching upon Topize's reacquaintance with the law two summers ago. Gordon was in no doubt this was the reason for the second visit.

'It's funny,' Sparks was saying, 'when the incident occurred back in that July we had no idea it was you involved.'

'Nor would you.'

A silence hung. Gordon would never willingly bring up his family in conversation.

'The insult was to your wife,' the young man said, 'and the complaint made by the proprietor at the request of several of the other diners. Indeed, you are not mentioned in the report.'

'Maintaining a low profile,' Sparks said.

Again, Topize made no answer. He wanted them to get to the point.

And then it came – Hughes-Roper. A man selling a property was assaulted after showing a prospective buyer the premises. As a consequence the police were interviewing everyone who had expressed an interest in the building. Gordon admitted he was interested but his offer was rejected.

How did he feel about that?

He shrugged.

So what.

The police went quiet.

Beneath Topize's genial exterior, his mind raced. How the hell did they find out about this? Hughes-Roper would never have gone to the police. On the contrary, the man had since called to say the place was his if he wanted it. Not that he could pursue it, with all this carry-on. *How?*

'Are you looking to open a nightclub?'

'Forgive me, gentlemen, but what is this really about? An important senior policeman such as yourself, Inspector Sparks, would not trouble himself to come all the way out here over an assault first thing on a Saturday . . . nice to see you again, though it is.'

'Detective Kenton here had already informed you of Colin Cooper's demise, I believe. What he hasn't told you is that Cooper was an erstwhile employee of Mr Hughes-Roper.'

This took a second to sink in.

'Doing what?'

'A beater,' Sparks said quickly.

'I don't follow?'

'With the shoot – beating, you know, shooing the birds from the hedgerows for the gunmen – basically a farmhand.'

'That is a part of this country's cultural heritage I know nothing about,' Topize said, puzzled. 'So anyway, what's the score – suspicion is cast my way? When I just try to help?' He glared at the young one. 'That how it is? What does me giving some ol' building a dekko mean to you anyways?'

'I take your point, Mr Topize. Unfortunately, though, the person who viewed the building after your offer was rejected ended up in hospital.'

The soldier boys had mentioned some collateral damage – Hughes-Roper's companion, tougher material than he, had interrupted the scene, slipped and taken a dive. No mention of a hospital, though.

'Who?'

'That's not your concern.'

'Maybe it's a good job I didn't get it then. Place is clearly jinxed.'

The police said nothing.

'We are exploring every avenue, Mr Topize. You have a past connection to Colin Cooper, you had a dispute with his employer over a property sale, the property owner gets a nasty visit, and a third party interested in the same property ends up in bandages down the County Hospital. See how this looks to us?'

Topize felt his anger rising. 'That shit outside the restaurant was over two years ago, goddammit!'

'But Cooper was in hiding for months,' said Kenton. 'His friend told us, for fear of reprisal – he was out of circulation for a spell. Maybe, after that, you bided your time, left it to blow over and allowed him to let his guard down?'

'Man, I have forgotten all about that. Bigger fish to fry. I'm a businessman. Jesus.'

'So enlighten us here, what are your interests, the holiday game?' Sparks said evenly.

Recalibrating his thoughts, Topize reckoned the chief of police himself turning up on his doorstep was not a cause for major alarm: if they seriously marked him for murder, they'd bundle him into the back of a van as soon as look at him.

No, laughable though it was, the old copper was here out of sentimentality. Instinct told him the police were reaching in the dark. However, here they were, and they had questions he would have to answer. Gordon breezily explained his business, the back and forth across the Indian Ocean, the beauty of Mauritius. 'You should try it,' he suggested to Sparks, 'get you some winter sun?'

'One day perhaps,' Sparks agreed, 'but back to Copford Grange. What exactly would you want with a place that big, with all this other activity?'

'What the good goddamn has that got to do with anything!'

The problem here for Gordon was he could not divulge what lay behind the manor without opening the proverbial box of frogs. He had to play this smart.

He told them the place had caught his eye first in the newspaper and then in the estate agent's window. In fact, Silvia had seen it on her way into Colchester and telegrammed him in Mauritius telling him she'd found the perfect building for what they had in mind.

'I'm sorry,' he said. 'Please, I want to help, but I still don't understand why all this fuss over some old building, when I see for the first time in nearly thirty years the man who saved my life?'

CHAPTER 38

Lowry woke, eyes focusing slowly on an unfamiliar ceiling. For a second he'd not remembered where he was. He shifted in the bed. Light passed through a chink in the long, dark curtains and touched the smooth shoulder beside him, turning the skin to gold under a black negligée strap.

How had they ended up here, in Colchester, having dined in Coggeshall?

He remembered the third bottle of wine.

Then it came flooding back.

I am not ending this night in another woman's bed.

And so she had called for a taxi.

Propping himself up on his elbows, he felt strangely good, giddy. He checked his watch. Jesus, it was nearly nine. The heavy curtains had lulled him into believing it was still early. Sparks would have set off already. He'd head over to Queen Street and wait. Moving further upright, he felt the effect of the cheap red wine.

A hand reached out and touched his thigh.

'I don't expect you to hang around all day, there's not much to see.' She turned over, pupils dilating in deep grey eyes as they caught the sunlight. 'But leaving right now would be considered the height of bad manners.'

Surprise brushed the faces of the two men in the Capri when they saw the familiar Saab in the Queen Street car park. The desk sergeant confirmed Lowry was in the vicinity but had stepped out. Sparks grunted and said he'd give him fifteen minutes before returning home. The chief was dissatisfied with the morning's outing. His conscience was troubled. The only thing they had achieved was to wind the man up.

Kenton followed the chief up the stairs, but turned off at CID. He wanted to take another look at the file on the junkie found in the Dutch Quarter. The pathologist's photos in particular. He hadn't admitted it to himself at the time, but he was sure he recognised the man from the Bugle. Indeed, he thought they may have shared a bifter round the back of the pub. What use this was he didn't know, but it was probably nothing good. He had thought to mention it to Lowry, but given the lecture he'd received on his dope intake, he'd held out. He longed for nothing more now than to mong out on the couch with a large one and Pink Floyd on the turntable. All the more so for having held off his usual morning blaze. He'd just have one more flick through . . .

He pushed open the door to discover a tall, tanned man in a dark suit at his desk with the file in his hands.

'Hello?'

The man did not look up.

'Excuse me?' Kenton said.

'And you are?' He turned, presenting an unshaven face, high cheekbones and a squint.

'Kenton, Detective Kenton.'

'Freathy, Inspector Freathy, drugs squad.'

Kenton swallowed.

Freathy placed the file on the desk. 'Ever since the New Year's drug haul went missing, we have been monitoring Colchester's drug fatalities.'

'Oh.'

'My, it's busy today,' Gabriel said breezily, coming into the office. 'I've just seen Lowry and Sparks . . . Who's your friend?'

'This is Inspector Freathy from the drugs squad. My colleague, Detective Gabriel.'

'Toxicology reports are missing,' Freathy said.

'They're not in.'

'Are these your Rizlas? Mind if I take one?' the detective asked. He picked the slender, green pack up off the desk and pulled two papers out. 'Be so good as to notify me when you have it – the toxicology report.'

Freathy handed him his card and left.

'That was all a bit odd,' Gabriel said.

'What are you doing here?'

Unknown to Kenton, Gabriel had a habit of coming in on Saturdays when the office was quiet, and catching up on paperwork.

'Right now I'm about to drive out to see Howard Osgood. Keep me company?'

It was not in Gabriel's nature to leave anyone troubled if she could help it. She bottled up her emotions but believed this unusual and followed the maxim 'a problem shared'. Except Kenton was not forthcoming; he barely uttered a word as they got into the car.

'I suspect he was from County,' Gabriel said as she drove, attempting to draw him into conversation. 'They're taking a hard line on drugs. Two officers were suspended for using in Chelmsford last week.'

'Great . . .' he said unenthusiastically.

'Sparks'll have nothing to fear with his athletic tribe. It'll be that Greenstead gang from last winter. My aunt thinks it was hushed up by the military. The drugs. Never found.'

Osgood's place was near Peldon, a village on the mainland, bordering the Strood, the road across to Mersea Island. The house was on a rise, set back from the road behind a neat lawn the size of a football pitch. The building itself was an ugly, modern affair, outsized Doric columns fronting plain brickwork, whacked up in a matter of days, probably. The message was loud and clear: biggest is best.

They parked on a gravel driveway large enough to turn an articulated lorry.

'Right, you okay to wait here?' Gabriel wanted to make amends and pay a personal call on Osgood to put his mind at rest. Kenton wouldn't help, not in his current frame of mind.

She climbed out of the car, alone. As the doorbell chimed deep within the house, she glanced back at Kenton, his schoolboy face behind the windscreen. What on earth was going on with him?

A woman of indeterminate age with a warm smile opened the door.

'Ah, Mrs Osgood, I presume? I'm Detective Gabriel.'

Osgood's wife placed a cup of tea neatly on the corner of the table. Osgood's house was spacious and done out in heavy red and purple. They had the exact same Laura Ashley curtains as her aunt over in Saffron Walden.

Osgood didn't speak until his wife left the room.

'I appreciate you coming out, in your own time,' he said, face creasing into a worn smile. She had phoned ahead, before setting off.

'I owe you an apology, Mr Osgood . . . I leapt to conclusions.'

'Forget about it.' He sat back. 'Just catch Colin's killer, else I'll never hear the end of it.'

'We're making progress.'

'What business would soldiers have roughing up Hughes-Roper?'

'They were paid to do it; it's complicated.'

'Try me.'

Gabriel took a breath. She would not reveal Drake's suicide. Here was a tired, ageing man, ready for the quiet life, not the thug she had seen flicking a man half his age into the water earlier this week. 'You were right to suspect the attack was aimed at Mr Hughes-Roper. He had upset a prospective buyer for the same property you'd just seen and it seems you were unfortunately caught up in the dispute.'

'Dispute, eh? Who would take offence with a fella like Hughes-Roper, I wonder?'

'A Mr Topize.'

'Topize, as in Gordon Topize?'

'Yes ... why, do you know him?'

'Only by reputation ... I don't – I never met him.'

Gabriel noted a reaction and said, 'You seem troubled.'

'It's a blast from the past, that's all – he, from what I recall, was a bit of a face, Jack the Lad ... thought he'd buggered off back to where he came from.'

'So did everyone at the station.'

'I bet.'

'He was known as Whitethroat.'

'Yes ... yes, I'd heard that.'

Queen Street HQ

'Suit, even at the weekend, eh?' Sparks wondered why Lowry was in.

'I have news from the garrison.'

Sparks listened intently, nursing a tumbler of scotch. That Topize was more deeply involved did not surprise him; he was almost pleased. Certainly relieved. Pushing back his chair, he stretched his legs out, ankles up on the desk. 'Hmm, makes sense to me,' he said. 'Send some black fellas out to put the wind up the man, and Hughes-Roper wouldn't hesitate before reporting it. But send a pair of squaddies in civvies to do the job . . . might try him at his own game.'

'Topize was certainly not afraid to let him know it was him. Show-off that he is.'

'Right. So Hughes-Roper makes his move in the form of Colin Cooper, striking directly at Topize himself, who promptly dispatches him into the Colne.'

'Exactly, though Cooper probably wouldn't have acted alone . . . you need to poke that posh plum a bit, get him to spill the beans.'

They sat in contemplative silence.

'You seem different,' Sparks said after a while. 'Happier?'

'Just the same. Here,' Lowry reached beneath him and produced a bottle, 'happy birthday.'

'Ah, I'd forgotten! You needn't have.' Sparks was more than appreciative. 'Great stuff, this Scallywag!'

'No bother; I'm not cooking you supper though.' Lowry smiled. 'How is Antonia?'

'Good, she's good. Speaking of, I should go, though.' He finished his drink. As men they were unable to communicate further beyond this brief exchange.

'Who's the Clint Eastwood with the black Granada in the car park?'

'Drugs squad sniffing around, Inspector Freathy. Nothing

to worry about. One final thing – are we a hundred per cent sure Topize hired those boys? He won't come easy.'

'The landlord at the Robin Hood confirmed the soldier's story.'

'All right, send out the boys in blue. He's yours when they bring him in. My stroll down memory lane is done.'

'He recognised you this morning, right? Did you share a moment?'

'Huh. Seemed to, yeah. Against the odds: I had way more hair in them days, and a natty pencil moustache, like Errol Flynn. He, on the other hand, looks the spit of the day I scooped him up – trim as you like, healthy.'

'Sunshine for you.'

The chief adjusted his feet on the desk. 'Life's treated him well, can't argue with that. Though it can't just have been hanging out in paradise; there's been some lurking in the shadows over the years, I dare say – why the hell else would he be living out in Dingley Dell. You should have seen his gaff. Like Snow White's cottage. Devil of a job to find it. There lies a man not wishing to be seen. How a man that private came to be parading around in a spit-and-sawdust sort of joint like the Robin Hood plotting with soldiers, I can't understand.'

'Where would you expect to find him?'

'Good question. But I know where he'll be tonight. Downstairs.' Giving the thumbs-down motion to indicate the cells, Sparks picked up the phone to issue the order.

'I should go.'

'No. Uniform will pick him up.'

'If you're sure . . .'

'And leave him to stew overnight.'

'Okay,' Lowry agreed.

For all his flippancy, Sparks felt disappointment heavy in his stomach. The Scotch had done nothing to numb it. He'd expected more from Topize. But why? Just because he saved his neck back in the day, didn't mean he'd reformed him in some deep way. Hell, it's only natural to hope for the best for a man with all the cards stacked against him, black and an immigrant at a time of deep national tension. But stuff him, a night in the cells without explanation never did anyone any harm.

'In the meantime, lean on that posh wally – if he's one of Enoch's boys, you'll draw it out of him. Pompous git of his kind, he can't keep it too far below the surface. And beat him down on the price of that boat while you're at it.'

Lowry watched Sparks reverse the Rover and waved him off. Two marked Cortinas and a Comma van left shortly after him, bound for the Stour valley. The sight of the black Granada reminded him to check in with the duty sergeant about this bloke from drugs squad. Lowry was not so dismissive as the chief – Freathy wouldn't have expected the chief to be at Queen Street on a Saturday, so his choosing the weekend to 'sniff around' gave rise to concern. As if reading his mind, the desk sergeant said Detectives Kenton and Gabriel were taken by surprise too. Lowry asked the sergeant to contact Gabriel and have both of them meet him tomorrow at Copford Green at half past eleven under the old cart lodge; he had not let on to Sparks, but he had the perfect plan to lean on Hughes-Roper.

The lugubrious bluesy opening to a Traffic tune twanged as Kenton bombed through the door of the Bugle. The troops had shipped out the night before, so there were only a handful of doleful regulars at the bar. He needed a drink to take the edge off – no way could he just go home and mellow out after running into the drugs squad.

Kenton stood before the bar, as if seeing the place – the place he'd spent many, many hours in – for the first time. Finding the drugs squad officer in CID had shaken something loose. His personal life and professional duty had come together, called into question, and it was deeply unsettling.

Down the far end, Julian was casually pinging darts. Kenton bought a pint. He'd not seen the plumber since the discovery of the dead junkie and they got chatting over a game.

'Don't worry, dude, he was mixing his intake – got the balance wrong. Wait . . . you here in an official capacity?'

Julian's playfulness did not alter his mood.

'501?'

Kenton, needing to take his mind off things, agreed. 'Nearest the bull,' he said, somewhat sourly.

'Lighten up, mate. I only ask cos some of your friends've already been in here.'

'Very funny.' He lined up for the bull.

'I'm serious,' Julian said.

The dart hit the metal on the twenty-five ring and came spinning back at him, skittering across the floor with such ferocity the few heads in the bar turned in his direction. Kenton tingled like ice.

CHAPTER 39

'Well, this is all very jolly on a Sunday. Magnificent, huge hayloft up there supported on these rickety old timbers, surprised it's still standing.'

But for all his enthusiasm, Kenton did not appear that jolly as the three of them converged under the lopsided ancient timber structure by the grassy verge. Lowry had asked Kenton to come for observation, but he also wanted to distract the young detective, stimulate him. 'This must be seventeenth century if it's a day, and of interest to that historical mind of yours – but nothing compared to what's in store,' Lowry said.

Gabriel lingered back, hands in pockets, and smiled across knowingly.

'Why, where are we going?'

'Church. Hop in.' He moved to the Saab. 'Quite unique, but it's a short drive.'

Lowry had taken note of a crucifix on the wall at Hughes-Roper's and had marked him as a religious man, probably central to village life. It was Remembrance Sunday and Lowry had a hunch he'd be in the thick of it.

What better place to quiz a person on extreme views than at church? Copford church was little way out, screened by a cluster of oak trees, and shared parking with the local cricket club.

'I'll wait here.' Gabriel rested against the Saab as the church bells began to sound beyond the trees.

'Very deep roof,' Kenton remarked at the expanse of warm red tiles reaching up to a steep apex, dwarfing the squat, stone masonry walls.

'Wait until you see inside,' Lowry said, and moved purposely up the path. Kenton quickened his step to keep up. As he did so, he heard the strains of a hymn from within.

Inside, Kenton was awestruck. The beauty of the wall paintings and ceiling decoration – he had never seen anything like it. The two of them stood at the back in silence. As the hymn came to an end, Hughes-Roper stepped forward to read a lesson. Kenton began to listen as it drew to a close. He had heard it before. The man spoke eloquently, in possession of the words:

Who is wise and understanding among you? Let them show it by their good life, by deeds done in the humility that comes from wisdom.

When the service had ended, they stood discreetly outside the church porch, overhearing the vicar converse with members of the congregation as they left. Kenton heard Hughes-Roper before he set eyes on him.

'Ah, Inspector Lowry. The police are much like the clergy, eh? No rest on a Sunday.' He joined them on the pristine grass, nodding and smiling as people passed him by.

'Only on special occasions.'

'Much like our ever-diminishing flock, then,' he said dourly. 'Did you catch the service?'

'The tail end, yes. We heard your lesson.'

'Ah. Very good. Now what brings you out here?' He gestured them further on to the grass with his walking stick. 'May we take a stroll through the churchyard?'

'A unusual building,' Kenton said, 'must be ancient?'

'Norman, bequeathed to my ancestors by the bishop of London in 1548, along with the Hall.'

'Impressive.'

'And it's been in the family ever since?' Lowry drew along him.

'No, the Hall changed hands years back; I live in the lodge where you visited me on Friday. The chapel belongs to the Church.'

'You are a pillar of the community.'

'I do my bit, yes.' Hands behind his back, holding his cane as they walked, he had the demeanour of a headmaster patrolling school grounds; less proprietor than lofty custodian.

'Simply – and literally – divine,' Kenton said. 'I've never seen medieval paintings like that before – most were covered up.'

'Frescoes, in fact. Impressive, aren't they? The outlines were executed in wet plaster in 1130. One of the county's – the country's – best-kept secrets, here in plain sight for all to visit.'

The images covering the walls and ceiling were a mixture of iconography and signs of the zodiac in rich red, yellow, blue and gold; more like art you might expect to find in a cathedral than a parish church.

'Somehow more surprising under such a – well, frankly innocuous roof,' Kenton said.

'Appearances, eh? Famously deceptive,' Lowry said.

'Ah, inspector, is that slight directed at me, I wonder.'

Lowry didn't answer. 'They say the skin of a Viking invader was nailed to the north door.'

'You're local, to have knowledge like that. I should have guessed, otherwise you'd not have been in the pub the other day. Yes, that is apparently true.'

'How did they know he was a Viking? He'd have been a distance inland?'

'His skin was fair.'

'Sorry,' said Kenton, struggling to keep up. 'I'm missing out here – a human skin, nailed to the church door? Why?'

'As a warning.'

'To who?'

'Invaders.'

'Isn't that rather, er, heathen?' said Kenton. 'For a church, you know?'

'Heathen or not, one must protect what one has from unwanted visitors.'

'And you, Mr Hughes-Roper,' said Lowry, 'what would you do with the skin of a foreigner – a Mauritian say, such as Mr Topize – to prevent him taking possession of your property?'

Kenton froze. But Hughes-Roper did not rise to the bait.

'Ah, so that is what this is about.' Hughes-Roper continued to amble gently through the churchyard. 'That I refused the sale of the Grange. The Viking who was nailed to our chapel door doubtless had fairer skin than you, Inspector Lowry, but that did not give him the right to enter and take what was not his. Likewise, a man can decide to whom he wishes to sell his property.'

'Copford Grange, have you sold it?'

'It remains on the market. Are you interested? I did offer to sell to Mr Topize, as it happens. But he has since changed his mind – unbelievably . . . did you know that?' They did not. 'Now, inspector, where's all this leading?'

'Are your ideological beliefs aligned to Colin Cooper's – and did he carry out any other jobs for you, beyond scattering game birds?'

'What a preposterous suggestion. He couldn't spell the word.'

'A man is dead; a man connected to you and to Gordon Topize.' Lowry was losing his cool. 'I can't make it any simpler. You know exactly what I mean.'

Hughes-Roper stopped at an ornate headstone.

'I am a blue-blooded Englishman, is that a crime? No. Colin Cooper and a number of his ilk were found up at the port where there were demonstrations. They were protesting about immigrants. Rather than them waste their energies, I took a few on. Now, if you are insinuating that I ordered Colin to rough up Mr Topize after his henchmen roughed up myself and his uncle Osgood, I'm afraid you're wrong. But . . . but . . .'

'But what?'

'Colin knew of the attack. I was – and you may not believe it, Mr Lowry, but it's true – I was distressed. And out of loyalty to me, if not to his uncle, he may have taken matters into his own hands.'

'See, that wasn't too painful, was it? Thank you for your cooperation.' Lowry strained to smile; he had the information he needed. Whether or not Hughes-Roper was complicit was another matter. 'You'll be delighted to know Gordon Topize has been arrested for the murder of Colin Cooper. Had you been more straightforward, we may have arrived at this conclusion earlier. If you'd be so good as to come into the station to make a statement, that would be appreciated.'

'Very good,' he said, as they had reached the low stone wall and gate on to the road. 'Oh, inspector, you are not wearing a poppy. Wait a second, there's a collection in the porch.'

'No, thank you.'

'How can you forget those brave men and women?'

'Who said I had? Good day, Mr Hughes-Roper.'

*

'I suppose that was some sort of lesson?' Kenton said as Gabriel rejoined them. If there was one thing he hated, it was to be thought naive. His middle-class upbringing had fostered an unsophisticated view of heroes and villains.

'Take it however you want. Thought you'd be interested in the frescoes. They are unique.' Lowry said.

'Yes, yes. Thank you. Sorry. I thought . . .'

'Hey, forget about it. I wanted the company, too – don't trust myself with our friend there.'

Lowry then updated Gabriel on their conversation with Hughes-Roper as they watched him shake hands with elderly parishioners.

'Strikes me,' she said finally, 'if you did lay a finger on him, angels would sweep down to protect him; if ever a man thought himself untouchable, he's standing right there. Do you think Cooper acted alone? I wouldn't trust him to post a letter.'

'He might've acted under his own impetus. He was a hot-head – you saw him in action, Jane, firing off at his uncle.' Lowry said.

'Yes – but he was hardly effective – Osgood flicked him into the river as if he were a wasp round a Coke bottle.'

'True, true . . . but there is a connection with Topize.' Lowry replied. 'That's all I was after.'

'Cosseted I may be,' Kenton said, 'but all the same, I still don't think Gordon Topize is the sort of fellow that would risk getting estuary mud on handmade leather shoes . . .'

'That's a fair point.' Lowry would now head back to interview Whitethroat. 'How Cooper ended up there is baffling, you're right. Like you, I don't have Topize getting his shoes dirty, and there's nothing we know of that would place him there. Right, thanks; see you both Monday.'

'I think I'll have another gander at those frescoes,' Kenton said.

'Mind if I join you?' Gabriel said.

Kenton's beaming face said it all and Lowry departed alone to Queen Street, feeling for the first time in ages he'd done something worthwhile.

CHAPTER 40

Topize was marched into the interview room. After a night down in the cells he appeared surprisingly well-groomed. Uniform had made it known to him that he had been connected to soldiers involved in an assault in Copford. But that was all they'd let on.

'You cannot keep me here,' he announced.

Lowry stood waiting.

'Yes, we can. You're a prime suspect.'

Topize took these words in and remained standing.

'A night here gives you – and us – pause for thought. Away from the day-to-day distractions.' Lowry circled him. Topize was wearing tailored trousers and shirt. His shoes were handmade as Kenton had said.

'It is only natural you'd look my way for Cooper's murder,' Topize said, while Lowry stood behind him. 'I can't pretend I don't think the world is a better place for it. But you're wrong. It was not me.'

'When was the last time you saw him?'

'I already told you – I ain't seen him since two summers

ago, when he was bogging at me through the restaurant window.'

'How do you feel about the water?'

'The water?' he answered loudly. 'What d'you mean, the water?'

'The sea, Topize. Boats.'

'Gotta catamaran.'

'Where, West Mersea?'

'Jesus, no – you mad? Mauritius. I get on a boat, it ain't gonna be on that murky freezin' puddle you lot go nuts for.'

According to Topize's passport, which Lowry now held in his hand, he had left the country shortly after the incident two summers back and not returned until Christmas – rendering Cooper's retreat from public view pointless. Topize wasn't here; he was hiding from a ghost. Lowry tossed the navy blue passport across the table.

'What are your business interests here?'

'You know,' he waved lazily, 'a couple of shops. Hair and beauty, man.'

'That's your wife's concern. What do *you* get up to – when you're not fraternising with the army in Osborne Street, that is?'

'I operate outta them joints too; we work together. My wife deals with a lot of pampered folk all day in her salons, people with money and time on their hands, but you can tell from this,' he picked up his passport, 'I ain't here that much. Heck, why am I dealing with you? Where is Chief Sparks?'

'Otherwise engaged.' Sparks was at the hospital all day, it being a Sunday. 'So you'll answer to me. How do you spend your time here? At home?'

'Alphamstone? Not a lot happening there. The Indian Ocean, that ma home.' He laid on a thick accent, light green eyes twinkling like a cat. 'That cottage for her.'

'So why come back now?'

Topize spoke easily about his tourist business and the growth in long-haul exotic holidays. 'People go to Spain for two reasons – to eat tapas and to die. Young people with money want exotic locations: tiny islands like mine, or Bermuda the other direction. All these yuppies need somewhere flash to spend their cash. The movies sell it like a big, real-life ad; since *The Deep*, say, scuba has grown massively . . .' he chuckled. 'Same man who give us *Jaws* and make people run away from the water, send them diving in a couple of years later. Or perhaps it's Jacqueline Bisset's impressive aqua-lungs causing folk to reach for a snorkel, eh?' He spoke with the silver tongue of a salesman.

'And this brings you into contact with military personnel, how?' Lowry said.

'I beg your pardon?'

'The men you sent to frighten Hughes-Roper. How did you come across them? The Robin Hood – not being funny, but I don't have you as a regular.'

'Ah – I see. They got to relax when not chasing Irishmen.'

'You're not telling me you have sent squaddies on holiday

to Mauritius?' The impression he had from Oldham, it was feast or famine with the infantry; either broke from gambling or had more money than they knew what to do with – even so, what Topize was offering was at the luxury end, surely.

'One or two made inquiries,' Topize said cagily and sat down. 'Long haul is the future; won't be exclusive forever and before you know it, the cabbies lining the Costa del Sol will all be filling jumbos bound for Goa.' Lowry knew nothing of the travel business; he couldn't even manage a weekend in Sussex, let alone get on a plane to travel halfway round the globe. He let the matter go.

'How long did you plan to be back here in Essex for?'

'Few business matters to attend to, then I leave in two weeks. All being well.' His eyes followed Lowry. 'I can show you the airline ticket if you want.'

Not enough time to close a property deal. Why the interest then?

'What about the Copford building?'

'The location has appeal – out of the way but with great access; the main artery from the east into London. People will travel. But I ain't interested now, I let him know that.'

'The traffic flow for entertainment is usually in the opposite direction.'

'Depends what's on offer. No matter.' His voice trailed off. 'Will you be charging me?'

'Possibly.'

'No way, man.' He rose, aggrieved. 'You got nothin' linking me to those that duff up Hughes-Roper.'

'You just told me you were trying to flog them a holiday?' Lowry watched Topize's expression closely as he moved around the room. He was twitchy, uncertain – confused, even. 'No matter, we aren't interested in that. We are holding you on suspicion of the murder of Colin Cooper. The brush with Hughes-Roper and Osgood is material only in that it led us to you.'

His lip trembled in rage. 'But I told you I didn't do it! There is no proof!'

Topize was close to blowing a gasket, which encouraged Lowry to push on.

'You maimed his friend, took the man's finger. That Cooper was in hiding with his uncle, Howard Osgood, for a period, means nothing. He insulted your wife – family is everything, you believe that. Revenge is all the sweeter for the wait.'

Topize flipped the table up as if it were made of balsa. Two Uniforms rushed in to restrain him as Lowry exited, returning upstairs to his desk. The man had a rage on him, and Lowry could easily imagine him lashing out . . . only, Cooper's was not a violent death and his body was unmarked, apart from a tiny bruise at the back of his head.

On Monday morning, Lowry examined the photos of Cooper's body, looking for anything to give him an inkling as to how he ended up in the water. He must have been on a boat.

Topize didn't have a boat here. Hughes-Roper, on the other hand, did. And he was selling it. What was Lowry missing? He may have established there was a connection, but there were plenty of reasonable explanations for that.

'There's a lady here to see you, guv.' Barnes appeared at his side.

'Not now.'

'Oh, I think you'll want to see her.'

Lowry glanced up. 'Well?'

'Mrs Topize.'

'Really? Show her up, sergeant, show her up.'

Lowry peered into the interview room, where a woman in her late forties sat clutching a handbag. She wore her peroxide blonde hair in a bob, old style from the sixties. He recognised her but couldn't place her.

He entered the room and asked politely how he may help.

'It's about my husband.'

'Of course. Can we offer you anything – tea, coffee?' She glanced apprehensively at the uniformed officer, as if a warm beverage was the last thing he might be capable of, before shaking her head. Lowry dismissed the PC and sat opposite the woman.

'Forgive me, but have we met before?'

'You came into the salon last week. I run a hairdressers', Maravanne, in the town centre.'

'Ah, yes, my apologies. You sat at the till, told me your girls don't date squaddies. It's decent of you to come forward like this, but I am not sure it'll help. Your husband has a short fuse, which does him no favours.'

'He's a very proud man, Mr Lowry.'

'Of that I need no assurance. And quite right too; a man like him must have faced numerous obstacles that many would find insurmountable to get where he is today. With a temper too, it can't have been easy.'

'Oh, he does have a tantrum now and then. He doesn't mean anything by it—'

'That's good to know. A police station is not the best place to start smashing up tables.'

'Please don't laugh at me; I've come to help him.'

Lowry leant back. 'I'm not laughing – that's straightforward, sound advice: don't lose it in the nick, you might not get out anytime soon.'

She looked to her lap, embarrassed. He thought she might cry, but no, she raised her head and said, with steely countenance, 'Not everyone has been through what he's been through.'

'I can only imagine.' Lowry gave a slight nod. 'How did you two meet?'

'At Turner Village, my little brother was there. He was what you used to call a little bit slow. Now they call it something different, more polite . . .' Her eyes rolled, searching for the word. '*Remedial*. Anyway, I met Gordon when he was treating John.'

'Treating him?'

'Helping him to speak.' And then, should there be any doubt, added, 'English.'

'And your brother?'

'He passed away, pneumonia, while he was there. Weak chest.'

Lowry knew of Turner Village. His wife had spoken of it as the site adjoining the new General being built – the old hospital for idiots, architecturally laid out in a 'colony' style, comprised of villas and plenty of open space. Part of the old Eastern Counties Institution set-up, catering for the mentally handicapped across the entirety of East Anglia for a time, long before the huge Severalls asylum out on the north Essex plains. Not nearly as forbidding as that austere colossus transpired to be. Lowry'd seen the patients at the Village – unfettered human shells drifting freely across the relaxation quadrangle and gardens. Jacqui would say half the country's crazies wind up in Essex.

Mrs Topize went on to describe the younger Topize as diligent and hard-working, but impatient to get on. Months had ticked by and promises of education and qualifications grew ever more elusive; the only thing the NHS had to offer the likes of him was longer hours.

'Over time Gordon grew bitter, realising he would never get beyond the level of nurse. He felt cheated – what's the word – less of a man – and that's when the need to strike out took hold of him. He came here with the dream of becoming a doctor. That just wasn't going to happen, and he soon learnt he was not in a progressive part of the health service. He was just as trapped as the inmates. It's not easy working with people like my brother. Gordon wanted a diversion and needed to prove himself; the prospect of remaining a male nurse for the rest of his days was ... well, you've met him.' She half flinched, then smiled reassuringly. 'He never really did anything that bad, but the local boys resented him muscling in on their turf. It was bad enough with the army, soldiers nicking their girls, let alone foreigners.' She touched her hair lightly at the back, indicating that she was once a prize herself. 'But look at him now. He's a successful businessman and people envy him.'

Her husband's story told, or a version of it, she stopped talking; clearly that was all she'd come to say. She was neatly turned out, taking great trouble over her appearance – in that aspect she was in accord with her husband, simmering down in the cellars beneath them. Unlike him, she was petite, compact with a small, delicately upturned nose, softly spoken and of calm disposition. She sat there neatly, looking around at the cracked ceiling and the ancient pipes running alongside the discoloured frosted-glass windows.

'I've not been here in a long time,' she said.

'This room – the police station?'

'My father disapproved of my seeing Gordon and made me report here every week, this room, and give an account of myself to the sergeant, like a common criminal.'

'Seems a bit extreme.' Though so unbelievable as to be true, he thought.

'That's what you'd think, isn't it? The police back then thought him right to do it.'

'When did you marry?'

'1965, in Sudbury.'

'Hence living on the border.'

'Yes, Gordon couldn't quite accept defeat on that level and leave the county.'

'But at the same time didn't want to be found.'

'That, and it was dirt cheap. We've been there ever since. Before that incident with the skinheads no one knew where we lived. Or cared. We opened the first hair salon in Sudbury, where I trained as a stylist the year my father died. Then last year we opened Maravanne. Speaking of, I must be off now before I'm missed.' Silvia Topize paused, and added, 'Gordon is not a violent man, just because of what happened to him, his . . .' She gestured to her throat. 'He never has carried a knife or gun, that I know. The nickname they gave him – it sounds so, so horrible . . . like, oh, I don't know, some gangland flick-knife wielding yobbo.' She paused and noticed Lowry's expression. 'You disagree?'

'Names have different associations for different people. To me, it's just a bird.'

'Never heard of it,' she said, doubtfully. 'What's it look like; is it pretty?'

'Not especially – brownish with a grey head and white throat – but they do sing beautifully.'

'All right, we live in the country; I'll have a look out for one when I hang the washing out.'

'Oh, you won't see one now, they're in Africa for the winter. They return in the spring.'

'Don't blame them. People think Gordon's African – the names they used to call him back then. Jungle bunny and the like; there isn't even any proper jungle in Mauritius.'

'There's a lot of ignorant people out there, Mrs Topize.'

She took the remark with a frown. 'Well, if that's all . . .'

'I only wanted to meet you,' she lingered over her words, 'see if it would help.'

And in that moment Lowry saw why she had come forward on her husband's behalf. Why she had endured the discomfort of having to talk – which was clearly not in her nature – and the distress of being reminded of the past. She did it because she believed it would count – that she, a white woman, could tell Lowry everything was okay, and he would believe her. As if she were reporting in to please her father.

'Please, inspector, can we keep this visit a secret? He'd have my guts for garters if he knew I'd been in here. As I said, he's a very proud man.'

'Mum's the word.'

'Thank you, Inspector Lowry.'

'Nick, please.'

She held out her hand. 'Silvia.'

CHAPTER 41

'Bold of her to come in,' Lowry said. He was pressing Sparks for a decision on charging.

'Doesn't mean a thing; he probably put her up to it.'

'I thought you were on his side.'

'I'm not on anyone's side.' Sparks shrugged. 'He's a wily little fucker, he'd not be where he is today if not: I'd not put anything past him. I'd prefer he were innocent, how could I not? Saving his skin all those years ago ... only for him to murder some dopey kid all these years later? I'd hate to think it. But how can you tell? He's a chip on his shoulder the size of the Mary Rose.'

'I don't see it that way – he's just pleased he's made it in life, and he is cocky to make sure the whole world sees he had the last laugh. Up until last year, one of the hotels in Coggeshall still had a sign outside saying *No fruit pickers, No gypsies, No blacks.*'

'Things change, I agree, but I'd still give the gypos a wide berth; by the time they're good for business, I'll be long gone.' Sparks mused.

'We can't charge him just because he's black – there's no evidence. Apart from the Hughes-Roper thing, but that was just venting off steam, anger at prejudice he can do nothing about. Like you said, he's chippy.'

'Where's his alibi?'

'He told uniform he was at home, which is hard to disprove. . . it's almost as if he's sulking.'

'Sulking? We'll give him something to sulk about. Jesus, he's got to be pushing sixty. Doesn't he realise how serious the situation is?'

'Yesterday he was angry – but it was aimless, like a child . . . frustrated with himself more than anyone in particular.'

'You've changed your perspective. His missus give a good sob story?'

'No – don't leap to the obvious, that's all. Topize is complex and contradictory. Yes, he lied, but so has everyone else . . .'

Sparks pulled an expression of pain and held up his hands. 'Don't start on all that psychology nonsense . . . I'm not listening. Topize either tells us what he was up to during the period in question or we are nailing him. If there's one thing I learnt when Antonia had her fall, it's don't fanny about – life's too short. Know what I mean?'

Lowry drove out to see Osgood at his large, modern house outside the village of Peldon. The man had softened and was almost genial. The riddle of his attackers had been solved and Gabriel's visit had transformed him.

'Colin was involved with an assault in the summer of 1981. Your sister told us you had protected him from possible reprisals.'

'There was some silly thing up on North Hill. I don't know the details. But yes, she wanted him off the streets, so he worked in a pub of mine in Harwich. Nobody was going to find him there.' He chuckled throatily.

'How long for?'

'Only three months or so, as a live-in pot man and cleaner.'

'That was good of you.'

'He's family.' Osgood conceded, 'Besides, the regular pot man was doing a spell in the clink for nutting a drunk fisherman.'

'How many properties do you own round here?'

'A handful. A couple of pubs and bars. Used to have more residential properties, inherited from my old man, but can't be doing with the hassle.'

'The flat in Rowhedge?'

'Yes, that's mine – my father's originally – it comes with a mooring and that's why I hang on to it. He owned a fair slice down there towards Fingringhoe; a boatyard down on the south quay, all mothballed for donkey's years. An eyesore slab of concrete I couldn't bring myself to get rid of, until now – the whole lot went under the hammer. The Hippodrome is going to cost a pretty penny to sort out, so I could do with some cash . . .'

'Where?'

'Only the old dock, which has not seen any proper use in

years. The old man used to have a lot more – acres of sand
and gravel pits up by Geedon Creek near Fingringhoe. He
bought it after the war, from an old soldier who'd gone mad
in the desert, he reckoned. Got it dead cheap.' Osgood took a
thoughtful sip of his drink. 'The sun might've made him soft
in the head, but you couldn't blame the fella for wanting rid
of the land: it was worthless. After the war, nobody round here
wanted sand and gravel. My dad tried his hand at boatbuilding,
set up shop on the old quay. But again, post-war was hard
times: who had the money or time for sailing?'

'So, that boat of yours?'

'One of his.'

'And the sand pits, what happened to them?' But Lowry
didn't need to ask. He already knew the answer.

'Ha, he sold it to the army in the end: the military, not the
individual. They use it for manoeuvres and the like, part of
the firing ranges.'

'Yes, of course.'

'Well, he held on to the dock, for the boatbuilding, like I
said, but it didn't work out and the sheds are now ruins. The
auction was on Wednesday, when Colin was found ... but
I still needed the extra cash, the Hippodrome needs more
spending on it than I'd allowed – didn't tell Colin when I
listed it, in case he panicked and thought his flat'd be next.'

'You got a decent price for it, then? If you were looking
at Copford.'

'Nah, peanuts. Brownfield site, in this economy, you gotta

be kidding.' He sniffed. 'I saw the posh boy's place just to keep an eye on the competition. He did a good pitch, think he was impressed with the plans I had for the high street.'

Lowry's father was yet again an unwanted presence in his mind. It wasn't so much Armistice Day or Remembrance Sunday, though of course that had set a tone. No, it was the conversation with Osgood; he was right to say the land surrounding the ballast quarry had changed hands after the war. The Lowry family were the ones who sold it. They had owned the sand pits then. The sale, however, was not made by a soldier gone 'soft in the head', but by Elizabeth Lowry, his wife; Lowry's mother.

When war broke out and set in properly, the business of sand and gravel extraction had been significant in Fingringhoe and the surrounding area. The many airfields that were established across East Anglia during the war effort all needed solid foundations to prevent the airplanes sinking into the ground upon landings. The farmland outside Great Tey, for instance, through which Lowry used to jog. Forty years ago, that land had been surfaced with ballast excavated from his father's own quarries for the use of American fighter planes based there.

Lowry's father was in the tanks during the Second World War, and by early 1945 he was missing, presumed dead. In a fit of panic, Mrs Lowry sold off half a dozen hectares to provide for her and her son, who was only two years old. Nick Lowry was conceived after the Second Battle of El Alamein when Thomas was home on leave, before preparing for D-Day. The signs of his father's unravelling were already evident, his mother had told him. Unimaginable to contemplate his old man, trapped in a metal box, baked alive in unbearable heat on the desert battlefield. No surprise he stepped away from reality; so many did.

When Thomas reappeared in October 1945, he was in a bad way. Crippled by dipsomania, his wife now believed him to be on the verge of madness. Unable to help, she watched him drink the proceeds of the quarry sale, periodically disappearing and then finally leaving for good when the money ran out. With no money coming in, Elizabeth and her son were destitute. The parish took pity on them, found a new council house at Greenstead. There was an army pension, but that travelled with Thomas, his whereabouts unknown.

To this day, Lowry did not know whether his father was alive or dead.

'How was Mr Osgood?' Kenton disturbed him from his memories.

'All right . . . responsive.'

'You're not convinced it was Topize, are you?'

'The pressure is off Howard Osgood.' Lowry swerved the question. 'I went to ask him about his hiding Cooper in Harwich, that's all, but we ended up talking about his property – he had industrial land at Rowhedge up for auction near the flat.'

'Makes sense actually. Cooper had the local newspapers lying open at the property pages in his flat,' Kenton said, moving towards the window and blinking in the low sunlight. 'That's all the papers are full of these days, isn't it? I remember thinking it odd, wondering why'd he looked to be interested in moving out; that flat's nicer than mine! Then I noticed it was business lots he was looking at.'

Lowry thought Kenton was brighter today, not so edgy. 'Cooper didn't know about the forthcoming sale though – Osgood didn't tell him, didn't want to spook the boy. So that is even more peculiar. Why would he be leafing through the property pages?'

Cooper's flat was exactly as Kenton left it, though tinged with a damp feel having been left empty and unheated. There was no evidence that his mother, for all her fuss, had visited the property, and the newspapers lay as Kenton had last seen them.

Lowry picked up the uppermost paper. One month old. Open at a page of lots just beyond the south quay.

'These are Howard's, I bet. Though his name would not be attached to the auction.'

'Is that relevant?'

'No, not necessarily; just that the seller's identity is not made known at this stage.'

Lowry placed the newspaper back on the kitchen table. 'This paper is a month old – the auction date was last week, Wednesday. Again we come back to your original observation: why was Cooper interested in the property pages at all? That is the poser.'

'Gotcha,' said Kenton, vexed. 'Wednesday. The day he died. God, that's a sorry coincidence.'

'Shit for Cooper, obviously,' said Lowry, 'but perhaps a rather good thing for Gordon Topize.'

'Yes, I doubt he'd be after a nightclub and some industrial wasteland at the same time, not with all the other pies he has fingers in. Somehow I can't imagine him involved in this.'

'Topize is an anomaly in this whole business. His actions seem irrational and spur of the moment – and because of that, he stands out, attention gets diverted his way. What's going on *here* is thoughtful, considered. This is the action of a man who has plotted his moves – Osgood, I mean. Cooper was a young hothead and must have thought there was something in it for him.'

Lowry left the flat. Outside he crossed the road on to the cobbled quay where the brown slab of a Thames barge slowly made its way downriver.

'What if the land was worth a little more than mere peanuts?' Lowry said to himself.

As Kenton joined him, they drew the attention of an elderly lady who approached them.

'Excuse me, do you know the young man that lives there?'

'Yes, we do.'

'Tell 'im to get that vehicle mended.' She pointed to a dirty Ford Cortina.

'That's Cooper's,' Kenton said. He jangled the keys at Lowry.

'What's wrong with it?' Lowry asked the woman.

'Blinkin' eyesore, that's what's wrong with it, makes the place untidy. If I've told 'im once, I've told 'im a thousand times, get it going or get it gone.'

'Didn't he use it for work?' Lowry said.

'It's not moved an inch.'

'Ah, you see, madam,' Kenton started to explain, 'Mr Cooper has been unable to drive it—'

'I know that,' she interrupted, 'you listening to me or what? It's broken. No way he could get to work in that thing, had to ask me where he might fetch a bus to West Mersea.'

'Mersea?' Lowry snatched the keys off Kenton, opened the driver's door and climbed in. 'When?'

'Ooh, it was pension day. Tuesday.'

They'd not considered Mersea at all. He tried the ignition, dead as a doornail. 'Flat battery.'

'Tell me, love, did you not see the posters? This one, for instance,' Lowry said, pointing towards a phone box, mortified they had missed this lead. The woman muttered something about her eyesight and carried on her way.

'Sorry, I didn't think to try starting the car,' Kenton said.

'Not your fault; unless a motor is up on bricks you imagine it runs.'

'West Mersea? Did Osgood have a pub over there?'

'No. But Hughes-Roper has a boat.'

CHAPTER 42

Sparks announced the sailing boat to Antonia. His welcome-home gift for her.

'Oh, honey, thank you. I always dreamed . . . you are divine.' His wife beamed up at him. She had regained some of her colour. He helped adjust the pillows, getting a whiff of the extremely potent blooms on the bedside table as he did so. Evidence of his mother-in-law.

'I don't know about that,' he replied, though he'd like to think the extravagant gift would aid her recovery. He'd need to dry dock it and scrub the hull. It'd not touch the water until the spring, April, May possibly. Where would they be by then? He reached down to touch a lock of her hair and smiled. He sat holding a birthday card she had managed to acquire through the ward staff. 'You just get yourself right again.'

'The doctors say we will be able to try again. In time.'

Antonia was often called petite and now, looking even more tiny and fragile after the ordeal, Sparks doubted she would ever be robust enough. The doctors had told him she had lost a lot of blood. If he had his way, he'd wrap his wife in bubble wrap and cocoon her out of danger the rest of their lives. He knew this was not the modern thinking and she'd never hear of it.

'That's grand,' he said eventually.

'Have you spoken to Mummy?'

'Err . . . yes.' Dotty had installed herself and her husband at the George. 'She's insisting on staying in the hotel. I said there's room at the house—'

'No, no. She can't possibly. The house will be in a frightful state.' Her mind transported her to Creffield Road where she imagined – not without a tinge of relish – all manner of domestic horrors. 'Have you done any washing since I've been in here? There was a huge pile on the landing. Not that it'd dry . . . Wait. Have you even changed your underwear? Seriously, Stephen . . .'

Lowry was waiting for him under the hospital portico. 'How goes it?'

The chief's face had softened in some indeterminate way. He lit a cigarette and stared out across the car park with a lost, dewy-eyed expression Lowry'd seldom glimpsed other than at the end of a session of heavy drinking.

'She'll be home Wednesday, Thursday latest.' Then, composing himself, he added, 'Yes, she's recovering in leaps and bounds.'

'Great,' Lowry said, 'that's terrific news,' as they walked towards the exit and Lexden Road, bypassing Sparks's Rover.

The chief rubbed his hands together enthusiastically: the Hospital Arms was in his sights. 'You know you mentioned the port being run down and town hall knowing it?'

'Did I?' Sparks pushed the pub door open.

'When we were down there hunting out Cooper's associates.' Lowry followed him in. 'You're right, there's nothing doing: zilch coming in or going out. Customs house people reckoned the port will shut completely. Do you know anything about it?'

'No, just idle speculation.' Sparks ordered two pints of Guinness. 'Be no surprise though if they did.'

'When would we hear?'

'We wouldn't. Never get wind of half the decisions made at town hall. One year the bin men turn up on Wednesday, the next year it's a Thursday. One day you can park a car in the high street, the next you can't.' Sparks continued, dismissive of the mechanics of the town in which he played no part. 'My mate Nigel, the accountant, sits in on those committee meetings; he's always relaying snippets. Remember he said some dick proposed to charge for parking at the hospital? Same people make the call on the port and by and large, who cares, right? The writing is on the wall there. One day you'll realise you'll not seen a boat for a while, and that'll be that.'

'Customs men saw a surveyor down on King Edward's Quay.'

'There you go then – sizing up another bridge.'

'What, the decision's already made?'

'Probably. Why the interest?' Sparks asked.

'Rowhedge and Wivenhoe might see some development if that happens, right?'

'Possibly, the river is wider there.' Sparks raised an eyebrow. 'Yes, conceivably it could increase.'

'And the land might see some move upwards in value – if it was currently worthless . . .'

'Where are you heading with all this?' the chief asked.

'Can you get the names of the committee?'

'Sure, sure.' Sparks paid for the drinks. 'Hmm, she is pleased with the boat. Should've seen her face when I told her. Be a while before she can get out on it. Not the same as a baby, but something to look forward to all the same.'

Lowry placed a hand lightly on Sparks's shoulder and smiled. 'It's a nice thing to do,' he said, and let the chief savour the moment. The news that Cooper got a bus to Mersea the day before he wound up dead could wait until they reached Queen Street.

Gabriel wandered around Mersea port. Lowry had said to try everywhere from the Victory to the chandleries – meaning boat repair shops – and the two sailing clubs. She followed two men carrying what she took to be a rolled sail between them into a hangar, where sat a boat. She showed them a picture of Colin Cooper. Nothing.

There wasn't much life here. The island had a small fishing fleet, dead at this time of day. And of course, there were the world-famous oysters. Recreational sailing was over for the year. Nevertheless, she questioned the few people aboard, and after strange looks from one or two fishermen, she entered the yacht club, itself deserted.

A white-bearded man in a crisp white shirt addressed her peremptorily, and for a second she wondered whether it was one of those stuffy, old male-only establishments.

'Police,' she said loudly, 'I'm looking for someone.' She addressed him as if he was evidently elderly and hard of hearing, hoping it would cut him down to size. 'This man, have you seen him?'

He held the photograph at a distance and squinted. 'Working on the boats?'

'I doubt it.'

'Sorry, can't help you then.'

She wandered over to a noticeboard, which was behind glass and displayed an assortment of cards: boats for sale, crews wanted, regatta dates.

'Why's it behind glass?'

'Folks pay for a week.'

'Oh, I see, stop people putting up notices for free?'

'Anything you looking for in particular?' He didn't like her snooping around, that much was obvious.

'Only this man. Are you sure?'

'Doesn't look the type of chap we'd encourage in here.'

She doubted whether he could see the photograph at all, given the milky cataracts making his eyes swim. She was wasting her time. She stepped up to the bar. 'You're right, you'd not have his kind in here – skinhead, Doc Marten boots up to here.' She tapped her shin.

'Ah ... that rings a bell. A bovver boy. There was a chap like that in here looking for Mr Hughes-Roper. He was late – missed his bus.'

'They'd arranged to meet here?'

'No, the skipper had said to meet down on the jetty. The lad was late and panicky and was after directions. Didn't want to miss the tide.'

'Why so?'

'Oh, he wanted to be out at high water to get a close look at the banks of the Colne.'

Sparks may have been distracted by his wife's imminent return home, but back at Queen Street he still remembered to call his buddy in the finance department at town hall. The accountant, himself a member of the planning committee, was able to reel off the entire board over the telephone. Sparks replaced the telephone in its cradle with a satisfied air.

'The port is to be mothballed. Gradually, so there's no outcry from local preservation movements,' he told Lowry, 'and yes, our friend Hughes-Roper is on the committee, the same committee that gave Howard Osgood the nod to develop the Hippodrome. There was a vetting process whereby Hughes-Roper would have learnt of Howard's property portfolio and Rowhedge, his business interests, etc.'

'Right. I'm getting the gist. Armed with the info he'd been

given from the go-ahead on the Hippodrome, Hughes-Roper then approaches Howard about his own property out at Copford. Why? To suss him out before buying the disused dock? Ensure he goes ahead with the sale by tempting him with more? None of this is a big deal; a bit shifty maybe,' Lowry said. 'He bids for it anonymously at auction – the auction being the day before they were stopped on the road by the squaddies. Why? Why would he want it?'

'There's more,' Sparks interrupted. 'The port of Colchester will silt up and shut, but the river can be used further up. So, to entice business to stay in the area, there's a large development grant to be had for commercial proposals along the south shore. Hughes-Roper knew about it all.'

'That's it then. Howard would have been in the dark – had he known, he may have held on to it.'

'Probably.'

'Cooper. Cooper is mixed up in this.' Lowry relayed the property pages lying open in the flat. 'He was the link. Colin got a bus to Mersea Island the day before we discovered him at Wivenhoe – Gabriel's there now.'

'Aha. We're starting to think Mr Hughes-Roper might have nudged him overboard?'

'The more so now – though it's still not clear to what purpose. Let's have a gander at your boat.'

Sparks's phone began to ring.

'I've not paid him for it yet, we agreed next weekend . . . how would Hughes-Roper get Colin Cooper out on there?

369

Remember the fuss it takes? Weaving through boats and buoys through the marshes to reach the mooring. Can't just jump on it like Howard's.' He snatched up the phone. 'Sparks. Uh-huh. Put her through.'

Lowry turned to let him take the call and took in the assorted paraphernalia that cluttered the chief's office. Cricket bats, boxing gloves, a rifle, the boxing photos. On top of the trophy cabinet there was a black-and-white photo of himself and Sparks. Lowry was in boxing shorts and Sparks in a training vest. They were jubilant. He'd never noticed this before. The date at the bottom was 1976.

'Miss Marple calling from Mersea,' Sparks called out. 'Cooper was due to meet Hughes-Roper there – she reckons they were out scouting the shoreline.'

'Right. Let's get him.'

'And what about our Mr Whitethroat?'

'Let him out after my chat with his missus.'

Sparks's wiry eyebrows shot up. 'What? Ha! Good on you – was difficult for me, you know that, this whole episode with him.'

Lowry had taken a gamble. He had had to make the decision: the chief had been in a tumble and would not have known how to deal with Topize. 'We going or what?'

'Hold on a sec,' Sparks picked up the phone again, 'let me call the Mersea nick – get the launch out there and seize my new boat.'

CHAPTER 43

As suddenly as everything had blown up, so things quietened back to normal for Howard Osgood. As if a mirror, the weather had settled too; the tumult of the change of the season over the last few days had ebbed and the ground took a quiet in-breath, ready to draw down the last of the year's foliage. The pace of life seemed as gentle as the birch leaves drifting languidly to the grass in the still autumn day.

Howard had awarded himself a day at home, a day to think things over and tend his plants. He'd even got the mower out; the incline of his land allowed the rain to drain and this break gave him the opportunity of one last cut before the year's end.

The respite in the weather would be temporary; gales would arrive and peace in the Osgood garden would not last. The man, however, was ready for calm of a more permanent nature to settle in his life. The past week had wrecked him at some core level and now all he wanted was to slow down, maybe retire even, once the club was up and running. He'd hand the day-to-day over to Trevor.

The problems that had presented themselves in the wake of

Colin's death made Howard realise his empire was unmanage-able without significantly more manpower. He only had Trevor on the payroll full-time. Kevin, the old sea dog, was a pal of his father's and maintained *Nomad* for a pittance. And at this time of life, he'd not the stomach for staff, and the rigmarole of finding people he could trust. It all took time, time he did not have. Or time he'd rather spend elsewhere. Colin may have been a royal pain in the proverbial but he was family, and a decent driver come to that. Trevor, quiet, dependable Trev, had unexpectedly seized upon Colin's absence to start complaining about his lot.

Owning the Hippodrome was a childhood dream, the desire sweeter than the reality. His true happiness was being on the boat with Gill. That and the greenhouse, his only truly private domain. Selling the old man's dock at south quay would be the beginning, the tip of the iceberg; much more downsizing was on the horizon.

'Who'd have thought the great Howard would have green fingers?'

Topize stood in the wooden arch.

Ever since Gabriel mentioned the name Topize, Osgood had been expecting an encounter, but he hadn't figured on the man rolling up at his house unannounced. Thankfully Gill was at a coffee morning, if things turned nasty.

'Fuchsias,' said Topize. 'Beauties, ain't they? Like dancing ballerinas, but no scent – all finery but no soul.'

'Gordon. I wondered when you might appear.'

'No answer at the front door, but I saw the Audi. I hope you don't mind?' Topize lazily stroked a fuchsia bell with a thin, gloved finger. Always the performer, thought Osgood; gestures and manners. All affected.

'Not at all.' He waved the secateurs, his grip on which tightened. He was suspicious, on his guard.

'I think there has been a misunderstanding.'

'Oh, how so?'

'You think I killed your nephew.'

'There's reason to suspect so, maybe, wouldn't you agree?'

'Young Colin ain't a fan of my kind.' He grinned, a glint of gold could be seen. 'But his passing has nothing to do with me. Though you can be forgiven for thinking otherwise – the police made me for it. And I had implicated myself.'

'Oh, how so?'

'A public school boy by the name Hughes-Roper.' He sniffed. 'I wanted to buy a property of his. Copford Grange.'

'Ha, so that was you behind that slapping, was it? Those lads damn near put my back out. What the hell for?'

'Get back at you, of course. Buying the cinema. That did rankle, there's no denying it!' Topize took his hand from the flower. 'I was angry, and I should've let it go after the duel. What do I want with a nightclub? I made a mistake.'

'Duel?'

'My idea of justice.'

'Eh?'

'Those guns we posted. What you do with them?'

Everything started to fall into place. 'You telling me you sent those squaddies to have a shoot-out at my front door? Just because I own a property you wanted?' He stared in disbelief. 'Someone was killed – what the hell!'

'The young men of this town need to be taught a lesson,' Topize said, matter-of-factly and without further explanation, 'long overdue. And where better than the high street for a duel? Sends a message. Dropping the guns in your letterbox was a nice touch, eh? Just to rattle you up a bit while you is busy trying to renovate that place of bad memories.'

Osgood grunted. 'All that was a long time ago, though . . . Memories, as you say. And look at you now.'

'Don't be fooled – it's still as hard as it ever was. Dealing with your rich friend, a case in point.'

'He's not my friend. Did you really *want* a nightclub?'

'Actually, yes, for years I tried to get approval for places in the town centre, been refused permission each time. And then you waltz in and steal the show – it was hard to bear.'

Osgood didn't believe him. 'Hold on – you've been abroad on and off for years. Were you even in the country when the theatre was up for grabs?'

'That is not the point,' he said stiffly. 'Silvia filled me in. Told me you'd bought the old place. *That man*, she said. *That. Man.*'

Howard winced. Topize was going to lose it. He'd witnessed it before. Perfectly civil one minute then raging the next. That was what had frightened Howard all those years ago, when he'd cornered Gordon at the side of the Hippodrome. That's what made him lash out with the knife.

'Then this old manor house, the Grange, comes on the market, some distance from the town centre, out of the way, and I have an idea – a vision, if you will. You can keep your drunk teenagers – already three venues to entertain them – all noise and plastic cups. That shit ain't for me. My plans are upmarket – exclusive, for singles. Or folk that wish they *were* single, if only for a night – think how many dudes who'd cruise down here on the prospect of meeting bored, lonely ladies.

'My wife runs a hair salon, as you know. She hears tedium and frustration day in, day out. Many women crave a spark, a bit of excitement, before it's too late and they are left no alternative but to end their days serving up beans on toast to some fat slob they married years before.'

'Smart,' Howard conceded, though he struggled to picture the clientele – yet again, evidence he was losing touch, a new generation he didn't have a handle on. 'What about the holiday business, though?'

'That's up and running. I know I come and go, but when I'm here – as I must be, for my family – I have to stay busy. Otherwise my mind gets to thinking. Otherwise I start to get angry. Otherwise I start reaping revenge on the man who left me to die, who now taunts me even more by celebrating the very place it happened.' He said these words lightly, disarmingly out of context.

'I'm sorry.' Howard bowed his head, now convinced Whitethroat was armed. 'I was just a silly kid then.'

'Ha, yes, like your nephew, eh? Nothing changes, does it? Jealousy breeds hatred.'

Osgood could not argue with this, though Colin wouldn't have troubled himself on the finer points of jealousy – *if they're black send 'em back* was where it began and ended for him. Back in the fifties, the rage Howard and his friends felt was more primal; Howard was running with some lads who were envious of the silver-tongued Creole muscling in on their girls. That, and the fact that Gordon had more entrepreneurial flair in his little finger than Howard's greasy-haired mob had between them. Though the situation was different thirty years ago, the outcome was the same. Colin's juvenile assault was rooted in fear, the same as Howard's back then.

'Time teaches us the error of our ways.' His eyes sought Topize.

'Time! You white people have time; people like me have only one chance – swerve from what is acceptable and forever a villain. Youth is youth. I must protect my own.'

'You have kids?'

'I do. Family is precious.'

'Colin was my family.' Howard was convinced Whitethroat had killed his nephew and had come for him. Why had the police released this lunatic?

'So, I came to make peace – more, in fact, but . . .' Topize said, turning back to admire the fuchsia. 'You don't seem pleased to see me?'

'Don't get me wrong, Gordon, but your shirt jars with the flora.'

'Not against this purple and red beauty – does it have a name?'

'Black Prince.' While Topize investigated the shrub, Howard unobtrusively lifted a small wicker box from the seed shelf and placed it on the bench between them.

'How cool.' Topize smiled. 'A worthy rival – I am plain by comparison! I must get one!'

'Now, not wishing to be rude, but I'm a busy man. Maybe we can cut to the chase?' He did not want Gill returning to witness what was surely going to happen.

'I want to sort this out for good. I don't want this bad blood between us. I must move on. We both must. Will you hear me out?'

'Go ahead.'

'An act of great rashness caused me a lot of aggro and landed you in hospital, for which I apologise. You have lost your nephew. For that loss, in which I had no part, I am sorry too,' he said humbly. Then he reached out towards Howard – palms up, arms wide, welcoming – and continued. 'I have a daughter who, because of my travels, I cannot keep in my sight as well as a father should . . . and she is at an age, a vulnerable age. She requires protection. And so I ask you – would you assist me? What greater sign of trust could a man offer another, than to open up his arms and ask him to mind his kin? I have withdrawn my "interest" in Copford Grange. All I want from you is peace and your help. Like the old English kings and queens, eh? Forging alliances with the noble houses of France and Spain, right?'

Except Osgood's greenhouse was no Granada, and he wasn't a nobleman, just an old cynical Brit who'd had enough bollocks in a week to last until the millennium.

'Of course,' he said, slowly edging towards Whitethroat's outstretched arms, 'but to confront a man unannounced in his own home is downright rude. An Englishman's home is his castle – you know that? I remember Colin told me you had a penchant for fingers, so let's see if this brings us any closer.' And with one deft move, he caught Topize's little finger in his secateurs and squeezed with all his might.

Gordon jerked back and Howard staggered forward towards him and then let go of the secateurs. Disorientated, he turned round for the box with the stashed handgun, but it was now out of reach and he fumbled, knocking it towards the glass. As he twisted round to scrabble for it, his leg twinged, and in the midst of the scuffle, he received a hard kick in the rear end from Gordon's designer shoe, sending him crashing forward. Hands splayed, he attempted to save himself from a fall, but his weight and velocity were too much for the fragile greenhouse. His left hand smashed through the glass. The force of his fall did not push the entire pane out – the glass was three millimetres thick and toughened – and much of the lower square remained intact. Howard tried to free his arm, and tore a diagonal gash to near his elbow joint. He sunk to his knees, upending the bench. Shock powered through his body. He screamed an almighty howl of pain.

In the fug of blood and chaos he could see the Smith & Wesson in the corner out of reach and Gordon standing above him, his smooth features contorted, clutching his gloved finger.

'Damn, man, that hurt,' Gordon said eventually, wincing. He bent down to inspect Howard's wound. 'Jesus, that a bad cut. You gonna lose a *lot* of blood. Maybe all you got. Tch.'

Howard made to get up but was too weak and slumped feebly to the ground.

'Call an ambulance,' he wheezed. 'I beg you.'

'Hmm . . . let me think. I am not sure I want to interfere.'

Howard's watering eyes – or was it tears – tried to focus on the face bearing down on him. Was that a grin? His breathing grew laboured. His nostrils filled with the dusty aroma of potting compost mixed with his own plasma.

'Yes, you know, I think maybe this was meant to be. Can't imagine a thing more fitting.' And with that, Gordon stepped out of the greenhouse.

Gordon put the garden gate back on the latch and walked around to the front of the house. It was possible he had overdramatised his proposal and Osgood thought him laying trap. 'Only trying to be sincere,' Topize said to himself. 'Still, if ever the hand of a divinity was involved in delivering justice, that right there was it.'

If he managed to get off the property unseen it would be Allah's will that Howard Osgood fell on the glass. Slicing himself, as he had sliced Gordon all those years ago. Gordon was not in any way seriously religious, but these things were said. Unfortunately this time it seemed there was no guardian angel, as Sparks had been for him, to alter the course of events.

Topize remained on the driveway for a moment, listening. The girl's info was good. A pleasant, still afternoon. Howard's house was remote, like his own, if more exposed. The road was visible, but too far off for passing cars to witness the comings and goings. Osgood would surely bleed to death, like Gordon himself nearly did. Not a sound, other than a bird in a Pyracantha bush near to the side of the vulgar Roman columns supporting the fancy porch.

Birds. Silvia said the oddest thing to him yesterday – that his old nickname, Whitethroat, was a bird's name. Who'd have thought. Gordon came up with the name himself, thought it sounded tough. He wasn't a bird. He was a lion.

'A lion among men,' he said, removing his glove – he didn't think his finger broken, but the glove was scuffed. 'Ruined,' he muttered, then edged himself down into the Scimitar and drove off humming 'Virginia Plain'.

CHAPTER 44

Hughes-Roper was not in his Church Street office, nor at his Copford farmhouse. The gardener informed Lowry and Sparks that the boss was out entertaining some gentlemen up from the city.

'London?' Sparks said.

'That's what he told me.'

'What sort of gentlemen?'

'It's none of my business and I don't ask.' The man had a stoop from years of weeding rosebeds and shovelling horse crap.

'Where?' Lowry said.

'Fields out near Eight Ash Green, you'll find 'em.'

Sparks frowned, but Lowry thanked the man. 'Let's go. I know where.'

'Maybe we should wait until he's back?' The chief climbed into the car.

'It's not far,' Lowry said. 'See how his lordship feels about showing off when we roll up.'

'Yeah, well, we don't want to screw up. We've got good cause to pull him in so no need for a scene – the man has a certain status whether we like it or not. No point ruffling feathers of connected city types; that won't do us any favours down the line.'

The gardener tugged his flat cap as Lowry kicked the Saab into reverse.

'City gentlemen?' Lowry said. 'Not the likes of Osgood then.'

'Frankly, I don't give two hoots.' Sparks glanced across at him, one hand on the wheel, the other resting on the gear knob, which was back and forth as the car forged through the hedge-lined lanes. Lowry was on a mission. The Saab surged again as they hit a straight. Sparks, stroking his bottom lip, wondered at a darker motive. Lowry's dislike for the landowner was out of kilter with his usual professional demeanour – only now, minutes away from a confrontation, did it dawn on Sparks that Lowry had never taken a personal angle on a suspect until now. Sparks would be the first to admit that in-depth analysis of a man's psyche was not his strong suit, but even he could see the man at the wheel, this man he knew better than any other, was searching for someone to punish.

What for?

The dreadful loss he'd endured this past week had enabled Sparks the perspicacity to see things clearly. Months had rolled by, and alongside the shame and anger of a failed marriage and an unfaithful wife, Lowry had doggedly accepted everything and everyone the Essex police force had thrown at him. If only Sparks had seen this earlier – but sometimes you can't see a precipice until you're right on the edge. Here, in the car, he worried his friend may do something uncharacteristically foolish. Antonia's fragility and losing their child had boosted his patriarchal need to protect those around him, and Sparks knew he should be here at Lowry's side and wouldn't change places for the world, even if it put himself in danger.

'He's a gentleman, Mr Hughes-Roper, it'll be fine,' Lowry said, sensing the chief's unease.

'Unless provoked.'

'Maybe.'

The narrow road disappeared around another hedge. 'All these farms look identical,' Sparks said, fidgeting. Stay cool. Danger was good. And he had had the foresight to come armed. The radio crackled into life. The West Mersea police had boarded Hughes-Roper's boat.

'Anything untoward?' Sparks clicked on the radio handset.

'Nothing. Except it appears to be missing a winch handle on the port side.'

The boat had winches pocketed either side of the cockpit, for trimming the sail. Sparks reckoned the gear piece at the end happened to match the size of a ten-pence piece.

'Hmm. I'll have to knock him down on the price,' Sparks said under his breath.

'Sorry, sir, didn't catch that. Say again?'

'Nothing,' he said, loud enough to be heard. 'Jolly good. Well done.' He hung the handset back on the dashboard. 'Reckon Colin was nudged overboard then,' he said across to Lowry. 'Knocked him off from behind with a winch. Would explain the mark on his neck. And watched him drown, dropping or throwing the handle in after him ... Why, though?'

'My guess is Colin tried to squeeze Hughes-Roper for a cut for handing him his uncle.'

'Sounds fair. And ol' Marcus was having none of it.'

They drove past another set of farm buildings, high-sided with corrugated roofs, some open-faced, framing unused equipment like museum pieces. Sparks was not familiar with the agricultural calendar or what any of this machinery was for, but he did know the shooting season – more or less – and in England, most species of bird fell between September to the end of January. Except for the poor pigeon, when all year was open season.

'Here we go.' A pair of tatty Land Rovers, a number of smarter black Range Rovers and a couple of mud-spattered XJ6s were parked up behind a patch of wilted corn. The cereal here was grown to give game birds cover on a field perimeter, and was left to rot down rather than be harvested.

'I'm not an expert on what city gents drive,' Sparks said, 'but these look remarkably like carriages from the East End.'

These friends of Hughes-Roper weren't on a sightseeing tour of the Essex countryside.

'It doesn't matter,' Lowry said.

'Did you know?' Sparks said. He'd been unable to quantify his unease, but now it was staring him in the face. They were about to interrupt a shoot and this was a reckless move in anybody's book.

'They say a lot of East End villains have acquired the taste for this sort of thing,' Lowry said, with forced jollity, 'and why wouldn't they want a ready explanation for having a twelve-bore rattling around in the car boot? Not scared, are you?' he said as he switched off the ignition.

'Fuck off.' Sparks shoved open the heavy Saab door, secretly pleased – he'd take a straightforward villain over a poncy city man any day. 'But I'm not traipsing through mud in these.' He raised a tasselled loafer.

'Fair enough, we'll wait here.'

Back against the car, taking in the sun, Lowry passed the hip flask. The beaters had already returned and trundled off down the track in one of the Land Rovers. A low, cold light fell across the field.

'At least it's stopped raining,' Sparks said.

'That's something,' Lowry agreed. 'Not wishing to put a dampener on things, but I don't think we'll ever get to convict Hughes-Roper, you know. That Cooper was seen on the dock at West Mersea doesn't prove anything; they weren't seen together – all we have is the word of an ancient yacht club steward and a missing winch handle.'

'I know,' Sparks said with an air of resignation. 'I guess that's why we're here.'

Lowry believed Cooper's final falling-out with Howard was the fuel he needed to betray his uncle. Sadly, it was to prove fatal. Colin had been courting Hughes-Roper, trying unsuccessfully to cut himself some action.

'You'd think Colin might have worn a life jacket,' he mused. 'That boat of yours is tippy – what was he thinking, venturing out in open water?'

'Probably wasn't thinking at all, from what we know of him. Anyway, you can ask Hughes-Roper for yourself. Here we go.' Across the farm forecourt came a dozen or so men wearing a mixture of Crombies, such as Sparks wore, and Barbours. None, however, were in any way like the set of country toffs Lowry'd seen in the Woolpack when waiting on Becky. A different breed altogether. The shooters regarded the two policemen with extreme suspicion – the surprise on the faces of the heavies was unmistakable. They'd come for a jolly old day out in the country, to blast the hell out of a few unsuspecting partridges and enjoy the hospitality of the local Hooray. The last thing they were expecting was an encounter with the Old Bill.

'See, dear Marcus would never think we had the nerve to nick him in a situation like this.'

Lowry wanted to mete out a crushing humiliation. Either that or he would be pushing a likely armed suspect and putting them all in danger. Either way, Sparks was ready. 'Wotcha,' he called gaily, eliciting apprehensive nods. The visitors milled around like uncertain schoolboys, waiting for someone to tell them what to do.

Hughes-Roper eventually materialised, bringing up the rear, a face like thunder. Lowry lit a cigarette. The landowner strode forward, positioning himself between two enormous men. Sparks reached down to touch the cool of the handgun in his overcoat pocket.

'What in the Lord's name are you doing here?' barked Hughes-Roper.

'Do you gentlemen have licences for these weapons?' Sparks asked politely.

'This is private land. It's none of your damn business,' Hughes-Roper said angrily, lifting his shotgun. 'You are trespassing.'

'Call the police,' Sparks mocked.

'We'd like to ask you a couple of questions,' Lowry said.

'What is it now?'

'How about the fact that you took Colin Cooper under your wing, then nudged him into the Blackwater when he ceased to be of use?' Lowry said, unperturbed by the gun barrel pointing in his direction. 'Or did he threaten to tell his uncle the true value of the dock?'

This got the attention of the shooting party.

Hughes-Roper laughed loudly, the shotgun twitching in his hands. His companions glanced at one another.

'You boys invited down here for an investment opportunity?' Lowry smiled, catching a glare from a stocky little bullet-headed man on the verge of speaking.

'Lower the gun,' Sparks commanded.

'Two Essex coppers disappear. Would anyone care about that, I wonder?' bullet-head said.

'What, at the hands of a couple of little squirts like you?' Sparks said. 'Nah.'

'We could take them back, chuck 'em in the Docklands

an' no one'd be any the wiser.' A large man stepped forward, raising his gun.

'Another Jack the Lad?' Accepting the situation for what it was, Sparks had decided he'd make the most of it and enjoy himself. 'Fancy your chances?'

Lowry stepped forward, skirted round behind the big fella, who'd taken Sparks's bait, and approached two older men at the back in camel-hair coats. The big man had tilted his head to one side but continued to face Sparks and lay on the verbal. Both of the older men held shotguns. 'Nice,' Lowry said, admiring one. He reached for the barrel, asking quietly, 'May I?' The man offered no resistance. Lowry took the weapon. Swiftly grabbing the breach with his other hand, he raised the gun and, moving forward, logged the butt hard into the side of the big man's head. The man fell to his knees and then slumped face first into the mud. A brawl ensued. Two men set about Lowry. He took a punch to the gut from bullet-head, at the same time as a jab to the kidney from another. The two old lags in camel hair watched on.

A gunshot halted everything.

Lowry spun round to see a flurry of pheasant scatter low over the corn.

'Pointing guns at a policeman,' Sparks said, 'is very naughty indeed.'

Between them Hughes-Roper lay twitching in the mud.

CHAPTER 45

Jane Gabriel took the emergency call to the Peldon house.

Howard Osgood's death was made real more by the distraught appearance of Gill Osgood than the collapsed form in the greenhouse. The warm disposition of the woman who had brought her tea in the living room only days before had transformed into one of anguish. The widow sat in the chair Gabriel herself had sat in at the weekend, relaying over and over again how she'd told her husband to watch his diet – salted peanuts for some reason played a large part in this unhealthy regime – then interrupting herself with a barrage of self-incrimination for failing to look after him.

From what Gabriel had seen, Howard was not the sort that would be dictated to, least of all over something as perfunctory as food. She rose as a WPC entered the room to take over. She saw Sutton, the scenes of crime doctor, through the window. He was in the greenhouse at the foot of the garden.

'Thank you,' Mrs Osgood said, in no more than a whisper.

'I'm sorry.' Gabriel bent forward, hand out, almost touching the woman's shoulder.

'For coming to see him, tell him everything was all right; he was worrier, not that you'd know.'

The crisp air came as a relief to Gabriel as she stepped on to the patio.

'Ah, there you are.' Sutton walked towards her. 'Well, he's dead all right, as the medics said.'

Osgood's wife had made a panic-stricken call for an ambulance on discovering her husband earlier that afternoon. It was the ambulance crew who in turn radioed the police, leaving the body – approximately – as they had found it. Gabriel and the doctor stood together at the greenhouse threshold surveying the interior. There was so much blood inside. The crime scene doctor then moved round to the side of the wooden frame and examined the broken glass lying outside, considering the trajectory. He adjusted his tortoiseshell spectacles and scratched his beard, but said nothing.

'A complicated scenario,' Gabriel offered.

'Not for me,' he said, bald head jutting forward, held apart from his lean frame on a long neck. 'Bled to death. Pints of it in there, sliced both ulnar and radial arteries, accurately, like this,' with middle and index finger he ran a slash vertically across his forearm. 'Many suicide attempts get it wrong; this fellow opened himself up good and proper. If he fell as a result of a heart attack, as his wife suspects – and he may well have – he was carrying a few pounds more than was good for him, and by the smell of him, liked a drink and the odd cigar. His weight would have contributed to his punching through this tempered glass, three millimetres, tough, and once penetrated, strong enough to withstand in the form of lethal, jutting fragments, capable of tearing the flesh—'

'Yes, I get the picture,' Gabriel interrupted. 'The deceased was recently knocked unconscious in an attempted assault out towards Copford.'

'Yes, yes, I read that . . . interesting . . .' Sutton tapped his thin chin thoughtfully, 'perhaps delayed shock to the system, all too much for the old bugger. Anyhow—'

Raised voices could be heard from the house. Visitors. Gabriel recognised Colin Cooper's mother.

'There's blood here on the path. Smudges.'

'Yes, the scene is compromised somewhat. The medics. Which is a nuisance as there is the one complication.' He pulled out a bamboo cane from a tomato plant tub and, with a grunt of exertion, he crouched and pointed to the far corner of the frame with the stick. 'And that, there, is it.' A black object slid down the cane into Sutton's gloved hand. 'A snub-nosed Smith & Wesson is not a bit of kit generally recommended by the Royal Horticultural Society – or Mr Percy Thrower, for that matter.'

Gabriel re-entered the house through the back door into the kitchen. The two women paused in their grieving and turned towards her expectantly.

'A handgun was on the ground in your husband's green-house,' Gabriel said levelly.

Gill Osgood sniffed and said, 'A stubby little one?'

Gabriel nodded.

'It was his; I found it one day in the vanity unit in the en suite and wouldn't let him keep it in the house – I don't want guns in the home. In any case, I didn't want the cleaner to come across it and think she was working for a gangster. Has it . . . ?'

'No, it has not been fired. Well, I'll leave you in peace, Mrs Osgood.' She made to go. 'But if there's anything I can do, don't hesitate to call.'

A smile through her tears. 'I will do that.'

'And Mrs Osgood, your husband was not a gangster.'

She said this sincerely, but still Gabriel found it hard to accept that the man she saw flick Cooper into the Colne could be bested by a bag of KP nuts and the odd cigar.

Lowry and Sparks watched the last XJ6 pull away, chucking up mud as it went. The sun had sunk behind an ominous bank of cloud blotched with crimson, and it had grown chilly.

'Think we just scraped by without causing a scene there,' Lowry said, needlessly adjusting his tie.

'His connections won't help now,' Sparks sniffed, 'and they'll think twice about troubling themselves with Essex again.'

'Amazed you let them get away.' There had been a stand-off – Sparks and Lowry versus three men holding shotguns – but a diplomatic truce was easily agreed as Hughes–Roper lay on the ground between them. 'Threatening to bury you in the

Docklands? A kid spits on the pavement within a hundred yards of your loafers and he'd be looking at a six-month stretch in Hollesley Bay . . . you must be going soft.'

'Soft? Don't catch me fannying about with a pair of binoculars, do you? No, best those fat slugs are out of the way. Reckon there'll be a few questions to be answered for matey here, and rather nobody ask their opinion.'

'Was he really going to shoot?'

'He turned his gun on you. One hundred per cent. Don't fret, it'll act as a deterrent.' Sparks spun his gun on a finger like a cowboy before it disappeared inside his Crombie.

The bullet entry point was near the heart. 'No way he'll survive that. You could have just winged him at that distance.'

'Aim ain't what it used to be, I guess.' The chief was a county champion marksman. 'Perhaps I need glasses?'

'You already have them.'

'Oh, yeah,' he said, disinterestedly. 'Well, no point hanging around. It's starting to rain.'

Lowry scratched the back of his head. A blackbird sounded an alarm call in the hedgerow. Hughes-Roper, still on the sodden field, suddenly spluttered blood; his mouth opened dramatically in the act of sucking mud, like a landed fish. He was trying to talk. Sparks placed his hand on Lowry's chest. 'No, you call this in from the car. Any last words, I'll take them.'

CHAPTER 46

Lowry stood at the window, report in hand. He had arrived early but found the power out and could do nothing until there was sufficient daylight.

The office lighting had fused due to water damage, and the inner reaches of the building were in total darkness. The rain was not heavy and a pale grey sky shed a decent enough light on the sheet of paper, allowing him to re-read his own account of the events in the field at Eight Ash Green.

The shooting party held us at gunpoint until inside their respective vehicles to make their escape. We have reason to believe they were from a South London criminal fraternity. It is our conjecture their intent was to establish shipping arrangements via the deceased's recently acquired property on the Colne.

The words did not sound like his own. He had laboured too long over them. He wasn't used to bending the truth to this extent on official documents. After a while, he could read through it no more. What did it matter really? What happened with the shooting party made no difference, they were not – and never would be – forthcoming. The real meat was Hughes-Roper and whether the death was warranted. That he was holding a shotgun was in their favour, that it was not loaded was not. To Sparks's mind this was immaterial; why take a chance when the thing is pointing at you?

At ten, Gabriel had opened the office door with news of more death. It seemed inescapable. Howard Osgood had been found dead in his garden the day before. Lowry was surprised and saddened to hear of Howard's passing. Their last conversation had struck a chord perhaps, stirring up thoughts of Fingringhoe and his childhood. The sand pits he'd raced over with boys from the village. Not that he chose to dwell on it.

He sighed. Water started to cascade off the guttering on to the window. He tossed the report on the desk. There was no way he could account for those last seconds in a way that put his mind totally at ease, so he told himself to leave it.

A knock at the door. Gabriel poked her head round.

'Come in, I'm done with this. What news?'

'We've spoken to the cleaner, who saw nothing.'

Howard had managed to keel over in the brief window that his wife was out with friends at her weekly American-style coffee morning in Tollesbury, as she was every Tuesday morning when the cleaner came, from approximately 10.15 till around 12.30.

'She didn't hear anything either. Busy hoovering. There

she goes.' Gabriel tapped the windowpane lightly with a long finger.

Lowry watched the cleaner cross Queen Street leisurely swinging a red handbag. She disappeared from view up Short Wyre Street, the narrow seventeenth-century lane, entering the old town, built on the earliest Roman foundations. Seconds later he was surprised to see Kenton dash across the road in the same direction.

'Hello. Where's he scuttling off to?'

'Good grief.' Gabriel's shoulder touched his. 'I think he believes he's scored.'

'Why?'

'Miss Lindsay March, the cleaner, is also a part-time hairdresser – she gave him a short back and sides.'

Lowry smiled. 'Tch, well . . .' but he chose not to comment, unsure of how things stood between them. 'Where? Hairdresser where?' he said, recalling all the salons he'd been round the previous week.

'In the old town, Scheregate Steps. Anyhow, Sutton was uncertain whether she was even in the house when Osgood died. He was found in the greenhouse as you know and Miss March claims not to have known he was at home.'

'Keen gardener, was he?' Lowry asked.

'Likes to potter about, yes. And spent a lot time outside, chiefly in the greenhouse at this time of year – to escape "getting under her feet", as she put it.'

'And the gun?'

'Wife insisted he keep it out of the house. I couldn't pinpoint whether it dislodged when he fell or . . . or whether he had it out at the time.'

'Why would he have it out?'

'To clean it?'

It was plausible Osgood could have stumbled. He had fallen badly on to the road when he'd been with Hughes-Roper the other day. It was equally plausible he could have had a seizure or heart attack, given his heft and high blood pressure and eating habits. The timing though, while the wife was out, raised questions.

'What are the odds he tripped up – had a fit or whatever – the second his wife left the house?'

'Hmm. I don't know,' she turned from the window, 'he's a lot on his mind. Dr Sutton says most strokes occur in the morning. The three hours after waking when the body is coming to terms with the stress of the day.'

'Pruning geraniums is hardly demanding.'

'Fuchsias,' she corrected. 'I don't know – some say when you finally relax, that's when you're most vulnerable. He's dead; it's a shame.'

Studying her profile in the weak light from the window, he caught purple under the eyes suggesting lack of sleep. She had fine skin, unblemished like a child's, if not for the tiredness. That handful of words Marcus Hughes-Roper had breathed into Sparks's ear flashed through Lowry's mind. *'Colin. The girl on the quay. Saw him go over.'* Should he tell her? If there were to be an inquiry, it may come out that her witnessing Cooper being knocked into the Colne by his uncle had been a humiliation too far for him – made to look small in front of a pretty woman. That's what they deduced from the man's last gasp – that something had fused in Colin's simple brain, making him turn away from his uncle and – fatally – towards Hughes-Roper. It wouldn't do any good telling her now.

'Are you all right?' she asked.

He was aware he was staring. 'Yes; fine. There's been a tiny complication on the Cooper case. A shooting accident yesterday. Anyway—'

'Yes . . . I heard about Hughes-Roper.'

Lowry got up and fetched his coat from the hat stand.

'Where are you going?' she said, surprised, expecting an explanation.

'I have a theory I need to explore.'

'Care to share?'

'In time,' he deflected.

'Right,' she said stiffly. 'Freathy called, by the way. I heard the conversation with the desk sergeant.'

Kenton slowed his pace as he entered Eld Lane; he didn't want to appear out of breath, as if he had literally chased after her, which of course he had, racing out of the station without delay.

He'd fancied Lindsay from the moment he sat down and was greeted by her warm, wide smile in the salon mirror.

They had chatted about the weather, then she said she liked to cycle and be outside, and he'd told her he was the same and regaled her with the story of his failed windsurfing attempts, which made her laugh. He'd ended up with more than a trim in an attempt to keep her talking. However, in the end, all he had the guts to do was tip her generously and leave, unsure whether their connection had been real or if she just had a winning way with customers.

Events at Queen Street soon eclipsed everything and he had thought no more about it, until Sunday. After their outing to the church in Copford, Gabriel had put him straight once and for all. She was fond of him but he was a colleague and their ages were too close – she had used every possible excuse not to make a go of it. The cinema only last week? She even had an answer for that – the dead soldier had taken his girlfriend to see that film and she had merely been curious.

To be honest, this came as a relief. He felt he was released, and not at all upset, which he put down to his affections being pulled elsewhere. Kenton's surprise was matched by Lindsay's as they came face to face in Queen Street's interview room. The hairdresser did not baulk at the sight of him, which Kenton took as an encouraging sign – he'd not told her he was with the police – and he was sure he saw a twinkle in her eye. For the first time since arriving to Colchester, with this woman, he felt a spark. And boy, did he need it after Freathy had put the willies up him good and proper.

Lindsay might be a tiny bit older, but so what? He'd not

met a soul outside Queen Street since he'd moved here (apart from the tawdry crew in the Bugle). People did meet and date through work, but this was different. It wasn't as if Lindsay was a suspect. Just helping them with their inquiries. Kenton was lonely and craved company – his return to work would have been quicker if he'd had someone to share his trauma with.

He ducked left on to the cobbles and descended under the dwelling built in the Roman wall. Lindsay was on the threshold of the salon before he caught up with her.

'Hi,' he said breathlessly, 'I thought, I mean, I wondered if—'

That broad white smile of hers halted further words.

'*Detective*,' she said, mockingly, 'you are a dark horse . . .'

'Well, I . . . I don't tend to lead with my profession. Some people find it off-putting.'

'Only to a crook, surely. Do I look like a crook?'

'No, no . . . of course not. Err, can we . . . can we . . .'

Lindsay reached out to still him. 'I get out at five; meet me on the corner near the Clarence pub.'

He rubbed his hands in expectation.

'Oh, good, good! See you then!'

He walked away feeling light of heart, excited like he hadn't felt in a long, long time. A woman wanted to meet him, straightforward, no blurred lines like with Jane. He might even enjoy himself for once.

CHAPTER 47

There was a man in overalls in the corner of Sparks's office; only the hump of his back was visible. Try as he might, the chief couldn't ignore him and as a result was only half paying attention to what the fellow from the drugs squad was saying.

Sparks cleared his throat and reached for the pack of Embassies lying on his desk. 'Sorry, run that by me again.'

He also had Merrydown to contend with. The ACC was expected later that afternoon. And once he had her out of his hair, he'd go and collect Antonia, who was to be discharged sometime today.

'The man in West Stockwell Street is twenty-three-year-old Gary Chilcott from Billericay.'

'Billericay Dickie, eh? Well, that's great that he's been identified.' The electrician – for that's what Sparks had him down as – started rattling around in his toolbox and then proceeded to make a scraping sound on the floor.

'The man was in possession of several methadone scripts and sizeable quantities of cannabis resin from North Africa. We understand the purpose of his being in Colchester was to sell these for more potent narcotics; Billericay has cleaned its act up.'

'How do you know that?' He puffed hard on the cigarette. 'Might be on day trip, see the sights? We have plenty to see here,' Sparks said, caustically.

'Be serious, Superintendent.'

'Oi! Do you mind!' His outburst caused Freathy to flinch. 'We're having a conversation here.'

'Sorry, mate,' came the muffled response.

'Thinking of moving us,' Sparks said aside in derision.

'Anyway, to continue with what I was saying, Chilcott is not the first user to come down to Colchester to score. As you are no doubt aware, there's all manner of narcotics flooding in from the continent. A lot has been picked up in New Town, coming in from the coast or through the Hythe, where it's disseminated, cut, whatever—'

Sparks stood, and talking over the officer, said, 'Right, that's enough. For what it's worth, there will under no circumstances be any computer terminal in this office, so you're wasting your time trying to run wires all the way up here.'

The man rose. 'I'm a chippy and these here floorboards are riddled with woodworm; it's a wonder you ain't crashed through the ceiling below.' And with that, he picked up his toolbox and left.

'Bleedin' cheek.'

'Chief Sparks, please can I have your attention.' Freathy narrowed his gaze. 'What I have to say is important. One of your officers is a regular of an establishment we currently have under surveillance.'

Sparks sat down. 'What surveillance?'

'The Essex coastline is reckoned second longest in the country, did you know that? After Cornwall. Some argue that Kent holds the number-two spot. The reason it can't quite be narrowed down is Essex is riddled with obscure inlets, shifting sands, all the nooks and crannies. In short, a drug smuggler's paradise.'

'I'm well aware of that,' Sparks said defensively. 'Jesus, I've been catching drug smugglers up the Colne and off Mersea since you were in short trousers. Where is this surveillance going on?'

'It's not just the Colne and West Mersea. As I said, New Town is where it all funnels.'

'On whose authority?'

'The assistant chief constable.'

'Why the bloody hell don't I know about this? Since when?'

'Calm down, Superintendent; since January when a large haul brought in from Germany went missing. County deemed it worth keeping a covert operation down here, given the region is overstretched.'

'Overstretched, who says?'

'Back to the point, if I may: one of your officers has been seen in New Town buying resin.'

The door went. 'Piss off,' barked Sparks, expecting it to be the carpenter.

Freathy rose as Merrydown entered. 'Ma'am.'

'Charming as ever, Sparks,' the ACC said. 'Sit down, Graham.'

'We weren't expecting you this early, ma'am,' Sparks said.

'I'd like a word with Inspector Freathy. Alone.'

'Be my guest.' Sparks accepted something was afoot, but there was no point challenging his boss until he was in position to. The only thing was, she would not yet be apprised of the Hughes-Roper incident. He would need to play this carefully; he left his office with good grace. What was it with people? Why did he feel the constant pressure to convince them he was doing his job?

Lowry watched Kenton bound up Scheregate Steps energetically and jog back along the walkway in the direction of Queen Street. He certainly had a spring in his step. Lowry was nervous for Kenton. The drugs squad's purpose down here had yet to be explained. Lowry had not been asked to speak to Freathy himself – he must be after Sparks. There was trouble heading for them at Queen Street, of that he was certain. If there was backlash over Eight Ash Green, their position would be weakened in protecting themselves. Lowry pulled up his collar and made for the salon.

One thing at a time.

If the cleaner also worked at Maravanne, which it seemed she did, Lowry would lay bets on Gordon having paid Howard a visit that morning, knowing the old man was alone. A gun on the floor was enough of a signal. Lowry chose to approach

Topize's wife; her calm disposition would make her easier to deal with than Gordon himself, no doubt brittle after his recent dealings with the police. After all, it may be a coincidence. Barging into the salon, he bumped Lindsay as she was slipping off her coat, catching her arm above the elbow.

'Excuse me, miss, might I have a word with you and the manageress?'

'Do you mind?' she said indignantly.

But Silvia was not behind the till filing her nails; in her place was a schoolgirl in uniform pivoting round and around on the chrome stool. Lowry turned to the row of three women snipping away. He released the cleaner's arm.

'My apologies, I'm after Silvia Topize.' He appealed to the hairdressers and their customers alike. 'It's in everyone's interest that I speak to her.'

Just then the door opened, and Silvia walked in, collapsing an umbrella.

'Ah, just the lady. Mrs Topize? We've met – Inspector Lowry. May I have a word? Outside will be fine; maybe a cup of tea?'

'That depends – what is it you want?' She stepped aside to let a customer in.

'Please?' He gestured to outside.

Lowry came straight to the point. Silvia Topize was indignant. She claimed to have no idea who Howard Osgood was, or that Lindsay supplemented her salon wages with cleaning work. Why would Lindsay pass on details of clients to her husband?

'We look at connections: I wouldn't be doing my job if I didn't follow this up.'

Rain caught her mascara, causing it to run. To passers-by they could be taken for a couple having an argument.

'Yes, of course, sorry, you took me by surprise; the last few days have not been enjoyable. Thank you for getting Gordon out, I know it was you.'

'He was innocent,' Lowry said simply.

Lowry ushered her to a café on Eld Lane and found them a corner table against the large misted window. Wishing to regain her trust, Lowry asked about those first dates with Topize; the business at the police station with her father, the timing. She wiped the moisture from the glass as she answered his questions.

'Let's start with how he got his nickname.'

Yes, she knew Gordon was attacked by the Hippodrome, she said, carefully dabbing her eyes, but not who by. He was proud, and sharing that would show her he was vulnerable. This defiance, to forget and move on, sealed her love for him.

The tea sat before them untouched. Silvia pulled out a compact to check her make-up. The door went and two soldiers entered, dripping wet. Silvia darted a quick, hesitant glance before returning to the mirror.

'Tell me,' Lowry said, observing the two lads who couldn't have been more than seventeen, 'when I came in the salon at the beginning of last week, you said none of your girls dated soldiers.'

'Yes, that's true as far as I know.'

'But strangely your husband has come into contact with soldiers.'

'Gordon?' She said, surprised.

'Yes. It's a unisex salon, right? I had assumed until an hour ago it was female-only, you know, I'm old-fashioned: in my experience women use hairdressers and men the barbers'. But a male colleague of mine visited you only last week.'

'We don't take squaddies. There's a sign on the door. I pointed it out that Monday.'

Why did this rattle her so? Lowry had not paid enough attention to Gordon's story connecting himself to the military; it was now glaringly incongruous. Lowry had missed something. Randomly he asked, 'Was a soldier responsible for Gordon's attack in 1955?'

'Good heavens, no, it—' She stopped herself, too late.

'You know who it was, don't you? It was never reported. Gordon said nothing . . . I wonder why. Maybe he's dead, the attacker?'

Her eyes said not.

And then he thought he knew; he'd answered his own question. So sure was he, he didn't mention it.

'How can you tell – a squaddie, I mean?' he said, changing tack.

'Easily, like I said before.' She placed the cup unevenly on the saucer. 'As a copper, I reckon you know well enough.'

'Okay, on the level, how would Gordon sell soldiers holidays if not through the shop?' Lowry smoothed a paper napkin neatly. 'I'm curious. I know many soldiers on leave go back-packing in the Far East, but really? Have they enough cash to jet away to Mauritius? That's what he said.'

Her bottom lip wobbled ever so slightly. Here was a woman in an uncomfortable situation. Lying was alien to her, as was confronting difficult circumstances. She lifted the teacup to disguise her unease, but it trembled in her hand and she placed it back down immediately.

Why?

Gordon had been released and Lowry'd not pressed her on the cleaner, yet there was something else she was holding out on, just below the surface. He waited. The soldiers took seats near the counter.

'Why, Mrs Topize, would your husband have reason to come into contact with soldiers? Because I don't believe it's for travel.'

An old woman entered with a small dog in a tartan coat. The soldiers sat quietly minding their own business.

'Saffron . . . our daughter.' Her mouth skewed on the word.

Lowry was unaware Topize had a daughter.

'She was in the shop when you came in just now.'

'Working?'

'No; she was sat on the stool waiting for Lester to let her in next door.'

'In school uniform?'

'Yes, though she has a change of clothes.' Silvia Topize nodded. 'She works – worked – at the salon Saturdays, sweeping up and making coffee, chatting to the customers. Fifteen years old.'

'Go on.'

'Fifteen going on twenty-one if you'd seen her properly. She has started singing for a band too; one of the girls heard her and said her fella was looking for a backing vocalist. One thing led to another, and before I knew it, we were seeing more male traffic than usual at the shop – so up went the sign.' She tried the tea again but the cup became unsteady. Lowry moved to take it. She swiftly pulled out a handkerchief and blew. 'Gordon had been away. Found out when he got back she had been dating a soldier. Staying out, God knows where. Shock of his life, I can tell you, seeing her in kitten heels. Went ballistic.'

'I see – define ballistic?'

'Had words with the lad involved,' she said archly.

Lad – singular.

'What sort of words?'

'Inspector, I don't ask my husband his business, and there are perhaps things he doesn't tell me for my own good.'

'Fair enough. When I came by last week, asking if any of you were or had ever dated soldiers . . .'

'I am not going to incriminate my own daughter, am I, inspector? Besides, that had stopped since Gordon put his foot down.'

Silvia Topize could not allow herself to see how the dots joined up. And a tea room in Eld Lane was not the place to show her.

'Mrs Topize, thank you. But I will need to speak to your husband.'

'He's on the golf course this afternoon.'

'In this weather?'

'It's due to clear up, so he says.'

'I wouldn't have him down as a golfer.'

'Business.' She shrugged.

'What sort of songs does your daughter sing?'

'Old ones from the sixties, soul and R'n'B, you'd know them for sure. There's this black girl blues singer she idolises, sang for the Mod bands back in the day. Kinda legend.'

'PP Arnold,' he said.

'That's her.'

He reached inside the donkey jacket and pulled out the small sachet Oldham had given him. 'These were found. Each one in separate places.'

The earrings lay on the plastic check tablecloth between them.

'I wondered where they'd got to.'

'Yours?'

'Saffron's forever "borrowing" my make-up, jewellery, head scarves, clothes.' She sighed. 'Where did you say you found them?'

*

410

Lowry watched Silvia Topize hurry down the lane. The sun had come out as she said it would. He had chosen not to elaborate over the location of each earring. That she acknowledged they were hers was something; did it exonerate her?

He thought back to Drake's suicide letter, the wording *'and if asked to perform the task again, I would not hesitate.'* Was that it? Gordon simply asked the soldiers to duel for his girl? At some point Oldham should be informed, but now Lowry was curious about Saffron Topize, who was the cause of all this mayhem. He'd paid no attention to the schoolgirl in the salon. What sort of girl could inspire such absolute action from suitors and father alike?

CHAPTER 48

DC Daniel Kenton's afternoon ran smoothly. He was excited at the thought of his date later. How quickly things change. He smiled to himself as he typed up Lindsay's statement. Then he became aware of raised voices coming from the Uniform section beyond CID. He stopped typing. He heard Merrydown's name.

The phone rang and interrupted his eavesdropping.

It was the desk sergeant.

A man had walked in off the street with two pistols. Would he come down?

Hell. Not more. Not right *now*.

'What have we here then?'

The two sleek black guns lay on the seat of an old wooden chair. The table belonging with the chair was propped up in pieces against the wall, having been demolished by Gordon Topize.

'Standard service revolvers,' Barnes said. 'Cylinder's empty.'

Both policemen looked at the unshaven man in his mid-thirties who had brought them in.

'They were shoved through the letterbox of the Hippodrome. I worked for Mr Osgood, until he . . . you know.'

'Understood. Doing what?' Kenton asked, pulling out another chair.

'Sourcer – fixer – maintenance. Right-hand man.'

'I see.' Kenton laced his fingers.

'Yeah, I opened up the morning those soldier boys had that shoot-out in the high street, to let the decorators in. Geezer must have ditched these through our door in case he got stopped by you lot.'

'Right, right. Yes, of course,' he said.

'What you been doing with 'em since then, eh?' Barnes asked.

'Boss weren't sure what to do with them. Now he's gone, guess there's no point hanging on to them. Guns only bring trouble. They're clean – I mean we'd not handled them, if you want to test for prints . . .'

Lowry entered the room, slipping off his donkey jacket.

'Hi,' Kenton said.

'Sun has come out,' Lowry said as if it bore significance. Then he noticed the guns. 'Ah,' he said.

Kenton filled him in. 'Why ditch the guns at the Hippodrome? It's a huge risk – what if we can identify fingerprints?'

'They wore gloves. Maybe it was part of a plan, though.'

'Plan? I can't think of any good reason other than a fit of panic.'

Lowry did not say anything.

413

The chief's face appeared in a crack in the door. 'Nick, can I borrow you a moment?'

The pair stood outside in the car park, Sparks's suggestion. Lowry took this to be a bad sign. The ACC's gleaming Jaguar and the drugs squad's black Granada were in their field of vision. The afternoon sun had some warmth in it.

'Nice to feel it on your face, isn't it,' Lowry said, closing his eyes and absorbing the sun's rays.

'Yes. A lull before the next deluge,' Sparks said.

'Are you referring to the weather or – something more?'

'It'll be fine,' he replied. 'Hughes-Roper we can duck and dodge, chuck in sweeping allegations about corruption at town hall if it comes to it. We have to paint this guy as a real villain, capable of anything.'

'Uh-huh. And Freathy?'

'That is not as straightforward.'

As if Hughes-Roper *was*.

Lowry heard him out.

That the drugs squad operated in clandestine fashion did not surprise him. They had to. Never mind corruption at town-hall level, the police were not above taking the occasional bung, turning a blind eye. Equally, sometimes they were simply too close to the detail to see the bigger picture; detachment helped reveal things that went unnoticed otherwise. And in this case, they found Daniel Kenton.

'What can we do?' Lowry asked.

'It's tricky. Mitigating circumstances, perhaps . . .'

'You don't sound convinced.'

'If he'd had his wits about him, he could have nailed these guys the drugs squad are after.'

'Kenton was on sick leave.'

'That won't wash, a good policeman doesn't get sick – and if he does, he gets his medication from a GP; he does not buy lumps of cannabis resin in a pub under surveillance by the Drugs Squad. Freathy had a man in the circle, some pub in New Town. Talk about drawing attention to himself.'

Lowry took this on board. He had warned Kenton but never expected anything of this magnitude.

'The only chance we have is Gabriel.'

'How so?'

'Aren't those two at it? She could plead with her aunt.'

'I wouldn't put it like that. I don't like to pry, but it seems their relationship is up and down. Not sure he saw anything of her while he was on leave.'

'Well, that's where we're at,' Sparks said decisively. 'A shame, I was warming to the lad; we had a jolly old time with Topize, out in the back of beyond.'

'There have been developments there, too.'

Lowry briefly outlined his cup of tea with Silvia. 'The missing piece to the whole jigsaw is Saffron Topize, Gordon's fifteen-year-old daughter.'

'Bloody hell.' Sparks sniffed. 'He returns home from Mauritius to find his little 'un's been having it off with half the garrison. Not surprised he's a bit miffed. Sure I'd feel the same. And it's them same squaddies he gets to nobble Hughes-Roper and Osgood ... well, who'da thought? That is ... impressive.'

'Canny. If Topize forced these boys into staging a duel – or maybe he didn't need to force them? – it would explain a lot, but I don't think we can have him for it. I'd probably do the same myself ... but there's still a tiny piece missing and I need to see Topize to find it. I have a hunch—'

Sparks lit a cigarette and looked him square in the face. 'By all means talk to him. But easy does it. Whatever you're looking to uncover, and I'm sure you'll tell me in time, let it go – short of murder, that is.' He looked at the floor. 'Give the guy a break while we still have some power.' There was sadness in his voice, but the chief checked himself. 'Be interesting to see what you make of his gaff. I'd never picture him there in a million years. Kenton is right, muddy as hell in this weather, not ideal terrain for his fancy threads.'

'He's not at home. He's on the golf course.'

'What? Jesus, what's the world coming to?' He started to laugh. 'Ha! Raving iron!'

Lowry didn't fall for this shot at humour. He sensed a sadness underneath it.

'Why did you shoot Hughes-Roper? Level with me. At that range, it's too close; you could have disarmed a wimp like that with one hand behind your back.'

'I could see *you* were gunning for him, that's why, you

twat. You were on a mission, and don't even try and deny it. There's no need you ballsing up your career just yet. My days are numbered. I belong to another time, with this crumbling old place.' He gestured to his surroundings. 'You've got some good years in you yet.'

'You could lose your job. Merrydown has yet to prove herself capable of understanding.'

'We'll see, she'll come round; might need to don the ol' pussy snorkel, if it comes to that.'

Again, making light of the situation did not convince Lowry they'd come through the other side. There was one tiny glimmer of hope: Merrydown had been sympathetic when she heard Antonia was in hospital. But how far would, should, her sympathy extend? He would not put money on Sparks's charms winning through.

They grew aware they were being observed. Freathy was in the shadow of the rear entrance to the building. 'The assistant chief constable is ready for you, Superintendent,' he said.

'Don't forget to pick up your wife,' Lowry said.

Sparks placed both hands on Lowry's shoulders and smiled. 'I want you to take a break from this now – see Whitethroat by all means, then get away from here for a few days. Take that bird of yours. Becky's a good one. Let this blow over. That's an order, got it?' He approached the back door, and as he reached the threshold, he paused. 'I'll suspend your arse if you turn up here tomorrow, got that? Besides, this place is hazardous – the floor's all rotten.'

'Never rains but it pours.'

'Something like that ... Give Gordon, well, give him my best, I s'pose.'

'Oh, wait.' Lowry had just remembered. 'Will you mind my cat?'

'Mind your what? Oh yeah, sure – be nice for Antonia to fuss over. Drop him off.'

And with that he went inside.

Lowry remained motionless. He glanced at his watch; there was not much daylight left. If he were to catch Topize on the golf course he'd better go. Wide open space had its appeal. Kenton would still be with Osgood's man, logging the handguns – he'd catch him later. Lowry would be back before five-thirty, and hopefully by then he'd have a plan.

CHAPTER 49

Moisture filled the air on the golf course and the green shimmered beneath a fine haze of evaporation weaving up into the sunlight. Breathless and tranquil as any autumn afternoon could be. Topize pulled out a wedge. He could chip this baby in. He took position, taking his time. Gentle with his stroke. Calm, and . . .

'In there!' Paula, his PA, shouted joyfully. She was young, cute and clever. Other members of the club frowned at him employing a girl. He took pleasure in rattling convention. The time he was in America, he insisted on a white driver, to make a point – the reversal of fortune. It was a cheap shot, but he liked and could afford it. The guys on the next hole glanced back disapprovingly. He tweaked his cap in their direction. He was, inevitably, the only black member of the club and he and Paula made an unusual pair. Paula was originally a stylist from the salon, but she'd always had greater ambition than hairdos. She had nudged her progressive father to nominate Gordon for the Lexden Golf Club; it was her vision that together they could gather business there.

Paula played too and they came during the week, figuring only those rolling in top lolly could afford time out on work days to avoid the weekend rush of the plebs. So far though, they'd not got close. Nobody would talk to him. Early days, but he was beginning to think he would no more likely take a holiday booking from these lazy Essex wide boys than he would sprout feathers and fly. It had, however, given him the ingenious idea of starting a golf club in Mauritius. He'd seen it when in Florida too. People actually flew across the Atlantic to play this dumb game.

He exchanged clubs with Paula. He rubbed his little finger, swollen beneath the golfing glove. He was, ironically, a natural at this game in which he took no enjoyment.

'Nice one, Gordon.' Today Gordon was up against his lawyer, Gavin Holmes, with Paula caddying. Following his brush with the law, there were a few precautions he needed to iron out. Gordon beamed at his companions and clapped his hands but stopped when he caught sight of a figure crossing the green. 'Hello, what do we have here . . . ?' A man in a grey suit. 'The police?' Only Silvia knew he was here. Anxiety rushed through his veins. 'Good job you're here,' he said to Holmes, but his worry was not for himself but his daughter. The policeman was not in any hurry but that slow confident stroll did not give him any reassurance.

It was Lowry, the cool quiet one who had released him from custody. Maybe he was panicking unduly. 'Afternoon, Gordon.'

'Inspector. I didn't realise you were a member,' Topize said cordially. 'You'll have to do something about that suit.' It was the same one he'd seen him in before. He wondered at the policeman's salary.

'I need to have a chat.'

'We're among friends. This here is my lawyer and business associate.'

Lowry considered Paula and Holmes.

'It's about what happened in 1955.'

Topize watched his lawyer take his shot. 'Bad luck, Gavin. Maybe this policeman make you miss, eh?' Holmes shucked a wary eyebrow and moved forward and tapped the wayward ball in. 'That a long time ago. You a boy then.'

'Indeed. There's something else too; a man we are both familiar with was killed yesterday.'

Topize held the club horizontally, testing its weight. They had him. Shit. He didn't know how . . . but that's all it could be. He sized up the policeman; he was big but probably out of condition. He could make a bolt for it, sprint across the green. Lowry'd not catch him. If they took him in for Osgood, he didn't think he'd ever get out. All the euphoria of getting away with it through divine intervention seemed silly now, childish when confronted with the pale grey suit on the green. Stay cool, he told himself, and casually strolled on to the next hole, the three others following. It was pointless to flee. An innocent man does not run, and certainly not an innocent black man – if there was such a thing in the eyes of the police.

'Your daughter sings, I gather.'

'My daughter? What she to you. You leave her outta this, you hear me?'

The policeman was playing games. He'd got to Silvia, how else would he know to find him here? Topize placed the ball in the tee.

'It would be great if we, just you and I, could have a peaceful chat.'

Gordon stood erect, arching his back, and surveyed the green ahead and all the shots it seemed now that he would not get to take today, or perhaps ever again. Way off down towards the banks of the Colne, a mist wreathed the trees bordering the course, marking the onset of evening. The groundsman had said the furthest holes had become waterlogged due to excessive rain over the last few days. How could a course not be designed with adequate drainage in a country with such persistent rainfall, he wondered, and took a deep breath of chill air. Still, this afternoon – for a spell, it was dry. He thought of home in Alphamstone and of Silvia and Saffron, safely hidden from the scum of the world. The dirt and squalor of towns in this country were fit for business only. They had moved to Alphamstone decades ago to escape Silvia's father, and though the danger had long since passed, he'd grown to love the place where nobody gave them a second look and the annoyance of leaf mulch underfoot had long been offset by the freshness of the air.

He exhaled a heavy sigh of resignation. Nevertheless, he positioned himself ready to swing.

'Yes, Marcus Hughes-Roper was killed in a firearms incident,' Lowry said.

As the ball careered way off course into the rough, Gordon muttered, 'Oh. Oh dear.'

'Yes, an unfortunate accident.'

'Guys, why don't you two carry on while I have a word with the inspector? Come to the clubhouse with me, Mr Lowry.' He spied two fatties in a golf buggy checking his PA out. 'Keep an eye out for business, Paula – you got me?' They'd buy a holiday from her. He should use her more. 'Jus' careful with those there clubs.'

As they walked, the policeman stopped talking, prompting Gordon to lead. 'Okay, so you mention my girl, which I guess means you speak to Silvia, right?'

'We had a cup of tea, yes. You're a lucky man to have such a wife.'

'Thank you,' he said politely. This guy was a hard read, not like the old sentimental one. Topize was uneasy but he didn't feel threatened.

'Two service revolvers were posted through the Hippodrome letterbox; you happen to know anything about that? Not the guns themselves, which were sourced through the garrison – I mean who had them? And why they then ended up inside the old theatre?'

'You talk in riddles,' Topize said dismissively. The only way to handle this dude was to outcool him.

'I'm helping you out,' Lowry offered.

'You have kids, inspector?'

'A son, I don't see much of him now. Separated from his mother.'

'Ah, I am sorry to hear that. Children are life; they give so much. So precious. You know what we are prepared to do to protect them, eh?'

'Indeed. You have more than one?'

'Jus' the girl. Silvia and me been together a long time, we try and try for many years but nuthin'. One of us weren't right. We give up . . . But then bang! One day after near fifteen years, she pregnant – jus' like that. Amazin'. A gift.' He shook his head in disbelief, as if this miracle only happened yesterday. They reached the clubhouse, but instead of entering the building, Topize sat on one of the worn wooden benches outside facing the green. 'People will only stare inside, we are more comfortable out here.' He breathed in deeply, arms aloft in a stretch. 'I didn't force those boys to shoot it out, merely suggested honour demanded it, which they readily accepted.'

'And the winner collects her hand, that it?'

'Hell, no, she underage – I'd ground her forever if I could.'

'You've nothing to fear on that front. The other soldier slit his wrists himself soon after.'

'Jesus, really? That a damn shame, they were fine boys. Brave as hell. They fall in love with my girl, and she was wrong to torment them. String 'em along.'

'Why a duel, then?'

'One, the ugly one, Lawrence, came to the house. That was

a mistake. *My house.* Lurking around – at night. At times, when there no rain or wind, it dead quiet out there, not a sound apart from an owl or maybe a fox, so hear anything at all, you wonder what it is. Anyway, I hears something. At first I thought it foxes – I tell Silvia it *is* foxes, go back to sleep. But I swear it was a voice. Immediately, I think we being robbed. It was dark; I took the axe I used for logs, went out there and find this goon on my lawn talking up at Saffron's window, trying to wake her up. Jesus, I went crazy.'

Topize wielding an axe in the moonlight would have been a sight to behold.

'Bet that gave Drake a bit of a start – what was going on?'

'It sure did. He found out she seeing this other dude, William Cousins. So I gave him a piece of my mind, I tell you, but real quiet. "You oughta be ashamed of yourself!" I hiss, not wanting to wake them inside. Saffron sleeps with her Walkman on, by the way, so he wasting his time. I says to him, "Your problem with that William Cousins – so I advise you to go fight it like real men, don't come round here bothering us in the middle of the night or I'll come at ya both with this here axe." Or words like that – I was angry, you see.'

'I can imagine. That's as strong a form of "suggestion" as I've ever heard. What did your daughter have to say on her two-timing?'

'She deny everything. Still, I lock her in her room till *I* calm down. Trouble is, anything I say only hold while I'm around; her mother too busy and Saffron rebel all the harder if I tough on her, that's why I encourage her to sing. But sing safe.' He stopped to reflect a moment, then said, 'How the land lie with military police? That them, not you – the duel, I figure.'

'You're in the clear as far as that goes. They want no more of it.'

'Good, good. They got better things to do.' Topize thought he was reaching an accord with this policeman. 'I do not deny I wanted to make it clear to the young men of this town they are not to mess with my daughter. But soldiers, they come, they go, more like stopping an incoming tide with a sandcastle wall . . .' He sighed and raised a finger. 'However, the flip to this was those particular young men were shipping out very soon – and with them, the memory of me. And so that gives me an idea, when I meet them later . . .'

Lowry lit a cigarette, noticing for the first time a large black man in a leather coat standing against the dark of the conifer border.

'To send Mr Hughes-Roper a message.'

'Yes, a message, that is indeed how it was.'

Topize's loquacious manner was galvanised by his need to share, displaying his quick mind; it was as Lowry thought – the risk of all the fanfare at the Robin Hood was incidental to his way of thinking. All he saw was the fact the lads would be gone within the week.

'We can skip all that, now, back to the original question of 1955.'

'What about it?'

'It only occurred to me after retreading all this business with you and Cooper two summers ago – it wasn't you that reported it, but the restaurant manager. Still, family is all important, are they not?'

'The number one.'

'By not reporting that crime – any crime – the coast is clear for personal retribution. Your name wasn't even on the incident sheet.'

'Hell, we done with that shit, man.'

'Bear with me. Roll back nearly thirty years ago to the attack that earned your nickname, Whitethroat. The records say an "unknown assailant". But it was a close encounter; you'd have seen your attacker close up.' Lowry sat forward and ground out his cigarette. Topize wore a tan leather blouson not dissimilar to Sparks's the day they looked at the boat, and an open neck shirt, leaving his scar visible. 'What would you say to the accusation that you knew all along the identity of the man who cut you, but chose not to say? Waiting for a time when you might strike back, even if it meant waiting decades.'

Topize half closed his eyes towards the sinking sun setting the sky ablaze. 'We'll never know, will we.'

'Your wife knows. I suggested a soldier was responsible, which she abruptly dismissed – too certain. And it was far too convenient that Mrs Osgood was out when Mr Osgood stumbled in the greenhouse.'

'You wouldn't believe me if I told you.'

'Try me.'

Topize's stare remained in the distance to the west, beyond the green, his eyes catching the reflection of the sunset where the sky was now vermillion-streaked on the horizon.

'I did pay Howard a visit, correct; whether the wife was there or not was of no consequence. I came, as you might say, "to bury the hatchet". A man like me, who spends half his time out of the country where his wife and child live, cannot be distracted by the fear of enemies. Yes, I had dreams of reprisals over the decades. Yes, I wanted a nightclub – and all the more so when I learn of Howard buying that same building where he left me to die. My rage! This I learn of by letter; Silvia wrote of it, enclosing the newspaper clipping.' Lowry winced – of course she knew who Osgood was. Sparks was right, he was going soft. 'But,' Topize tempered his tone, 'but when I land at Heathrow, only my wife there – and Winston, him standing there.' He flicked a finger in the direction of the trees. 'No Saffron? I say, where my princess? Silvia say she out, consorting with the infantry . . . this news troubles me and changes things.'

'Over setting up a nightclub?'

'It clouds my horizon. At first I am not sure, still wanting to do everything. When Silvia send the Hippodrome clipping, I wrote back saying be on the lookout for prospective proper-ties and arrange appointments for viewings upon my return, which she duly does – the one I am keen on is Copford. So, when the first problem – the soldier Romeo – presents itself on my doorstep,' he allowed himself a brief smile, 'I take the opportunity to deal with it as quick as I can. *Then* I can follow up on the property. The shock on the estate agent's face when I went in for the particulars says it all. Surprise, surprise, my viewing is cancelled!'

What followed, Lowry knew. The soldiers, skint, agreed to rough up Hughes-Roper before shipping out to Ireland. That Howard Osgood was in the car at the time was, Topize declared, 'A bonus'. He clapped his hands.

'Mr Hughes-Roper, he then sees the error of his ways – I can have the building . . . but by then, no, I am for making friends with Howard. Maybe he even keep an eye on Saffron for me? Can't make her report to you, inspector, like Silvia did, eh? So. That's why I drive to Peldon.'

'And?'

'No answer. The car outside, I see a lawnmower on the grass, a big one with a seat, so I reckon he in the garden . . . I find him in the greenhouse face down. Very nasty.'

'Tragically so; you didn't think to call an ambulance or the police?'

'Ha, you are a funny man, Inspector Lowry. You policemen turn up and find a black man in a rich white man's home? They think this black fella push him through the glass. I have to think carefully; it's not easy being me.'

CHAPTER 50

Lowry left the entrepreneur to finish his round of golf and made his way back to Queen Street. Whether he believed all or some of what Topize said, he'd need to weigh it all up. The police verdict on Osgood's death was yet to be pronounced. The scenes of crime doctor would await the post-mortem on Osgood, but the leaning was towards a seizure. Forensics had found nothing. Topize had not left so much as a footprint. It was unlikely to be recorded as suspicious.

He would do as Sparks told him, but only once he was satisfied Kenton was okay. If he wasn't, that was another question, as he could think of no way out from what Sparks had said. He knew it.

As he entered the Queen Street building, there was a strange sense of emptiness. Gabriel was waiting for him in CID. The overhead lights were still out and only the desk lamp was on.

'How bad?'

'Rumour is we're in for a shake-up,' she said, 'but not yet.'

'Kenton?'

'He's okay, gone for the day.'

'Where did he go?'

'He was due to meet that woman, the cleaner. Hairdresser. Whatever she was. He's fine, honest.'

'Where's Sparks?'

'Picking up Antonia from hospital; he said you're not to be here.'

'Right.' They stood facing each other. He'd couldn't read her expression in the shadow, but there was an uncertainty to her voice which made him ask, 'How about that drink?'

She averted her gaze. 'Not now, some other time.'

'Sure?'

'Yes, sure. I must go, I only stayed to pass you this message – chief's orders, you know. You have a nice couple of days' break.'

'Okay,' he said. The sash window remained a good eight inches from the sill. 'You might want to put some cardboard up, stop the rain coming in?'

Gabriel waited until she could no longer hear Lowry's feet on the stairs before turning off the desk light. She had not let on that Sparks had told her Lowry was also in trouble. It was fifty-fifty whether they came for him tomorrow, depending how the chief fared with the ACC and the chief constable himself in the morning. The chief constable had pushed for them to convene this evening, but deferred to Merrydown, who insisted they postpone until the following day. Her aunt had allowed Sparks to collect his wife from the hospital first, which presented Gabriel with a window of opportunity.

Precisely what Lowry'd be up for was unclear to her at present. Perhaps covering for Kenton – who'd been suspended – or for Sparks? Or for something she knew absolutely nothing about? Sparks had given her very precise instructions on what she was to say, which she'd followed to the letter.

Whatever thoughts and emotions she had – and there were many conflicting ones tumbling around her head – she sealed them away at the back of her mind. She had to steel herself. As she climbed into the car and prepared herself for the drive across the country, she recalled Sparks's parting words.

'You might have a word with your aunt about the situation here.'

'What does that mean?'

'That's for you to judge.'

That was all he said before himself climbing into his Rover to get his wife. All she did know was that she didn't want anything to change, including losing Sparks from Queen Street. A bore and ruffian he may be, but he understood this town, and this town needed him.

Kenton was going to be late, but he couldn't run for it. It was a matter of pride. He couldn't be seen running out of Queen Street after having just been suspended. A week on full pay, pending investigation. He'd gained respect from Uniform, at least – couldn't suspend everyone who took the occasional bifter, they told him as he tidied up. He wanted to believe this but wasn't sure. Jane's expression as he left the building did not inspire confidence. Uniform foolishly thought Sparks had the last word, but clearly he wasn't the top authority any more. The chief's policy of challenging everything he disagreed with filtered down, so the rest of them had no idea what was right or wrong.

The further he got from Queen Street, the faster he walked, and soon he was pegging it down the cobbled lane. She wasn't there. Bloody hell, he was only ten minutes late. He hurried down Scheregate Steps, thinking maybe she was still at work, or maybe she'd said five-thirty, not five.

The hair salon was locked. He rattled the door. Nothing. Cursing, he stepped next door to the Candyman. The jazz bar didn't officially open until seven, but he heard a female voice coming from within and the door was ajar.

'All right,' he said to Lester, ducking into the bar. Pink half smiled, as he sat chatting to a fat man on a bar stool. At the far end was a slender woman crooning gently, warming her vocal chords while a bunch of lads went about a sound check with guitars and a keyboard.

Lester slid Kenton a Scotch. He took it and mooched forward, watching the singer sway. Things were verging on the cataclysmic. Maybe Lindsay only agreed to meet him to keep him sweet – knowing he'd write up her statement – but with absolutely no intention of showing up. The electric organ kicked in and the singer's vocals soared with it. She had impressive range. She was a half-caste, traditional mulatto – or, as they now said in universities, of mixed parentage. It was irrelevant; she was strikingly glamorous in a sequin one-piece. He knew the number, it was a Small Faces tune – Lowry's favourite, in fact.

'Hey Lester,' he called over to the proprietor, 'let me get the lady a drink.'

'No,' came the firm reply, 'she don't take kindly to young men buying her drinks.'

Charming. The girl put down her microphone as the guitarist stopped to fiddle the amp. She looked vaguely familiar – had he seen her before or did she remind him of some pop star he'd seen on the telly? He ignored Pink, sidled up to the girl and asked her what she fancied. Hell, it wasn't as if the day could get any worse.

CHAPTER 51

Pushkin sat in the cat box on the kitchen work surface, pupils dilated with dread at the prospect of travel. Being black, only his bright green eyes were discernible in the dark interior of the carrier. Lowry contemplated the creature from across the kitchen. There were loose ends. His inclination was to let them drift for a few days, take all the unanswered questions with him to the south coast, and in the meantime, trust Sparks.

Topize, at least, was free to do whatever he needed to do – stay here, go to the Indian Ocean, play golf, whatever. There would be no questions surrounding Osgood: it would not amount to a murder investigation. Sutton had only confirmed the cause of death was murky, difficult to parse – a stroke, likely; his weight was enough to puncture the glass. He heard the toilet flush upstairs.

Lowry ignited the hob and bent down to light his cigarette. The cat blinked at the smoke.

'It'll do us good to have some time apart.' The animal issued a plaintive mewl as Lowry went to stand on the front doorstep.

Becky came to the doorway. 'Whatya doing out here?'

'Cat doesn't like it.' He waved the Navy Cut.

'Well, I'm ready when you are.'

'Grab him then and jump in the car,' Lowry said. He finished his cigarette and then went around the house locking up, checking the windows and unplugging the VCR.

Last time he'd shut up the house and left the cat in care was the family holiday in 1981. He thought about his son, Matt. The boy would not speak to him when he called last night. Jacqui had turned Matt against him when Nick asked for the divorce. To do that to a teenage boy . . . He hoped in time his son would be more generous towards him than he had been towards his own father when he left. At least Lowry had never bullied Matt the way his father had bullied him. He sometimes wondered if the reason he had trouble relaxing was that any source of pleasure he'd found as a child had been taken away from him, almost in spite.

'Your binoculars, do you have them?' Becky asked, holding the cat box.

'Ah, no, forgot.' As he re-entered the house he heard Becky tell Pushkin that his namesake was a blackamoor whose grandfather was African and black just like him.

At least Pushkin wasn't going to leave him. But he did worry about leaving the animal with Sparks. Lowry must insist he keep the animal inside the house, those roads round Lexden were busy . . . not like here. And it was just as likely that Sparks would flatten the cat himself, swinging in to park the Rover after half a dozen pints in the social.

He hadn't got a litter tray. Damn. Maybe if Antonia was mobile she could go and buy one if he slipped her a few quid. There's no way Sparks would—

'Nick . . .' Becky called from the hall, concern in her voice.

He turned back and saw the two Uniforms in the doorway.

ACKNOWLEDGEMENTS

Gwyneth Hambleton, Debbie Munson, John Gurbutt, Jon Riley, Sarah Castleton, Olivia Hutchings, Rich Arcus, Sharona Selby, Felicity Blunt, David Shelley, Sarah Neal, Patrick Janson–Smith, Myles Archibald, Steve Oakley, Mike Bulmer-Jones.